Praise for the Liver

'A love letter to Liverpool
with a touch of Peaky Blinders.'
SE Moorhead, Author of Witness X

'A thoroughly enjoyable debut.'
Catherine Fearns, Author of the Reprobation Series

'A truly British and Irish thriller.'
Readers' Favourite, Reviewer

'I was hooked from the first chapter.'
Readers' Favourite, Reviewer

JACK BYRNE was born and raised in Speke, Liverpool to an Irish immigrant father and grandparents. He is an advocate of Irish and Liverpudlian history. *The Liverpool Mystery Series*, including *Under the Bridge* and *Across the Water* follow our heroes, Vinny and Anne, across Liverpool and Ireland as the mysteries of the past collide with their investigations in the present.

Follow Jack on Twitter @Jackbyrnewriter
And find him on www.jackbyrne.home.blog

JACK BYRNE

ACROSS THE WATER

NORTHODGE
PRESS

Northodox Press Ltd
Maiden Greve, Malton,
North Yorkshire, YO17 7BE

This edition 2022

2
First published in Great Britain by
Northodox Press Ltd 2022

ISBN: 978-1-915179-01-2

This book is set in Caslon Pro Std

For Jack Kavanagh and Rita Hunter

Chapter One

Vinny

Wicklow, Ireland, 2010

Ireland was coming toward them, a spectre emerging from the mist.

'This is it.' Vinny stood in front of the rain-spattered window. 'Time to find out what happened to my dad.' He shifted his weight as the ship rolled with the waves.

'You make it sound like you're going to jail or off to fight in a war,' said Anne.

'How do you know we're not?' asked Vinny.

The public address system played a recorded message asking passengers to return to their vehicles. All around them people were spurred into action.

'Shall we go down to the car?' Anne asked.

'Can we go on deck first?' This was Vinny's first trip to the land of his ancestors. The land of Gaelic and Guinness, songs and stories, war and revolution. He wondered which one he would find.

She smiled. 'Sure, I guess it's all part of the experience.'

It was mid-May, but no one had told the Irish weather. A slanting rain came in from the land, whipping the sea up, and smacking the sides of the ferry. The wind swirled and buffeted them as Vinny opened the lounge door. Leading the way to the front, guided by the cold wet handrail. He pulled his grey North Face jacket together, the zipper slowing over the slight protrusion of his stomach. Pulling the hood down, his short brown hair parted in several directions at once.

'Welcome to Ireland,' Anne shouted. Younger and slimmer than Vinny, she would've liked her father's afro. Instead, her looser curls gave her a Latin look.

Vinny laughed. 'I don't think it wants me here.'

Anne linked her arm through his while leaning closer and he moved his arm around her shoulders, pulling her in. Without Anne, he'd never have discovered his dad hadn't abandoned him. In fact, he'd gone on the run. Vinny watched the grey shore loom closer. It looked like any other piece of land the world over, but he knew it held a personal truth he'd been denied. But would it be a truth he wanted?

'Come on, let's go,' Anne turned, leading Vinny back inside. 'Excited?' she asked.

'Yeah, just to get off this thing.'

They sat on the darkened car deck with the engine off as the ferry made its final manoeuvres into position at the dock. Amid the shouts and hand signals of the seamen, the great door began to open and grey daylight swept in.

Anne's phone vibrated. She reached into her bag. 'Vodafone.'

The car swayed as the ferry door clanked and groaned into place. Vinny's phone beeped as well. He checked his message. 'Same,' he swiped to get onto the satnav when it beeped again.

'What time are you in?' his eyes narrowed.

'What is it?' she asked.

'A message from my Uncle Martin.'

'That's quick. What does he want?'

'Asking if we've arrived.'

Anne turned the ignition, the car stirring into life, before she followed the line of traffic leaving the ferry. 'We have now,' she said as the car bounced off the bottom of the ramp. 'When are we supposed to be seeing him?'

'I thought maybe tomorrow or the day after?'

Anne was negotiating the car out of the ferry port, accelerating away from the boat and toward the exit. 'Give him a ring.'

Vinny tapped the phone, holding it flat out in front of him on speaker. It rang once, twice.

'Hello, hello,' a surprised voice rang out.

'Martin, it's Vincent, Vinny.'

'Hello, Vincent. We're here in Wicklow waiting for yeh.'

Vinny looked at Anne who managed to shrug while turning onto the main road.

'Oh, right I thought we were seeing you later in the week in Tipperary.'

'Well, something's come up, like.'

'Ok, can you tell me what it is?'

'Well,' - there was a pause - 'Maybe it's better if we show you. We're at your hotel.'

'Give us an hour and we'll be there.'

'Right you are, see you in an hour then.'

'Ok, bye,' Vinny swiped to bring the satnav back up.

'What was that about?' said Anne, looking for the slip road to the N11.

'What could he mean, "something's come up?"' Vinny thought aloud. 'And why drive all the way from Tipp? Okay, go straight on, a bit, then I think we can get onto the motorway.'

Vinny swiped the screen, enlarging and reducing the image on his phone. Anne concentrated on the traffic. Vinny reached across for Anne's hand. She was changing gear and moved her hand back to the wheel. She managed to give his hand an awkward squeeze between movements.

'Here, take this turn,' Vinny pointed.

Anne swerved to join the flow of traffic. Her lips were pursed, deep in thought.

'What is it?' he asked.

'If you fail to prepare, then prepare to fail.'

'The hotel's booked,' said Vinny.

'Not just the room. The investigation.'

'More advice from the great Anthony?' Vinny's eyes widened.

'Yes, as it happens. It might be a cliché, but it's true, and there's no need to sneer. Anthony's been a good editor for me, a mentor,' Anne paused to let the recrimination sink in. 'This is serious,' she paused. 'So, what do you know about your dad's death? Time? Place?'

'All I know is what my mam told me. It was a motorbike accident not long after he arrived back in Ireland.'

'April 1974, right?'

'Yeah, the last time he was seen in Liverpool was late April.'

Anne laid out the facts. 'He came back to Ireland, to Wicklow, but he was from Tipperary?' she turned toward Vinny.

'He was on the run from Liverpool, so my guess is that Jack Power, the boss under the bridge, set him up with his contacts in Wicklow after they killed Mark Riley; they wanted him out of the way quickly.'

Vinny knew his dad was a murderer, and he hated the whole gangster thing, turning thugs into icons. If it took a village to raise a child, he believed it took a culture to create a killer.

'Okay. Well we'll see what your uncle has for us when we arrive,' said Anne.

'Local papers may be on their last legs, but I'm glad I've got the best journalist in Liverpool on the case with me.' Vinny smiled.

'We'll see,' said Anne. 'And as a journalist, I might have to move to do my job,' the two-lane highway was busy but the traffic was flowing.

'Is this the Novo-media thing again?'

'Partly yeah. The North has been ignored, everything is dominated by London.'

'That's not completely true. You've got Granada, the BBC in Salford.'

'All the decisions and the jobs are in London,' Anne countered.

'Then go to London if you want to be near the "power."'

Jack Byrne

'It's not that, I just want a career near to where I live. Is that so bad?' She made eye contact briefly, then back to the road.

Vinny looked sideways at her. 'Doing videos on YouTube?'

'You've got to start somewhere.'

'I don't want to argue,' said Vinny.

Anne turned to face him again. 'Who's arguing? If I get offered the job, I'll take it.'

'Fine. Watch the road,' he pointed ahead.

The road curved round to the left and began a climb. Within minutes they'd reached the top of the hill.

'Look, there's the sea,' to the left, the greenfield and hedgerows fell away to reveal the open expanse of the Irish Sea. A mass of glittering blues and greens with the white caps of waves breaking throughout. 'Great isn't it?'

'You weren't saying that when you were on it,' said Anne.

'Yeah, well. I can appreciate it more from here,' he smiled.

'Isn't that always the case? Everything looks better until you're in it.'

'Are we still talking about the sea?' asked Vinny.

'What do you think?' she asked.

'This thing with my dad has always felt like unfinished business. We know he did a runner from Liverpool after killing Mark Riley, but what happened when he came back? It was probably just an accident like they said, but I need to know.'

'I hope that's the only piece of unfinished business. Somehow, I don't think your dad spent his last days in a cottage, walking a dog on the beach. We turn up in Ireland asking about a death. God knows what we're getting ourselves into.'

'Well, we're about to find out. The next exit takes us to Wicklow.'

* * *

Five minutes after leaving the N11 they drove into the town, taking a left down toward the sea. The hungry cries of gulls

5

welcomed them to Wicklow. 'Looks okay.'

A brick-built timber beamed pub with whitewashed walls next to the shallow but fast-flowing River Vartry. The arches of the stone bridge spanned the water, which came down from the mountains and out into Wicklow Bay.

'No, it's lovely,' Anne corrected.

Vinny retrieved his bag from the car, and Anne trundled her roll-along case behind him. Two men stepped out of a brown pick-up close by.

'Vinny?' An older man with a healthy shock of grey hair approached him, hand outstretched. A heavy-set young man with curly brown hair and a stocky, solid build followed him closely. 'This is your cousin Sean.'

Vinny shook hands with Marty and then the younger man.

'This is Anne.'

They both nodded hellos at Anne.

'Are you coming in?' Vinny asked.

'I think your man in there would rather we waited out here, didn't like the cut of our jib,' Martin said.

'Ok, look, give us a minute, we'll get rid of the bags and be back out.'

The swing doors opened onto a reception area. Through a side door, they saw the bar, a long room full of tables and chairs, filled with the dark brown glossy wood of country pubs. There was a hatch counter in front of them and the stairs off to the left. As soon as they entered the area, a figure appeared behind the counter.

'Good Morning. I'm Mr McDonagh, General Manager. My assistant Sheila is off today, so I'll book you in.'

'Great. Vincent Connolly.'

'Ah yes, Mr Connolly, you've had some visitors already.'

'So, I believe,' said Vinny.

'I asked the gentlemen to wait outside. Passports please,' McDonagh's tone was of disturbing efficiency.

'Yeah, I heard.' Vinny handed over his and Anne's passports;

he wasn't smiling. Unsure why the manager had slighted his visitors. The manager ignored him and tapped away at a keyboard, eyes fixed on the screen. 'Yes, I have you here, double room. If you could just sign the register for me.'

Anne and Vinny completed their paperwork, left their bags in reception much to the manager's disapproval, and went back outside to the car park. The sun was fighting its way through the clouds, the air fresh and cool.

Martin was waiting by the entrance, pacing back and forth in short bursts. Vinny knew something was wrong. 'I know it's no way to say hello, but you'd better have a look,' he led them over to the back of the pick-up. Sean reached in and pulled out a tyre.

'From my dad's motorbike?' asked Vinny

'You said Sean here could try and fix it up. Well, he got started on it straight away, had his eye on it for years he has.'

Sean held up the tyre and poked his finger through a hole. 'The front tyre,' he said.

'Puncture?' asked Vinny.

'Not a hole clean through like that,' said Marty.

Sean handed the tyre to Marty and dug in his pocket. He pulled out a small tin and broke open the lid. He held a piece of metal between his fingers, about two centimetres long; one end was rounded like it had melted. 'This was still inside the tyre. It must've hit the rim.'

'A bullet?'

'Yeah, that's what it looks like.'

'Jesus, did no one say anything at the time?' asked Anne.

'No one looked. It was a motorbike accident, no reason to think anything else,' said Martin.

'Have you told anyone about this?' asked Anne.

'Yeah, I called the Gardaí,' Sean replied.

'He had to,' said Martin.

Vinny took the bullet and weighed it in his palm. 'This was no accident. My dad was murdered.'

Chapter Two

Paddy

Liverpool, 1974

He kept the door open with his foot to combat the smell of piss and held the coin above the slot. Once it dropped, there'd be no going back. Beep… beep… beep… the coin hovered, beep… beep… beep. Fuck it. He pressed the 2p, and with a mechanical click, it was swallowed by the machine.

'D. I. Barlow,' the voice that answered was clipped and distant.

'Mr Barlow. We need to meet,' Paddy's head was banging. He'd drunk too much at the funeral the day before.

'Who is this?'

'It's me, Paddy Connolly,' he called from the Parade. The public box was outside Damwood Hall. There was a beat of silence.

'Mr Barlow?'

'Why are you calling me?'

'You said if it was important,' Paddy walked a fine line between respect and hatred—respect that the bastard was using everybody, and hatred for the same reason.

'I said if it was urgent. I hope you're not playing games.'

'I'm not. It's fucking important,' Paddy's stomach churned, head aching.

Barlow was no longer distant.

'Don't take that tone with me,' he snapped.

'Fuck you, then, we'll wait and see what happens,' Paddy raised the receiver, about to slam it down in anger and frustration. Barlow's voice was distant but urgent.

'Wait... wait.'

As Paddy placed the receiver back to his ear, an old man appeared all coat and cap. He shuffled up to the box and waited. His dark eyes looked out from under the cap directly at Paddy. Who was he? For fuck's sake. Paddy glared at him, then turned his back and looked across the road at the public swimming baths. He couldn't trust anyone.

'What is it?' Barlow asked, then added, 'No, don't tell me here, I'll meet you. Where are you?'

'In Speke. How about the Dove?' said Paddy.

'No. Not in a pub.'

'Down the Yonk,' Paddy used the local name for the riverbank.

'Where?'

'The Yonk, Oggie shore.'

'Okay, half an hour.'

The line went dead. Paddy stared at the phone before replacing the receiver. It was done. The old man shuffled forward; a young woman was behind him now in the queue, collar turned up against the cold and damp.

The old man pulled the door open. 'It stinks,' for a second Paddy thought he knew that he'd been talking to the police.

'It does,' Paddy replied unnecessarily. 'Of piss,' he walked around the back of the flats where his car was parked and slid into the driving seat. Jesus - he had to do something; he didn't have a choice. It took a couple of minutes to get from the Parade to Dungeon Lane, along Central, and then Eastern Avenue. The compass point names indicated an estate without history or identity. He left the main road, turning onto Dungeon Lane, an older place of farms and functions, now squeezed up against the airport runway.

He parked next to a burnt-out car on a rise overlooking the riverbank. He lit a ciggie; unable to distinguish whether it was his hand or the flame that shook and waited. Across the river was Stanlow Oil refinery, an island in the Mersey. It had once been home to monks, the first settlers in the area. Now it was an international oil terminal. To his left beyond the lighthouse in Hale stood a jungle of interconnecting pipes in the ICI chemical works of Runcorn. This place stank some days, and all their shit went in the river. He peered into the burnt-out car next to him, a Ford Cortina, no telling how old. Some poor bastard was looking for it. He'd even seen posters on lampposts, looking for stolen cars like lost dogs. Fuckin idiots, he thought.

He heard the Inspector's car coming down the lane before he saw it turn round to face the river. Fuck him too.

The Inspector skidded to a halt a few yards away, tyres sliding over the greasy earth. Paddy watched him get out of his car. His square frame and movement marked the DI as ex-military. 'This is your kind, off the estate,' Barlow said, pointing to the burnt-out car.

'Kids,' said Paddy in explanation, then added. 'Where the fuck are your lot when they're needed?' His only form of defence was attack.

'Don't get lippy with me. Here, give me one of those,' Barlow reached out.

Paddy threw the ciggie packet to him.

'There was a problem. A young guy got done in.'

'What do you mean, "Got done in?"' asked Barlow.

'What do you think I mean? He's dead,' Paddy threw him his lighter, annoyed at the interruption.

'Are you sure?'

'What kind of stupid question is that? If he's not dead, then he's fucked because we buried him.'

'Where?' Barlow lit his cigarette and handed the pack and lighter back. 'Wait, don't tell me, I don't need to know,' they were side by side facing the river, as though for a second, despite everything, they were on the same side. 'Weren't you at the funeral yesterday?'

'You know about that?' Paddy asked.

'Of course, we know. The news of a soldier's suicide gets around. Such a waste. You and all the boys were there.'

'Yeah, strange day. We ended up burying two bodies yesterday. The legal one, at Allerton cemetery. Then the other, private burial, you might say.'

'You mean a hole in the ground?'

'What else?'

Paddy stared out over the Mersey. The tide was in, and the river slapped at the banks below.

'What happened?' asked Barlow.

Paddy turned to face him. 'It was Charlie Power's fault, the fuckin eedjit,' Paddy's accent slipped back into his native Tipperary. 'He was to give the man a slap and he fucked up, and the fella come at me with something so I had to knock him on the head. Turns out he'd a skull like an eggshell, so here we are.'

Barlow tried to sound casual. 'So, what do you want me to do?'

Paddy didn't hide his anger. 'Get me out of this. You're the reason I'm still involved. You know I wanted out. "Stay," you told me, "it'll all be alright. I'll look after you." Well, we're both fucked now.'

'Stop panicking. Who was he?'

'Mark Riley. He was calling Jack Power a snitch. He was in the Blue Union passing remarks. So, we got a call.'

Barlow walked back and forward. 'Is he local?'

'No, he was a sailor, off one of the boats in the docks. He'll not be missed, not around here anyway.'

'That's good. They'll think he jumped ship, happens all the time. No one here'll be looking for him,' he paused then added, 'For now,' after another pause, 'So what's the problem?'

Paddy drew heavily on his ciggie. 'You're a cold bastard. He'll have a family like anyone.'

Barlow stopped and stood in front of Paddy. 'You've got some bloody cheek. I'm cold? You're the one who killed him.'

'I was doing my job, unlike you, you bent fucker.'

Barlow's finger jabbed the air. 'Listen here you Irish...' he stopped himself. 'If I turn you in, you'll go down for life.'

'You won't, though will you?'

'And why not?'

'Cos people would find out about your deals with Jack Power,' this was Paddy's trump card. Barlow and Power helped each other out. Barlow was vulnerable. The DI laughed, 'I can handle Jack Power. You're the one who should be worried, with what you know, you can take them both down. Jack and Charlie, they won't like that.

'Why else do you think I'm here?'

'Watch yourself. You're a threat,' Barlow was pacing in front of Paddy. He pulled the last of his cigarette and threw the stub on the ground. When he spoke he was calmer, logical. 'This isn't about some deckhand, or you and Jack Power, small-time hoodlums. Your Irish mob are blowing up pubs, killing women and children,' Barlow lit another ciggie and pointed. 'You see that river, don't you? One wrong word and you're in there, never mind prison, do you understand me? They'll find Lord Lucan before they find you.'

Paddy could see the wheels turning as Barlow laid out his plan.

'If you do as I say, you can clear out. Start fresh somewhere else. Where's the body?'

'Buried. We tried to get it through the docks, but the union guys wouldn't let us.'

'Those commies have got the docks sewn up. They're worse than you lot,' Barlow paced around.

'You're gonna have to get out of here.'

'Where? Where can I go?' asked Paddy.

'You're lucky the Powers didn't bury you as well,' Barlow

kicked the ground and a puff of dust rose to meet his words. He stopped pacing, face brightening. 'Go back to Ireland. I can help you.'

'I don't want to go to Ireland. Why the fuck d'yeh think I'm here?'

'Look, you go, six months, maybe a year. I'll make sure everything's quiet here, and you can come back.'

'For fucks sake,' Paddy rubbed his face. 'I'll go to London, Birmingham.' He didn't want to leave his son, Vinny.

'That's no good.'

'Why?'

'You've got two problems—the normal plod, get pulled for speeding, drunk and disorderly, anything, they could ship you back here. Second, as long as you're in England, you're a danger to Power, you could snitch. You've got to get clear. Til' we know no one's looking for this guy.'

Barlow paused before adding, 'Anyway, we can use this,'

'You mean, you can use it,' Paddy spat on the ground. He could see his options disappearing in front of him.

'This can work out for both of us,' Barlow spoke faster, excited by his idea.

'Do you know Wicklow?'

'A bit,' Paddy admitted.

'You know Conor Walsh?'

'I've heard the name.'

'Course you have. He's Jack Power's guy over there,' Barlow rubbed his hands together.

'So?' asked Paddy.

'So, you want a life with your missus and kid back here. Get out for a while, let this settle down. You do a job for me, and I'll make sure it's clear when you come back. I'll guarantee there's no hassle with the Powers, a clean slate. You can do what you want.'

'Can you do that?' Paddy stared at him, unconvinced. Could he make all this go away?

'Where've you been living? We can do what we like now.

PTA means we have all the power we need. Jack and Charlie will do what they are told.'

'PTA?' Paddy asked.

'Prevention of Terrorism Act.'

'Jesus,' it was Paddy's turn to pace. He was excited and frightened.

Barlow sat on the bonnet of Paddy's car. 'This is your chance. Not many people get a second one, a get out of jail free card. It's either this or you spend the next year looking over your shoulder, 'cos if our boys don't get you, sooner or later the Powers will twig just how dangerous you are to them.'

'Okay. Okay. Let me think,' he tried but couldn't. His thoughts were like the swirling eddies in the river below.

'Nothing to think about. Shit or bust, mate.'

'I'm not your fucking mate, and what favour? What do I have to do?'

'Are you too stupid to realise?'

'Realise what?' asked Paddy.

'That right now, I'm the only thing keeping you alive. "I'm not your mate?" Is that what you said? If that's what you think, then go on fuck off now,' Barlow pointed toward the estate. 'Go on, go.'

He grabbed Paddy's arm and pulled him from the bonnet, pushing him toward the driver's door. 'Go on. See how long you last.'

'Ok, OK.' Paddy put his hands up, and his head down. 'What do you want me to do?'

Barlow spoke quietly but firmly. 'Here's the deal. You get Conor Walsh. I give you a fresh start here.'

'What do you mean, "Get him"?'

'I want him knocked off his perch. I don't care how you do it. Get some dirt on him, double-cross him, do what you like, but I want him gone. I'll get Jack Power to open the door for you, he'll arrange for you to hide out in Wicklow. Don't tell Power we've spoken, he'll make like it's his idea, you just need to go along with it.'

Paddy nodded. He didn't know what else to do. 'How do I get rid of him?'

Barlow tapped the side of his head. 'You're gonna have to use this. I can get you in there. Then it's up to you. Give us something solid we can get him on, launch a coup, give him a knock with a hammer. I don't care, do whatever you have to. You do this for me, and I guarantee this is all done, gone, clean. You'll need your wits about you; he hasn't survived this long by being stupid. If you're not careful, we'll be digging another hole in the ground.'

'What's this guy done to you?'

'Not just him, all of them, like a cancer eating away at the state. The virus of rebellion we've got to snuff it out. You're my penicillin.'

'What?'

Barlow wiped his hands as if cleaning them. 'Just get it done. Power will be in touch with you.' He took a few steps toward his car and stopped, then he turned to face Paddy. 'When you get across the water, remember who your real boss is.'

'What about Carol and Vinny?' Paddy asked.

'You do what you're told, and they'll be fine.'

Paddy nodded in defeat.

Barlow got in his car. He revved the engine, spun the tyres, and threw up a cloud of dirt as he pulled away.

Paddy looked out over the river. The sky darkening, the tide had turned; water would rush out to sea. He would soon be going out with it, through the estuary, and across the water to the land of his birth.

Chapter Three

Paddy

Liverpool, 1974

'Must've been a hell of a crack you gave him?'

Jack Power was in his armchair. Charlie was behind the cocktail bar in the corner. They had rigged beer pumps with kegs underneath. Like a real bar, spirits were arrayed in a line of optics. The front room of the three-bedroom house in Speke had been turned into a mini pub. Paddy hadn't been offered a drink.

'It's no good, you know.' Jack's original Irish accent had been replaced with a guttural Scouse. It sounded over the top to Paddy, like Jack had practised it.

'I couldn't do anything, Jack. After he laid Charlie out, he came at me.' Paddy wanted it clear that the only reason he had to hit the guy was that Charlie had fucked up.

'A hammer to the head?'

'I picked up the nearest thing to hand. I didn't know he'd crack like an egg.'

Charlie stifled a laugh.

'You can shut up as well. You were supposed to be in charge.'

'One of those things,' Paddy said.

'My arse. Now the two of you have to disappear. We don't know who's going to come sniffing round, and I don't want either of you picked up. Both of you could've been seen outside

17

the Blue Union. What a fucking mess.' Jack pointed to Charlie who was pulling himself a pint. 'Charlie's off to family down in London.' He pointed at Paddy. 'Where are you going?'

'I thought I'd see it out here, you know keep a low profile.' Paddy knew what was coming. The door opened and Teresa, Jack's missus, popped her head in.

'Hello, love.' She beamed at Paddy, eyes twinkling at her sometime lover.

Paddy half-raised a hand, 'Hi.'

'What do you want, can't you see we're talking,' snapped Jack.

'I'm sorry love. Is Paddy staying for something to eat? I can put an extra pie in for him.'

Paddy didn't wait for Jack to answer. 'Oh thanks, but I promised the little one I'd be home.'

'Oh, that's nice. See that, Jack, a family man.'

'Will you get out woman.' Jack spat the words. Teresa pulled a face before closing the door.

'What are we going to do with you? That's the question. We can't let anything about the other night get out. You'd be done for murder, you do know that? Self-defence won't wash with them.' Jack was making a big deal of giving it lots of thought.

'I know, I can never say a word. You know me, Jack. How long have I been with you?'

'I know, I know. That's why I've pulled a few strings for you. I've found you a place to keep your head down. It wasn't easy mind, but I managed to sort you out in Wicklow. What do you think of that?'

Paddy opened his eyes wide in mock surprise. 'Wow' - he paused for effect - 'Wicklow, I mean, I don't know anyone.'

'We've sorted all that,' Charlie spoke up. 'Jack has called in some favours. You'll be going to work for Conor Walsh.'

'I've heard the name, but don't know the man.'

'You soon will. He takes no prisoners, an old IRA man from back in the day. You know what they do with snitches.'

Paddy frowned, 'There are no snitches here.'

'That's right because they know what they'd get,' said Charlie from the corner.

The silence hung for a minute before Jack exclaimed. 'Ok well, time for you to pack a bag. I've got you on a ship tonight from Garston. The Esmeralda, Gerry the skipper, is an old mate of mine.'

'Tonight?' Paddy's surprise was genuine this time.

'Yeah, tonight, you gotta get out of here. Charlie will drive you.'

The clock above the mantelpiece chimed 8 pm. The little fella would be bathed and in bed now.

Charlie drove the Escort down Western Avenue toward the Pegasus. Hundreds of Escorts came off the line every week in Fords, so it was a popular car locally. In the offices of Liverpool council, there were plans for an extension of Western Avenue all the way to the river, with a promenade and Lido. The plans never made it onto the estate; they were filed away until money was available. Twenty years later and there was no sign of money ever turning up.

The car swung around the roundabout and along Central Avenue, finally circling the Parade and turning into the maisonettes.

Charlie made a show of looking at his watch.

'He's catching the tide at ten. You're gonna be on that boat. Get a move on.'

Paddy got out of the car and before he reached the flat, the door was open. Carol stood with arms folded. 'What's going on?'

Paddy brushed past her. 'Let me get inside will you.'

'What's going on? Why is Charlie waiting for you?'

'I've got to go away for a while, just a few weeks. Will you close that door?'

Carol closed the door. 'Go where?' One of his favourite songs was playing.

'London, I've got a job. A few weeks work. It's good money, so I'll be able to send some back. It's all a bit of a rush.' He passed the living room

'What work? What are you gonna do in London?'

Paddy grabbed a sports bag.

Carol pulled at one of the handles. 'Do you think I'm stupid? You're not going to London; you're running off to Ireland.'

Paddy pulled the bag away from her and climbed the stairs. Carol followed him. 'At least tell me the truth.'

Paddy stopped halfway up. 'Shush, woman, you'll wake Vinny.' He stepped into the bedroom, opened a drawer and pulled out a couple of shirts. Carol was following him. He went into the bathroom, opened the cabinet and threw his shaving gear into the bag. He moved to the top of the stairs, then stopped. He gave the bag to Carol. 'Give me a minute.' He turned and put his hand on the door to Vinny's room. 'Please.'

Carol went down the stairs. Paddy slipped inside the room. The curtains were drawn, but there was a starry night light that projected the solar system onto the ceiling. By the light of the stars, Paddy looked at his son sleeping soundly. He could hear Johnny Nash 'I Can See Clearly Now' playing downstairs. Life was so much easier before Vinny. He didn't have to care for anyone or anything, then Vinny arrived. Now he would stand in front of a bus for this guy. Getting out was the least harmful. Jail or death, this little guy didn't need to deal with either of those. With luck, six months and he would be back. He leaned down and let his fingers brush the soft skin of his cheek. 'See ya, mate.' He turned and left the room.

Carol was waiting for him at the bottom of the stairs. 'This is because of the mess with that fella?' She held out the bag. 'I put some socks and underwear in.'

'Thanks, love. I have to get out. Three, six months. I can send for you and Vinny.'

'Where?'

'Wicklow.'

'Don't bother.' Carol let go of the bag and opened the door. Paddy leaned in to kiss her. Carol moved her head back out of the way.

'You know if you go to Ireland, you won't come back,' she said as he left. Paddy walked straight to the waiting car.

Charlie turned the engine over and they pulled out back around the shopping centre, the Parade. Paddy scanned the street. Teenagers were gathering outside the off licence, the only open shop in the steel shuttered Parade. They passed the large three-storey family houses on Central Avenue, half a dozen or more kids was not unusual among Irish Catholics. The dual carriageway Speke Boulevard took traffic straight from the M62 past the Speke council estate and into Liverpool proper. They would turn off under the bridge in Garston Village. St Michael's church on an outcrop towered over the approach to the docks. With the church at one end, three pubs in its short span and the docks at the other, King Street was a journey through history. Starting and ending as Liverpool history does with the river, and through it, the world.

'It's all laid out for you. You cross the water to Arklow, make your way to O'Malley's pub and you'll be delivered from there to Wicklow.' Paddy had arrived at Stalybridge dock twenty years earlier, angry and hungry. He swore he would never go back.

Chapter Four

Vinny

Wicklow, 2010

'Ready?' Anne asked.

'Yeah, I think so.' Vinny strapped himself in. 'You okay driving?'

'I'll be fine.' Anne turned the key, and the engine started. 'Your uncle knows we're coming?'

'Yeah. It's weird calling him my uncle. I've only just met him.'

Anne reversed and then turned out of the car park. They went up into town and then turned left at the crossroads. The road out of town to the South took them past Wicklow Gaol. The imposing structure was now the town's busiest tourist attraction. The drive south also took them past the Black Castle, the oldest built structure on the coast, a legacy of England's first invasion. The road weaved between the coast and the rich farmland it bordered. Away from the sea's blue expanse, the land and road rolled in soft curves up, over, and between hills.

'It's beautiful,' said Anne.

'And deadly,' said Vinny.

'You mean your dad?' asked Anne.

'Him as well, but these country roads, crossroads, villages were all perfect ambush country. Police stations out in the sticks had no chance.'

'Are you nervous?'

'Not really. I'm still kinda putting things together. It's different now we are here.'

'What do you mean?'

'I'm a historian. I know all about the 1916 Easter Rising, the War of Independence, how the British forced them to sign away the North to get peace. Then the civil war.'

'Yeah, and…'

'It's always the same. There is the grand sweep of history, society, and government, but then there are the individual stories. Like my dad, and the thousands like him who left.'

'Isn't it supposed to be the individual stories that make history?' Anne asked.

'No. It should be, but it's not.' Vinny looked across at Anne. 'Actually, they become history if they are told. That's what you do.'

'Me?' asked Anne.

'Journalists, yeah, you start from the other end. You tell people's stories, and that's the news, but it's also the first step in recording history.'

'So, we are doing the same job?' asked Anne.

'Maybe, but from different ends of the spectrum.' They drove on in silence for a while, an unfinished conversation lingering in the air. Vinny asked, 'Can we pull over?'

'Are you okay?'

'Yeah, I just want to stretch my legs.' Anne pulled over at the entrance to a field. There was no gate, so once out of the car, Vinny walked into the field. Anne opened her door but remained in the car.

When Vinny returned, he approached Anne's side. 'I know you want to move on.'

Anne angled her head slightly. 'From the job, yeah.' She paused. 'I've done it for six years now. If I don't move, I'll get stuck.'

'Like me, you mean?'

Anne got out of the car. 'No. It's not about you.'

'Because I don't want to move.' Vinny bent and picked a blade of grass. He split the base of the blade in two. 'I'll be at Liverpool Uni for as long as they'll have me, till I retire.' He pulled the two strands of grass apart till he held one in each hand.

'We're at different stages,' Anne said.

'Is this about age?' Vinny asked.

'Between us, no? Not in that way, but in a life sense, maybe, yeah. I want more than The Chronicle, a change.'

'More than me?'

'Oh, come on, self-pity doesn't suit you.' Anne laughed. 'No, strike that, actually it does.' She reached across and put her hand on his. 'You're the original emo kid who never grew up.'

'I was never an emo kid.' Vinny half-smiled. 'But you're right, don't let my lack of ambition hold you back.'

'It's not a lack of ambition. You've done it. A history professor is all you wanted to be. Well, now you have it.'

'Whoopidy doo. I get to talk about what dead people did.'

'Speaking of which, shall we go and see what happened to your dad?'

He gave a half-laugh. 'Ooh, that was brutal.'

'I know, welcome to the new me. Come on.'

Vinny let the separate blades of grass fall from his hands.

* * *

Ballyglasheen Cross, the sign said. Anne drove through another small village. 'We're nearly there. Just a couple of miles now. Look at that name. You don't get more Irish than that.'

Miles of hedgerows and trees lined both sides of the road between the villages. When the growth dropped away, the crest of gently rolling hills led off beyond Tipperary and into Waterford. They passed a Magners plant. 'Look at the size of those tanks.' Vinny pointed. 'Do you think they're full of cider?'

'What else? There's a roundabout coming up. Where are we going?'

'Okay, straight through, there's a couple more, keep going.

Across the Water

We're getting into the town now. I'll tell you when to turn.' Vinny consulted his phone. 'We're a minute away.'

* * *

Vinny rapped the tarnished brass knocker. He couldn't help his anxiety. He looked around and guessed the house was a council property. The bit of garden in the front was overgrown. Anne reached forward and squeezed his hand. He mouthed the words 'Thank you.'

He heard a rustling from inside and then finally the lock being turned. Marty opened the door.

'Hi,' Vinny started but didn't finish.

'Good to see you again. Come on in, come in.' Marty stepped back.

Vinny led the way. The living room was small but comfortable, an armchair faced the TV, and a sofa ran along the back wall. The house had the odd familiarity of the unknown, the sofa and chairs, the TV, the tiled mantelpiece. Vinny realised he had travelled back in time. Everything was the same as in the mid-seventies. The decor and furniture were the same as his mum's house used to be in Speke. The most obvious difference was the lack of a crucifix or the more common sacred heart of Jesus.

'Sit down, sit down.' He ushered them toward the sofa.

Vinny sat awkwardly on the edge of the sofa; Anne sat back.

'Is Sean not here?' Vinny asked.

'He's on his way,' said Marty. 'You look like your dad. When I saw you at that hotel, and as I'm looking at you now. It's my brother Patrick I'm looking at.' He shook his head. 'Oh, I'm forgetting me manners. Will you have a tea?'

'No, I'm fine thanks,' said Vinny. 'I came to sort out what we're going to do.'

Martin looked toward Anne. 'Sorry I'm terrible with names.'

'Anne,' she volunteered. 'It's Martin, isn't it?' she asked.

'It is. Marty to me mates.'

'Good to meet you again. You know, if it's okay with you, I wouldn't mind a tea,' Anne said.

Marty straightened his arms on the chair to lift himself.

Anne smiled, 'No, let me do it.' She rose from her seat. 'You two men can say hello properly.' Anne winked at Vinny.

'If you're sure. There's a kettle on the side, and all the stuff is there.'

Vinny knew Anne was playing a role.

'No problem.' Anne took her coat off and went into the kitchen.

'Well, this is a turn-up. You could've knocked me over when Sean told me what he'd found.'

'Do I really look like him?' asked Vinny.

'You do. Like father, like son, you can't break that connection. Patrick's your dad alright. Anyone who knew him would say that.'

There was a knock on the door.

'Oh, that'll be Sean.' Marty went to open the door.

Vinny heard the voice from the front door. 'Here yeh go, Marty.'

'Come on in. They're here.' Marty came in carrying an oven dish covered in cellophane. He raised the dish. 'Your aunties think I'll starve if they don't feed me. Here, come in, Sean.'

Anne popped her head into the room. 'How do you like your tea Marty?'

'Milk and three sugars.'

Anne's eyes widened. 'That's not good for you, you know.'

'Oh, I know, love, but there's no one here to stop me.'

'Fair enough, three sugars it is,' she disappeared again.

Vinny shook his head; Anne knew exactly how to play to Marty's stereotype.

'A lovely woman.'

'She is,' Vinny smiled. 'I guess he's buried here?' Vinny asked, redirecting Marty from Anne to his father.

'He is a couple of miles up the road. It was a small affair, just me and your aunties. They look after the grave. I'm not one for that. They did tell me about a flower that was put there each year, but it's stopped now.'

Anne came in carrying a tray with three mugs of tea.

'You found everything then.'

'Yeah, I usually do. Three sugars.' She smiled at him.

'Here, love,' Marty lifted a small side table and placed it in front of the sofa.

'Did I hear you say something about flowers on your brother's grave?' asked Anne.

Marty took a drink of tea, issued a satisfied sigh and placed the cup back on the table. 'Yeah, every year for a while. I don't know how long, to be honest. Vinny's aunties looked after the plot.'

'No card or message?' asked Anne.

'No, nothing.'

'What kind of flower was it?'

Marty pursed his lips together as if the act of memory required a physical prompt. 'A lily, I think, white.'

'Ok, thanks,' said Anne.

'So,' said Vinny. 'Now that we're all here.'

'Here, you'll be wanting these.' Marty pulled a brown manila envelope out from the side of his chair.

'It's the papers, like, from the Gardaí.'

Vinny opened the envelope and spread the contents on the table in front of him.

Anne leaned over and identified them. 'Death certificate, accident report, undertaker's bill, stonemason.'

'So, no suspicions were raised at the time?' asked Vinny.

'No, an accident. He come off the bike, his head was bashed in. That's it really,' said Marty. 'We didn't think of anything.'

'No, why should you?' said Vinny. 'No helmet?'

'Didn't have to in those days,' said Marty.

'If Marty hadn't kept the bike, we would never have known,' said Sean

'It didn't feel right getting rid of it, not scrapping it, anything like that. That's why I asked you if Sean here could have it.'

'You called the police?' Anne asked Sean.

'Yeah, they sent two guys out, detectives.'

'What did they say?' asked Anne,

'Not much. They looked at the tyre and the bullet, and said it could have happened anytime over the last years, someone using the bike as target practice.'

'I guess that's true,' said Vinny.

'Except I know, it's been here in my shed, no one has touched it, and certainly not for target practice. Nobody has been near it until Sean started work on it last week.'

'Inertia,' said Anne.

'In what?' asked Marty.

'Inertia. It takes more energy to start something, so until they have to, the police will let things rest.'

'Do we want them involved?' asked Vinny.

'Not sure yet,' said Anne. 'At the moment it probably means we know more than they do. It also means they are not looking. It would be nice to get some background on what your dad was doing.' Anne picked up the documents from the table.

'The question is who would want to kill him and why?'

'She knows her stuff,' said Marty.

'And I can make a good cup of tea.'

'That you can love.'

'Can we take these?' asked Anne,

'Of course, they're all yours.'

'As to the 'who and why.' Marty shook his head. 'No idea.'

'What will you do?' asked Sean.

'Try to find out what he was doing in Wicklow,' said Anne.

Vinny changed tack. 'It wasn't easy to find you. All I had was the old service card from my dad's funeral. If you'd have moved…'

'I haven't been far, all my life within ten miles. Sure, I've been up to Dublin for a couple of weeks' work, but no, I'm here now, nothing will shift me.'

'I'm gonna get going,' said Sean. 'My mum made me promise to invite you over.'

'Yeah, well, now I know I've got aunties.'

'And a shower of cousins,' said Marty.

'Tell your mum we'll see her before we head back,' said Vinny. Marty nodded and Anne waved as Sean left.

'Here, let me show you.' Marty raised himself and crossed the room. He picked up two framed photographs and handed them to Vinny. 'The first is me with Maeve and Ciara. That's some years ago now, mind you. The other is Christmas a couple of years back. It's the two families together.'

The second photo showed a chaotic scene of kids and adults squeezing into the frame, the younger children brandishing toys, teenagers looking like they wished they could be anywhere else. The adults, including Marty, held drinks, a Christmas tree in the background sparkled with pinpricks of light. He couldn't help comparing it to the dull Christmases of his youth, just him and his mum.

Vinny smiled. 'Nice. No Paddy though. He was lost by then?'

'That's right, another one.'

'Another?' asked Anne.

'Lost lives, this place is full of them.'

Vinny looked at the earlier picture of Marty and his sisters. They stood in a line. Although they were all smiling, there was something sad and off about the slight distance between them. Vinny thought of Charlie, how he loved to climb all over him. Unfortunately, that was happening less and less as he grew up and away. The guilty McDonald's meals on Saturday afternoon no longer impressed his son.

'And you, Marty? No kids?'

'Never married. No, it wasn't for me.'

'So, my dad.'—Vinny put his mug down—'I didn't know anything really. My mum refused to talk about him. I think she never forgave him for leaving the way he did. Is there anything you can tell us? Anything about his background here that might help us.'

'I think he meant to go back, but then he had the'—he paused before adding— 'the accident.'

'Why do you say that?' asked Vinny.

'There was nothing for him here. He'd been in England so long since he was a young man himself. As soon as he could, he got out of here, and I can't say I blame him.'

'Why's that?'

'A lot of boys joined the army and went to sea or off to England; anything to get away.'

'Away from what?' asked Anne.

'Here.' Marty spread his hands.

'People left looking for work?' said Vinny.

'There was that, but with your dad and a lot of others I knew, they wouldn't stay here after what happened to them.'

'What happened?' Vinny looked at Anne. 'What do you mean?'

'Your dad, and me and your aunties, we didn't see each other as kids. Well, the girls did. Thank God for that. They had each other. But your dad and I, well, they split us up.'

'I'm sorry,' Anne said.

'No, you're alright, love. I can talk about it. They can't hurt me now, or your dad.'

Anne reached over and held Vinny's hand. As Marty continued talking, his grip tightened as the story unfolded.

'Our mam died. Later on, I did some digging and found it was cancer, breast cancer, but thirty-five she was.'

'So young,' said Anne.

'Aye love, well when she died, our dad was working over in England, so the authorities put us in Ferryhouse, me and your dad in Ferryhouse, and the girls went to a cousin of our mam .'

'What's Ferryhouse?' asked Vinny.

'Saint Joseph's was its proper name; an industrial school ran by the Fathers. It was somewhere between an orphanage and an approved school, I guess. Kids who had nowhere else to go or were too much trouble for their parents. Anyway, that's where we ended up.'

'You said you got split up,' said Anne.

'We did. I was older than Patrick, old enough to work. So, they had us on the farms roundabout. We would work all hours, no money mind you, in all weathers. Sometimes we went back to the school to sleep, sometimes not. It all depended on the farmer if you were treated alright, but there's no hiding it. There were some miserable bastards, used us like donkeys.'

'That sounds terrible,' said Vinny

'Yeah, well, that wasn't the worst of it. The boys back in the school who had to put up with the Christian Fathers, well, they had it worse.'

'My dad was one of them?'

'He was... awful things, awful stories come out later, about what went on, what they did to those boys.'

'It must be hard to talk about,' said Anne.

'Not so much for me, love. The girls get upset, your aunties like, and well, we don't know what they did to your father, how badly he was damaged. But for me, it's just anger. I've no sadness or regrets, any of that stuff. I don't think back on it. It's in here,' he said, slapping his chest, 'and up here.' He touched the side of his head. 'And that's where it's staying. I'm not letting the bastards out. Excuse my language now, but bastards is what they were. Well, they never broke me. I'm here, and they'll all be in the ground by now. And I hope to God none of them are up there'—he raised a single finger— 'because I'll tell you this, if they are up there, then I'm turning round and going straight down to the other place because it couldn't be any worse than what them fellas do.'

'So, my dad left?'

'He did, but your father was a fighter son. You should be proud. He broke a stick over one of them fellas, all the other kids cheering and whooping. He clouted the fella good and proper. Then, of course, he had to run, or they would've killed him.

'I was with your aunties at the time. We had found each other. My oldest sister, Maeve, was just married and had a little house, and I and my other sister lived there all together like, for a couple of years. We was making up for lost time, you might say. I went back to the school and told Patrick where we were. I don't know if that's what started him off, but, well, he clouted the fella, and next we knew, he was on our doorstep. We had one night with him, and the next morning he was off. And didn't the Gardaí come looking for him, doing the dirty work of those bastards? Council, Gardaí, the courts, they were all in it together.' He paused, took a breath, and clapped. 'But your dad got off, and, well, here you are.'

Vinny sat back in his seat.

'Are you okay?' Anne asked Vinny.

'He'll be fine. He's a fighter like your father, eh son?'

Vinny shook his head. 'Can I er… use your toilet a minute?'

'Of course, you go out the door there up the stairs, and it's facing you.'

Vinny climbed the stairs quickly. He closed the door, sat on the toilet lid, and put his head in his hands. Jesus Christ.

For years he had been angry, betrayed, and abandoned by his father. He had listened to his mum, calling him a loser, no good, for years. The absence was a real, physical thing, an empty space where his father should have been. Now that space was filling, He could feel his father's pain. He didn't know if it was being in the place his father grew up, or just his imagination, but he felt the anger, confusion, and betrayal his father must have suffered as a child. How the priests, the police, and the courts had treated them. Vinny had no right to be angry at his father, his old schools, Saint Christopher's and Cardinal Allen, might not have been perfect, but fucking hell.

He pulled the chain, splashed some water on his face. As he dried it, he looked in the mirror. He wanted to see his father's face. All he saw was his own.

Anne stood when Vinny went back into the living room. 'Are you okay?'

Across the Water

'Yeah, I'm fine.'

They sat down.

'Marty was just saying we should meet your aunts,' said Anne.

'Yeah, that would be good. Maybe next week, eh? Before we go back?'

'Do you want to see your dad's grave?'

'Yeah, but maybe next week for that too. It's a lot to take in.'

* * *

They were quiet getting back to the car.

'Do you want me to drive back?' Vinny asked.

Anne went to the passenger side, opened the car and climbed in. 'A lot to take in.'

Vinny was in the driver's seat. 'Yeah, not half. I don't know what I was expecting, but Marty was a nice guy.' Vinny was about to start the car but looked at Anne.

'What is it?' she asked.

'The stuff about my dad in that home.'

'Yeah.'

'I always thought I was the victim, you know, he abandoned me kinda thing. Then when we found out all the stuff about him killing Mark Riley. It was like this guy was a monster, some kind of nutter, and now…'

'Now… you don't know what to think?'

'Right, okay, yeah, he killed someone, no excuse for that, but what kind of life led up to it?'

The evening was bringing a grey mist with the growing darkness. In the absence of conversation, the slap of the windscreen wipers filled the car. Anne was thinking of white lilies.

Chapter Five

DI Barlow

Liverpool, 1974

'Who do you think you are? SAS, MI5? You need to get a grip. Your job is here in Liverpool.'

'I can bring down an IRA gun route,' said Barlow.

Commander Marsh paced the room. 'No, you can't. Pass your intelligence on to someone empowered and qualified to act on it. Keep your fantasies for your missus, not your job.' Cdr Marsh sat down, his finger prodding the walnut veneer of his desk. 'This country is falling apart. Didn't you notice the blackouts? It wasn't so long ago I was sitting in my living room playing cards around a candle with my kids. Birmingham officers got the Shrewsbury 24. They sent the two guys to jail for picketing, and where were they from?'

'Liverpool.'

'Yes, here'—he banged his desk—'Scousers shutting down half the country's building trade and you're playing catch the Paddy.'

'We've got experts for that, Military Intelligence, MI6. Jesus Christ, there's a whole load of letters and numbers, secret government departments, after them. You think you're going to make the difference?' He stood up again.

'Do this job not the one in your head,' he pointed out the window. 'We've got seamen, dockers, car workers, train drivers, you name it, all organising to overthrow us. If you think Wilson is bad, you haven't seen anything. If we don't stop them, these people will be running this city, this country before long.'

'We're on it. DS Jones has a project. We're into everything, the docks, Standard Triumph, Fords.'

Cdr Marsh's voice dropped an octave and he spoke slowly and clearly. 'No. DS Jones doesn't have a project. DI Barlow has a project, or DS Jones, who's doing what he's told might become DI Jones. Am I making myself clear?'

'Crystal.'

'Go after them. I want reports on who's meeting who, who's planning what, who's running this stuff. Who's on the shop floor? Who's coming in from outside? That's your job. You come across any Irish intelligence; you bring it in and hand it over. I've got a security and policing strategy meeting at the end of the month, and I want something to put on the table.'

Barlow was silent.

'The correct response, Detective Inspector, is "Yes Sir."' The Commander leaned back in his chair. 'You're good, John. I don't want to lose you.'

'Then give me the tools to do the job, sir. The Met have the SDS, they've got agents everywhere. It should be national; we should have it up here.'

'The Special Demonstration Squad infiltrate radical groups in London with undercover officers. They've got national resources. We're not the Met.'

'No, we're in Liverpool, even more reason. Do you know how many Commies and Trotskyists are back and forth over to Belfast? They're not separate anymore. It's not trade unions or politics — it's both. They're the same thing. The only thing missing is, throw a few criminal gangs in there and we're really fu....knackered.'

* * *

Barlow left the door open and walked past the secretary. He was shaking his head. Marsh didn't have a clue.

Lose me? He'd be lost without me.

Barlow drove back through town, up through Park Rd. He didn't trust this place—it was enemy territory. Just like Speke, no respect for authority, or each other, no wonder the place was falling apart. No one cared.

He wasn't going to let this go. He'd been working on the Powers for years. He didn't usually care what they did Under The Bridge in Garston, but the Irish connection was too good an opportunity to miss. Connolly was stupid, facing life for the murder of Mark Riley, and desperate enough to go along with it.

It was a good move—anyone from military intelligence could see that. He slapped the steering wheel, and it was quick thinking. Other bosses would be congratulating him. If he could get rid of Walsh, that would bring him the attention he deserved. MI5, Industrial Relations Department, there was plenty of money in those corridors of power. He needed a win to make it happen. He could prove they could handle undercover agents as well as London.

He passed a bus and stopped at a crossing. The engine of the Ford Capri was throbbing. He pressed the accelerator to hear it roar. A woman with her hair in rollers under a headscarf glared at him. He waited till she was near the pavement, slipped into first gear and pulled away, missing her by inches. He smiled into his mirror as she waved a fist.

He drove along Aigburth Rd toward Garston, and a few minutes later took a right into Cressington. He wanted a house in Crosby or Ormskirk, somewhere outside the city, but this would do for now. Twenty years in the Special Branch, the problem with these specialised units was no room for promotion. He was a DI and would be until Commander Marsh dropped dead or retired. He hoped it would be the former.

He pulled into the gravel drive. His detached house was far enough away from the people he watched and still affordable. He turned the engine off and sat back. It was always the same. The posh boys ruled the roost. Oxbridge, public school, they didn't really have a clue. For Barlow, the Communists were less of a problem. They were too busy fighting among themselves. It was the Irish. It had always been the Irish. That's what the Specials had been set up for, the Special Irish Branch was a unit of the Met.

He kicked his shoes off in the hallway. The cream carpet was still spotless a year after they had it installed, wall to wall. Cost an arm and leg, but kept the missus happy.

'Hello. Good day?' she asked.

'Yeah, not bad. Is Julie in?'

'She's out with Graham.'

'The blond lad who needs a barber? We'll have to keep an eye on him.'

'He's ok. His parents go to St Michael's in Garston.'

'Under The Bridge? You make sure she's careful, you know what I mean.'

'Of course, I do. You don't have to worry, Julie's a good girl.'

'They're all good girls till some lad pushes his luck and they end up in the club. Why can't she find a boy at University?'

'I'm sure she will; give her time. Sit down; I'll bring you your tea.'

'Well, he'd better not try anything, cos he'll know about it if he does.

The shrill tones of the telephone broke his thoughts. 'Get that, will you?' he slumped into his armchair, TV remote on the arm.

* * *

'It's Mike.' His wife held the phone out for him.

'How'd it go with the big C?' asked Mike.

'Same old shit, watching his back. I told him you were doing a good job on the industrial stuff, so we need results.'

'I've got something on tonight.'

'Where?'

'In Halewood, just after ten.'

'Mind if I tag along?'

'Course not, boss.'

'Great, pick me up at the house.'

Barlow slumped back in his chair. His dinner had been delivered to the side table next to his armchair. He flicked on the TV.

All around was chaos, Heath was out, there would be a minority Labour Government, the IRA were on the rampage, and politicians were talking about 'power sharing' between Northern and Southern Ireland. The country was sliding into anarchy.

He heard Mike pull up outside, 'Ok, I'm off love. I won't be late. Make sure Julie's home before I am.'

'She will be. You be careful.'

'I'll be fine, see you later.'

* * *

Barlow climbed into the passenger seat.

'Saved me from an evening with Des O'Connor, either that or watching as the country falls apart.'

'Don't know which is worse,' joked Mike.

Barlow snorted.

Mike drove along Aigburth Road and down through the village.

Across the Water

The airport terminal was on their right. Barlow looked at the impressive Art Deco entrance and air control tower. This city could really be something. One of the biggest ports in the world. The Mersey was full of ships when he was a kid. Unions were destroying it all; the dockers were on strike more than in work, the car factories were always out. The country was being ruined. Blacks and Irish, the twin evils of Liverpool.

Mike followed Speke Boulevard and then onto the Ford Road itself, built to connect the factory to the M62. The road separated the Speke estate from the forty-four acre site.

'Why are you going this way?' Mike took the slip road to the factory. They drove around the perimeter road to the Halewood exit.

'There's a power struggle going on. The Convenor of the Assembly Paint and Trim and is in with the left, but not everyone's happy.'

'What's on?' asked Barlow.

'Terry Connor, a shop steward, someone snitched on his brother. We've got statements, burglary, and robbing cars.'

'Hardly crimes of the century.'

'I'm doing what you said, trying to turn him.'

'What time does he get off?'

'He's on the afternoon shift. He finishes at 10 pm.'

They parked on Leathers Lane, not far from The Leather Bottle pub. Barlow never felt comfortable here.

'Does he go for a drink?'

'Nah, not unless they're having a meeting.'

At five past ten, the road suddenly got much busier as the factory shift ended. A few cars parked up near The Leather Bottle. Others were dropped from shared cars. They would have time for a pint before last orders unless there was a lock-in, but that was usually on payday.

'There he is.'

Instead of going into the pub, the man they were watching got out of a car and waved it off. He crossed the street and headed toward the maisonettes.

'Ready?'

They waited till he was just yards away, then both jumped out at once. The worker stopped and took a step back.

'Don't run, you won't get far,' said DS Jones.

'What do you want?'

'Get in.'

DS Jones moved forward. 'Get in the fuckin car.'

'We just want to talk,' said Barlow.

'I've told you I'm not interested,' Terry said to DS Jones.

Barlow opened the rear door. 'Terry isn't it? DS Jones here has told me all about you. You have thirty seconds to get in, or I go down there and arrest your brother. I'll drag him out of the house in front of your mum, dad, and all the neighbours.'

'You bastard.'

'Yeah, that's right. So, are you getting in?'

Terry looked up and down the road before sliding into the back of the car. Barlow and Jones got in. Jones was in the driver's seat. Barlow took the back seat next to Terry. Jones started the car.

'I told you I'm not interested,' Terry said. 'Let me out.'

'We don't care if you're interested or not. DS Jones here was being nice to you. You give him information. We look out for you.' Jones swung the car right and headed back up toward the factory. He took a left along Higher Road to Hunts Cross and accelerated. Barlow spat the words at Terry. 'That deal is gone. These are my terms. You tell us what's going on, and we don't lock your brother up. I've got him for stealing cars, burglary—you name it, your rat of a brother is up to it. You know it and I know it.'

Jones took a right then a quick left and parked the car outside The Hunts Cross Hotel.

Barlow turned round. 'It's not your mates. They're ok. It's the commies. You know who they are. They're not into unions like you. They're all about South Africa, Portugal and Ireland.

What's that got to do with you? The ANC and IRA, what's that got to do with better wages? Eh? You tell me. 'Cos I tell you what I think. I think they are using you. Do you support the IRA?'

'No. Of course not.'

'That's right,' said Mike.

'You're a shop steward right?'

'Right.'

'You are part of the Speke… what's it called?' Barlow asked Mike.

'Speke Area Trade Union Committee. Its rank and file,' he answered. 'Yeah, I've been to a few meetings, they gave out leaflets at the shop stewards meeting. It's not just Fords.'

'Who else is on it?'

'The Railway, Evans Medical, Mothaks, Dunlops…'

'There you go, that's the one,' said Barlow.

'What's going on with it?'

'It's a union committee. They talk about union stuff.' Terry's eyes bored into Barlow.

'What's up with the assembly plant at Ford's?' Mike asked.

'Alan Harvey wants to stop redundancies. That's what they're arguing for.'

'That's the left-wing line?'

'Yeah I guess so'

'I don't get it, don't they all want to stop redundancies?' asked Barlow.

'The right-wing is against compulsory redundancy, but they don't mind getting a few grand for voluntary redundancies.'

'Ok, that's a good start. But we want more, regular reports. What's going on in and outside the factory.'

'If I tell you to fuck off?'

'Then say goodbye to your brother. Oh, and your dad works for the council?

'Yeah, Parks and Gardens.'

'Mike here doesn't see you the night after the meeting; your dad can kiss his job goodbye as well.'

'You fucking bastards.'

'That's up to you, Terry. You can have us as bastards or mates, you decide. Now get out of the car.'

'Can't you take me back?'

'Walk, it'll give you time to think.'

Terry slammed the door and walked off.

There were few people around. No one walked these streets for pleasure, and those with purpose had long gone. The streetlamps threw halos of light within the darkness. A nervous dog scuttled along the pavement.

'Let's get out of here,' said Barlow.

Traffic was light leaving the area. Mike was driving. 'Fancy a pint before I drop you?'

'It's getting a bit late.'

'We'll be ok in the Garston Hotel, friendly landlord.'

'Yeah, go on then.'

The Garston Hotel at the top of St Mary's Road was a large purpose-built hotel and bar, long past its glory days, but it was still busy. The new container docks and rail terminal behind it provided its daytime patrons. Its location at the top of the village also meant it was the last pub before Aigburth.

'Things are changing and we have to keep up with it or we'll become paper chasers.' Barlow was holding forth.

The jukebox was blasting out 'This Town Ain't Big Enough for the Both of Us' by Sparks.

'We have to act. It's not just intelligence - it's counterintelligence. We are swimming in hostile waters and need suppression tactics. In Kenya, Aden, even in Cyprus, we armed and trained locals to do the fighting.'

'You had the army,' said Jones.

'Of course, we did, but that was the last resort. The idea was to show two local sides fighting, and we were there just to keep order, stop them killing each other. You have to create a narrative, tell a story.'

'This is not Kenya or Aden.'

'That's where you're wrong.' Barlow paused to increase the impact of his words. 'Everywhere is Kenya or Aden.' Barlow held his fingers out and counted off. 'We have an active hostile population, an organised minority trying to overthrow the legitimate power, same forces, same tactics.'

'And Terry?' asked Jones.

'Terry, like Paddy, is the first step. We destroy them from the inside. Get them in, then activate them.' Barlow drained his pint.

'To do what?'

'I don't know yet. We will have to wait and see. It depends what opportunities we get. I have to check in on Paddy to see what he's up to.'

'Do you want another?' Jones stood.

Barlow checked his watch. They were the last two customers in the bar. It was past closing time. 'Last orders have gone, haven't they?'

'What's the use of having power if you can't use it?' said Mike.

'Exactly,' said Barlow. 'Make mine a double.'

Chapter Six

Paddy

Wicklow, 1974

Paddy left the body of Mark Riley under the earth in England as he stepped back onto Irish soil. He walked along the quay at Arklow, passed the trucks waiting with loads of timber to be shipped to the Matchworks in Garston. If he ever wanted to make the same journey and see his son again, he would have to deal with Conor Walsh.

His feet slapped the wet stone. His smart shoes and crumpled suit were out of place on the dockside.

'Are you right, Paddy?'

'I'm grand.'

'If you go into the town there, find O'Malley's and ask the bar fella. It's all organised, you'll get a ride. You'll be right.'

'Thanks, Ger, you're a good man.'

'Take it easy now.' Ger spat into the harbour, his phlegm carried by the gusting wind.

Paddy pulled his jacket tight. He shivered in the mid-morning gloom. He wanted a hot bath. The cabin below deck was cramped and damp; he hadn't been warm since he left Garston. In Speke, the little fella would be up and about now. Carol would be cursing him. Maybe he could send for them. She might change her mind about Ireland. If he could get himself sorted in Wicklow. Why not?

Because she hated the idea of Ireland, that's why, for fucks sake. But he could see the little fella, he would organise, Michael his mate would help him. Michael was a good guy. Fuck the Powers.

There was a body in the ground because Charlie Power couldn't deliver a slap on his own, and now the bastard Barlow was on his back.

It was a short walk along the quay. He crossed the stone bridge into the town proper, then on to O'Malley's. The cars and trucks were English, but the names on the shops and businesses were Irish. He wasn't sure why he noticed that, but he did.

He'd get up to Wicklow and see Walsh. He was the Powers' contact in the town. Jack said he'd have a word with him, but after what happened, he didn't know if he could trust Jack. None of them trusted each other. Talk about dog-eat-dog, fucking rabid dogs might be more like.

Walsh worked with The Powers, but Barlow wanted to get rid of Walsh, and Paddy was to do whatever it took. He would need his wits about him; there would be nobody putting the flags out for his return. Paddy didn't know how much this guy Walsh was into the struggle in the North - he wanted to keep away from that. It was enough to have the English police on his back without all that shit.

O'Malley's was a typical Irish pub, shining bar, and grimy floor. The stones were swept regularly but never cleaned. Pubs were not houses, and the customers didn't appreciate being fussed over, keep the niceties for your grand hotels. In a pub, they wanted a fire to take the chill off, a pint to take the edge off, and a chat to forget the shite.

'Good morning. What'll you have?' The barman had a thin grey face.

'A ride to Wicklow,' said Paddy.

'Ah, right, that's you. Is it Conor Walsh's man?'

'It is indeed, I was told it's all organised.'

'It is, your ride will be along in good time.'

'In that case, I'll have a pint and a whiskey to put some warmth in my blood, while I'm waiting.'

The barman shouted, 'Kathleen, will you come and sort out the fire?' He turned to Paddy. 'She'll build it up for you now, see if we can't get a blaze.'

'That's very good of you.' Paddy walked across to the fire to warm himself.

When Kathleen appeared from behind the counter, the woman too young to be his wife, moved through the empty bar as if through a crowded theatre on her way to the stage. Her movement spoke to Paddy, and when he looked into the grey eyes he was gone.

Paddy lifted her hand from the logs. His touch was tender. She met and kept his gaze. 'Let me help you with that now. You don't want to be getting splinters there.'

He selected a log from a basket beside the fire and placed it in the grate. He picked up a long iron poker and brandished it like a sword stoking the fire. 'Let's put a bit of life into this thing.' Paddy stirred the embers.

'It looks like you know what you're doing.' She glanced nervously at the bar.

'I do indeed Kathleen, rest assured of that.'

'I will,' she turned, went back behind the counter and disappeared.

Paddy moved back to the bar where his drinks were waiting. 'It's a fine place you have.'

'It was my father's before me.' The barman had a cold, precise air about him. Every movement and word was measured and controlled.

Paddy took a drink of the pint, the dark stout slipped down easily, followed by a shot of the whiskey.

'What time will that ride be?'

'He'll be along when it's time.'

The harsh bell of the phone interrupted their conversation. The barman turned and disappeared into the back. He came out wringing a towel between his hands. 'It'll be the morning before you get up to Wicklow. There's a problem.'

'What problem?'

The barman ignored his question. 'Colm will have let Mr Walsh know. We've rooms here. You're best sticking where you are till it's sorted.'

Paddy wondered what kind of problem, somehow, it didn't feel right. 'I don't have towels and such. I wasn't the best at packing.'

'Kathleen will provide all you need.'

'Looks like I've no choice,' said Paddy.

'That's right.' The barman agreed. 'I'll get Kathleen out of the shop, you have your drinks, and it'll be ready for yeh.'

Paddy carried his drinks over to the table by the fire. The chair was straight back and hard, but the warmth more than made up for it. He'd had a rough night; he would never make a sailor. Gerry said the crossing was fine, so God knew what it would be like rough. He needed to adjust, let his head catch up with his feet. Liverpool was behind him

* * *

Paddy climbed the stairs, his energy draining with each creaking step. God, he needed a lie-down. The whiskey that warmed his bones was now closing his eyes. Straight ahead, the barman said.

The bed squeaked too; everything in this place had its voice. He drew the curtain over, closing out the sight of Arklow's parade ground and statue. He collapsed onto the bed, pushed off his shoes, and he slept.

Paddy opened his eyes to the half-light of late afternoon. He needed new clothes; at least he had a clean shirt in the bag. It would take a while, he had to let his head settle, it was all too recent. Mark Riley was England's ghost. Ireland had enough of its own. Mark would be lost among them. Mark was visiting Paddy more often, now the heat of the moment was well and truly cooled. When he relaxed and his mind wasn't filled with immediate needs and dangers, he would picture Mark's father waiting for a son who never came back from the sea.

Swinging his feet out of bed, he pulled on his trousers. There was a knock on the door before the knob rattled, and it opened.

'I brought you a towel. You'll be wanting a wash and a shave.'

'Could you not have waited?'

Kathleen stood before him, her hand extended, holding a towel. 'Oh, excuse me, I didn't take you for the shy type.'

'I'm not but, you're lucky I'm just after putting on my trousers.'

'You've got nothing I haven't seen before…' she paused.

'Paddy,' he said.

'Paddy. One of Mr Walsh's boys?'

He accepted the towel without answering. 'A shave would be great.'

'I'll bring your water.' Kathleen turned with a swish, and Paddy knew he was onto something. He took the towel into the bathroom across the hallway. The shaving mirror above the sink was balanced on the ledge of a small window, the bubbled glass was opaque, and behind it, the evening was grey before the black of night.

He turned the tap and half-filled the bowl with cold water.

'Here you go.' Kathleen held a steaming kettle with a tea towel around the handle.

Paddy took it from her, careful not to spill the boiling liquid. She leaned against the door frame as he added the boiling water to the bowl. He soaped his brush, getting a good head of foam. 'Jeez, it must be boring down there if this is exciting for you to watch.'

'It is. My dad has me stuck in the shop or helping in the bar all hours.'

'A lively-looking girl like you? You must have the local lads queueing up. Shouldn't you have a man of your own by now?'

'The chance'd be a fine thing since my mam passed, my da has me as his maid, cleaner, cook, and skivvy.' Kathleen reached forward. 'Here, give us that kettle. He'll be listening out for me on the stairs.'

Paddy grabbed her hand and pulled her in toward him, their bodies touched, and he leaned forward to kiss her. She held back for a couple of seconds before accepting his kiss.

She pulled away from him and picked up the kettle. Taking a step back, she said a little louder than necessary, 'If you need anything else, let me know.'

'Thank you, you've been very good, Kathleen,' he said.

Kathleen wiped the trace of soap from her face as she left.

Fresh shirt, shit, and a shave, and he was ready to turn the page.

Eddie, the barman, nodded as Paddy entered.

'I could be doing with a bite to eat now.'

'There's a chipper and a cafe down the main street there.'

Paddy hit the pavement. Eddie was a dark horse, looked like he could handle himself, but it would be worth the risk to have a go of that daughter of his, Kathleen.

He walked across the square, passed the statue of some fella pointing and leaning forward like he was about to fall over. Is the cafe that way? Is it now? Well if I were wearing a cap, I'd tip it to you. Thanks for the direction. He nodded to the statute.

Paddy walked the pavement on the main street, and car headlights flashed by him, the sound of engines rising and falling in waves, the few shops that were still open were lit up. It was just that turning point in the year when winter wouldn't let go and Spring was around the corner. New buds would arrive, and the long days with them, but now the town wore darkness like a blanket.

The line between normality and chaos was thinner than people knew. It wasn't so long ago they had the three-day week, power cuts, the whole thing was crazy. Even the governments couldn't get organised, the world was turning to shit, no doubt about it. The cafe was near the end of the main street. He would have a bite, then walk back up to the pub, a few drinks, a tap at Kathleen, then a decent kip.

He found the cafe and took a seat remembering the night before, he'd seen better jail cells than the boat. Everything was metal, which was cold before you started and couldn't get warmed up no matter what heat you threw at it. Then you placed it on top of the coldest water in the western hemisphere and shook it about for ten hours solid. No wonder old Ger was a pisshead. You'd have to be to keep sane. They finished a bottle of rum between them, it was only the alcohol that knocked him out, and everyone knew there was no rest in sleep when you'd more rum than blood in your veins. If he went back, it'd be on a proper ferry with a bunk and all, no more tin cans. But Ger was a good man. Paddy knew he wasn't the only parcel that went out on The Esmeralda through Garston docks.

He checked his pocket, he had plenty of cash for now, but it wouldn't last forever. He'd do a swap with the bar fella to change some money over. Wicklow was next, to get the measure of Walsh. At some point, he'd be on the road to Tipperary but there would be no 'sweetest girl I know,' like the song. If he saw the beast that took his virginity, he would give him a crown of thorns to go with his crucifix.

The empty cafe supplied meat and two veg with mashed spuds and lashings of gravy to line his stomach for a couple of pints later. Eating out was a luxury. It might be 1974, but the swinging sixties had passed Arklow by; there was no gurning, steaming espresso maker. You could have your tea with or without milk and sugar. Like religion with or without God, it didn't really matter as long as the performance was good.

Across the Water

He walked back to the pub at a brisk pace. The evening had deepened, turning the night black, the shop lights were out now, and the halos of the streetlights pointed the way down the road, somehow highlighting the darkness in between.

The door to O'Malley's was in the centre of the building. There was another door further down that must be to the shop Kathleen mentioned. The pub and shop combination was a common feature of smaller towns in an attempt to make both profitable.

The fire had warmed the bar, and Paddy felt at home. It didn't take much; his anxieties and troubles were all in the mind; the body could take its pleasure in the physical things, a warm bar, a good pint, and a soft bed, preferably one that wasn't dancing its way across the Irish Sea.

Eddie was serving, two customers were holding up the bar, Paddy was happy to wait his turn.

'Did you find a bite?' Eddie asked.

'I did, the little cafe on the main street.'

'Ah, that would be Rooney's. He's had that a couple of years now, but who would want to go to a cafe when you've got food at home?'

'That's like saying who would want a pub when you've a drink at home?' the customer receiving his pint said.

'Well, you've a point there,' Eddie conceded.

'I'll have a pint of the dark stuff,' Paddy said.

'Niall, this here's Paddy, using one the rooms upstairs, and this is Jim, the local undertaker.' Eddie nodded to the second customer.

Paddy wouldn't have had him for an undertaker. He looked shiftier, like an office worker, a clerk or something.'

'How are yeh?' asked Jim. His thin face suited his thin tie.

'I'm good and yerself?'

'You know how it is, coming out of the winter.'

'Yeah, I forget what it's like. It'll be a busy time for you then?'

'Oh, we got our share, what with the flu's and the cold.'

'Have you been away a while, have you?' Jim asked. He reminded Paddy of a dog with its nose in the air twitching for scents.

'A good while, nearly twenty years since I was here.'

'Are you coming from Liverpool?' asked Niall.

'I am,' said Paddy.

'That's a wicked place, that Liverpool.' said Jim.

'Have you been?'

'No, but I've heard all about it, didn't me two brothers go over there.' Jim nodded to agree with himself.

'So why is it wicked?' Paddy provoked.

'Well, there's people over there would steal the eyes out of your head given half a chance and then sell them back to you one by one.'

Paddy laughed and raised his glass. 'It's good to be home.'

The three men raised their glasses.

Paddy caught sight of Kathleen through the doorway behind the bar. Her smile was all the invitation he needed.

'Would it be alright to leave me a pint awhile? I need to check something in my room.'

Eddie lifted the hinged countertop at the corner of the bar.

Once behind the bar, with Eddie's back turned. Paddy lifted a quart bottle of Power's whiskey from the shelf and slipped it in his jacket pocket. At the stairs, he motioned for Katleen to follow him from where she looked out the back kitchen. Once upstairs, he pulled her into his room. He pressed his mouth on hers, and his hand slid up under her skirt and enjoyed the feel of her smooth, round bum.

She pulled her head away while simultaneously pushing his hand down. 'Jeez, ye'll get us both killed, yeh mad bugger.'

'Kathleen, I hope you're not bothering our guest up there,' Eddie shouted from the bottom of the stairs.

There was silence and then a creak as he started climbing the stairs.

Kathleen pulled herself free. 'No, father, I'm just wiping

down the bathroom.'

She slipped out, leaving Paddy alone and frustrated. He opened the whiskey, took a swig then put the Powers under his pillow.

He squeaked his way back down the stairs.

'It was a great occasion. Gun carriage, salutes, I'd have to say they did him proud,' Jim said.

'What was that then?' asked Paddy as he came through the bar.

'Dev's funeral up there in Dublin. I went up for the day. The whole city was out.'

'Yeah, well, another of those sanctimonious bastards, if you ask me.' he took a drink of his pint and placed it firmly back on the bar.

Jim, about to take a drink, stopped and put his pint down. 'You can't be saying that.' He looked around the room for support. 'Not with De Valera giving his life for the country.'

'I'll say what the fuck I like,' said Paddy. 'I don't know about giving his life for the country, but didn't he give the country to the church?'

'A bit of respect for the dead, and him being President and all,' said Jim.

'You're a great one to talk about respect. Wasn't you just warming your hands at the winter and the money you made off the auld ones?' Paddy said with half a smile on his lips.' I was doing no such thing,' said Jim.

'And him being President.' Paddy threw the phrase back at them. 'Wasn't him and his bollocks fighting for the country that didn't know what to do with it when they won?'

'You're showing your ignorance now. They were fighting for freedom,' said Jim.

'He's a guest of mine Jim, let's keep good order in here,' said Eddie, wiping down the bar and shaking his rag as if shaking away the tension.

'I don't care who he is - he's no right speaking like that, no right.' His head back and nose up, Jim blinked his disapproval.

'Was it not freedom them fellas was fighting for? Isn't that what you said?' Paddy insisted.

'It was our freedom from the English.'

'My freedom to call them sanctimonious bastards,' said Paddy. He slapped his empty pint pot on the bar. 'Oh, and how did that freedom from the English thing work out for your brothers in Liverpool?' asked Paddy. 'Another in there, please Eddie, and give this man whatever he's having.' Paddy couldn't be arsed getting angry with this fella. He would need to save that for Wicklow.

'That's what I like to see,' said Eddie, nodding.

Jim snorted half a reply, but wouldn't argue with someone who had just refilled his glass. Paddy stretched out the hand of friendship. 'I hear you boys are ok at Hurling.'

'Now then,' said Jim. 'At football too, winners of the Kavanagh cup in '73.'

Niall clapped his hands and Eddie's rag was tucked in his waist.

'The rocks are a championship team in the making,' said Jim.

'Ah but can we beat Glenleavy?' asked Niall.

Paddy relaxed, drank and watched the conversation flow naturally back into its course. The more he drank, the less concerned he was with Kathleen or dead Presidents.

When he finally laid his head, she was nowhere to be seen. Probably hiding, he thought, resisting temptation. She was a nice bit, but nothing to write home about. The thought made him laugh. As if he could write home to Carol about a bit in Ireland, wouldn't that just do the trick and get her over.

He remembered the little fella. It wasn't so bad now. It was kind of good knowing he was safe, warm, and had a mam that would look after him. Paddy wasn't selfish. Sure, he would like to swing him about by his arms or tickle-dry him with the towel, smell the sweet soap off his skinny wriggling body, but he could wait. He'll be a good lad, a smart fucker, better with me out the way. I'd be dead or in jail in Liverpool. When he thought about it, his chances were no better in Ireland, but at least he didn't have to worry about the kid seeing it all.

Confused, sleepy, and half-drunk, he thought he was back in Speke, the little fella climbing into bed with him, the same soft skin and sweet smell. Until the hand slid inside his pants and began stroking him. Fucking hell, she had some balls.

She had his balls in her hand. There was no light, and the bed squeaked like a mouse in a cat's jaw. But he did the business. Kathleen was no mug. She pushed him off before he fired his ammo. Fair enough. He thought she'd be washing the sheets anyway.

* * *

'Morning.' Eddie nodded when Paddy appeared in the kitchen.

'It's a good room and good bed you have up there. You wouldn't believe the wonderful dream I had.'

'That's grand. Sit yourself down. Kathleen will do your breakfast now. Then you can get off to your business in Wicklow?'

'I will indeed,' said Paddy

'And what business would that be?' asked Kathleen.

'My business.' Paddy nodded. The realisation dawned his business was life and death.

Chapter Seven

Anne

Wicklow, 2010

'This is nice.' Anne opened the curtains. 'It's like everything you imagine, the sea, the green fields and hills.'

Their room had a low ceiling and an uneven wooden floor. The Bridge Hotel wore its age well; the wood creaked and breathed. Vinny was leaning out of bed, his laptop open on the bedside cabinet. 'An old place like this, bound to be full of ghosts,' said Vinny.

'Well that's what we're here for.' said Anne.

'It appeals to the romantic in you,' Vinny looked up from his screen.

'Well, something has to.'

'Are you having a go?'

'No. I'm saying we should try to enjoy being here. Let's make this about us as well, not just the past. It's not often we get away.' Anne crossed the room and climbed back on the bed.

'The A-team, remember that?' said Anne.

Vinny pulled her in toward him, his arm around her, 'Did I really say something as cheesy as that?'

Anne smiled. 'Yeah, when we found out about your dad.'

'It was true, we made a good team. Hardly conventional though bonding over a dead body, a victim of my dad.'

'Past tense?' Anne turned to look at him.

'You know that's a journalist's question?' He leaned over and kissed her, Anne accepted the kiss then clapped as she got up off the bed. 'How about a walk, maybe down to the seafront. Then we can work out what we're doing?'

Vinny closed his laptop. 'Sounds good.'

'Have you found anything,' she nodded toward his computer.

'General background stuff so far.'

'Like?'

'The name is Viking, means Viking meadow, and St Patrick landed here.'

Anne laughed. 'Impressive company then.'

'How about you? Plans?'

Anne pulled the brown envelope they got from Marty from her bag, 'There's a couple of things in here I want to check.'

'So, a bit of fresh air first, a walk to clear the mind?'

'Sounds good.'

* * *

The Bridge Hotel was next to the shallow fast flowing Vartry, the water gurgled and bubbled over the pebbled riverbed. Left out of the hotel would take them to the enclosed harbour, with the lighthouse at the end of the jetty and boats tied up, it had the feeling of a postcard. Right and across the bridge meant a walk along the Murrough where the sea and land were contested space. Anne and Vinny crossed the stone bridge, took a left, up ahead the long spit of land between the river and the sea. On their right, the neat terraced houses were fronted by well-kept gardens, no doubt home to workers and fishermen in the past, now holiday homes, Airbnb, or city workers. The town had a feeling of being between things — between Dublin and the South, between the sea and the mountains, between a working town and a tourist resort. Somehow never managing to be fully either.

A large concrete sea defence wall separated the beach from the road. The waters were lively out beyond the pebbled shore. The concrete wall was for times when the power of the sea rose to threaten the quiet town. But not today. The sea defence wall didn't stop them from getting battered by the wind. Unsure where to, go it swirled about them pushing and pulling in all directions. They struggled against it for a few minutes before turning back, braced and refreshed.

On their way back into town, Anne spotted something. 'What's going on there?'

An older woman with a shock of white hair wearing a light pink woollen coat sat on a bench; a younger woman in a three-quarter length puffer jacket stood in front of her remonstrating, as they got closer, they heard the younger woman, 'Come on now. Let's be going.' Her accent was guttural and harsh.

'Will yeh leave me alone? I'm doing no harm now.'

'You're not to be out here, you know that.'

'Ahh, get away with yeh. I've been coming here for more years than you've seen.'

'I am in trouble if Mr Simon comes.'

The old lady answered with a wave of her hand, 'Leave me alone, will yeh. You've no right bothering me.'

They were in sight of the pub. Anne and Vinny were behind the bench. The older woman was facing away from them and toward the river.

'We should get back,' said Vinny.

'Is everything okay?' Anne asked the younger woman.

'It's nothing to do with us,' said Vinny.

The young woman rolled her eyes. 'It's Miss Carrol here. She's not allowed out on her own.'

'I'm not on me own, am I Karla? You're here bothering me.'

'I have work, not to be chasing you.'

'We are in the nursing home, Riverside.' Karla pointed across the river. 'There, she's not let out on her own.' The young woman twirled a finger, pointing at the side of her head. 'Crazy'

'Nursing home, more of a bloody lock up,' said the older woman.

'Where is it?' asked Anne.

'There, see, the white gate.' She pointed.

'How would it be if I walked her across to you in a few minutes?' Anne offered.

'I'm not sure. I don't want anything to happen.'

'I promise, I'll just sit here a minute with her, and then we'll walk over. How would that be?'

'That'll be fine if you get this one out of my face,' the old lady replied.

The young woman shook her head. 'She's such a terror.'

'Are you sure about this? Vinny asked.

'Yeah, of course.' Anne assured him.

'Five minutes? If you're no back, I call Mr Simon.'

'Don't talk to me about that shower...'

'I go back.' The younger woman waved her hand and turned.

'No problem, we'll be over in a minute. I promise,' said Anne

They watched the woman walk a little further and cross the footbridge, a second structure that spanned the river.

'You go on,' Anne urged Vinny. 'I'll catch you up.'

'If you're sure.' said Vinny.

Anne nodded and shooed him on. Vinny walked on to the pub. Anne moved forward and sat next to the old woman.

'That's a lovely coat, can I?' asked Anne.

'Of course, pure wool, you know, it's one of the few things I've got left.'

'I bet you were a real stunner back in the day?'

'Oh, you'd better believe it.' She lifted her chin and tilted her head as she spoke. 'The belle of the ball.'

'I can believe it,' said Anne.

'You know we're going to have to go across the river there.' Anne pointed to where Karla was entering.

'I know. Just a minute more. It's so nice out here. I love the sound of the river and the sparkle of the water.'

'Shall we get you back over the river?'

'Go on then, we don't want anyone having a heart attack, do we?' she said.

'Do you have a bad heart?' asked Anne.

'Not me dear, Karla, my stalker.'

'Oh right, come on then.' Anne stood and offered her arm.

She leaned heavily on the arm of the bench as she stood and reached out to Anne for support. 'Thank you, dear.'

'It's a lovely town,' Anne said. To the left, a little further was the three arch stone bridge that was used by vehicles. Closer on the right was a concrete pedestrian bridge.

'The Parnell Bridge,' she said, indicating to the right.

'Ok,' said Anne. 'Sorry, I'm not too big on my history. A politician, wasn't he?'

'A home ruler and a lover, a great mix to be a rebel and in love.'

'Sounds exciting,' said Anne. They reached the bridge and began crossing. The shallow river gurgled.

'It wasn't for want of trying, not on my part anyway,' the old lady said.

Anne had lost the thread of conversation.

'Oh, we loved the Black Castle, our favourite spot. '

'Is that local?' asked Anne.

'Oh dear, you are a stranger. Are you with a young man?'

'Man, not sure about the young.' Anne smiled,

'Get him to take you up to the castle. I can't get up there these days.'

'Thanks for the suggestion. I will.'

They had come off the bridge and were approaching the nursing home, 'Riverside Lodge.'

Anne lifted the latch on the gate and walked the old lady through to the entrance. The front door wasn't locked, and Anne held it open. Once inside, she saw Karla talking to a man in a silver-grey suit. Karla immediately left the conversation and rushed to the front door.

'In the shade,' said the old lady as she entered the atrium, 'Move him into the shade.' She pointed at a forlorn-looking plant, a straight green stem with leaves edged in brown. He needs to rest.

'Come in, we move him later,' Karla responded sharply and ushered the old lady inside.

Anne waved. 'Bye.'

Karla didn't wave back. Anne let go of the door.

Anne felt the man's dark eyes on her as she walked up the path to the gate. As she opened the gate she turned quickly, he was looking directly at her and speaking on the phone.

* * *

Vinny was on his laptop when Anne got back to the room. 'How did you get on?' he asked.

Anne took off her coat and hung it on the door. 'Fine, I like her. She's a character.' Ann didn't mention the suited man. She moved across and stood behind Vinny. 'Have you found anything?'

'Maybe, there's a local history group. I've sent an email, to see if the main guy fancies meeting up. You never know.'

'I want to check something out; can we meet somewhere a bit later?' Anne rifled through her bag for her phone.

'Sure, are you ok? You seem a bit... I dunno, distant?' said Vinny.

'I'm fine,' her thumbs tapped the screen.

'The old lady mentioned The Black Castle.'

Vinny turned and googled it, a picture appeared on his screen. 'Do you have any other suggestions?'

'No, that's fine. I've got all the info on the castle here.'

'So, you can give me a guided tour?'

'Yeah, why not,' said Vinny.

'Ok, while you do your research I want to do something. I'll text you when I'm done?'

'Yeah, do you want me to come?'

'No, it's ok.'

'I'll meet you there.' Anne pointed at the screen.

* * *

The County Council building Whitegates was impressive with a modern design which had recently been extended. Anne liked the feel of the box-like cruciform structure; it had the openness of large glass panels set in the brown structural stone. The central courtyard had a less impressive wave curl sculpture. It was a couple of minutes from the hotel, the distinct advantage of the town was that everything was within walking distance.

'Good morning. I wonder if you could help me?'

'Good morning, if I can.' The receptionist was bright and attentive. Anne had a flashback to her earlier self.

'I would like to find out the ownership of a property here in Wicklow, is that possible?'

The bright open face contracted in thought for a second, 'Mm, let me see, we don't really have that information here. My guess is you would need the Property Records Office in Dublin.'

'Oh right, that's a shame.'

'Where is the property and how old is it?'

'It's in town here, Strand Street and as for age, I've got no idea really, 1800s maybe early 1900s. My grandad lived there you see, I didn't really know my Irish family and I'm trying to find out a bit more.'

'Oh, that's lovely; I think the PRO in Dublin really is the place.'

'Oh right, not sure I've got the time to get up to Dublin. But thanks anyway, you've been really helpful.' Anne looked at her badge 'Cara.'

'Hold on. Look, I might be able to help, could you hold a minute?

'Of course, yeah.'

Cara tapped at her keyboard and began a conversation, through her headpiece. Anne turned away from the desk and checked the Police report of the accident pulling it out of the manila envelope. The address was clear.

Patrick Connolly, 10 Strand St. Wicklow.

Cara stood and motioned for Anne to follow; she led Anne behind an office divider to a desk with two computers.

'Our client access points.'

'Right thanks.' Anne wasn't sure what she was supposed to do.

'I can log in into the Public Records Office database, using guest access, you can do a quick search and see what comes up - how would that be?

'Fantastic.' Anne's face lit up.

Cara sat down, and her fingers danced over the keyboard, a few screens later, she got up. 'It's all yours, just log out when you finish.'

'Thank you so much.'

'No problem,' Cara leaned in, 'My boyfriend is from Grenada.' she gave a conspiratorial wink and marched away.

Anne wondered if people ever noticed that things were happening because they were white. She quickly found her way around the database and typed 10 Strand Street in the search function. She briefly wondered what other databases Cara's civil service guest password gave her access to, but decided against trying to find out, just yet. She had to spend a few minutes navigating the site but eventually found what she was after; she pulled out her notebook, made a few entries and logged out. She waved to Cara as she left the building.

If they were going to find out who killed Vinny's dad they would have to find out what he was doing in Wicklow. Now she had the first piece of the jigsaw, the owner of 10 Strand St.

in 1974 was one Conor Walsh. She crossed the courtyard and was back on the street, her peripheral vision caught two men in a parked red car. She didn't turn her head, but she did fix the image in her mind. Her years of reporting had taught her men in parked cars were usually up to no good, even if they were police.

The walk up through town didn't take long, Anne passed Wicklow Gaol, set back from the road, its imposing entrance and solid high walls made it the most formidable structure in the town, the gallows set above the entrance made its gruesome historic purpose evident.

In front of the goal in the market square was Billy Byrne, a leader of the 1798 United Irishmen rebellion, immortalised in the square that saw him executed, hung by the authorities in one age, and raised in bronze in a future era, both events happening within yards of each other but centuries apart.

She walked up the hill to meet the wind blowing around the cliff-top. The castle was now protected and revered; a couple of cannons were mounted in front of the historical site. She didn't know if they once belonged to the castle, huge black guns whose destructive power was meant to smash through the wooden hulls of enemy vessels.

She waved to Vinny, who stood in the centre of the ruins, his hair filled with wind, seemed alive.

'Not much left of it,' Anne raised her voice to compete with the wind.

'No, but the location is impressive.' Vinny leaned into the gusts.

Anne slipped her arm through Vinny's. 'Absolutely, imagine being here when the thing was in one piece.' At the very edge of a rocky cliff, there was nowhere to retreat for the castle defenders. All except the crude steps cut into the steep craggy cliff, leading straight down into the sea.

Vinny moved among the remaining half-formed walls. There was very little left, jagged grey teeth in a rough semi-circle, exposed on the end of a rocky outcrop. With the sea on three sides, its occupants must have felt secure.

'It was built by Fitzgerald, Old English,' Vinny said.

'Did you say 'Old?'"

Vinny waved. 'I'll tell you later.'

Anne smiled. The wind carried his words out to sea.

It looked like they had cut a slice off the top of the hill to make the castle. Its floor was solid rock, the walls built from the same stone, a realignment of nature, to create the unnatural. To her right, she could see the cliffs weave in and out, grass-topped and lapped by the green sea at the bottom. There was a shingle beach, although no obvious way to get down to it.

To her left she looked down on the harbour, the two man-made arms reaching out, a couple of ships bobbed inside its protective grasp, the lighthouse finished the picture-postcard image. The town looked like it was slipping into the sea, coming down the gentle slope to meet the water. She thought of the old lady and her lover; this was one of her favourite spots. She could see why. The sea and the land, the ruined castle, and the busy town. The rocky cliffs and castle ruins provided unlikely shelter for wildflowers among the nooks and crannies and in between fallen stones. Anne looked again, and it dawned on her: lilies. Everything clicked into place. She wouldn't say anything to Vinny till she was sure. As they crossed the grassy area back to the road, Anne noticed the now familiar red car and its occupants.

* * *

The hotel bar was a long piece of polished oak and was rightly the pub centrepiece.

'Good afternoon, what would you like?' The mop-haired barman wiped the counter.

'A Guinness, please.'

'Sure thing, do you have a room?'

'Yeah, we've been here a couple of days.'

'I can put your drinks on your bill if you'd like?'

Vinny thought for a second, 'Thanks but I'll pay as I go, easier to keep count.'

'Oh, I know. I have to ask; the manager.' Ronan nodded toward McDonagh in reception. 'Much bigger bills he tells me when people pay at the end.'

'I can believe it.' Vinny reached across the bar. 'Vinny, Vinny Connolly.'

The barman wiped his hand on his apron. 'Ronan, good to meet you.'

Ronan pulled the dark liquid into the Guinness glass. 'No rushing it now' — when it was around ninety percent full, he placed the glass below the counter next to the pump — 'We'll just let it settle a minute.'

'And a white wine, my girlfriend will be joining me in a few minutes.'

'You're on holiday?'

'Yeah, we've got a couple of weeks, kinda family research thing as well.'

'Oh, there's lots of that going on these days. Where are you from?'

'Liverpool.'

'Oh right. Excuse me a minute, will yeh?' Ronan went to the other end of the bar. Vinny watched as he poured a glass of wine and a half-pint. When he returned, he finished the Guinness and made sure it had a good head. 'There you go.'

Vinny lifted the pint to his lips and took a good long drink.

'I can see you've made yourself at home.' Anne entered the bar and took a barstool next to Vinny.

Vinny smiled, 'Why not? That's yours.'

'Oh, thanks.' Anne took a sip of the wine and nodded at Ronan. 'Well, I've got two bits of news and half an idea.'

'Sounds interesting, come on then.'

Ronan moved away and wiped the bar, large clockwise circles, from the centre of the bar moving closer to Vinny and Anne.

'The house your dad lived in, the address on all the paperwork, it was owned by someone called Conor Walsh. Have you heard that name before?'

'No, don't think so.'

'Well we've got time, we'll find out who he was. I also have half an idea about flowers.'

'Nice one, if I can meet this local historian guy, I'll check that name with him to see what he knows. What's the second bit of news?'

'I'm being followed.'

'Jesus, by who?'

Anne took a drink of her wine. 'Two guys in a red car. I saw them twice when I went to the council, and up at the castle.'

'Coincidence?' asked Vinny.

'In Wicklow? You can walk from one end to the other in ten minutes, who'd be driving round? And sat there.'

'Fair enough. Who though? We haven't been here that long.'

'Police?' Anne paused. 'Your cousin Sean reported the tyre and bullet, a possible murder, you're next of kin. Maybe us being here in Ireland is making them nervous?'

'I couldn't help overhearing, are you guys ok?' asked Ronan.

Vinny looked at Anne, she nodded.

'We're here trying to find out what happened to my dad.'

Ronan stopped cleaning the bar and tucked the towel into his apron; he was deep in thought as Vinny outlined what they knew so far.

'What do you think?' asked Vinny.

Ronan was slow to reply, choosing his words carefully, 'In Ireland, history is life and death, and history isn't over, for us, it's just a different part of the present.'

Chapter Eight

Paddy

Wicklow, 1974

'That was grand,' Paddy pushed his plate forward.

Kathleen reached for it.

'Ah, just hold on a second,' he ripped off a piece of bread and wiped the plate clean. 'There, finish the job properly.'

'You've a big appetite.'

'Isn't that the truth?' Paddy slid his hand up under Kathleen's skirts as she reached across the table for the plate. She straightened up quickly and slapped his arm away with her free hand. 'Greedy as well by the looks of it, but I decide when and where.'

There was a wheeze and screech of hydraulic brakes from outside.

'What's the racket?' Paddy asked.

'That'll be your ride.' Kathleen soaped the dishes in the sink.

'What is it? A tank?'

'Good guess.' She turned to face him. 'What are you up to? I bet however much you like, it won't be an honest day's work. Not for Mr Walsh.'

Paddy pushed his chair back; the legs screeched over the tiled floor. 'You're right about that.'

'You think you're a bad'un don't you?'

'I didn't hear you complaining last night.'

Eddie came through the back door. 'What's that about last night?'

'I was just saying, no complaints from me, best I've had in ages.'

'Well, we do our best, don't we, Kathleen.'

Kathleen remained silent.

'Are you ready for your ride then?' asked Eddie.

'I am.' Paddy stood. 'Thank you for your hospitality.' He nodded towards Kathleen.

She nodded back.

'Colm's waiting outside.' said Eddie

Paddy stepped out into the busy street, it was 9.30 am, and the day was up and dressed in Arklow. Business was going about its routines. Cars and vans rolled through the town, there was no panic or rush, but things had to happen, and so they were. In an hour, Paddy would be face to face with the man he had to bring down.

Colm had brought his vehicle to a stop by mounting the kerb allowing traffic to pass. The mud-spattered truck was a tanker of some kind, there was a round lid on top and a swaying black tube attached to the side. The smell of cow shit and diesel surrounded it.

Paddy walked round the vehicle and climbed into the cab. Colm wore a pair of brown overalls and black boots. His appearance matched the truck.

'Make yourself at home.'

'Yeah.' Paddy put his bag down by his feet.

'Did you meet Kathleen?'

'I did. She does a good breakfast.' Paddy looked at Colm for a reaction; there was none.

'I wouldn't mind being at her breakfast table meself if you know what I mean.' Colm winked.

'I do. I do indeed. A fine lady.'

Colm turned the ignition, and the engine chugged into life. 'She is. I've set me cap in that direction for a while now, for all the good it does me. I don't think she knows I exist.' Colm eased the truck out into the road, checking the mirrors as he went.

'Come on now - a big fella like you, she'd be lucky to get you.'

Colm expertly moved the truck through the gears and ran the wheel through his large hands as he steered them through the narrow town streets.

'Now, who's that fella there? I saw him last night. Doesn't he look like he's falling over?'

Colm looked across at the statue. 'He's leading the charge against the Brits, Father Murphy. You're a funny one, alright. You've no feeling for your country's independence?'

'Isn't the north still English?' asked Paddy.

'It is but south of the border, we're free.'

'You're free in the bit they let you have?'

'I'd say more in the bit we took.'

'What's it like being half-free?'

Colm replied. 'Better than being half in jail.'

Colm was silent for a while as the heavy lorry filled the small streets and worked its way to the edge of town. 'We'll be taking the Coastal road.'

The bright winter morning left a sheen on the road, a white dusting of frost the sun was burning off.

'Are yeh a Wicklow man?' asked Colm

'No, I'm Tipperary meself close to Clonmel.'

'I'm from Ballycoogue, a farmer.' Colm volunteered.

'Are you full back there?' Paddy nodded to the tank on the back.

'20,000 litres give or take.'

'Going North?' asked Paddy.

'They can't get enough of this up there, all the garages sell it. Mr Walsh has a place to treat it, remove the red dye, then sell it as British diesel with full taxes. Can't go wrong.'

Paddy looked out the window. Beyond a rise of fields, the

sea green and swelling stretched out to the horizon, which disappeared in grey mist. On the other side, the little fella would be in school now. He started this year, the first day in his short pants. Hair licked flat and shiny shoes. Carol took him, but she brought him upstairs and woke Paddy up so he could see him.

'I was on that night before last,' Paddy said, pointing. 'My insides nearly decorated the rusty tin I was on,' said Paddy.

'I'm land man meself, you wouldn't catch me on a boat. I like dirt under my fingernails.'

'I'm with you there, mate.' Although as he said it, he remembered the clogging mud as he buried Mark Riley. That shit got everywhere. He must have carried half a ton of it home.

'You do this for Mr Walsh?' Paddy nodded at the fuel behind him.

'This and a few other things.'

'What was the problem yesterday? Weren't you supposed to collect me then?'

'Ah, we got word the Gardaí were out in force, checking tankers. They've done their bit for a while so we'll be fine now. And what are you going to be doing for Mr Walsh?'

'I don't know, probably the other things,' said Paddy.

They drove on in silence, the morning growing older as they passed through the crossroads and cottages that claimed to be villages. They approached a sharp bend in the road.

Colm pointed to a small stone monument. They drove past too quickly to read the plaque.

'Did you not see the memorial stone?'

'No, I missed it,' said Paddy.

They were coming out of the bend and back onto a straight road.

'It was the War of Independence. The Dunbar ambush.'

Paddy looked at him with raised eyebrows.

'Mr Walsh was a youngster, a teenager- four soldiers killed and two IRA men. Mr Walsh himself doing the killing - Mr Carrol was the leader. They plugged some bigwig.'

'Right, well, now I know,' said Paddy.

It looked like they were coming into the town as houses began to line the side of the road. 'Are we here?' asked Paddy.

'Mr Carrol, he was TD for years. He's passed now, mind.'

'TD is an MP, right?' asked Paddy.

'A Teachta Dála.'

'That's what I said, an MP.'

Colm narrowed his eyes at Paddy. 'Yes, we're here. This is Wicklow Town. Are you going to Fizgerald's?'

'I am,' said Paddy.'

'Then sit tight. We'll be there in a minute.'

The truck trundled through the main square. Paddy noticed another statue, this time, the man held a pike aloft. A minute later, Colm pulled the truck up. He mounted the kerb so traffic could still pass him. 'Here you are then.'

Paddy opened the door and jumped down.

He walked round the front of the cab and was about to go into the pub.

'I'll tell you this for nothing' — Colm leaned out of his window — 'You've a lot to learn about your own country.'

Paddy stopped and turned to face Colm. 'Oh, by the way.'

'Yeah,' said Colm.

'You're right about Kathleen - she is good.' Paddy winked and disappeared into the pub.

The door closed behind him, and Paddy could taste the hops in the air. Though it was mid-morning outside, the half-light of good pubs bathed the bar.

He rapped his knuckles on the glossy brown bar. 'Hello.'

'Back here.' A voice came from out of the gloom toward the back of the bar.

Paddy made his way to the rear. Two men were in a booth.

'How are yeh. Would you be Mr Walsh?' Paddy extended his hand to the grey-haired erect figure.

As he shook hands, Paddy looked into the grey eyes of the

man he had agreed to betray. Conor Walsh didn't flinch and held his gaze, Paddy looked away first. It was too early for any kind of challenge. He would wait for the right moment.

The table between them was covered in papers, including a copy of An Phoblact/Republican News. Paddy ignored the younger man, broad-shouldered and flat-faced, who sat opposite Mr Walsh.

'And you are?'

'Paddy Connolly, from Garston.'

Mr Walsh leaned back. 'Right, Paddy. I've been expecting you, have a seat.' He indicated the booth seat opposite him.

Paddy waited. The younger man didn't move.

'Smart looking fella can handle himself and knows what's what. I'm to be careful though you've a bit of a wandering eye and a temper. So, I believe?' Conor looked up from his papers at Paddy.

'That'd be fair to say,' Paddy replied.

'Sit down.' He extended his hand. 'Hang on, let Stephen out there. Go and fetch us a drink. What'll you be having? I'm having a tea, but don't let me stop you imbibing.'

'Well, to warm the blood, a glass would help.' Paddy pulled out the quart bottle he lifted from O'Malley's.

'A tea for meself and a glass for our friend here.'

Stephen gave Paddy a withering look and rose from his place on the booth seat. Paddy sat down.

'I see you've come prepared,' Conor said, nodding at the whiskey.

'Always,' said Paddy. He placed the quart bottle on the table.

Conor spoke quietly and was relaxed. 'Now you've to keep yerself out of the way for a few months.'

'That's right.'

'Did you know the soldier?'

'Soldier? Paddy asked.

'The boy there that took his life, terrible thing.'

'Oh yeah. You know about that?' Unconsciously Paddy had raised his eyebrows.

'We might not be in it, but it's our war too, of course, I know.'

'Jim Doyle's son. I know his da, but not the boy,'

'A crime.' Conor Walsh shook his head.

'Tragedy,' said Paddy.

'A crime,' Conor repeated. 'When a boy of Irish parents is sent by The British Army to fight his own kind in the North - that is a crime.' Conor's tone made it clear he would brook no disagreement.'

'Just so,' said Paddy.

'Well, you'll do alright here son, we'll keep you out of the hands of the state. Your job is to do what you're told when you're told, and without bothering anyone. Pretty simple really. You come at the request of Jack Power, he's staked his reputation on you, so you won't want to let anyone down.'

'You've no problems on that score, Mr Walsh.'

Stephen brought over an empty glass for Paddy and a steaming mug of tea.

'That's lovely,' said Mr Walsh.

Paddy acknowledged Stephen, poured himself a shot, and knocked it back. Stephen sat next to Paddy.

'A splash of water would be fine,' Paddy said to Stephen

Mr Walsh nodded. Stephen went back to the bar and returned with a small water jug.

Paddy's 'Thank you, Stephen' was condescending enough to put him in his place, for now.

'We'll have to get you settled. You must be tired after your journey?'

'It was a bit rough, aye.'

'No problem, Stephen here will take you to your digs. I say digs, but it was my old house. The lowest part of the town meant for the lowest class of people, but we've never accepted their rules. '

'Of course, Mr Walsh.'

'You can drive Paddy?'

'I can,' Paddy answered.

'That'll be useful, and have you served at a bar?'

'That I haven't, I've only been on the drinking side so far, but I'm good at learning.'

'That's the spirit. We'll get you helping out here until I find a good use for you.' He issued orders to Stephen. 'Take Paddy down the house, get him settled? Are you okay for money?'

'I am. I changed some in the pub I stayed at last night.'

'That's great, then get settled, have a rest, get your bearings, and I'll see you up here in the morning to start work at the bar. Stephen will tell you anything you need to know.'

'Nice one.' Paddy stood.

'I'll be watching you.' In defiance of his words, Mr Walsh flicked his eyes to his paper.

'Thank you.' Paddy walked toward the door and knew those cold grey eyes were on his back.

Stephen collected his jacket from a hook behind the bar.

Outside, Colm and the diesel tanker were gone, no doubt wending his way north. The whiskey and the morning sun, combined with the knowledge of the task in front of him, made Paddy feel light-headed.

'C'mon then, let's get you sorted.' Stephen stepped ahead and crossed the road.

Paddy had to move quickly to catch him. 'How far is it?'

'Just five minutes down the hill here.'

'Are we in a rush?' Paddy asked.

'Nah, but we've nothing to wait for either.'

Paddy increased his pace. 'How long have you been with Walsh?

'That's a stupid question.'

'Why's that?'

'He's me uncle. Wouldn't I be with him anyway? It's family. I take it you're not a family man yourself then?'

'I've got a little one across the water, a brother, and a couple of sisters back in Tipperary.'

'And you've not been to see them?' Stephen stopped and turned to look directly at Paddy.

'No,' said Paddy.

'Families should be close. If you can't trust your blood, who can you trust?'

'No one,' Paddy replied.

'Exactly.' Stephen nodded and turned to walk.

They walked past a split in the road. Railings and shrubbery protected an obelisk on a triangular island.

'See the car?'

Paddy looked out as a silver Hillman Avenger was passing them, two young men in the front. 'Yeah.'

'Tommy Carrol, he's in the passenger seat.'

'And…?'

'Look out for him. You don't want anything to do with him or his auld man.'

Paddy watched as the car passed by. He raised his hand in mock salute. The figure in the car turned to stare at him.

Stephen shook his head, 'For fucks sake what did you do that for?'

Paddy shrugged. 'Just saying hello.'

'Don't fuck about with such things; you're not five minutes here.'

'This pub here's the Bridge Tavern.' Stephen pointed to his right. It was hard to miss the imposing building. It looked like it had been extended and had two wings to it. 'A nice pint in there, and the people are sound. The only place you should stay clear of is 'The Grand', Peadar Carrol's place. He's what you might call a bit up himself, and he and my uncle don't see eye to eye.'

They crossed the town bridge, a solid stone three arch affair. The Vartry underneath was clear and fast-flowing down from the mountains and running out into the sea.

They turned right into Strand Street just beyond the Bridge, a narrow street with terraced houses on both sides. It was overshadowed by the ropeworks. In the past, the dirt floor houses were home to the town's poorest. Now renovated and rebuilt, they were homes to those left in fishing, the ropeworks, and the other industries still operating on the Murrough.

The small terrace was a two up two down.

'Here, this is yours.' Stephen opened the door to the bedroom.

'Who's the ugly fella with the 'tash?'

'That's James Connolly.'

'Is it now?'

'That's Mr Walsh's, don't move that.'

'Alright, well, I'm gonna have a lie-down.'

'Oh right. I'll be downstairs if you need anything.' Stephen turned and went back down the stairs.

'Righto.'

Paddy shut the door. He read the quote under the picture.

'The worker is the slave in capitalist society. The female is the slave of that slave.'

'I hope so, brother,' said Paddy.

He lifted the framed picture off the nail it was hanging on and turned it to face the wall.

Paddy threw his bag in a corner, kicked off his shoes, and laid back on the bed. Wicklow didn't seem too bad, a small town with small people. Conor Walsh was smart and capable. Paddy knew those eyes wouldn't flicker or turn away from whatever was in front of them. Fair enough, but Paddy had been set the task of bringing him down and he was prepared to do whatever it took.

He made sure the door was shut, then let his thoughts turn back to Kathleen. She knew how to move.

t was grand,' Paddy pushed his plate forward.

Kathleen reached for it.

'Ah, just hold on a second,' he ripped off a piece of bread and wiped the plate clean. 'There, finish the job properly.'

'You've a big appetite.'

'Isn't that the truth?' Paddy slid his hand up under Kathleen's skirts as she reached across the table for the plate. She straightened up quickly and slapped his arm away with her free hand. 'Greedy as well by the looks of it, but I decide when and where.'

There was a wheeze and screech of hydraulic brakes from outside.

'What's the racket?' Paddy asked.

'That'll be your ride.' Kathleen soaped the dishes in the sink.

'What is it? A tank?'

'Good guess.' She turned to face him. 'What are you up to? I bet however much you like, it won't be an honest day's work. Not for Mr Walsh.'

Paddy pushed his chair back; the legs screeched over the tiled floor. 'You're right about that.'

'You think you're a bad'un don't you?'

'I didn't hear you complaining last night.'

Eddie came through the back door. 'What's that about last night?'

'I was just saying, no complaints from me, best I've had in ages.'

'Well, we do our best, don't we, Kathleen.'

Kathleen remained silent.

'Are you ready for your ride then?' asked Eddie.

'I am.' Paddy stood. 'Thank you for your hospitality.' He nodded towards Kathleen.

She nodded back.

'Colm's waiting outside.' said Eddie

Paddy stepped out into the busy street, it was 9.30 am, and the day was up and dressed in Arklow. Business was going about its routines. Cars and vans rolled through the town, there was no panic or rush, but things had to happen, and so they were. In an hour, Paddy would be face to face with the man he had to bring down.

Colm had brought his vehicle to a stop by mounting the kerb allowing traffic to pass. The mud-spattered truck was a tanker of some kind, there was a round lid on top and a swaying black tube attached to the side. The smell of cow shit and diesel surrounded it.

Paddy walked round the vehicle and climbed into the cab. Colm wore a pair of brown overalls and black boots. His appearance matched the truck.

'Make yourself at home.'

'Yeah.' Paddy put his bag down by his feet.

'Did you meet Kathleen?'

'I did. She does a good breakfast.' Paddy looked at Colm for a reaction; there was none.

'I wouldn't mind being at her breakfast table meself if you know what I mean.' Colm winked.

'I do. I do indeed. A fine lady.'

Colm turned the ignition, and the engine chugged into life. 'She is. I've set me cap in that direction for a while now, for all the good it does me. I don't think she knows I exist.' Colm eased the truck out into the road, checking the mirrors as he went.

'Come on now - a big fella like you, she'd be lucky to get you.'

Colm expertly moved the truck through the gears and ran the wheel through his large hands as he steered them through the narrow town streets.

'Now, who's that fella there? I saw him last night. Doesn't he look like he's falling over?'

Colm looked across at the statue. 'He's leading the charge against the Brits, Father Murphy. You're a funny one, alright. You've no feeling for your country's independence?'

'Isn't the north still English?' asked Paddy.

'It is but south of the border, we're free.'

'You're free in the bit they let you have?'

'I'd say more in the bit we took.'

'What's it like being half-free?'

Colm replied. 'Better than being half in jail.'

Colm was silent for a while as the heavy lorry filled the small streets and worked its way to the edge of town. 'We'll be taking the Coastal road.'

The bright winter morning left a sheen on the road, a white dusting of frost the sun was burning off.

'Are yeh a Wicklow man?' asked Colm

'No, I'm Tipperary meself close to Clonmel.'

'I'm from Ballycoogue, a farmer.' Colm volunteered.

'Are you full back there?' Paddy nodded to the tank on the back.

'20,000 litres give or take.'

'Going North?' asked Paddy.

'They can't get enough of this up there, all the garages sell it. Mr Walsh has a place to treat it, remove the red dye, then sell it as British diesel with full taxes. Can't go wrong.'

Paddy looked out the window. Beyond a rise of fields, the sea green and swelling stretched out to the horizon, which disappeared in grey mist. On the other side, the little fella would be in school now. He started this year, the first day in his short pants. Hair licked flat and shiny shoes. Carol took him, but she brought him upstairs and woke Paddy up so he could see him.

'I was on that night before last,' Paddy said, pointing. 'My insides nearly decorated the rusty tin I was on,' said Paddy.

'I'm land man meself, you wouldn't catch me on a boat. I like dirt under my fingernails.'

'I'm with you there, mate.' Although as he said it, he remembered the clogging mud as he buried Mark Riley. That shit got everywhere. He must have carried half a ton of it home.

'You do this for Mr Walsh?' Paddy nodded at the fuel behind him.

'This and a few other things.'

'What was the problem yesterday? Weren't you supposed to

collect me then?'

'Ah, we got word the Gardaí were out in force, checking tankers. They've done their bit for a while so we'll be fine now. And what are you going to be doing for Mr Walsh?'

'I don't know, probably the other things,' said Paddy.

They drove on in silence, the morning growing older as they passed through the crossroads and cottages that claimed to be villages. They approached a sharp bend in the road.

Colm pointed to a small stone monument. They drove past too quickly to read the plaque.

'Did you not see the memorial stone?'

'No, I missed it,' said Paddy.

They were coming out of the bend and back onto a straight road.

'It was the War of Independence. The Dunbar ambush.'

Paddy looked at him with raised eyebrows.

'Mr Walsh was a youngster, a teenager- four soldiers killed and two IRA men. Mr Walsh himself doing the killing - Mr Carrol was the leader. They plugged some bigwig.'

'Right, well, now I know,' said Paddy.

It looked like they were coming into the town as houses began to line the side of the road. 'Are we here?' asked Paddy.

'Mr Carrol, he was TD for years. He's passed now, mind.'

'TD is an MP, right?' asked Paddy.

'A Teachta Dála.'

'That's what I said, an MP.'

Colm narrowed his eyes at Paddy. 'Yes, we're here. This is Wicklow Town. Are you going to Fizgerald's?'

'I am,' said Paddy.'

'Then sit tight. We'll be there in a minute.'

The truck trundled through the main square. Paddy noticed another statue, this time, the man held a pike aloft. A minute later, Colm pulled the truck up. He mounted the kerb so traffic could still pass him. 'Here you are then.'

Paddy opened the door and jumped down.

He walked round the front of the cab and was about to go into the pub.

'I'll tell you this for nothing' — Colm leaned out of his window — 'You've a lot to learn about your own country.'

Paddy stopped and turned to face Colm. 'Oh, by the way.'

'Yeah,' said Colm.

'You're right about Kathleen - she is good.' Paddy winked and disappeared into the pub.

The door closed behind him, and Paddy could taste the hops in the air. Though it was mid-morning outside, the half-light of good pubs bathed the bar.

He rapped his knuckles on the glossy brown bar. 'Hello.'

'Back here.' A voice came from out of the gloom toward the back of the bar.

Paddy made his way to the rear. Two men were in a booth.

'How are yeh. Would you be Mr Walsh?' Paddy extended his hand to the grey-haired erect figure.

As he shook hands, Paddy looked into the grey eyes of the man he had agreed to betray. Conor Walsh didn't flinch and held his gaze, Paddy looked away first. It was too early for any kind of challenge. He would wait for the right moment.

The table between them was covered in papers, including a copy of An Phoblact/Republican News. Paddy ignored the younger man, broad-shouldered and flat-faced, who sat opposite Mr Walsh.

'And you are?'

'Paddy Connolly, from Garston.'

Mr Walsh leaned back. 'Right, Paddy. I've been expecting you, have a seat.' He indicated the booth seat opposite him.

Paddy waited. The younger man didn't move.

'Smart looking fella can handle himself and knows what's what. I'm to be careful though you've a bit of a wandering eye and a temper. So, I believe?' Conor looked up from his papers at Paddy.

'That'd be fair to say,' Paddy replied.

'Sit down.' He extended his hand. 'Hang on, let Stephen out there. Go and fetch us a drink. What'll you be having? I'm having a tea, but don't let me stop you imbibing.'

'Well, to warm the blood, a glass would help.' Paddy pulled out the quart bottle he lifted from O'Malley's.

'A tea for meself and a glass for our friend here.'

Stephen gave Paddy a withering look and rose from his place on the booth seat. Paddy sat down.

'I see you've come prepared,' Conor said, nodding at the whiskey.

'Always,' said Paddy. He placed the quart bottle on the table.

Conor spoke quietly and was relaxed. 'Now you've to keep yerself out of the way for a few months.'

'That's right.'

'Did you know the soldier?'

'Soldier? Paddy asked.

'The boy there that took his life, terrible thing.'

'Oh yeah. You know about that?' Unconsciously Paddy had raised his eyebrows.

'We might not be in it, but it's our war too, of course, I know.'

'Jim Doyle's son. I know his da, but not the boy,'

'A crime.' Conor Walsh shook his head.

'Tragedy,' said Paddy.

'A crime,' Conor repeated. 'When a boy of Irish parents is sent by The British Army to fight his own kind in the North - that is a crime.' Conor's tone made it clear he would brook no disagreement.'

'Just so,' said Paddy.

'Well, you'll do alright here son, we'll keep you out of the hands of the state. Your job is to do what you're told when you're told, and without bothering anyone. Pretty simple really. You come at the request of Jack Power, he's staked his reputation on you, so you won't want to let anyone down.'

'You've no problems on that score, Mr Walsh.'

Stephen brought over an empty glass for Paddy and a steaming mug of tea.

'That's lovely,' said Mr Walsh.

Paddy acknowledged Stephen, poured himself a shot, and knocked it back. Stephen sat next to Paddy.

'A splash of water would be fine,' Paddy said to Stephen

Mr Walsh nodded. Stephen went back to the bar and returned with a small water jug.

Paddy's 'Thank you, Stephen' was condescending enough to put him in his place, for now.

'We'll have to get you settled. You must be tired after your journey?'

'It was a bit rough, aye.'

'No problem, Stephen here will take you to your digs. I say digs, but it was my old house. The lowest part of the town meant for the lowest class of people, but we've never accepted their rules. '

'Of course, Mr Walsh.'

'You can drive Paddy?'

'I can,' Paddy answered.

'That'll be useful, and have you served at a bar?'

'That I haven't, I've only been on the drinking side so far, but I'm good at learning.'

'That's the spirit. We'll get you helping out here until I find a good use for you.' He issued orders to Stephen. 'Take Paddy down the house, get him settled? Are you okay for money?'

'I am. I changed some in the pub I stayed at last night.'

'That's great, then get settled, have a rest, get your bearings, and I'll see you up here in the morning to start work at the bar. Stephen will tell you anything you need to know.'

'Nice one.' Paddy stood.

'I'll be watching you.' In defiance of his words, Mr Walsh flicked his eyes to his paper.

'Thank you.' Paddy walked toward the door and knew those cold grey eyes were on his back.

Stephen collected his jacket from a hook behind the bar.

Outside, Colm and the diesel tanker were gone, no doubt wending his way north. The whiskey and the morning sun, combined with the knowledge of the task in front of him, made Paddy feel light-headed.

'C'mon then, let's get you sorted.' Stephen stepped ahead and crossed the road.

Paddy had to move quickly to catch him. 'How far is it?'

'Just five minutes down the hill here.'

'Are we in a rush?' Paddy asked.

'Nah, but we've nothing to wait for either.'

Paddy increased his pace. 'How long have you been with Walsh?

'That's a stupid question.'

'Why's that?'

'He's me uncle. Wouldn't I be with him anyway? It's family. I take it you're not a family man yourself then?'

'I've got a little one across the water, a brother, and a couple of sisters back in Tipperary.'

'And you've not been to see them?' Stephen stopped and turned to look directly at Paddy.

'No,' said Paddy.

'Families should be close. If you can't trust your blood, who can you trust?'

'No one,' Paddy replied.

'Exactly.' Stephen nodded and turned to walk.

They walked past a split in the road. Railings and shrubbery protected an obelisk on a triangular island.

'See the car?'

Paddy looked out as a silver Hillman Avenger was passing them, two young men in the front. 'Yeah.'

'Tommy Carrol, he's in the passenger seat.'

'And…?'

'Look out for him. You don't want anything to do with him or his auld man.'

Paddy watched as the car passed by. He raised his hand in mock salute. The figure in the car turned to stare at him.

Stephen shook his head, 'For fucks sake what did you do that for?'

Paddy shrugged. 'Just saying hello.'

'Don't fuck about with such things; you're not five minutes here.'

'This pub here's the Bridge Tavern.' Stephen pointed to his right. It was hard to miss the imposing building. It looked like it had been extended and had two wings to it. 'A nice pint in there, and the people are sound. The only place you should stay clear of is 'The Grand', Peadar Carrol's place. He's what you might call a bit up himself, and he and my uncle don't see eye to eye.'

They crossed the town bridge, a solid stone three arch affair. The Vartry underneath was clear and fast-flowing down from the mountains and running out into the sea.

They turned right into Strand Street just beyond the Bridge, a narrow street with terraced houses on both sides. It was overshadowed by the ropeworks. In the past, the dirt floor houses were home to the town's poorest. Now renovated and rebuilt, they were homes to those left in fishing, the ropeworks, and the other industries still operating on the Murrough.

The small terrace was a two up two down.

'Here, this is yours.' Stephen opened the door to the bedroom.

'Who's the ugly fella with the 'tash?'

'That's James Connolly.'

'Is it now?'

'That's Mr Walsh's, don't move that.'

'Alright, well, I'm gonna have a lie-down.'

'Oh right. I'll be downstairs if you need anything.' Stephen turned and went back down the stairs.

'Righto.'

Paddy shut the door. He read the quote under the picture.

'The worker is the slave in capitalist society. The female is the slave of that slave.'

'I hope so, brother,' said Paddy.

He lifted the framed picture off the nail it was hanging on and turned it to face the wall.

Paddy threw his bag in a corner, kicked off his shoes, and laid back on the bed. Wicklow didn't seem too bad, a small town with small people. Conor Walsh was smart and capable. Paddy knew those eyes wouldn't flicker or turn away from whatever was in front of them. Fair enough, but Paddy had been set the task of bringing him down and he was prepared to do whatever it took.

He made sure the door was shut, then let his thoughts turn back to Kathleen. She knew how to move.

Chapter Nine

Anne

Wicklow, 2010

Anne was up and dressed. 'Vinny.' She shook his shoulder gently. 'Vinny.' He looked out of it.

The evening before, she had one drink and left him in the bar. He staggered in at some point during the night.

She let him sleep and went down, it was just after nine and she had an hour before breakfast service finished. She left the hotel and turned left up toward the main street. There were two florists in the town. One at the southern end of the High Street and a second over by the Lidl. Walk or drive? Drive. She wanted to be back in time to get breakfast.

'Good morning, how can I help you?' The woman was in her mid-thirties and wore an apron over her velour tracksuit.

'Well, a bit of information really. Sorry, I'm not actually buying right now.'

'Ok fine what can I do for you?'

'Lilies,' said Anne.

'Yes.'

'Do you sell them?'

The woman behind the counter was individually trimming the stems of Gladioli. Her eyes narrowed. 'A strange question.'

'Why?'

Across the Water

'You do know where you are?'

Anne raised her eyebrows.

'Sorry love, lilies are a national symbol in Ireland.'

'Oh right, sorry you must think I'm stupid.'

'No, you're foreign how would you know?'

Anne tried to hold it back, but she couldn't, when she spoke her tone was harsher than she meant.

'How do you know I'm not Irish?'

The woman picked up a stem with each sentence and cut. 'One, you didn't know about the lilies. Two, your accent. And three your…'

Anne interrupted. 'Colour.'

The lady smiled as she put the flowers down. 'Well you did ask. Can I help you with anything else?'

'No thanks,' Anne replied and left the shop. This was one of the few occasions where someone came right out and said it. How many times, you just never know, you feel it, sometimes even see it in their eyes, but you can't prove it. Here the stupid woman actually said it. She should have recorded the interaction.

She opened the car and climbed in. She put the key in the ignition and sat, staring out the window. She felt like going back to the hotel and waking Vinny. This was her life. This was why she was still in the newsroom, she hadn't been promoted to features, or recruited to a national, or picked for the dance group in school, or snogged by the arsehole Davey Jennings. She wiped away the tears that crept from the corner of her eyes,

'Don't give up, keep going,' that was her dad's mantra. He was dead now, he was a part of the L8 defence committee after the riots in '81. He campaigned for Nelson Mandela's release and the end of Apartheid. He made his contribution. I keep going for you Dad, for you.

She turned the ignition and moved out into the morning traffic.

The second florist was just setting up, she had metal frames on both sides of the shop door and was busy bringing pot plants and buckets out from the shop to arrange the display.

'Hi.' Anne tried to sound bright and breezy.

'Good morning love.'

'I have a couple of questions if it's ok?'

'Sure, how can I help? As long as you don't mind me moving while I talk.'

'No, of course not, and thanks. Ok so lilies, do you sell many?'

The woman stopped, 'Shedloads of Calla lilies in the run-up to Easter, then not many at all, it's a popular flower.'

'This might show my ignorance but why Easter?'

'The lily commemorates the Easter Rising 1916, most wear pins these days not buttonholes, but the flowers are still popular for decorating houses.'

'So, would you remember someone buying one later in the spring, May?'

The woman smiled. 'If it was a regular annual thing, and she was a bit of a character,' she paused before adding. 'I would and.... do.'

* * *

Anne got back with ten minutes to spare. It was a self-service buffet, but Ronan was on duty laying and clearing the tables. 'Morning. You were out and about early.'

'Is Vinny down?' Anne asked as she scanned the room.

'Not yet.'

'I guess you saw more of him last night than I did.' she smiled.

'Yeah, he was after having a few in the bar.'

'I guessed that,' said Anne.

'Here, let me get you a table.' Ronan led Anne to a table near the window.

A few others were occupied. Anne nodded good morning as

she passed

Ronan checked his watch. 'Vinny's gonna miss out if he's not down soon.'

'I'll give him a ring,' said Anne. As she pulled out her phone Vinny appeared in the doorway.

'Why didn't you wake me?' Vinny asked as he sat down.

'I did.'

Vinny rubbed his hand over his face. 'Oh, Ok. Sorry. Yeah, I guess I had a few last night.'

Anne had a light breakfast of cereal and orange juice. Vinny avoided the full Irish and went for bacon on toast.

'The flowers,' said Anne. She had Vinny's attention and waited till she had drained her juice. 'Your Uncle Marty said a flower was left every year, for a long time on your dad's grave.'

'Yeah, any news on that?'

'A bit, I think I know who and why.'

'Well, I haven't been completely useless, chatting to Ronan over there. It turns out Conor Walsh was a pretty well-known local guy.'

'Well known for what?'

'He was in the old IRA before independence when the republican movement split he opposed the Treaty and was against partition Ronan said he was known and feared as a big man locally.'

'This thing gets more interesting all the time, if your dad was living in his house.'

'We can assume they were working together,' said Vinny finishing her thought. 'Ok, you've got me curious. How about the flowers?'

'I'd rather show you. If I'm right, it won't take long.' Anne got up from the table.

'Where are we going?'

'To visit someone.'

* * *

They left the hotel and walked straight ahead parallel with the river. They had gone about a hundred yards when Vinny said, 'It's the old woman, isn't it? We're heading to the nursing home.'

Anne turned to face him. 'Yeah, I'm pretty sure, but we'll find out now.'

'How did you work it out?'

'First, your uncle said about the lilies. Then the old lady recommended the Black Castle as a place she shared with her old lover.'

'Her lover was my dad?'

'I think so, when we went up to the castle there were wildflowers in the places protected from the wind. I saw a lily and it just clicked. Then this morning I went to the local florists, and luckily one remembered her. From years ago, but I assume she hasn't been able to get around on her own for a while.'

'You're right, you're too good for The Chronicle.' Anne looked away quickly, she didn't want Vinny to see the disappointment in her eyes. She had to prove how good she was.

She saw the familiar pink checked coat from the last encounter, on the same bench facing the river. 'There she is,' Anne pointed across the river. 'Let me go and speak to her. I don't want to give her a shock seeing you.

'What am I supposed to do?'

'Give me a few minutes with her, if we go into the nursing home follow us in. If not, come over after five minutes.'

Anne crossed the pedestrian bridge.

'Hello, have they let you out again?' Anne asked.

'Escaped, haven't I. The buggers can't keep me locked up.' The old lady's face lit up.

'Are you alright here, not too cold?'

'I'm fine, don't you worry about me.'

'That's a lovely coat.'

'It's mine. You can't have it.' She pulled the coat together as if protecting it.

'No, no, I don't want it, just saying it's lovely.'

'It's not their fault, not really.'

'Who? Whose fault for what?' Anne asked. 'Do you mind if I sit down?'

The old lady didn't respond to her request, so Anne sat.

'The women, they have to look after us, all us old biddies, half of them don't know what day it is. Those Poles and Romans earn their money.'

'Romanians,' said Anne.

'Yeah, and the Poles. It's not easy leaving your country. These lot are ignorant.' She waved her hand around. 'See all these.' She waved toward the terraced houses.

'I'm sure you don't mean that.'

'Oh, I do, curtain twitchers, not everyone mind, there's some good people here and there.'

'Yeah, how about we get you back home. Maude, isn't it? I'll walk you back. How about that?'

'Here, take my arm,' Anne said as she stood.

'I s'pose it is getting a bit chilly. I can say I've had my airing for the day.'

'You can,' Anne took her scarf off and wrapped it around her. 'Your name is Maude, Maude Carrol? Karla called you Miss Carrol last time we met.'

'They rub it in, don't they, all the same here, never married, you see, so it's always Miss this, Miss that. I never missed anything, so I don't know what they're going on about.'

'Okay. Here, take my arm.'

They walked slowly toward the pedestrian bridge across the river.

'Maude, I am, and I'm not so gone as people think, I'll tell you that for nothing.'

'I'm sure you're not,'

'You've no idea, have you? You must be English. It's not your fault.'

'No idea of…?' asked Anne.

'Gonne, Maude Gonne one of my heroes. See, I'm too clever for my own good. That's what my father always told me, bastard, that he was.'

'I'm sure you don't mean that.' Anne expressed her surprise.

The old lady stopped, 'You called me Maude? How do you know my name?'

'I'll explain when we get inside, come on, let's keep moving.'

They crossed the river and walked along the pavement. When Anne left the hotel, the air was fresh and cool. The sun had now decided to show up to chase away the morning chill. Anne saw Vinny and waved to him.

'Let's get you inside and I will explain everything,' said Anne.

The painted wooden gate wasn't locked and swung easily to allow access into the garden. Bordered by a privet hedge, the yard were well kept and mature, with a lawn and flowerbeds around the edges and a circle in the centre. A couple of benches painted green and white like the gate added to the relaxed atmosphere. Their feet crunched on the gravel.

Anne rang the bell and gripped Maude's arm tighter.

'Why didn't you tell me?' Maude asked.

A few seconds later, the door buzzed open.

'Let's get you in,' said Anne.

As Anne passed through the entrance with Maude. She noticed the flower Maude had placed on the ledge was looking stronger, the brown had gone from its leaves, and the bulb at the top was growing larger.

A sign pointed the way to the reception. Ahead of them, the narrow hallway opened up into a wide space. Immediately on their left was an opening, a half door through which Anne saw Karla, the woman who had been outside with Maude.

'Hello again.' Anne waved.

'Hello.'

'We met outside, by the river,' Anne said.

'Hello.' Maude's high sing-song voice rang out. 'I've got a visitor.'

The Polish woman's eyes widened. 'Ten minutes, okay?'

Maude kept turning to look at Vinny, who had entered and was now behind them.

'Please this way.' She led them straight ahead, upright armchairs were distributed randomly around a large lounge. French windows allowed light to stream through and showed a further part of the garden, more lawn, and flowerbeds.

'Of course,' Anne said. 'Thank you very much.'

Karla and Anne helped Maude into the lounge, removed her coat and settled her in a chair.

Anne pulled a chair over and placed it in front of Maude. The other residents were not taking much notice. Anne saw Vinny waiting by the doorway.

Karla brought tea for Maude and placed it on a side table.

'Maude, can I ask you some questions?'

'Of course, dear.' She reached out for the cup that sat on the table next to her.

Anne was quicker and handed her the cup to save her stretching.

'Thank you, although I shouldn't, goes straight through me, no bladder control you see, straight through like the river outside it is.'

'The flower in the entrance Maude, it's special to you, isn't it?' Anne said.

'Yes, dear.'

'You bought flowers every year for a long time, didn't you?'

Maude was quiet. She reached out for Anne's arm. 'Who are

you?'

'You mentioned The Black Castle; do you remember that?'

'Yes, of course, I do. I'm not ga-ga yet, not by a long shot. Makes me think of Paddy.'

Anne looked around and lowered her voice. 'Paddy Connolly? He moved back from Liverpool.'

'Yes, my Paddy.' Maude closed her eyes for a second. 'Such a shame, we didn't have long. Strange how you can live your life more in a few weeks than all the other decades put together. Do you know what I mean?'

'I'm not sure,' said Anne.

'Oh, you would know. If you had, you would know.'

'If I had?' asked Anne.

'Loved, dear, if you had loved.'

Anne sat back, stunned for a second. It felt like Maude had just delivered a gut punch.

She collected herself. 'Patrick Connolly.'

'Yes dear, Paddy.'

Anne motioned for Vinny to come close. 'Here.'

'There's someone I think you should meet.'

Vinny stepped in front of Maude. 'Hello, nice to meet you, I think you knew my dad.'

A figure in a suit had been buzzed-in and was marching down the hallway toward them.

Karla had appeared next to them. 'I think you'd better leave now.'

'Come closer,' Maude asked Vinny. He squatted down next to her.

She reached out and held his hand, she didn't look shocked, her face was calm and relaxed. 'Such a fine man.' She wiped away a tear as she said, 'Paddy would be proud. I knew you would come one day. Paddy's love wouldn't let you go so easy. I know, I know.'

The suited figure was on top of them now. 'What the hell are you doing here?'

Karla tried to explain. 'You see, this lady from England met your… Miss Carrol.'

Simon Carrol gave her a withering look. 'Shut up, woman. I know who she is. I asked who the hell gave them permission?'

Maude's voice became shrill and hard. 'They wanted to get rid of him. He knew too much. You see, your dad was never in anyone's gang. They thought he was. They thought they controlled him.'

Vinny and Anne stood.

'I'm sorry, Mister Carrol,' said Karla.

'Who is 'they' Maude?' asked Anne.

'My father and Conor Walsh, thought they controlled everyone. He usually did, but not Paddy.'

'Get her out of here.'

Anne grabbed Maude's hand.

'Get your hands off her.' Simon reached down and pulled Anne's hand away

'You should know not to mess with me. Now get out.'

Vinny pulled Anne away. 'Come on.'

'Out, now!' Simon Carrol shouted. Other staff had arrived

Anne stepped toward him. 'I don't care who you think you are. You know what? This isn't over.' She let her words hang in the air.

Maude clapped. 'You tell him, love. Cowards the lot of them.'

Chapter Ten

Paddy

Wicklow, 1974

Paddy left the house and walked toward the bridge. The house was on The Murrough between the river Vartry and the coast. It protected the town from the worst the Irish sea could throw at it. This was home to the industry, workshops, smithies, and ropeworks that, in the past, kept the ships afloat and the town alive.

Beyond the bridge was the town proper. Walking up the hill to the Grand Hotel was not just walking through time from where the Vikings landed 800 years before; it was climbing through the social classes. Those with money lived furthest from the noise, smell, and sometimes danger on the quayside. For Paddy, the situation was reversed. Each step nearer the pub was closer to the dangerous reckoning he knew would come.

Paddy had a drop while getting ready, and the alcohol was warming his insides, giving him an edge of energy. This place was too small for him, family history existed here like an aura, a living thing following people around. Everyone knew everything, that didn't mean there weren't secrets, here secrets were not the unknown, but the unspoken. He liked the anonymity of Speke, twice as many people on the one estate as there was in this whole town, easier to get lost. Tonight, was his night off from working the bar. When he was on shift, pulling pints and serving drinks he was dancing, spinning for this and that, sliding one way then the other. Always listening, for who, what, when and where.

He turned left at Halpin's obelisk, crossed the road. Fitz's pub was just a couple of minutes away. Halpin was the most famous of the town's mariners; he laid the telegraph cable across the Atlantic, connecting Ireland and Europe with America, once he perfected the trick he repeated it between Australia and New Zealand and many other places.

The bar was nothing special; wooden lettering announced its presence, 'Fitzgerald's.' A mixture of green and brown tiles decorated the outside, below the big windows shaded with curtains. He entered and was immersed in the smell of hops as usual, except now it was accompanied by music and voices, both worked so well together it was hard to tell where one started, and the other stopped. The jukebox had a range of popular and traditional tunes. Rebel songs were best live. The clientele was a mix of ages, family groups around tables at the front and in the booths toward the rear.

The bar was an L shape flipped around, the short end from left to right, and the long end was formed on the right and ran up the back of the pub. Fitz's was busy. The stools along the bar, the tables, and booths were all taken. Cigarette and pipe smoke filled the air.

Stephen was behind the bar, white shirt, black trousers, with a black waiter apron tied round his protruding middle. 'I'll have a pint when you're ready, barman.'

'Here, pull it yourself,' said Stephen.

'Sorry mate, my night off.'

'Well, sir, the Kilkenny's is a nice pint, not as heavy as your Guinness.'

'I think I'll go for that.' Then added, 'It's rocking tonight.'

'We've people in from across the water.' Stephen nodded to the front of the bar. 'Dorans, Kavanaghs, Hunters, Sinnots, Malones, a whole heap of them.'

'Mr Walsh's back there.' Stephen nodded. 'He said for you to join him when you get in.'

'Sure thing.' Paddy carried his pint toward the rear of the pub. Mr Walsh was in his usual booth, halfway down the bar with a good view of the entrance.

Conor was dressed in a collar and tie with a sharp suit for a man his age. The wide lapels showed it was recent and expensive. 'Give us a minute, will you, lads.'

The three younger men who shared the booth picked up their drinks and moved away. Paddy nodded as they left and then took a seat.

'Everything okay at the house?'

'Yeah, thanks very much. Am I to pay rent?'

'Don't worry, you'll earn your keep.'

'I hope so. I'm not one for sitting round doing nothing.'

'That's good to hear. You're good behind the bar, but hopefully, that's not all you're good for. Otherwise, you wouldn't be here.'

Paddy took a drink of his pint.

'You're a Tipp man, I'm told.'

'That's right,'

'Any family?'

'In Tipp, a brother, two sisters, a boy in Liverpool.'

'A boy, you're lucky, girls are a headache.'

'Parents?' he asked.

'Mam died when I was a kid. Da' disappeared in England somewhere.'

Conor snorted his disapproval. 'It just never ends with that place. Should've finished the job when we had a chance.'

'What job is… Oh, right, you mean kicked them out like all the way.' Paddy would have to be quicker on the uptake.

'Too right, leaving them to control the North was the biggest mistake in Irish history. We should have struck hard when we had the opportunity.'

'You're right there.' Paddy was trying to keep in with him.

'Not much patriotism among Jack Powers' lot.' This was the first indication Conor wasn't a fan of the connection in Liverpool.

'No, I'd say it was all about the money.'

'Don't get me wrong, son. I've no complaints about making a few bob, but you can choose where you take it from. Do you get me?'

'Yeah, sure,' Paddy lied.

'There's enough parasites out there for us to make a handsome living without taking a penny from the working man. Diesel, insurance, shipping, security.'

'Absolutely.' Paddy wasn't sure what else to say.

He leaned back. 'You see that?' He pointed to a flag on the wall. There was a deep blue flag with an arrangement of stars.

Paddy had seen the flag before but didn't know what it meant.

'The Starry Plough, that's my flag. From the land to the stars until there's independence, there'll be no peace. You're following in the footsteps of two of our best leaders.'

'I am?'

'Larkin and Connolly made the same journey from England. Larkin from the docks in Liverpool. The Chartists Cuffay and O'Connor, black and Irish, always the Achilles heel of Empire.'

Paddy didn't know who he was talking about but understood enough to know why Barlow wanted this guy out of the way.

'You'll be alright with us Paddy, we look after our own, and from now on, you are one of us.'

Conor reached out and clasped Paddy's hand. Despite his slim frame, his grip was strong. This time Paddy held his gaze. There was steel in those blue-grey eyes too. The intensity quickened his blood flow. He felt his heart skip as Conor explained.

'If you're with us, then you can't be against us,'

Fuck, did he know something?

'We've never liked traitors Paddy, and we know how to deal with them.'

Paddy knew not to look away and kept his eyes fixed on

Conor.

'I know you understand me.' He released Paddy's hand but kept eye contact.

Paddy knew those blue-grey eyes were searching his own. 'Yeah, I understand.'

Conor nodded and the younger men made their way back to the table. Paddy took a deep breath.

'Say hello to the boys here. We've Seamus, Thomas, and Declan.'

The boys nodded.

Paddy was glad to be able to take a drink. He knew the boys. They'd all been in the bar over the past week, but this was different. He was being introduced by Mr Walsh.

Paddy didn't like Seamus. He was heavyset. A fucking farmer's boy, thick as pig shit.

The others were alright.

'I was in Liverpool. Fine old town, many a good night there,' Seamus said.

'You know it?' Paddy was surprised Seamus had not spoken to him directly before.

'Sure thing. You were in Garston with Jack Power, is that right?'

'Maybe.' Paddy took a drink.

'Oh, I know them boys, think they're it. Little gang robbing off the docks.'

'Okay now, whatever you think you know, how about you keep it to yourself,' said Conor.

'Yeah, right boss.' Seamus took a drink of his pint.

An older man in his early sixties who didn't carry his age as well as Conor approached the booth.

Conor dismissed them. 'Go on, then.'

The older man sat down as soon as they made space.

Paddy followed the boys to the front of the bar. The tables were taken so the boys stood in a group near the bar.

'Red or Blue?' Declan asked.

Paddy laughed. 'Everton man, all the way.' Seamus made a point of letting him know he knew Garston and Jack Power. He would have to be careful with that fucker.

'There's only one team in that city. FA Cup winners last season. The mighty Keegan and Toshack.'

'And you?' Paddy asked Declan.

'The hoops, I'm Celtic.'

'Bit further to go for games,' said Paddy.

'Nah, I don't get over, armchair supporter.'

'You're all local boys? Paddy asked.

'Yeah, we are, so you can't hide anything from us. You'd do well to remember that,' said Seamus.

'What would I want to hide?' asked Paddy.

'Why you left Liverpool?'

'Did you not hear Mr Walsh? Keep your thoughts to yourself.' Paddy turned to Declan.

'The flag up there on the wall, what is it? I've seen it like, but—' Paddy didn't get a chance to finish.

'Ahh, it's the flag of republican socialists, James Connolly, and Irish Citizens Army,' said Declan.

'That'll be the fella in my room now, on the wall,' said Paddy.

'Mr Walsh is big on him. He was in the War of Independence, you know,' Declan continued.

'Who? Connolly?' asked Paddy.

'No, Mr Walsh.'

'Yeah, I heard that,' said Paddy.

'So, he won't be wanting any English shite,' said Seamus.

'I didn't know shite had a flag,' said Paddy.

'Come on now, boys,' said Thomas.

'So, what were you doing living over there with the enemy?' said Seamus.

'Get the fuck out,' said Paddy,

'Fucking gowl,' Seamus responded.

'Seamus, don't be an arsehole.' Declan moved in front of Paddy, and Thomas put a restraining arm between the two men.

'He's coming,' said Thomas.

Paddy turned to see Mr Walsh moving through the pub, accepting greetings as he did so. Seamus took a step back. 'Just jesting with yeh.'

Paddy looked at Seamus. 'And for your information, I don't give a fuck, here or in England, I've always been surrounded by the enemy.'

Conor made his way past the boys to the right, and against the sidewall was a raised stage area.

'Ah, he's gonna give us a song,' said Thomas. 'He has a good voice on him, he does.'

Paddy moved aside a little and put his pint on the bar. Declan followed him.

A guy on the table next to the stage pulled out a guitar and began to strum.

'What's his problem?' Paddy asked, nodding toward Seamus

'Don't let him get to you. He likes to think he's second in command.'

'Second in command? Does he think he's in the IRA?'

'Something like that, always wants to be the loudest if yeh get me.'

'I do. Met his type before and brought them low,' said Paddy.

'Well, hold your horses. You've just got off the boat.'

'Nah, I'm fine. I'll not worry me head about him, but what the fuck is a gowl?'

Declan laughed. 'Gowl, it means you're a cunt.'

Paddy laughed. 'Well, he's right there.'

Conor began to sing, his voice, aimed for the soft tremulous tones of Christy Moore but failed.

'Do you want another one there?' asked Declan.

'I'll get it. What are you having? And while I'm there, see what the other lads want,' said Paddy

Across the Water

There was a generous round of applause, and Conor made his way back through the bar. He called out to Stephen to keep the jukebox off for the night. As if on cue, a fiddle and drum appeared, and a group of people near the stage found their rhythm.

Paddy finished his drink he wanted to get out of Seamus' way before he did something he'd regret. He slipped out of Fitz's bar and walked toward The Grand.

The main lounge had a veneer of respectability and wealth. The marble floor and wood panelling were paid for in a different age. The wealth and aristocracy of Ireland had relocated to England, landlords, and landowners not scared off by the War of Independence, had long since divested in outrage at an Irish government telling them what to do. An economic tit for tat meant an independent Ireland struggled as England cut down on imports and charged more for exports. Price rises and poverty were the effects across Ireland.

After the flight of English capital all that was left was imitation. The home-grown moneymen slipped into the vacated space. Most of Ireland was one generation or cousin away from the land, cow and pig shit; attempts at sophistication were never carried off with much panache. This was not to say the Irish did not produce their own luminaries of class and style, they did, but they were generally the Irish born descendants of the Norman invaders.

The room was full; the air was thick with smoke. The pipe smokers used to the hearth on the farm carried it with them into the hotel ballroom. Stuffed inside collars and ties, they sat with accountants, lawyers, shop owners, and managers, this meeting of town and country was the lifeblood of Ireland's economy and social life.

Paddy flicked his lighter open and lit his cigarette. With Brylcreamed hair, open neck shirt, and wide lapels, he cut a figure apart. He stank of England and its arrogance. In Dublin, there were pubs and bars for sailors and emigres, pockets full of English pounds, coming back to lord it over the locals. Paddy wasn't the first and wouldn't be the last.

There weren't many women unless there was a dance night or a show band. Otherwise, they stayed at home. Those who were out in a couple knew their value and had that rare thing, a friend in marriage.

Paddy approached the bar with his usual swagger. He ordered a pint and a chaser because he could afford it. He turned to scan the room. He saw what he expected until his eyes fell on Maude. He didn't know her name then but determined he would find out. For now, he watched her. She was unaware of his attention and sparkled as naturally as she breathed. She was slim and elegant her reddish brown hair just about contained in a bun. She wore a straight pale blue dress cut in the 60s —simple and clean lines, a round neck, and sleeveless. Her body moulded the material to follow its gentle curves. Eyes on the surrounding tables were drawn to her. Whenever their conversation dropped or attention flagged, eyes flicked back to her.

Paddy turned to the barman. 'Hey mate, who's the girl?' He nodded in her redirection.

'That's Maude.'

'Maude?'

'Daughter of Mr Carrol, he's the one in the middle.'

'And who's he?' But as he said it, he realised this was the Mr Carrol, the one of the ambush, parliament, and power.

'How long have you been away?'

'I'm a Tipp man meself.'

'Well, Mr Carrol is the town's TD. Nothing happens in Wicklow that Mr C doesn't have a hand in, and word to the wise. There'd be a long queue of fellas after Maude, and you are at the back of it.'

Paddy laughed, he left the back of the queue the day he broke a stick over Father Pearson's head, and he wasn't going back there. Anyway, he loved a challenge.

Chapter Eleven

Vinny

Wicklow, 2010

'This is Niamh,' Ronan introduced his friend.

'Nice to meet you.' Vinny extended his hand to the young woman facing him. The bar was filling up and the voices merged with the music.

Anne stood. 'Hi.' She offered her hand. 'Please sit.' Anne gestured to the chair next to her.

'I've got to go sort my stuff out. I'll be back when I'm set up,' said Ronan. He moved off to a tiny stage at the end of the bar.

'Thanks.' Niamh took the seat next to Anne. She spoke with a soft, rolling accent. 'This is your first-time seeing Ronan then?'

'Yeah, but I brought my earplugs just in case,' Vinny said.

'Vinny!' Anne gave him a playful nudge. 'It was good of him to invite us.'

'Oh no, he's not so bad. Actually, don't tell him I said that. We don't want his head getting any bigger than it is.' Niamh's pale blue eyes sparkled, and her lips curled into a smile. 'I'm on the table over there with my and Ronan's mother.' Anne looked across and two women waved.

'That's so nice, his mum comes out to watch him?' said Anne.

'Well, this is our local.' Niamh explained.

'Are you going to join us?' Anne asked.

'I wouldn't want to intrude.'

'Don't be silly, we could do with the company. Get Niamh a drink,' Anne nudged Vinny.

'Thanks, a wine, white wine.' 'Sweet or dry?' Vinny was up, out of his seat.

'Oh. He'll just give you the house wine. It's fine. Thanks,' said Niamh.

'Are you enjoying your stay?' Niamh asked.

Anne rolled her eyes. 'Let's just say I'm still waiting for the relaxing bit.'

'Yeah, I heard. Ronan's been keeping me updated. Pretty exciting stuff. I hope you don't mind him telling me?'

'No, Ronan has been really good, so It's no secret, well not from you. Although, I'm beginning to think there are quite a few of those around. Secrets, I mean.' replied Anne.

'You're getting to know the place then. You're a reporter?'

'Yeah, the local paper in Liverpool.'

'That sounds so great. I would love that.'

'It's not as exciting as it sounds, believe me.' Anne took a sip of her drink and placed it carefully back on the table.

'At least you are getting paid for writing. I write for our paper, it's a campaign thing People Not Profit, but I don't get paid.'

'That sounds really good, and if you apply for jobs, that'll definitely help,' Anne assured her.

'You think so?'

'Yeah, it makes a real difference.'

'So, are your family from here too?' Niamh asked.

'No,' Anne shook her head. 'It's a bit complicated.'

'You've an Irish name, though, McCarthy.'

'That's from my dad. He was Bajan, Barbadian.'

'Oh right, I've heard something about that, isn't it "redlegs" or something?'

'There are different things it's a bit of a mess historically, some of Cromwell's prisoners were sent over, as indentured servants, then there had always been some independent Irish finding their way to the islands, travellers, sailors, a few ended up with plantations, while others worked as overseers. I don't know, maybe I don't want to find out.'

'How do you mean?'

'Well, white Irishman and a black woman during slavery...'

Niamh winced. 'Yeah, I see what you mean.'

'He could have been a slaver who raped my ancestor, or he could have been an independent farmer, married for love.' Anne held her hands out palms up, 'Take your pick.'

'The Irish get everywhere,' said Niamh. 'So, my bet is a dashing pirate and Bajan beauty.'

Anne laughed. 'That'll do me.'

'Did I miss a joke?' Vinny returned with the wine. 'Here we go, one house white as ordered.' He placed the drink in front of Niamh.

'You'll have to show me some of your articles,' said Anne.

'Oh, would you have a look at them? That'd be so good.'

Ronan arrived and placed his hand on Niamh's shoulder. 'Niamh's a writer too.'

'Oh right,' said Vinny.

'Well, more like a wannabe,' said Niamh.

'Don't let her talk herself down. She's a great turn of phrase. The Irish Times would be lucky to have her.'

Niamh beamed.

'I didn't get you a drink,' Vinny apologised.

'Oh no, no trouble. Mine are on the house tonight.'

'Oh right. Perk of the job?' said Vinny.

'Payment for the job is more like.' Ronan went to the bar.

'Tough times?' asked Vinny when Ronan had left.

'No kidding,' said Niamh. 'The Celtic Tiger has been shot and stuffed.'

'Are things that bad?'

'Actually, that's wrong. It's not the tiger that's stuffed, but us.'

'Things are pretty bad in the UK too,' said Vinny.

'If I can ever afford kids, their taxes will be paying off German banks for generations to come. Desperate is the word. There's nothing else. Property and bankers; the twin evils. It's like in the old days, with people leaving. Everyone is getting out. Talk of the devil, look who just walked in,' Niamh said.

Anne turned and made eye contact with the man she recognised from the nursing home.

'Who?' asked Vinny.

'Simon Carrol,' said Niamh.

'You know him?' Anne asked.

'That's the guy from the nursing home,' said Vinny.

'Everyone knows him,' said Niamh.

'He warned me off talking to an old woman, Maude Carrol,' said Anne.

'That would be his Aunt.'

Two men followed Simon Carrol into the bar. They were around the same age as him, mid-thirties. The group headed toward the bar. The other men looked familiar to Anne.

'The Price brothers, his goons,' said Niamh.

'No one really has goons,' said Vinny.

'Oh, he does,' said Niamh. 'He's a property developer, or he was, he took over his dad's business.' She leaned in and spoke quietly. 'His dad and grandad were big men. Simon made loads of money building houses. Then he went bust. Lots of shady stuff. Have you seen the ghost estates?'

'Ghosts?' asked Vinny.

'Housing developments, half-finished, abandoned when the financial crash happened.'

'Sounds familiar,' said Anne.

'His grandad was in the War of Independence, local hero, and MP. Then his dad was in charge.'

'Was?' asked Vinny.

'Yeah, he's been dead a while. Simon ran the business, his dad built it up, he crashed it. He lives off his family's reputation. He's trying to get a new development off the ground, some woodland he wants to cut down for commuter housing. There's been a few protests.'

Ronan came back to the table with his pint.

'That's the guy we were telling you about,' said Vinny.

'Don't you do anything stupid,' said Anne.

'Like what?'

'Anything,' she responded sharply.

'Does he normally drink here?' Anne asked.

'No, he's a golf club type or up in Dublin. To be honest, I wouldn't know where he goes, but not here,' said Ronan.

Simon was attracting attention. People went over and shook hands. Like a pebble dropped in a pool, ripples were spreading.

'He's nothing special. We've met his type before. A big man in a small town,' said Anne.

'This is Ireland, the whole country is run by big men in small towns,' said Ronan.

'I'd better get up and do my stuff.' Ronan made his way to the stool he had set on the stage. A microphone stand and an amp were the only other equipment on view. His guitar leaned against the stool.

He picked it up and strummed. He adjusted the strings as he spoke into the microphone. 'Good evening. I hope you are all well? We have some visitors from Liverpool over. So, to welcome them. I thought I'd do an old favourite of mine and one of Dominic Behan's classics, 'Liverpool Lou."

The conversation continued around the bar, but not in a way to disturb the singing. The low-level chatter seemed designed to provide a warm backdrop to Ronan's voice.

'Liverpool Lou lovely Liverpool Lou, why don't you behave just like other girls do.'

'He's not bad,' said Vinny.

'Yeah, weird voice,' said Anne. She quickly followed up with, 'Sorry, I didn't mean that the way it sounded, it's kind of rough but gets all the notes.'

'Yeah, I know, distinctive is how I like to call it,' said Niamh.

'Agreed, that sounds better than weird,' said Anne.

'He likes the old songs, a bit of a traditionalist at heart.'

'Me too,' said Vinny. 'One of the few things I had of my dad's when he left was his record collection. The Clancy Brothers, The Bachelors, he was into American stuff as well, you know the old country style.'

Anne could see Simon Carrol approaching the table.

'Don't get Ronan started on that. He'll go on for hours.'

Simon was next to the table and spoke to Niamh. 'Still doing your demos and pickets are you?'

'I am,' said Niamh. 'More than ever if you must know.'

'Are you not going to introduce me to your friends here? Oh, wait, no need. Vincent Connolly and Anne McCarthy, Anne works for The Chronicle.' Simon said.

'That's right, and since you know who I am, you might as well know.' She paused. 'I'm here doing a follow up on the financial crash, looking at who's responsible, and who ends up paying for the greed of property developers and bankers.'

Niamh smiled.

'Ahhh.' Simon Carrol laughed. 'Good one that. Yeah, very clever. Well, Miss Reporter, this is not Liverpool, and here we don't like outsiders poking their nose in other people's business. Do you get my meaning? Stay away from my auntie.'

'Are you threatening us?' Vinny stood.

Up on stage, Ronan finished his first song. 'I'll be back in two shakes,' he said into the mic.

He appeared next to Simon. 'What's the craic?'

Simon took a step back. 'I'm just telling these two here to mind their business,' The Price brothers were on their way over. Simon raised a hand to stop them.

'And what business would that be?' asked Ronan.

Simon half turned to walk away but stopped. 'I'll be as clear as I can.' He lowered his voice, so the surrounding tables didn't hear. 'Why don't yeh fuck off back to England? You're not wanted here.'

'They've as much right to be here as anyone. They're as Irish as you.'

Simon laughed and pointed at Anne. 'That's a funny colour to be Irish.'

'Will yeh get the fuck out,' said Ronan.

Simon walked back to join the other two men at the bar.

Ronan went back to the stage. 'Like I said, we've got a couple of people in from across the water, and I've had someone tell them they don't belong here. Mrs Devine, isn't your Niall over there now?'

'He is,' a lady waved back.

'Anyone else, who else has got family across the water? This next song is for those away'.

'Our Gerard, Gerard Byrne is in the 'pool," shouted one man.

The voices came quickly, one after the other. 'Phillip May is in Coventry.'

'My uncle Joe Judd is in Birmingham.'

'My mum's sister went to London, never came back.'

'My lad is only just after going to Australia.' A woman near the front crossed herself.

'Right, ladies and gentlemen. Can we show a little welcome for our guests from Liverpool and in honour of everyone who's got loved ones across the water.' Ronan started the clapping. There was a generous burst of applause then Ronan continued, 'So in the spirit of friendship, I'll sing our own Pat Brennan's song 'Forty Years From Home.' What do you say, Mr Carrol, will you join us?'

Simon made a show of finishing his drink and slamming his glass on the bar. Ronan began playing the opening chords as Simon stormed out, quickly followed by the Price brothers.

Niamh stood and waved to him.

'Now that was well done,' said Vinny.

'But at what cost?' asked Anne.

Chapter Twelve

DI Barlow

Liverpool, 1974

The waiter brought the two pints of lager. Mike raised one to his lips, 'Just what the doctor ordered.'

'Are you ready?' The waiter stood a pencil poised above his tiny notepad.

Mike placed his pint back on the table, 'Shall we wait for him?'

'No, let's order if he doesn't like it tough.' Barlow checked his watch. 'Chicken Tikka Masala.'

'Is that the yoghurt one?' asked Mike.

'Yeah, you'll like it.'

'Three of them, please, we've got someone joining us soon.' Barlow indicated one of the empty chairs on the table. 'With rice and some naan.'

The waiter closed his pad and disappeared into the kitchen.

Barlow checked his watch again, 'I hope this guy is not taking the piss.'

'How's your man getting on, across the water?'

'Not sure. I know he's active. We've got another guy in there.'

'You've got another guy in the same mob? Why not use him to get rid of Walsh?'

'Who takes over after Walsh?' asked Barlow. He let the silence hang for a second. 'Connolly is disposable, we lose him, we haven't really lost anything. The guy we have in there now is long term, I don't want to risk him. I've set the Irish anti- terror boys on Connolly too, so they can keep an eye on him, but we have to be careful I wouldn't trust them as far as I could throw them.'

'What's going on with the Commander?'

'Marsh doesn't get it, he's living in the past. Wants everything separated, in little boxes. The world doesn't work like that. He's mad keen on the industrial stuff, thinks he was shown up, the Shrewsbury pickets were arrested and tried in Birmingham even though they came from here.'

'Does he know about Ireland?'

'No, and I need it to stay that way.'

'I don't get it, if Marsh doesn't know about Ireland, what difference will it make?' asked Mike.

'Believe me, other people are watching. Marsh is a jobsworth, but there are plenty of real operators dealing with this stuff. On the surface, it is as if they are separate theatres, England, Ireland, and Northern Ireland. Different rules, different organisations, different tactics.'

'But…' Mike anticipated Barlow.

'If I can deliver Walsh, it proves that operating from here we can have an impact there. Marsh won't like it, but it's one step closer to a unified command.' He paused. 'If I learnt anything, it is that you have to strike at the heart.' He slapped his chest as he spoke. 'The heart of revolution in England is the example of Ireland, if we let the fuckers run rampant there, they'll be here before you know. No point picking at the edges. Kill the heart and you take the life out of everything.' Barlow took a drink. 'They have always done it. We're one step behind, no scrap that not one step, half a fuckin mile.'

'Who do you mean?'

'Republicans, terrorists. The Kimmage brigade in 1916 men from Liverpool, Glasgow, and London took part in the Easter rising. After the treaty in 1921, we rounded up and sent back hundreds of guys from Liverpool and the North East called themselves The Irish Self Determination League. Even now, one of the Provo's big shots, Stephenson is from London. Calls himself something Irish now, Sean Mac Steven, some Gaelic name, doesn't matter, he was born here as British as me or you.'

The waiter came back with poppadoms and an array of chutneys and sauces.

Barlow moved his drink as the waiter laid the table. 'It's always been our Achilles heel. The British Empire ruling half the world and these bastards next door with their rebellions and risings. Set a bad example, always have.'

'Enjoy.' The waiter nodded and left.

Barlow continued, 'But we have some things going on now, the real shit, the gloves off.' Barlow broke off a piece of poppadom. 'The thing is it's all organised from the North. To have some people active in the South as well. Let's just say if I can pull this off serious people will take notice.'

Barlow was leaning back in his seat, Mike elbows on the table head forward listening to every word.

'What about the government in the South? I thought we were setting up Power Sharing, what's it called... Sunningdale.'

'The loyalists won't share power; you wait and see, they'd rather bring the house down. We don't share power with terrorists. The government in the South hates the IRA as much as we do, more in some ways.'

'Jesus,' Mike was shaking his head; he stopped and looked across the restaurant. 'Here he is,' Mike welcomed Terry to the table and pulled out a chair.

Terry was wearing a burgundy suit jacket with wide lapels, a cream open neck shirt and cream flares. His dark hair was combed over to one side; it was long enough to cover one eye when it dropped over his face. His eyes darted around the restaurant.

'Relax, you're safe here, none of your lot could afford the prices.' Barlow grinned.

'I'm meeting some mates for a pint later so I don't want to be all night.'

The waiter arrived and took his order for a drink.

'Don't panic, it's just a catch-up session, see what's going on in the underworld.'

'Underworld?'

'Yeah below the surface where you guys operate.'

Terry screwed his face at Barlow.

'Don't get on your high horse. I'm not talking about you, it's those others.'

'Come on get stuck in,' Mike and Barlow were breaking off bits of poppadom and dipping them in the sauces, spooning on the chutneys.

'There's talk of redundancies again, the men are not happy.'

'How many and when?' asked Mike.

'We're not sure yet.'

'The convenor of the body plant is arguing that as long as they are voluntary, there's nothing we can do. He's putting a resolution to the Shop Stewards Committee. Alan from the assembly plant is arguing against it, he says we were given a promise, we've improved productivity, flexibility, introduced team working, done everything they asked. The European division is also making record profits.'

'You gobshites, it's their company, why don't you let them run it?'

Terry broke his poppadom and the crumbs flew across the table. 'Because they're our jobs if we don't have these we can't live. They've made money off us for years, they can put some of it back in.'

'That's not how it works, can't you see if it costs Ford more to make a car than Honda or Nissan than they can't compete.'

'That's not our fault.'

'No, but it's your problem.'

'It's the system's problem.'

'There we go again, always comes back to this with you guys, never just a few quid more, or a longer tea break. You want to bring down the whole system.'

'Tell us about Alan the convenor,'

'What do you want to know?'

'Everything, is he married, kids? How old are the kids? What car does he drive, where does he live? Is he buying his house or council? Is he messing around with anyone? Is his missus? Does he drink, gamble?'

'He's married as far as I know. Lives in Halewood got a couple of kids.

'Well, find out, ask around. We're not giving you this curry for your culinary education.'

'My what?'

'Never mind. How about groups? Is he in any?'

'Yeah, not sure how much, but he's around Big Flame, they've got some guys, and women down in Dagenham, they have a Ford rank and file group, Dagenham, Bridgend, Southampton. They put in a newsletter to the factory, I dunno about once a month, telling everyone what's going on in the union, in politics.'

'That's the thing, find out about that, the rank and file group,' said Mike.

Barlow interrupted, 'Don't find out about it. Join it. Then you can tell us who the person on the outside is, the people in London and Wales.'

'What's Big Flame?' asked Mike

Barlow answered. 'Radicals started here in Liverpool. They took the name from a film about the dockers - from small sparks to a big flame.'

'There is something,' said Terry.

'What?

'Some leaflets were going round for a picket. Some stewards were talking about going.'

'What kind of picket? Did you bring the leaflet?'

'No, I never thought.'

The waiter had arrived; he waited until Barlow finished speaking before he leaned in and delivered the three main courses from his tray.

'For fucks sake, why do you think we keep you in shite curries and beer? In future, everything that crosses your path, newsletters, flyers, notes from your mum. They all end up with us. Ok. Got it?'

'Got it.'

Barlow began eating, spooning the rice into his mouth. When he spoke, bits of rice flew out. 'So, come on then, this picket, what is it?'

Terry waited until he had swallowed. 'It was at the University, some bigwig from South Africa is visiting, giving a speech or going for a dinner or something. There will be a picket, students and others.'

'No time or place?' asked Mike.

'No.' Terry shook his head.

'We'll find out, that's good though that's exactly the kind of thing we need. Is this Alan going on it?'

'Yeah I think so; he raised it at the meeting. Not everyone was happy,' Terry said.

'I'm not surprised, what the fuck has apartheid got to do with people in Speke and Halewood, fuckin loony tunes the lot of them.' Barlow clapped his hands. 'This is more like it. How's your food?'

'Yeah nice, I like this.'

'You've had it before then?'

The waiter who had returned to collect the empty chutney dishes smiled as Terry spoke.

'Yeah, you'd be surprised even curry has made its way to the council estates.'

'Don't be a smart arse.'

Terry cleared his plate, 'I enjoyed that, just set me up nicely for a few pints.'

'Where are you meeting your mates?'

Barlow slipped open his wallet under the table, and pulled out a tenner, he passed it across to DS Jones.

'Is this part of your report as well?' asked Terry.

'No, just want to make sure I don't bump into you later, and here.' He passed the ten-pound note over. 'Have a pint on us.' 'Oh right,' Terry took the money. 'We usually start in the Big House. Have a few and go down Back Bold Street there's a few places down there. This'll pay for the taxi home.'

Terry finished his pint. 'Can I go now?'

'Yeah go on.'

Mike stood to shake hands with Terry while Barlow remained seated.

When Terry had gone, Barlow said, 'That was good stuff, he might be alright this guy. Like a fish on a line got to reel them in, then let them out again.'

'Evening Mr Barlow.' The tall well-built man in a grey suit had an open neck shirt with a gold chain.

'Well if it isn't Jack Power, local businessman and all-round benefactor of the community.' Barlow stood and offered his hand.

Jack Power didn't shake it. 'I won't if you don't mind, don't want to get a bad reputation. Saw you with your minion there, he looked familiar, anyone I should know about?'

'DS Jones I don't think you've met Jack Power?'

'Not had the pleasure,' Mike nodded.

'No, not in your line of work Jack, there's real work to be done here, not chasing petty criminals.'

'I hope your curry chokes you,' said Jack, smiling. 'Well I won't hold you up, just wanted you to know that we also have eyes on you, Mr Barlow.'

'Isn't that your missus over there?

'It is.'

'Well better hurry back, don't want her getting lonely, you know what happens to lonely wives.'

'Very funny Mr Barlow.'

Jack returned to his table and his unhappy-looking wife.

Barlow finished his pint. 'A whisky to round things off?'

'Sure.'

'This is where the real police work is being done, the real threat is coming, and if we're not ready we'll lose.'

'What threat?'

'Get to know who the top family is, every estate has got one,' he held up one hand. 'Then find out who the activists are, the Commies and the Trotskyists,' Barlow raised his other hand, formed a fist and brought them together. 'Where these two groups meet, that's where you get your problems.'

'Why?'

'You won't find this in any of your handbooks or manuals, but that's it.' Both fists were pressed together in front of him. ''Cos they've got the balls, they're already lawbreakers, you mix that with politics and then my friend you have a revolutionary cocktail, just waiting to go,' His fists unfolded and fingers extended 'Boom. That is where we are, that is why Terry and Paddy Connolly are part of the same operation even if they don't know it. Revolutionary ideas are like a cancer- got to be cut out before they spread. He paused, then added. 'I fuckin love it when a plan comes together. Next step, bring down Alan H.'

'Why?'

'Firstly, because Marsh needs a win and I have to give it to him. Secondly and more importantly, our purpose is to Disrupt, Derail, Disorganise, we make sure they can't win. A negative goal. Make sure whatever they try to do fails, whatever leaders they find, fuck 'em up.'

Chapter Thirteen

Paddy

Wicklow, 1974

Paddy opened his eyes onto another Irish morning, sunlight flooded through the open curtains. His purpose broke through the fog of a hangover - on a proper job today. He swung his legs out of the bed, the chill morning air caught his skin, his body woke from legs up.

He was out of bed, socks and trousers on, and staring at the bathroom mirror shaking his head to get rid of the needles too much whiskey had left. Rum was his usual drink, not the white Bacardi or the heavy Lamb's Navy, but clear golden rum, the colour of the Caribbean sky at sunset. Well, that was what he imagined; Barbadian rum was his favourite, Cockspur, Lemon Hart, and best of all, Mount Gay, the night before whiskey had been a poor understudy.

Paddy splashed his face with cold water, the shock tightening his skin. He used the water to flatten his hair. Back in the bedroom, he picked up a jumper; he'd noticed the guys were more casual during the day. In Liverpool, Jack Power and the boys wore suits and ties day and night. He did the same and never really thought about it. Maybe it was to show that he didn't work, get his hands dirty for a living. Here people saved the good clothes for the evening and Sunday, so the jumper was under his jacket.

He wasn't nervous about the work; he knew he could handle himself and anything that came along. The stuff in the North, though, the IRA and UDA there, is no fucking about with that shit. But that's exactly what Conor Walsh was doing.

He heard Seamus beep and made him wait. Seamus was parked outside the house facing the bridge. Declan was in the passenger seat, Paddy climbed in the back.

'You took your time,' said Seamus.

'My time to take,' replied Paddy.

'What?'

'I think your job is to drive.' Paddy pointed ahead and relaxed back into the seat.

Declan tried to cover his grin.

'For fucks sake.' Seamus threw the car into gear, and the gears crunched. 'Fuckin bollocks.'

'You might want to chill out, mate,' Paddy knew Seamus didn't like him, but couldn't work out why. Was he worried about his standing with Conor? Surely, he couldn't be so insecure.

Seamus swung the car left at the end of the street and over the town bridge. He took a right at the top of the town and was on the coast road to Dublin.

'So, what's the job?' Paddy asked.

'Picking up a truck and delivering it,' said Declan.

'You mean hijacking, robbing a truck?' said Paddy.

'If you say so,' answered Declan.

'Yeah, I do.'

'The driver?'

'You're full of questions, aren't you?' said Seamus.

'He's sound he'll be in a cafe having his breakfast,' Declan said

'And the load?' asked Paddy.

'What difference does it make to you?' said Seamus.

'It makes a difference.'

'Why?'

Paddy could see Seamus looking at him through the rear-view mirror.

'Look, we don't know.' Declan had turned to face Paddy. 'But...if it's a truck, it's gonna be summat shiftable, ciggies, booze, electrics.'

'Fair enough.'

'You're a right cunt, do you know that?' Seamus said.

'I do. You're not the first and won't be the last to notice.'

'We've got to pick up the lorry and leave it in a shed up near the border,' Declan added.

'Near, not over, across?'

'Nervous, are you?' Seamus forced a laugh.

'Look, whatever it is with you two, can you give it a fuckin rest?' Declan snapped.

'Near, don't worry. You can pretend there isn't a war going on.'

'I'm not pretending anything, it's not my war, and I want to keep it that way,' Paddy said.

'You've been in England too long,' replied Seamus.

'Because you daft bastards can't make a country where a man can earn a decent living.'

Seamus shook his head. 'It's people like you who let the country down.'

Paddy snorted. 'Says the man on his way to hijack a lorry.'

'That's different.'

'That's bollocks.'

Declan slapped the dashboard. 'Enough now, fuckin eedjits.'

They drove on in silence. Paddy was happy to be in the back. These narrow country roads were a nightmare, twisting and turning every hundred yards. The morning was the kind of grey that dulls all the other colours around it. A fine drizzle floated through the air, and the wipers squeaked across the windscreen. They were nearing Dun Laoghaire and the ferry port.

Across the Water

* * *

The Rediffusion lorry turned into the car park, Seamus flashed his lights. The lorry parked away from the building, and the driver got out and went inside. 'We have to be quick. He's only stopping for a piss. You two are in the lorry. Get in. There will be a key in the ignition. Start her up and follow me.'

'Right, you make sure we're behind you, no tear arsing round,' said Paddy.

Declan snapped. 'Do you have to turn everything into a row?'

Paddy held his hands up. 'I'm just saying.'

'Come on.' Declan jumped out the passenger side and walked quickly toward the truck. Paddy caught him up. The mist had left the air damp, and Paddy's face was immediately cold and wet.

'Who's driving? Paddy asked.

'You,' said Declan.

'No problem.' Paddy felt the adrenaline flowing through his veins as he climbed up into the cab. He turned the heavy steering wheel, pressed the clutch, and ran through the gears.

'Come on, get a move on.' Declan stared at him.

'Okay, okay, just getting my bearings.' Paddy reached round the steering wheel, found the ignition, and turned the key. There was a guttural churn before the engine kicked into life. Paddy could feel the power as he pressed the accelerator. 'Okay, here we go.'

They rolled the truck out of the car park, Paddy crashing the gears as they pulled out into the main road.

'You okay?'

'Yeah, yeah.' It took big movements to manage the truck, the wheel, the gears; even the pedals all required strength as well as coordination.

Before long, they were rolling through the countryside, narrow roads with long curving turns. The morning had brightened a little. When Paddy lowered the window, he was struck by the smell of the country.

'What is it with you and him?' asked Declan.

'He winds me up.'

'Is it true you're after Maude Carrol?'

'Jesus, I've just set eyes on the woman.'

'You'd better get over her and this row with Seamus, and quick, cos he's been with Conor a good few years and you're just arriving.'

'Yeah, I know. I will. What's his story anyway?' Paddy asked, he was trying to build his picture of Conor's operation, looking for his weakness.

'His da and his uncle were with Conor in the old IRA; they were comrades like, they carried on after the Treaty during the civil war. Seamus's auld fella took a bullet, and his uncle buggered off to England after they lost, so he and his brother were left with a farm and his ma to look after. He's not a bad fella, really. He does the diesel, has his team for that. Most of the farmers in the county are reds.'

'What? Communists like?' said Paddy

'They're on the red diesel, you know, we sell in the North.'

'Yeah, I got a lift off Colm, one of his guys.'

'Oh, it's a great racket, not just farmers, even some garages are getting it now. And keep your eyes on the road there,' said Declan.

'I am.'

'How about your lot in Liverpool?'

'Ah, nothing too big, you know, stuff in and out the docks, we'd be doing this kind of stuff too.'

Paddy reached over and turned the radio on. He struggled as he drove to turn to the dial and find a station.

'Here,' Declan took over and tuned in to the BBC, Radio

Ulster. 'I like this one.' The Eagles were at the chorus of 'Your Lying Eyes.'

Paddy eyed Declan. Was he trying to say something?

'What? They're a good band.' His body jerked in time to the music.

'Never mind that, how far are we going?'

'Another half-hour will get us up near the border.'

'And we're just dropping it like?'

'That's right.'

'Who for?'

'Not our business. We do our part, that's it. Conor keeps things close to his chest.'

'But you know?'

'I have my ideas.'

'The boss wasn't exactly shy telling me what he thought,' said Paddy.

'Yeah, right, he's not shy about that no, but when it comes to the 'work."

'Are you the same are yeh, republican?'

'I'd like to see Ireland united, of course, I would.'

'Sounds like there's a but coming,' said Paddy.

'Hold on.' Declan turned the radio up as the presenter introduced the news.

Paddy reached out to turn it off.

'No, leave it.'

'Why, it's just shite.'

'Don't be stupid. We need to know what's going on,' insisted Declan.

The announcer read in a monotone voice. 'Two Catholics have been shot dead.' She named a town Paddy didn't recognise. 'RUC are on the scene, and the army have increased patrols in the area.'

'It means we have to be careful,' said Declan.

The roads and signs meant nothing to Paddy. 'Do you know

where we are?'

'I know we're near the border,' said Declan.

'It feels like we're going round in circles. These houses look the same.'

'That doesn't mean anything. They all look the same in every village round here.'

'Well, I hope we get there soon, is what I'm saying.'

'Calm down. Seamus knows the way.'

'Does he now?' asked Paddy. 'What the fuck is that?'

'Shit, a patrol.'

'Who are they?' asked Paddy.

'Shit, it's Brits.'

Paddy slowed the truck. 'Do you have a story ready?'

Declan said, 'Yeah, he pulled out a piece of paper.'

'For fucks sake,' said Paddy.

Seamus's car was two ahead of them, and the soldier flagged him down. He stopped; a soldier leaned down to his window. Seamus passed his paperwork, and the soldier said something to him. Seamus replied. The soldier took a step away from the car and spoke into his radio. He waited, a minute later, acknowledged something on his radio, then returned his papers and waved Seamus on.

They followed behind the next car as it approached the same soldier; again, he leaned down and spoke to the driver. The driver produced his papers; the soldier examined them, gave them back, and waved him on.

Paddy turned the radio off. He eased the truck forward.

The soldier signalled for Paddy to pull over to the side of the road.

'Oh, shit,' said Declan. 'What's on the paper?'

'Clones, Kilmichael Industrial estate Clones. Keep your shit together.'

Paddy pulled over and watched in the mirror as the soldier slowly made his way to the front of the truck, alongside the driver's door. A second soldier was making his way around the vehicle, occasionally ducking to check under the chassis.

'Where you going?' The voice was crisp and firm.

'Clones,' said Paddy.

Declan announced, 'Kilmichael Industrial Estate.'

'We must have crossed the border, without realising,' said Paddy.

'Yeh you 'ave.' the soldier's sharp face and alert eyes scanned them both.

'Scouser, eh?' asked Paddy. 'Where in Liverpool are you from?' He hoped it sounded casual enough.

The soldier eyed him suspiciously,

Paddy tried again. 'I've just come back from there, Garston.'

The soldier's eyes narrowed. 'No. You taking the piss? I'm from Speke.'

Bingo thought Paddy. 'That's where I was living, mate, behind the Parade. You?'

'Eastern Avenue,'

'Near the Dove and Olive?' asked Paddy.

'My local when I'm home.' The soldier grinned.

'Ah, know it well,' said Paddy. 'And now you're here?'

'Tell me about it.' The corporal looked back toward his patrol. Then focussed back on Paddy. 'Red or Blue?'

'Toffee myself, blue,' said Paddy. 'I'm so stupid I didn't even know I'd crossed the border. Are you King's?'

'Yeah.'

This would do the trick. 'Just with some of your boys the other week. Paul Doyle's funeral.'

'Fucking shit that.' The soldier shook his head.

'I know the family,' said Paddy.

'Yeah, alright, mate.' The soldier turned and shouted to the rest of the patrol, 'Make space. Let this guy through. He's one of ours.'

He turned back to Paddy. 'Take a left at the next crossroads that'll get you back over.'

'Fuck, how does this work? You don't even know what country you're in?' Paddy said, then added, 'Thanks, mate, I'd've been fucked if you hadn't stopped me. Stay safe.'

'Go on then, get out of here, and watch out though this place is crawling with Provos.'

'You got it, mate.' Paddy raised his window.

He pulled the truck back into the road and moved slowly through the checkpoint giving a thumbs up to the soldiers. 'Wahooo!' He punched the air when they were clear.

'For fucks sake, you were cool,' said Declan

'I was sweating my arse off.' Paddy laughed, as he raced the truck through the gears.

'You got us out of that, no kidding.'

His face changed when he said. 'Yeah, but who got us into the fucker?'

'There he is, pull over.'

Seamus had pulled off the road onto the verge; Paddy pulled the truck in behind him. Seamus was smoking a cigarette leaning on the boot.

'You stupid twat you took us over the border?' said Paddy.

'It's these fucking roads.' He shrugged. 'Like a maze.'

'You're supposed to know where you were going. Jesus Christ,' said Paddy.

'What's going on?' asked Declan.

'It's not far. I know where we are, a mile up the road, and we're there,' Seamus spat a glob of phlegm into the grass.

'You don't even know what country you're in.' Paddy sneered. 'Some patriot.'

Declan pulled Paddy away. 'Come on, let's get out of here.'

Back in the cab, Paddy turned to Declan. 'Has that happened before?'

Declan's answer, 'Not to me.' darkened his mood.

Across the Water

* * *

'Have a seat.' Conor was in his booth with a cup of tea.

'Thanks,' said Paddy.

'Heard you did well today. Quick thinking.' Conor took a sip of his tea. His movements were careful and precise.

'I was lucky. He was in the Kings, lots of Liverpool lads in that regiment.'

'More's the pity.' He paused. 'You're a smart guy Paddy, but for a smart guy, you do some stupid shit.'

Paddy shrugged.

'What's with you and Seamus?'

'Ah, I think he's mad at me being here like. That shit with the border.'

Conor raised his cup but stopped, putting it back down. 'What? You think he did it on purpose? No one is that stupid, not even Seamus. There's 300 kilometres of border up there. It's like someone threw a plate of spaghetti at the map. It was a bad mistake, but that's all it was.'

'You know better than me,' Paddy said but didn't believe it.

'You can't fight all battles on your own; you need allies. That's the problem with us, they split us up, tell us we have to look after number one. Get us at each other's throats. The same people across the water, Irish in the North, British in Ireland, Irish in the South, Irish in England. Different versions of the same thing.'

Paddy knew that's exactly what Barlow had sent him to do. 'I'm just trying to survive.'

'We all are, but it's a hard lesson to learn. You need other people to do that.'

'Come on,' said Paddy leaning back.

'What?' Conor raised his eyebrows. 'Spit it out. If you've got something to say, say it.'

'Don't get me wrong, I've got nothing against it - but what you're doing. Who are you kidding? You're not fighting for anyone except yourself.'

'Don't be so sure about that. Just because you can't see it. You're a good man, you've got balls, and you're smart. Don't waste it all on petty squabbles. There are bigger things to fight for.'

'Like what?' asked Paddy.

'Like your people.'

'I've got no people or the ones I have I haven't seen for twenty years.'

'That's where you're wrong, everyone who went through the life you did, everyone who is as angry as you, as frustrated as you, look around you, these are all of your people.'

Paddy had a grudging respect for this man Barlow wanted him to get rid of. He'd survived the country's baptism of fire and managed to carve out an existence separate from either church or state.

'You were lucky it was the Army. It could just as easily have been the UDR, UDA or the UVF.'

'Jesus, what did they do? Swallow the fucking alphabet, how are you supposed to know who's who?' said Paddy.

'You can't. British Intelligence are hand in glove with all of 'em and share responsibility for every drop of blood spilt by loyalists. Ruthless bastards have spent decades organising locals to kill each other. If you read their books they even boast about it, in Cyprus, Aden, Kenya.'

'Who's books?' Paddy was confused.

'Military Intelligence. They think we don't know what they are up to.' His blue-grey eyes bore into Paddy. He tapped the side of his head. 'But don't kid yourself, we know. We know exactly what they're up to.'

I fucking hope not, thought Paddy.

Chapter Fourteen

Vinny

Wicklow, 2010

Vinny and Anne waited while Ronan finished his lunchtime shift in the bar.

'I was surprised he knew who we were,' said Vinny

'And who I worked for.'

'So, he has checked us out, and it must have been him following you.'

'Him or his guys,' said Anne.

'Did you recognise the fellas with him?'

'No, I didn't get a good look at them. The question is why would he warn us off? What is he hiding?'

'The old lady didn't mind talking to us.'

'There's something going on with that guy.'

Ronan came out, putting his jacket on. 'What guy?'

'Simon Carrol, it was clear Maude didn't trust him, or her father,' said Anne.

'So maybe that's it? He's protecting his family's name and reputation.'

'Seems, a big step to take, to follow and try to intimidate people to protect a name.'

'I wouldn't underestimate how people value their family name.'

'We are talking about events from the seventies,' said Vinny

'Even so.'

'Do you want to come?' Vinny asked Anne.

Anne spoke quietly as if distracted. 'No, it's fine you go, he's your contact. I have other stuff to do.'

Vinny turned to Ronan. 'Are you sure you don't mind showing me the way? I've got sat nav.'

'I wouldn't be too sure of those things when you get among the hills, you lose the signal and you never know where you'll end up.'

'If you're sure?'

'No problem.'

The rain had never really gone away that morning; it was like an insect that couldn't decide where to settle.

Vinny followed Ronan's directions. 'Go straight up the hill here, and left at the obelisk. We'll go out through Hawkstow and on to Avoca.'

At the top of the hill, as they turned left, Vinny caught sight of the Price brothers; they were approaching Maguire's. 'You think it was those two following Anne?' he asked.

'If Simon was behind it, then yeah. I don't know what car they drive, but they are his boys all right. It would make sense.'

As they turned the corner, one of the brothers noticed them he tapped the other on the shoulder and pointed. They shared a joke and smiled as they watched Vinny and Ronan drive by.

'They give me the creeps,' said Vinny.

'I wouldn't worry too much; it's a game of cat and mouse. I don't think they'll actually do anything.'

'How do you know?'

'I know them, and they know me, they might be big lads, and not too clever, but they are not stupid.'

Vinny looked at Ronan, his face was set, his features firm. For the first time, Vinny wondered why he was helping.

Ronan turned the radio on and the car filled with Katy Perry's sugary pop, California Girls.

He groaned. 'No, please.' He turned the dial and ran through the stations, 'Here, we'll try this.'

'What are you putting on?' asked Vinny.

'Saimsa.' Ronan turned the dial.

'What's that?'

'Here, you'll find out.'

Within seconds, the familiar chords of traditional Irish music on fiddle and guitar filled the car.

For twenty minutes Vinny drove through the thickening country. The trees were greener, the hills were higher, and the road twisted through the rolling landscape. The windscreen was spotted with the memory of rain that came and went in flickers.

'Have we got five minutes for me to show you something?'

'Sure.'

'Just a bit further now, and we're at the meetings there's a pub, restaurant, and garden. If you pull over I can show you.'

'The what?'

'Meeting of the waters.'

Vinny pulled into a car park opposite the large stone building on the riverbank. As soon as they stepped out of the car, the sound of rushing waters surrounded them.

'Follow me.' Ronan led the way.

The air was fresh; a light breeze carried the remains of the rain. The sun appeared lazily between clouds. They walked through the public area with wet empty picnic tables and benches to the edge of the river. In an almost perfect Y, the rivers Avonmore and Avonbeg met to form the Avoca. A stone-paved area formed a triangle, allowing them to stand in the middle, a river flowing each side and meeting in front of them. The effect was powerful, the rivers fast-flowing and deep, the bodies of water churned as they merged, the flow increased in strength as the Avoca rushed away down the valley.

'You can see the line of ripples there, where the waters meet,' Ronan pointed.

Across the Water

There was something urgent, demanding in the waterway, nothing could hold it back, or divert it. 'My grandfather brought me here, told me that the rivers are our lives, those rushing waters, full of power and force, but it goes past so quickly it's gone before we know the power we had.'

'I can see where you get your songs from, your grandfather sounds like a character.'

'He was, I didn't really know him. My mam fell out with him and moved across to England. I was born there, we lived in London for a few years before she decided to give it a go back here. English and Irish the meeting of the waters,' said Vinny.

'You know I should make a song out of that... the two rivers, the two peoples?'

Vinny thought for a minute. 'But you're forgetting the wall.'

'What wall? There's no wall in these rivers.'

'They've always made sure there was a wall between English and Irish.'

'Ah, now you're spoiling the image,' said Ronan, he paused before adding, 'it doesn't last long, does it? Romanticism like, as soon as we get poetic, real-life kicks in.'

'You manage to be a poet, romantic, and a cynic, all in one go,' said Vinny.

'Ha, maybe it's in my genes, as they say.' He turned to Vinny, 'A strange old holiday for yourself.'

'I always knew it would be. I put it off for years. To be honest I would probably have never done it without Anne.'

'She's your engine.'

'Ha, that's a funny way to describe it. Not bad though I'll have to remember that. Come on. Let's get to Jackie O'Reilly.'

'Ok. I'll take you and leave you there,' said Ronan.

'You won't come in?'

'No, I know Jackie; he's a nice enough old fella, but he does go on. I'll let him bore the arse off you for half an hour. I'll have a walk-through town, maybe get a cuppa. I haven't been here in ages, did you know this is where they filmed Ballykissangel?'

'Yeah, that's why I've heard of Avoca, it's all the brochures.'

'Meeting of the waters, more likely though. It's where Ballykissangel was filmed, a beautiful place, fair enough,' said Ronan.

* * *

'How did you get on?' Ronan asked as Vinny approached his table outside the cafe.

'He's an interesting guy, told me a lot about Wicklow. The trade schooners that shuttled between Garston and Wicklow, the Munster and Leinster, the cattle boats letting off animals first at Birkenhead before the people at Garston. The main trade was in coal, timber, and bricks from Rathnew as well people.'

'Anything actually useful?'

'Yeah, he told me about the War of Independence, how Simon's grandfather led the IRA locally, then became the MP for the area. The split after the Treaty. His dad was a big man in the town too, so I guess you were right he does have a family reputation to protect.'

'Was Carrol the only one he mentioned?'

'No, there were a few others.'

'He gave me a pamphlet to read.'

Vinny showed Ronan a local historical society publication.

Looks riveting. Ronan smiled. He waved his hand at a buzzing insect. 'Fucking bugs.'

'Wait,' said Vinny

'What's up?' Ronan asked.

The insect landed on the table. 'Look.'

About half the size of a normal yellow jacket wasp, the insect had a black body, but its wings were a shimmering metallic blue and green. It walked on the table in a kind of search mode, as if it had a pre-planned method of scouring an area. It traced geometric shapes in quick-fire movements.

'The colours are amazing,' said Vinny.

Ronan raised a fist.

'No, leave it.'

'It's not a stinger,' said Vinny. 'They're parasites, inject their eggs into other insects, caterpillars or slugs, and the larva eats its way out, kills the host from the inside.'

'That's disgusting,' said Ronan.

'Very beneficial, actually. The wasp gets rid of pests.'

The wasp took flight, buzzed around, and landed a metre away, holding on to a stem of swaying grass. There was a flap of wings, and a flash of black, as a blackbird swooped and grabbed the wasp. Its broken body and wings wedged in the beak of the black-eyed bird.

'So much for the parasites strategy,' said Ronan.

'Back to town then?'

'Yeah, fancy a pint when we get back? I'm buying.'

'Can't argue with that.'

* * *

Vinny pulled into the Bridge car park.

'Okay, I'll show you a couple of pubs, if you're up for it?'

'Let me at 'em.'

'Anne?'

'She's ok, I messaged her. She's got some work thing this afternoon.'

They walked up Bridge St. Ronan nodded toward an obelisk. It was above the road on a plinth at the intersection of Bridge and Castle Street.

'You know what that's for?'

'I do, Halpin laid the telegraph cable man.'

'That's the fella.'

'But did you know his son built the auld Bridge pub back

there?'

'Now that I didn't know,' said Vinny.

'It's not often I get to drink in the afternoons,' said Ronan.

'I should say, me neither, but there are a couple of decent pubs close to the Uni.'

'Long liquid lunches are there?'

'Not often, but it has been known to happen.'

'How long have you been with Anne? You did well there,' said Ronan.

'Punching above my weight you mean?'

'I didn't say that.'

'No, but you meant it.'

'Ha, go on now.'

'We've been together five, six years now. Got together over a dead body.'

'Now there's romance for you,' said Ronan smiling. 'Go on, you're gonna have to explain that one.'

'It was when she started as a reporter. I was just doing my Masters. Her first assignment was about a body turned up on a building site. A long story as it happens, but she thought the body was my dad.'

'But it wasn't, though.'

'Turns out my dad put the fella in the ground.'

'Yeah, you told me that part.'

* * *

They came back out into the light of the afternoon. Vinny shielded his eyes. 'It always gets me, a pint in the afternoon, and the whole day seems weird.'

'No lectures after lunch?' asked Ronan.

'I've done seminars a couple of times, but never again. I think the students can tell, smell it on you. They're all giving you funny looks. It's not worth it.'

'Rather you than me.'

'Come on then, Maguires?'

'Yeah, what about the brothers Grimm we saw earlier?'

'Oh, they'll be no bother anyway.'

'Okay, you're the boss.'

'That I am.' Ronan led the way.

Maguires was one of the small family bars that were slowly dying out, a shop front, a single door, a partition to provide a snug and table and two chairs by the window, and the bar about three meters long —that was the pub.

'Heya Ronan.' The barman was wiping a glass, a tall slim fella with grey hair that looked like it was trying to leave his head, fighting to escape in all directions.

'Hi Jack, how's business?'

'Ahh, you know, not complaining.'

'I'm showing Vinny here a few pubs.'

'Oh right, well. You'd have to get Maguires in.' The landlord turned toward Vinny to continue his monologue. 'Started by my grandfather this place was when the old market was further up the street there, you'd have cows and sheep the whole lot in the square before the jail, and of course, the farmers liked a pint on market day too. I'm sure they deserved it, out in all weather and all.'

'I'm sure they did,' said Vinny.

'The usual is it? he asked Ronan.

'Yeah, two please.'

'No trouble.' He picked up a pint glass and held it under the Guinness tap. 'Where is it you're from?' he asked Vinny.

'Liverpool.'

'What job would you be doing?'

'I work for the University.'

'History professor,' volunteered Ronan.

'Is that right now?'

'Then you'll know all about that bastard Cromwell,' he said as he handed the first pint to Ronan.

'I do. I do.'

'Okay, shall we not start a new Anglo Irish war here.' Ronan took a drink of his pint.

'I'm not starting anything, by the time he left five per cent of the land, which was all the Irish had left. Did you know that? Of all the land in this country and just five percent for Irish Catholics, sure some Protestants had the land, and you had to be a protestant to leave it to your kids, did you know that?'

'I did, the penal laws, no voting, no universities, no professions for Catholics,' said Vinny.

'Well if you know all that you must be one of the few good English men. I'm a bit of a historian too.'

'I didn't know that,' said Ronan.

'Oh aye, regular at the local history group I am.'

'We've just been out to see Jackie O'Reilly,' said Ronan,

The landlord handed over the first pint. 'Oh, that man can talk the hind leg off a donkey.'

'His dad was Irish, here in Wicklow,' said Ronan.

'Well, then why didn't you say so, here's me giving it out about Cromwell.'

Vinny laughed. 'No problem' and he accepted his pint.'

'So, what did you say your da's name was?'

'Paddy, Paddy Connolly.' Vinny handed over a note for the drinks. 'And take your own.'

'That's very good of yeh. No. That doesn't ring any bells.' Jack rang the register and retrieved Vinny's change.

'He died in a motorcycle accident on the way to Tipperary,' said Vinny.

'Oh, now you mention it. Yeah, something like that everyone knows about. Wasn't here long that fella.' He was quiet for a second as if holding something back. He nodded to Ronan. 'I think he worked with Conor.'

Paddy couldn't hide the excitement in his voice. 'Did you meet him then?'

'No, no, nothing like that. Just the accident, I heard about that.'

'Ronan here will know about Conor.'

Ronan nodded and turned, disappointed Vinny followed him to a table.

'That was strange,' Vinny said.

'How do you mean?' said Ronan.

'Remembering my dad.'

'Well, here's the thing. You know your dad was a bit of a bad lad as you might say.'

'Yeah.'

'Well, Conor Walsh was well known in Wicklow.'

'He owned the house my dad was staying at. What was he well known for?'

Ronan took a deep breath. 'You name it. Everything from bank robberies to actual armed struggle stuff.'

'No.' Vinny looked shocked. 'IRA?'

'Not really, no. I don't believe so. He was involved in the War of Independence, but in the seventies, there were a few independent groups.'

'Wow, fuck, that sounds serious,' said Vinny.

'You're not wrong,' said Ronan. 'I'm not sure you want to go messing about in those waters if you know what I mean.'

'We're not, we're just talking, asking questions,' said Vinny.

'That might be fine in Garston, but let me tell yeh, asking the wrong questions about the wrong people can go south very quickly. Do you know what I mean?'

'Yeah I get it,' said Vinny.

'I'm not sure you do,' said Ronan. 'Here, history isn't a question of life or death. It is life or death.'

'No need to be melodramatic,' Vinny replied.

'Look, I just don't want to see you get into trouble. Speaking of trouble. Fuck, that's all we need.'

'What?' Vinny looked around and saw the two men enter. 'Is

it a problem?' asked Vinny.

'Who knows,' said Ronan leaning back in his chair and changing the subject loudly. 'Anyway, you're gonna have to get down to Brittas Bay. Maybe go to Avoca?'

The Price brothers were served at the bar.

'Come on, then. Let's down this one, maybe have one back at The Bridge and call it a day. I don't want your missus giving me a hard time.'

'You'd be used to that, wouldn't you?' The voice came from the bar.

Ronan rolled his eyes.

Vinny weighed up the two men and quickly decided he didn't fancy his chances.

'Are you ready?' Ronan asked Vinny as he emptied his glass.

'Yeah.' Vinny took a quick drink, leaving half a pint on the table. 'I'm ready.'

'Did you not hear me?' the taller of the two asked Ronan.

'I did, but not today, eh lads?'

'That missus of yours should keep this out of things.' He tapped the side of his nose.

'I'll be sure to tell her that now,' said Ronan.

He was up and out of his chair. He extended his arm to cover Vinny's exit. Vinny needed no encouragement and opened the door.

The men at the bar laughed.

'You have a good one now, boys,' said Ronan.

The taller man turned back to the bar, smiling, clearly happy with his victory.

Out on the street, Vinny asked, 'What was their problem?'

'People Not Profit, they've had some protests about a development Simon is involved in. Well, neither he nor they are Niamh's biggest fans.'

Ronan led the way along Main Street. The high street still had the variety of locally owned shops that had long since departed the small towns in England. Textile and wool, a hardware store, along with fresh meat from a butcher and bread and cakes from a baker.

'It's like going back in time,' said Vinny. 'Most high streets back home are either half empty or full of charity shops.'

'Just taking longer here.' Ronan stopped walking.

'What is it?' asked Vinny

'I've just realised something.'

'What?'

'You think Ireland is the same as England. Just we have different accents?'

Offended, Vinny stopped too. 'No. I never said that. When did I say that?'

Ronan walked on. The road split into higher and lower levels; traffic was one way. 'You didn't say it, it's what you think.'

Vinny caught up with Ronan. 'That's not true.'

'Come on, let's get to the next place.' Ronan set the pace, and Vinny struggled to keep up with the younger man. 'The end of this block here.' Ronan turned to face Vinny.

'Are you okay?' Vinny asked.

'Yeah, come on.' Ronan turned and walked ahead.

By the time Vinny had caught him, Ronan was going through the door to Ernie's bar. It was behind the statue he saw earlier in the week.

Ronan ordered two pints. 'I'll get these,' he said.

'It was supposed to be my treat,' said Vinny.

'I can buy a couple of pints,' said Ronan. 'Why don't you get a seat.'

Vinny sat down. The pub was similar to the last one, except larger, it was on the street corner. Vinny watched and waited as Ronan paid for the drinks and exchanged words with the landlord.

'Okay, come on, I know I've pissed you off. What's wrong?'

'You're a historian,' said Ronan.

'Yeah, you know that,' said Vinny

'Well, not all history is the same.'

'What do you mean? That's a weird thing to say. Of course, I know it's not.'

'What is Cromwell to you?' Ronan asked.

'The leader of the Parliamentary army in the English civil war.' Vinny sat back a bit. 'I know where you are going with this. In Ireland, he led the army in a brutal invasion and slaughter. So, he means two different things to the two countries?' Vinny lifted his pint and took a long drink.

'No, that's not the point.'

'Oh, right.'

'The point is there are families now that live in houses and own that land because of Cromwell, and there are other families who were dispossessed and remain skint today. Your civil war was 400 years ago. Ours was 100. That's three generations.

It means parents and grandparents fought and died, and sometimes killed each other. We know who was on what side to this day and who killed who. I can show you bullet holes in the walls. History in Ireland is not a separate subject; it is a living thing. And you are gonna have to start being careful because your dad was part of that. I don't know who he upset or didn't upset, but his hands weren't clean. You've already told me he was a killer. Do you understand me?'

'You mean he could have killed someone here?'

'I mean, you should be careful who you upset.'

* * *

'Come on then, back to The Bridge?' said Vinny.

'Nah, I think I'll call it a day if you don't mind. You'll be alright from here? To make your way back?'

'Yeah, no problem.'

'Are you okay?' Vinny asked.

'Sure, not used to the afternoon sessions.'

'Okay, see you later.'

'Sure thing.'

Vinny crossed the road to go down toward The Bridge. The sun was hiding, and clouds dominated the sky. He felt the chill of the breeze. Cars buzzed past as he walked on the narrow pavement. His head was full of warnings and threats; the longer he stayed in Ireland the closer he got to his father's world of violence and death. He stepped into the road to allow a mother with a pram to pass, a car whisked by so close when it swerved toward him he felt the brush of its metal; contact with its smooth surface spun him, the rush of air as he fell in its wake shocked him as the flash of red disappeared down the street. Adrenaline pumped through his veins, as the next car approached. Fuck.

He scrambled and stumbled toward the pavement and tripped on the kerb. His head hit the wall, and he crumpled to the ground. As he fell, the pamphlet left his pocket, and though his vision was blurred and his head was spinning, he could read the title.

Ambush at Dunbar.

Chapter Fifteen

Paddy

Wicklow, 1974

'Are you coming up to Fitz's?' Stephen asked.

'Yeah, but later, I want to check something out first. Which reminds me, have you found that priest, Father Pearson yet?'

'Yeah, the priest's house, St Nicholas, Carrick-on Suir.'

'I owe you a pint for that.' Paddy closed the door behind him and took the now familiar walk up the hill. The border run was still on his mind, it was a near thing. The truck would've been reported stolen by the time they reached the checkpoint. Seamus had dropped him and Declan right in it. It was either stupidity or malice and whichever it was Paddy didn't like it. He stored the thought away. Wicklow had a bit of life for a small town, and enough pubs to keep you occupied. More than Clonmel, he'd go down and see his brother and sisters soon too, which would be strange.

Now he was back, the memories of his family were stronger. Somehow, in Liverpool, they were in a different world, so he'd locked and bolted that room in his mind. The image of the locked door was sudden and revealing; he stopped walking and leaned against a wall. A series of locked doors, a long corridor with many doors, he knew each held an experience, a part of his life. The realisation both frightening and empowering. For the first time he knew where things were, he could also see the light shining under the door and through the keyholes. He found it harder and harder to ignore what was behind them. Could he open the doors one by one? Or would they all burst at the same time and flood his mind with what had been kept hidden, sweeping into the new rooms containing Riley, Barlow and Conor.

He smiled to himself because Vinny wasn't behind a door, he hadn't closed him off or shut him away. Somehow, he knew Vinny was the key to the other doors. Allowing the love of his son to slowly reveal the light behind each door. They would either be opened or burst. But not tonight. He'd heard there was a 'do' on in the Grand, and he thought it might be his chance.

The pale blue dress stood out between the various grey and black suits. Maude's life animated the part of the room she occupied. Everything else seemed static, she floated, her gestures like branches swaying in the wind.

The dull roar of voices competed with a piano being hit the other side of the room. Maude stood then made her way toward the bar. She moved with ease through the crowded room and turned faces in her trail like a wake. As she neared Paddy, three young men lurched toward the bar. They were a noisy swaying barrier through which Maude would have to pass.

'Hey lads, let the lady through,' Paddy said.

They looked at him and not Maude as she made her way toward them.

'What?'

'I said, make way.' Paddy extended his arm and pushed the guy nearest to him against the bar.

'Hey, bollocks, who do you think you are?'

The three young men glared at Paddy.

'That's a good question, Davey,' said Maude. Paddy couldn't help but notice her piercing blue eyes.

The speaker turned. 'Oh, Miss Carrol, sorry we didn't see you there.' He gave his mates a shove. 'Move out the way, let her through.'

She moved through the men who reformed behind her and

turned their attention back to the bar. She stood in front of Paddy. 'You're Conor Walsh's new guy. I've heard about you.'

'And you're Maude.'

'So now we know each other,' she said

'Do we?' he asked, he was enjoying the verbal fencing.

'I hope so.'

'Me too.' He gave a half bow.

She held out her hand. It was an unusual gesture. Her hand was palm down as if she was waiting for it to be kissed. He wanted to kiss it but instead, Paddy reached out for it and turned and shook it like he would a man's, even though it was soft and as smooth as silk. Shaking it was a sign of respect. He looked her directly in the eye.

She laughed. 'You like things your own way, Paddy.'

'Don't we all, and what is it you like, Miss Maude Carrol?' He felt the surge of electricity between them.

'Would you like to find out?'

'Oh, I promise I will find out.' He wanted to sound confident, but something about her kept him at arm's length.

She angled her head and a half-smile stole across her lips. 'Is that so?'

'It is,' he added. 'I hope,' in a show of humility.

She looked around. 'So, who are you with, Paddy?'

'I'm me own man. Am now and always have been.'

'Is that so?'

'It is.'

'Then you'll be happy to meet my father.'

'Well, now I'm not so sure of that.' He knew well enough who Paedar Carrol was. He hadn't been in Wicklow long, but long enough to know Conor would not be happy with what was about to happen.

'Come on now, are you scared or what?'

He wasn't scared but was nervous. She moved away a step and reached back for his hand. Did she know something he didn't?

Across the Water

Paddy downed his rum and allowed himself to be pulled across the room. They wove their way through the tables. When they approached her father's table, she slowed, as if her own impulses were weakening. He'd no idea what she was up to. The round table was a collection of stomachs with bulging suits and grey hair. Mr Carrol had a large frame, but age had diminished his ability to fill it. Paddy could see that Mr Carrol was used to being obeyed.

'Maude, what game are you playing now? Who's this fella?'

'How are you, Mr Carrol?'

'I'm fine, and what's up with you, my daughter dragging you across the room?'

'To be fair, I don't really know,' said Paddy.

'Well, will you enlighten us, Maude? What game are you playing here?'

'This is Paddy Connolly, from Liverpool.'

'Aaah, is that right? It seems to me men are travelling the other way to England. What reason would a feller have now for being contrary and coming the opposite way?'

'Missing the old country, sir.'

'Right, well, a bit of advice for you. If you want to make a go of things here in this town, you'll do two things.'

'And what would that be?'

'Get yourself a decent job and stay away from my daughter.' There was no malice in the words, it was matter of fact, but Mr Caroll looked Paddy in the eye and held his gaze as he said it.

Paddy held back the half dozen smart replies he could've made. 'I'll bear that in mind, sir.'

'You do that.'

Mr Carrol turned back to his company.

Paddy ordered drinks. 'What the fuck was that about?'

Maude looked shocked. 'Well, Paddy, best to know the score. That over there is your problem. You want to know me; I need to know you've got what it takes to look him in the eye.'

'Jesus Christ, where did they get you from?'

They shared a look and Paddy could see defiance and determination. 'My guess is the same place as you, Paddy. I'll see you about.' She turned and waltzed back to join her father's table.

Paddy shook his head, No doubt, no doubt.

He finished his drink and left. The alcohol warmed his blood and gave him an edge of energy. This place might work, after all. She was certainly something, he wasn't quite sure what yet, but he wanted to find out.

He turned right and walked along Main Street; Fitz's bar was just a minute away and busy. The stools along the bar and the booths were all taken. Cigarette and pipe smoke filled the air between, The Clancy Brothers played on the jukebox. Stephen was behind the bar. Paddy made his way over.

'The usual?' asked Stephen.

'Yeah.'

Stephen pulled and handed him the Kilkenny's. 'It's on your tab.'

Declan, Thomas, and Seamus were part of a larger group, about ten of them in all. Paddy reckoned they were the next circle in the ring of influence that began with Conor Walsh. These were the boys who worked for the main men.

'We might have something on, not sure if it's tomorrow or the day after.' Declan had joined him at the bar. 'I'll let Conor fill you in.'

Paddy knew Declan was full of shit. He didn't know anything.

'There's a call for you,' said Stephen.

Paddy put his pint on the bar. 'Me?'

'Yeah, come on, you can take it in the back now.'

Paddy noticed Declan watching as he lifted the hatch and went through to the back.

Stood between boxes of Tayto Crisps and peanuts, he lifted the receiver lying on its side. 'Hello?'

'Not getting too comfortable there, are you?'

'What?'

'Remember what you're there for.'

'Who the fuck..?' Paddy looked around to make sure no one

was listening. 'Is that you?' He didn't want to say Barlow's name.

'It is.'

'How the fuck..?'

'Never mind, but I'm watching, so make sure you deliver.'

'For fucks sake…'

The phone rang off.

Stephen popped his head round. 'Everything okay?'

'Yeah, yeah, a mate from Liverpool.'

'Oh, right.'

'Nothing wrong then?'

'No. No. He's just been to see my missus and kid, just letting me know they're all right like.'

'Oh, that's good of him.'

'Yeah, it was.'

Paddy moved back into the bar.

'A phone call? Who knows you're here?' asked Declan.

Paddy could see Seamus watching him.

'A mate, from Liverpool.'

The door opened, and the three lads from the Grand came in. They were younger than Paddy and obviously local; they were greeted by many in the group. Declan moved aside to let them in at the bar.

Paddy turned his back on them; he didn't want another round. He felt a nudge, not a real push, just enough to make him adjust his stance so as not to spill his pint. He took a step further away from the bar. Declan moved from beside the bar to stand with Paddy. There was another push, this time enough to spill some of Paddy's ale.

He took a deep breath.

Declan moved forward and put himself between Paddy and the men.

'Now, Pat, I'm gonna assume that was an accident like, and you'll be a man and apologise,' Declan said.

'I will not,' said Pat. 'This fella was sniffing round Maude Carrol and pushed us out the way to do it.'

Declan looked at Paddy.

Pat continued, 'So if he wants to be a man, he'll put his fists up like one.'

'Fuck off,' said Paddy.

He took a couple of steps and put his pint down on the nearest table.

Seamus was smiling and the volume and chatter receded as the confrontation took centre stage.

Declan took a step back, a challenge had been thrown down, and protocol demanded that Paddy answer. Pat moved toward Paddy. He tensed his muscles and straightened his back, presenting the largest frame he could. Paddy stood watching him move closer. He took a long drink of his pint and let the glass rest on the table next to him, his hand curled around it.

'Outside,' said Pat.

A few cheers went up from the men at the expected entertainment. As Pat was about to pass him, Paddy swung round, his whole top half turned 180 degrees in a smooth fluid movement and raised the hand with the glass as he spun. Pat's last step brought him to the perfect point for his face to meet the glass in Paddy's hand as it arced through the air.

The glass and remaining Kilkenny's exploded in Pat's face.

He staggered back a step, then put his hands up to his face and moved his head down. This was all Paddy needed, and he raised both fists high into the air before bringing them crashing down on the back of Pat's head. The force of the blow sent Pat sprawling forward. When he hit the floor, it was in a puddle of blood and Kilkenny's.

Paddy turned quickly, and a blade flashed in his hand.

'You bastard.' Pat's two friends moved forward toward Paddy, but the knife was enough to stop them in their tracks.

'Get him the fuck out of here.' The voice was Conor Walsh's. He had appeared from behind the bar. 'You two, Declan, get that fucker out.'

Across the Water

Pat's friends and Declan leant down to lift the man.

'Stephen, clear that shit up. Paddy, you get back here.'

Paddy followed Conor through the bar. People made way for them to pass by.

'Men put their hands up here,' Conor said as Paddy sat down in the booth.

'I don't care what people do here.'

'I can see that.' Conor shook his head. 'Jesus, what the fuck am I going to do with you?'

'Declan mentioned a job.'

'Did he? Well, he shouldn't. I'll be having a word with him.'

Stephen appeared with two whiskeys and placed them on the table.

Conor waited till he'd gone. 'This is not Liverpool. There is more fucking death here than you can deal with.' Conor clicked his fingers. 'Like that, that's how easy it is to die. So, you either sharpen up or fuck off. Am I making myself clear?'

'Yeah.' Paddy nodded. He liked Conor, but Barlow's voice was ringing in his ear.

'There are two countries here, and we don't mix them.'

'You mean the North?' asked Paddy.

'No. I mean Ireland. We are the shamrock and Guinness, the blarney stone and the ballads, but we are also an gorta mor and the black and tan war.'

'The angor what?'

'The Famine. Did no one teach you your history?'

Paddy threw back his whiskey. 'It's not my thing.'

'You're a strange one, alright. You can find your way home with us, but no games, no freelancing, keep your head down.'

'I got it,' said Paddy.

'Decide tonight. Declan will come for you in the morning if you get in the car.' He pointed toward the front of the bar. 'That ends. You do what you're told when you're told. Or it'll be me coming after you.'

Chapter Sixteen

Anne

Wicklow, 2010

'Can I come in?'

Anne stepped back from the door. 'It's Ronan.'

'Yeah, let him in.'

Vinny was propped up in bed with a plaster over his left eye. The left side of his face was a palette of purples and blues.

Ronan winced.

'Not a pretty sight,' said Anne.

'To be fair, I wasn't a pretty sight anyway,' Vinny screwed his face in a half-smile immediately followed by a grimace.

'Look, I'm sorry.'

'It's not your fault,' said Vinny.

Ronan was still at the door. 'Anne's right to be pissed off. I should have seen you back to the hotel.'

'What can we do for you anyway?' asked Anne.

'When the manager told me about the accident. I felt bad.'

'Guilty?'

'Yeah guilty, but not just for leaving him.'

'What else have you done?'

'Come in,' Vinny waved his arm. 'Guilty about what?'

Anne opened the door fully and made way for Ronan, she checked outside the room before closing the door behind him.

Ronan turned the chair by the dresser to face the bed. Anne sat on the edge of the bed next to Vinny. 'Do you know who did it?'

'No, I think it was a red car. I was so dazed I couldn't really tell.

'Did anyone call the police?'

'I was half-pissed. There would've been no point.'

'I wonder why that was?' Anne looked at Ronan

'It was both of us, no one forced me to drink,' Vinny said to Anne. 'But the car could've been the same one that followed Anne.'

'We need to find that car to make sure, but I think the only people stupid enough to try that in broad daylight, would be the Prices.'

'Why though? It doesn't make sense?'

'It does if you know the history,' said Ronan.

'Ok so come on, what are you guilty of?' Vinny asked again.

'Not being straight with you.'

'About what?'

'Conor Walsh…'

Vinny interrupted, 'The guy who owned the house my dad was in?'

'Yeah.'

'Who was involved with the IRA?'

'Yeah, let me finish.' Ronan collected himself, he leaned forward his elbows on his knees, his hands clasped in front of him as he explained. 'He was my grandfather.'

'Really?' Anne was first to respond, she looked across at Vinny.

'Why didn't you say something earlier? You know we've been talking about him.'

'I wasn't sure what difference it would make.'

Vinny raised himself a little. 'Wait a minute. Were you warning me off? All that talk about History is life and death?'

'Partly, well, no not really. I was saying this stuff can get dodgy very quickly, there are a lot of historic crimes that remain unsolved and unresolved, digging around is very dangerous.'

'So, you wanted us to stop?'

'No, look honestly. I didn't know my grandfather that well, what I told you out at "the meetings" was true.'

'Your name's not Walsh?'

'No, my mum married in London, it didn't work out but she kept the name. She fell out with her dad, went to London where she met my dad. They got married and had me. You know what it's like, it didn't work out, and so we came back here. I knew my grandad, but she never really got back on full terms with him.'

'So, when we arrived?'

'When his name came up concerning your dad. I was curious what you would find out. I didn't like Simon trying to push you around, and the Price brothers are dicks.'

'So, you were watching us?'

'I thought if they knew I was with you it would make them a bit more careful.'

'You wanted to protect us?'

'Well, I obviously didn't do a good job of that did I?'

'It wasn't your fault,' said Vinny.

'So, will you be straight with us now?' asked Anne.

'Yes.'

'That's why you didn't want to come in to see Jackie O'Reilly?' A few pieces were starting to fit together for Vinny.

'Yeah, because he knows my family history. And he would've connected my dad and Conor Walsh,' said Vinny.

'Probably. Have you read the pamphlet yet? asked Ronan.

'No, I didn't have the chance.'

'Well, I can explain it. Christ, I've heard enough about it over the years.'

'Was my dad working for your grandfather?'

'As far as I know, yes. That's what it looks like. To be honest, until you turned up I'd no idea who your dad was.'

'What was he doing for your grandad?'

'Again, I don't know. I know my grandfather, Conor, was into the national struggle and he wanted the Brits out of the North. He wasn't in the IRA but he was friendly if you know what I mean.'

'Go on then, explain,' said Anne.

'My grandfather and Simon's grandfather were the main guys in an ambush just south of Wicklow at Dunbar.

'It was 1920; the War of Independence was in full flow. There was an active IRA unit down in Arklow and Simon's grandfather set up the Wicklow unit. He was an ex-volunteer officer, so took command. Conor Walsh was younger, but as the story goes he took the actual lead in the ambush.'

'Who did they ambush?'

'They got word a bigwig from Dublin Castle , Brigadier Alfold from the Royal Irish Rangers was attending a ceremony in Wexford and would be travelling down through Wicklow.

'They set the ambush near the Price's farm. That's where their loyalty comes from, the two families have been connected since then. After independence Paedar Carrol became the TD, he looked after the Prices. They got permission to build on their land and they made money, so did Paeder as TD and a property developer.

'All very convenient,' said Vinny

'Yeah, it was. Anyway, the ambush wasn't a complete success, they killed all the escorts but Alford survived. Since he was the target, that wasn't so great. There were some other issues, that meant Conor Walsh and Paedar Carrol didn't get on.'

'Like?'

'Well, Allford claimed a gold watch was stolen from him, this might seem petty given that four soldiers were killed, but it gave the press a chance to call the volunteers, bandits and robbers. One of the Doyle brothers were accused of that, he skipped over to Liverpool right after the ambush, the other brother was killed.'

'I know some Doyles in Speke,' Vinny looked at Anne. 'Shit, and a watch, could they be related?'

'I've got no idea; you'd have to check it out. Anyway, the story went round that Paedar Carrol froze, that it was my grandad, a teenager, who took command and killed at least two of the soldiers. So, the whole thing was a bit messy.

'On top of this, when the truce was signed giving the UK the six counties in the North it split the movement down the middle. Paedar Carrol accepted the Treaty and went on to become the MP. My grandad rejected it, he fought on for a while, spent some time in jail but was eventually released. The anti-treaty people gave up after a year or so, but my grandad never really reconciled himself with the Southern state. So, Carrol and Conor Walsh ended up as enemies.'

'So, we think it was the Price brothers, who followed me and tried to hurt Vinny?' Anne asked.

'Yeah, stupid enough and loyal to Simon Carrol,' said Ronan

'But the question is still why is Simon Carrol so freaked?'

'It's got to be because of what Maude said, she said they all killed Paddy.'

'Her dad and Conor Walsh?'

'Maybe?'

'What if we find out it was your grandfather?'

Ronan shrugged, 'It is what it is? I know he wasn't an angel. I understand if you don't want anything to do with me. But I have nothing to defend here, I know Conor was a killer, could he have killed your dad? Absolutely, and if that's where this leads us, I won't get in the way of it.'

The phone on the bedside table burst into life, its ring tone breaking the uneasy silence. Anne answered and after replacing the receiver, she said to Vinny. 'The police are here to see you. They're waiting in reception.'

Chapter Seventeen

Vinny

Wicklow, 2010

When Vinny and Anne arrived in reception, the hotel manager, McDonagh was waiting with two plain-clothes officers.

'I'm Detective Sergeant Murphy and this is Detective Constable Hannity.'

Both produced their warrant cards.

'Mr Connolly?' Murphy, the taller and older of the two, took the lead.

'Yes.'

'Can we see some ID, please?'

'Can I ask what this is about?' asked Vinny.

'You can after we've seen some ID. We need to know we're speaking to the right person.'

Vinny flipped his wallet open and pulled out his driver's licence.

The second officer had his notebook open and scribbled the licence details.

He returned the licence.

'And you are?' Hannity asked Anne.

'That's my partner, Anne McCarthy. I would like her to be present.'

'Okay.'

'This way, gentlemen, please.' The manager led them down a

narrow corridor. He produced a set of keys and unlocked the door. He stood holding the door open as they entered.

Vinny entered first, followed by Anne. They took up a position at the end of the repurposed dining table and chairs; the nod to business use was the presence of framed posters urging "Positivity for Progress" and "Communication Equals Customers."

The officer with the notebook closed the door. In plain clothes, the officers fitted well in the room, as they wore the air of travelling sales reps. They all took seats.

'It looks like you've been in some trouble,' Murphy said to Vinny.

Vinny raised a hand to his face without touching it. 'An accident,' said Vinny.

'So, I believe. The manager was good enough to fill us in.'

'Then you know all about it.'

'Is there anything you want to tell us? It's not every day that someone survives a hit and run.'

'I wouldn't call it that.'

'Really? What would you call it?'

'Like I said, I had an accident.'

'Is there a reason you didn't report your accident?'

Vinny wanted to get off the subject. 'No, not really. Is this why you're here?'

Detective Murphy leaned back in his chair. 'You seem to be having quite an impact since your arrival here in Wicklow.'

'How can we help you, officer?' said Vinny, tired of the cat and mouse.

'Ok, I'll be straight with you. What're you doing in Ireland, Mr Connolly?'

'We're on holiday. Why?'

'Miss McCarthy, you're a reporter?' He ignored Vinny's question.

'I am, yes.'

'Are you working on a story now?'

'I'm sorry, why do you want to know?' asked Anne.

'I'm just trying to establish the purpose of your visit.'

'I've already told you,' said Vinny, 'I assume you haven't come here to discuss our holiday plans. So, do you mind telling us why you're here?'

'The Garda Siochana received a call from Sean Grogan. The call was related to the death of Mr Patrick Connolly in a road traffic accident in May 1974. We visited Mr Grogan and examined the motorcycle.'

'Right,' said Vinny.

'I believe you've been making enquiries about the accident, and the deceased is, sorry was, your father?'

'Yes, that's right.'

'Can I ask why you're making enquiries?'

'Because he was my father, and I've every right to find out exactly what happened to him.'

'He was tragically involved in a motorcycle accident, Mr Connolly. His death was certified as an accident thirty-five years ago. I'm not sure what can be achieved by questioning events from this distance.'

'Don't you have cold case units?'

'This isn't cold, Mr Connolly, this has been in the deep freeze for decades.'

'Yeah, I get that, but did you see the bullet?' Vinny asked.

'Yes, we have it, a .455 probably from a Webley, but…' He paused. 'Without a gun to match it, and establish the chain of evidence, it is impossible to know where that bullet has been for thirty-five years. Or at what point during those thirty-five years it was fired through the tyre of the motorcycle. Certainly, no one at the time of the accident drew attention to it. It's impossible from this distance to establish any causal link between the accident and the bullet.'

'I came to Ireland to visit my father's grave, pay my respects. I didn't expect to find a murder victim.'

'I wouldn't go around saying things like that.'

'No, I guess you wouldn't, but then he wasn't your father.'

'Okay, let me put this another way.' DS Murphy leaned forward. 'Don't go around saying things like' — he paused — 'There's no murder case here.' He looked at Anne. 'There's no story here and you can't harass elderly members of our community.'

'I haven't harassed anyone,' Anne replied.

'Is this why you're here?' asked Vinny.

'I've told you why we're here, Mr Connolly.'

'But this is it. This is the real reason?' said Vinny.

'You're here to tell me, us, to be quiet. To stop asking questions?' said Anne.

'We're here to advise you to enjoy your holiday and have a safe journey home.'

'Oh, right. Okay, so someone reports what they think might be a death in suspicious circumstances, and your response is to tell us to stop asking questions?'

'Okay, I think we've done all we can here.' DS Murphy stood.

'Hold on a minute, can I see your warrant cards again?' asked Anne.

The detectives looked at each other. DS Murphy took the lead and produced his card.

Anne took out her mobile phone and took a picture of it. 'And yours?'

The second officer produced his.

Anne took another picture. 'I wouldn't want to get your names wrong.'

The officers left the room. Although it hurt a little, Vinny smiled at Anne. 'What do you make of that?'

'I don't know, they don't seem very concerned about finding out what happened to your dad, but they also have a point after thirty-five years, are we really going to find anything?'

'We've found out a lot since we've been here.'

'Yeah, we're finding out how he lived, but not how he died. All Maude and Ronan can do is help us to build a picture of what was going on at the time.'

'It was interesting they brought up Maude,' said Vinny.

'The nephew Simon must've been on to them. Weird how they think them coming out to tell us nothing is going on would make us just give up,' said Anne.

'With some people, it would. They're used to getting their way,' said Vinny.

'The question is why?'

The Manager popped his head round the door. 'If you don't mind, I'd like to lock this again.'

They made their way back to the room, Anne opened her laptop and Vinny flopped down on the bed.

'What about Ronan? Are you pissed with him?' Vinny asked.

'Yeah, aren't you?'

'I'm not sure.'

'He's right about one thing though, asking questions is stirring things up.'

'Is that good?'

'I've got a feeling we'll find out.' Anne turned back to her screen.

'Any news?' Vinny asked.

'Yeah, they've offered me the job.' She stood up smiling,' I've got to confirm.' She looked up. 'I don't know if I should give them a call.'

'You're definitely going to do it then?'

'I guess so.' She tossed her phone onto the bed.

'Just like that, no hesitation, no discussion.'

'It's not like it's out of the blue. We've discussed it. I need this job.'

'What about us? You'll move to Leeds?'

'If that's what it takes, yes.'

Across the Water

'And us?'

Anne closed her laptop. 'You ask like it's my responsibility? If I take the job then yeah, we have to make some decisions.'

'You've already decided to go.'

'And what about you? Have you thought about coming with me?'

'I can't, you know that. My job is in Liverpool, and Charlie.'

'It's not like you see that much of him.'

'Oh right, have a go.' Vinny was taken aback.

'I'm not having a go, I'm being honest,' Anne said. 'You could get a job. Charlie could come for school holidays, you'd probably end up seeing more of him, and Helen would get a break.'

'You've got it all worked out?'

Anne threw her hands up. 'There's no pleasing you, is there? Either I want to go and leave you, or if I show how you could actually move, then somehow, it's all worked out so you can't refuse. The problem isn't me or this job. The problem, as usual, is you don't know what you want.'

'As usual?'

'Come on, Vinny, you got your dream job, now you're looking around and don't know what to do. That's why we're here. What's all this about? Looking for your dad, who's been dead for what? Thirty-five years?'

'I thought you were okay about coming?'

'I was. I am, but this isn't about your dad anymore. It's about you, who or what you are. I thought you had sorted it out.' Anne opened her laptop. 'Maybe you never will. That's why you think your job is more important than mine.'

'I don't think that. I'm not saying that.'

'That's exactly what you are saying 'you can't leave your job.' Or tell me, why do I have to make the sacrifice?'

'We said we'd deal with it when we knew for certain.'

'You were hoping I wouldn't get it?' Anne said.

'No, not really.'

'Not really?'

'Well, it would've made the decisions easier,' Vinny conceded.

'For you, but what about me? What about my career? My ambitions?'

'You could look for another job locally.'

Anne stood, 'I get it, I do. Do you know how hard I've had to work to get and keep my job? Coming from Liverpool Eight talking like I do, looking like I do. Watching these white middle-class kids come in and move on? Magazines, radio, TV, nationals, and I'm doing the same job I was doing six years ago. Six years of being the oldest cub reporter in the newsroom. When do I get to move on or up? I'm sick of it, really.'

'I thought you liked your job?'

'I do, but I'm not a crutch, for you or Anthony, I have a life, I'm a person, I'm not just here for you. You think I should organise my life around you, because you're the real professional, the white, educated historian. Your life is more important because you were the abandoned kid.' Anne paused, and her anger turned to frustration. 'You don't need to find your dad. You need to grow up and get a grip of yourself.'

* * *

Vinny pulled his coat tighter. He'd stormed out of the hotel and wandered the streets. He calmed down as he ate his fry up in a cafe, the sausage and bacon settling his stomach. Back out, he walked with a little more purpose. He knew the town square was at the end of the main street. It was chilly, but he needed time to think. It wasn't like Anne to raise his whiteness. She must've been pissed.

An old man sat on a bench facing the centre of the square. There was plenty of room, so Vinny sat down too. The space was dominated by a statue, they were too far away to read the inscription, but a man stood with one arm raised to the heavens, and holding a pike, an appeal, to who? Or what?

'Afternoon,' the guy in a flat cap nodded to him.

'Afternoon,' Vinny responded.

The old man pulled the last smoke out of a hand-rolled cigarette before dropping it on the ground and grinding it into the pavement. 'I know before you say it.'

'Know what?' Vinny asked.

'The ciggies, no good for me.'

'I wasn't going to say anything.'

'The missus was on at me for years.'

'Is that why you're out here smoking?' Vinny asked.

'Oh no, she's been gone a while now. Still don't smoke in the house, though.'

'Oh, sorry.' Vinny was referring to his wife but suddenly felt stupid, as if he was commiserating with not being able to smoke in the house.

'Don't be. She made sure she got enough curses at me in her lifetime to last well beyond her years. They're still ringing in my ears. That's what public benches were made for.'

Vinny looked at him

'For men to get out of the way of scolding women.'

'Who was that, then?' Vinny pointed toward the statute to change the subject.

'Billy Byrne from Ballymanus, they executed him.'

'What for?'

'1798 Rising. You're not a local then?' said the old man.

'No, I'm just visiting.' Vinny couldn't be arsed talking about his dad. Anne had hit home, she knew him better than he knew himself.

'Family?' the old man looked at him more intently.

'Not really, just a holiday.'

'Do I know you?'

'No, I'm from England?' Vinny said.

'A lot went over there, took the easy way out.'

'Easy?' Vinny asked.

'They got the jobs and money, come back here, in their new fashions flashing cash around.'

'I don't think they had it easy. What about the ones who didn't come back?'

The old man shrugged. 'Well, if they'd stayed here through the hard times, I'd have more respect for them, going over there losing their faith and traditions. Look at him up there, d'ye think he would have done that?'

'Probably not, but then like you said, he was executed. Is he your hero?' Vinny asked.

'I don't have heroes,' the old man replied.

'And you stayed here, never went to England?' Vinny asked.

The old man sat upright. 'I did not.' his posture softened as he added, 'Although to be honest, there were times I thought about it. Running away is always attractive.'

Vinny scoffed 'Like you from your missus?'

'Ha, fair point, but we can't escape the things we've done, no matter how far we run. So I stayed, with my missus and my mistakes.'

'At least you know yours, what if I don't know what they are?'

The old man shook himself and rose slowly. He turned before walking away and said, 'Give it time son, you will, you will.'

* * *

Vinny walked back along Main Street. No doubt his dad had walked this street. Did it make any difference? Did he feel any closer to him? Did he know him any better?

He used to love history. It was the means to understand the world. To know what went before, to know how we got to where we were. Recently, all it did was frustrate him. It didn't help decide what to do. Knowing the past was the easy part; determining the future, was the challenge. That was the difference. Anne had that ability. She knew what she wanted and took the steps necessary to get it.

Vinny pulled his coat in tight.

I guess part of it is being willing to lose. If I want something, I have to risk losing what I've got, to get it.

Like old Billy Byrne back there, he wanted a united Ireland free of British rule. He risked his life and lost. That was what Anne was doing. She wanted the job and was willing to lose their relationship. Meanwhile, Vinny sat on a bench, moaning about the decisions taken by others.

He put his head down as the wind whipped along the street. A flight of steps led down on his right, gulls squawked above and flew in loops and swirls. The stone steps took him to the quay. A couple of boats tied up, they bobbed on the lively river, the rigging tinkled as the parts moved in the wind.

When he looked up, Anne stood on the edge of a family group on the quayside.

'Hey,' Vinny said.

'Hi there.' She waved him over.

Vinny approached the edge of the quay. Anne linked arms with him.

'What's going on?' he asked.

'Look there.' She pointed at the dark, choppy water.

Vinny saw movement. A shape was swirling just under the water. 'What is it?'

It surfaced, and Vinny saw the whiskers and big eyes of a seal, a big seal. 'Wow.'

'It comes in every day to be fed.'

'Really, that's weird.'

The kids, with their parents, were excited and watched, amazed as the seal danced about beneath the surface, circled in whooshing movements. A fishmonger from a unit on the quayside approached a bucket in hand. He emptied the contents into the deep green water, the seal hoovered up the fish in seconds.

'Apparently, he's quite famous. Been on the telly and everything,' the father of the family group said to Vinny. 'I was telling your missus there all about him. A local character he is.'

'Yeah, I can see that,' said Vinny.

Anne gave Vinny a gentle pull. 'Come on then, shall we let him have his lunch in peace?'

'Yeh, sure.'

Anne held on to Vinny, and they walked arm in arm along the quay.

'I'm sorry about earlier,' Vinny said.

'Don't worry about it. Did you get something to eat?'

'Yeah, there's a little cafe.'

'Okay, good.'

'You should take the job. Whatever happens after that is down to us, we either make it work, or we don't; that'll be our responsibility. But you have to grab things while you can.'

'I agree. We'll work it out,' said Anne.

'I hope so,' said Vinny. 'And you're right about this thing with my dad, but I'm here, and I'm going to do all I can to find out, whatever it takes.'

Chapter Eighteen

Paddy

Dublin, May 17th, 1974 5.30 pm

The train rattled and wobbled its way along the coast; Paddy looked at the sea. The ever-present sea, even inland, its waves were felt in the half-empty villages, in the faces of old men whose sons were off to earn a bit. It filled the songs and poetry because it had taken from every family. More potent than politics, it outlasted everything; its pull a constant, leading people to new lives, death, or exile, most never came back.

The train clattered through the villages and towns of Greystones, and Bray, eventually it sliced its way through the overcrowded city, houses, bridges, and walls built within inches of the track. They resented the space the train took and so built right up to its face. The colours were reddy browns and greys, bricks and slates.

The passengers were the usual mix of hope and endurance. You could see the hope of youth turn line by line into faces of endurance.

The spring afternoon was as moody as Paddy felt; he walked out of Connolly station. Why do they celebrate failure? He knew the answer before he asked: because there are so few victories. Paddy looked at the name she had written down - The Shelbourne Hotel - Stephens Green. He was convinced she only invited him because she thought he would never show up to a party in Dublin.

Across the Water

He left through the main entrance. The station's Italianate central tower looked out of place on Amiens Street, busy with shoppers and commuters, the hands of the station clock marked 5.28 pm.

Dublin was busy and the streets were full. Women and workers, everyone had a purpose. He looked up at the unusually blue sky.

'Av ye got any change, mister?'

Paddy looked down at the boy, around ten; his big eyes darted around ready to move on to the next mark if this one went nowhere.

'Do ye know The Shelbourne Hotel?'

'I do, mister, av ye got change?'

'Here, you can have a shilling, if you get me there.' Paddy dug around and produced the coin.

The boy snatched at it.

'Not so quick, when we get there.'

'Right ye are, follow me. A shilling now, you promised.'

'I know yeah, a shilling.' The boy's hair was curly and uncontained. He wore jeans and a blue anorak underneath. Paddy could see a thick woolly jumper.

'Come on then, what are yeh waiting for?'

'Alright, take it easy.'

'What are you doing out here asking for money, shouldn't you be at home?'

'Nothing there mister, me mam'll be out at her mates, have you got a fag?'

'No, I haven't. What about ye da?'

'He's in the jangle.'

They walked side by side, the little fella chest out, arms swinging, commanded his space on the street.

'What's the jangle then?'

'The old jingle jangle my da calls it.'

'What's that when it's at home?'

'Mountjoy, he's doin a year.'

'What for?'

'I dunno, summat or other, that he got caught for, that's why yeh usually go.'

'True enough.' Paddy agreed.

'What're ye doing there like? It's a posh place, so it is.'

'Meeting a woman,' Paddy winked at him.

'Ahh going see ye tart are ye?'

Paddy clipped him round the head. 'Ye little bastard, what do you know about such things?'

'Hey hands off, I've had me share, don't you be worrying about that.'

'How far now?'

'Couple of minutes mate, straight on across the river now.'

The boy's presence suddenly made Dublin brighter; the troubles just something to be walked through, head up, chest out, the Dublin way.

Then the world stopped. The air shook with sound, faces gaped and grew wide with terror. Ahead the street disintegrated. In the flash, colours and shapes dissolved, cars and people and glass and bricks were flying through the air in pieces.

Paddy was on his back, for the longest time he looked up at the blue sky in silence. Slowly at first, then all at once, the sky disappeared in swirls of smoke and dust, the silence that burst his ears was now replaced with low deep moans broken with shrill cries. Someone helped him up, he didn't know who. The boy was not beside him.

He walked through the devastation, the blood in the gutter was not his, the leg on the sidewalk was a woman's, the headless body, a young girl. A handbag, a platform shoe. No boy. A man with a large piece of metal through him moaned. Paddy stumbled on, the dust and smoke and glass and bricks and bodies had now settled on the ground, scattered like confetti at a wedding. He walked on passing the blackened centre, some people were standing motionless, others laid where they were blown, some blown together, some blown apart. But no boy. People rushed to help, alarms and bells began to take over from moans and cries, and then again, the air shook and sky roared and again somewhere close by the street and the people in it were confetti.

Chapter Nineteen

DI Barlow

Liverpool, 1974

A paved courtyard stood in front of the main administration building of Liverpool University. Steps led up to the double doors and a suite of offices housing the Chancellor and other luminaries. Students criss crossed the courtyard in the early afternoon sunshine.

DI Barlow had a spring in his step, the anticipation of the day was building for him; any operation, no matter how large or small, brought the thrill of excitement. It was as much the planning and coordination as the event itself. Checking and rechecking the situation and possibilities, developing contingencies, this was his world. The world outside was in turmoil. In Ireland, the Ulster Workers Council were on the verge of a General Strike. Meanwhile, on the mainland, the Wilson's Labour government was hanging on by the skin of its teeth. There were no borders between Ireland and England; it was one fight and it was a time for action, not the armchair strategists of his Commander Marsh.

A DI from Admiral Street was given command of the police operation and had set up an office in the admin building. His uniform and peaked cap glistened. Barlow had contempt for these office boys, but you had to know how to play the game.

'Hi Tom, are they looking after you?'

'John, it's been a while.'

'Yeah, you all set up for this evening?'

'Should be, not expecting anything too rowdy. I was a bit surprised to see your request.'

'Yeah, there's someone we would like to get our hands on.'

'I've got the name here, why not just pick him up off the street?'

'More fun this way,' Barlow laughed.

'I never understand what you guys are up to.'

'That's the way it should be, Tom.'

'Anyway, we'll be ready.'

'How many are you expecting?' Barlow asked.

'Could be up to a couple of hundred, they've been advertising it pretty widely. Young Liberals, Labour Students, a few from L8 too.'

'Have you got your ducks in a row?'

'Absolutely, but being so close to Admiral Street and HQ we'll have plenty of backup on standby should things go south.'

'This gonna be a Command Centre?' Barlow looked around the large room. The Inspector stood and walked over to the window, 'Yeah, gives a view of everything from up here. Anything you need to tell me?' He asked.

'Like?'

'Well, it's not every day special branch ask for our help?'

'No, you can fill out your risk assessment; we have no relevant intel, no threats, all clear from us.'

'Good to know.'

'What's the plan?'

'Simple, get our special guest in and keep the buggers out. Will you be here for this one?'

'Yeah, with a small team we'll be here for the build-up, can you give us a separate room?' Barlow asked.

'I'll have a word and see what we can do.'

'Ok, much appreciated.'

* * *

Barlow, DS Jones, and DC Hyde were on the first floor of the admin building. Barlow didn't know whose office it normally was but it stank of pipe smoke, the colour of the ceiling was somewhere between mustard and HP sauce.

'If that's the ceiling, what are the guy's lungs like?' Barlow asked.'

'Are you trying to put me off?' DS Jones lit his cigarette.

'Wish someone would,' Lynda Hyde said.

The operation commander came into the office. 'All set up John?'

'Will be, you know DS Jones,'

He nodded. 'Sergeant.'

'This is DC Hyde, our spotter.'

'Spotter?'

'It's a nickname sir, not my actual title.'

'Should be though,' said Barlow. 'A bloody valuable asset.'

'My talent is facial recognition, to memorise and put names to faces.'

'Strange talent.'

DS Jones gave her a nudge, 'Tell him how you discovered it.'

'I addressed DI Barlow by name when he held open a door for me, in the station.'

'A station I'd never been in before,' added Barlow.

'He asked if we'd met, and I said he gave a talk at the Police College in Menlove Avenue. He was surprised I remembered his name from a couple of years earlier, and that was it.'

'Turns out she has a gift for this thing, Sir.' DS Jones interrupted, 'But that wasn't the biggest surprise though.'

'What was, Sergeant?'

'That he held open the door for anyone.'

The Inspector laughed at the well-practised joke. 'Well if you need anything, give me a shout.'

'Will do,' Barlow answered.

Uniformed officers had erected a barrier below keeping a lane open between the roadway at the approach to the square and the building entrance. The barrier sealed off the courtyard, police allowed protesters in, but once in they were caged.

The ambassador was due to arrive at 7 pm and an hour before the numbers were growing. This was the best time for Lynda and the police photographer, they snapped and catalogued as many people as Lynda could identify, and those who looked important. The Liverpool left outside the Labour Party was pretty small, and she was getting to know the faces and organisations. Big Flame, International Marxist Group, Workers Revolutionary Party, International Socialists. Then of course, there were those inside the Labour Party: The Militant Tendency. Detective Constable Lynda Hyde was unintentionally becoming an expert on revolutionary socialism in Liverpool.

By 6.30 pm the courtyard was relatively full, near the barriers the crowd was quite deep, although, toward the back, there was enough space for people to walk around. Barlow knew they had to complete the operation before the ambassador arrived, once he arrived the crowd would disperse rapidly.

'He's moving into the square now.' DC Hyde had spotted her man.

Barlow picked up his field glasses. 'Yeah, got him. Who's he with?'

'Don't know, they're both new to me, looks like he's got a boy with him,' said DC Hyde.

'The one on the right is Terry Connor, Ford shop steward.'

'Right, got him,' said Hyde. Then asked, 'Is that his son?'

'I guess so.'

'What do we do?' DC Hyde lowered her glasses.

'We carry on, what do you think?' Barlow was offended by the question.

'Hey up, Rory Gallagher, originally Belfast, now Liverpool Big Flame, well connected with republicans.'

Gallagher greeted the group including Terry Connor.

'See, that's what I mean.' Barlow pointed. 'Right there. Get me pictures of them with Gallagher; make sure you get Alan with Gallagher.'

'Done.' the police photographer was snapping away.

DC Hyde continued to name people for the photographer, her library of faces was growing.

'Ready?' DS Jones was impatient.

'Not yet, too early, too obvious.'

As the minutes went by, the crowd grew larger, the noise increased, the dignitaries began to arrive, and the surges against the barriers became more insistent.

'The ambassador's expected any minute,' said DS Jones.

'Get the squad leader up here,' Barlow ordered.

A minute later a Sergeant arrived.

'There, that's him. With the blue top, with short dark hair and a moustache.'

The Sergeant followed Barlow's directions and checked the photo he'd been issued till he identified the figure in the crowd. Toward the centre near the back of the press.

'He's well back, Sir, harder to reach.'

'Can you do it or not?' Barlow snapped.

'Yes. Sir.' The sergeant issued garbled commands over the radio.

'Are you ready?'

The photographers with their array of zoom lenses nodded.

The sergeant agreed.

'Go!'

'Go, Go, Go,' the radio crackled and Barlow heard the command at the other end.

From his window on the first floor, Barlow watched as two rows of white helmeted officers lined up behind the barriers.

Across the Water

In a practised movement, the barriers were moved aside and the officers in black overalls sliced through the demonstrators. The rows of white helmets cut rapidly through the crowd. They stopped when they reached their target, formed a semi-circle, grabbed him, and withdrew. The young boy was pushed aside. As they broke back through the police lines, Barlow was happy to see a body pinned between the officers.

'Get him inside,' Barlow commanded.

'Roger that.' The sergeant gave a thumbs up. Barlow looked across at the photographers recording the seizure.

'All good?'

'Yeah, we got some nice shots from downstairs too.'

'Great.'

Barlow put his binoculars down and turned to Mike. 'Let's go.'

'Wait.'

'What's up with you?'

'They got the wrong guy- he's still out there.'

'For fucks sake.'

Barlow turned to the Sergeant, 'You fucking missed him.'

'Who have we got, then?'

'I don't fucking know, there's the guy we want!'

'Shit.'

'What do we do with the fella we've got?'

'Keep him for a couple of hours then turn him loose.' Meanwhile, Barlow was pointing. 'Can you get him?'

The Sergeant called down on the radio, the lead officer of the snatch squad joined them, 'There.' Barlow pointed.

'Got him.'

'Not yet you haven't, but make sure this time you do.'

Minutes later the parallel lines of white helmets formed again, they followed the same procedure, there was more resistance from the crowd this time as they realised what the snatch squad were doing. Truncheons swinging and digging into people to force them aside. Snatch squads operated on the principle that a small well-trained, organised, and equipped force could assert their will over a large disorganised body.

The squad got their man on the second attempt.

'Check with the photographers. I want pictures on my desk in the morning.'

A uniformed sergeant appeared at the door. 'We got your man. What do you want us to do with him? Arrest him? Charge him?'

Barlow hesitated,

'Are you going down?' asked DS Jones.

The sergeant was waiting.

'We can't hold him here, we have no facilities. If you want to keep him we have to ship him out to Admiral Street.'

'Ok, I'm thinking.'

'Well, do it quickly.'

Barlow snapped back. 'What did you say?'

'Sir, I mean. Sir, the boss says we have to let him go, we have no right to detain him, unless we're going to charge him.'

'You're not thinking of interviewing him?' asked DS Jones. There was no reply so he added. 'You'd risk giving the whole operation away.'

'But think of the reward,' replied Barlow.

'You'd never turn him, Sir, not over this.'

'No, you're right, Sergeant.' Barlow turned to the uniformed officer. 'Arrest him, breach of the peace, take him to Admiral Street. Give him a caution and let him go. We've got what we want.'

As Barlow finished, all hell broke loose outside, the South African ambassador arrived in his chauffeur-driven Mercedes and despite the roars and best efforts of the crowd he made it inside, pelted with eggs and flour most of which covered his security detail. He was ushered into the building. The crowd didn't disperse however, remaining vocal and in high spirits. The reason for this became clear fifteen minutes later, the local paper caught the moment when an "END APARTHEID" banner was unfurled from one of the windows inside the room where the ambassador was being hosted. Inside students hired as waiters had managed to egg the ambassador, and hang the banner out of the window, much to the university's and DI Colman's embarrassment.

The crowd, having made their point, seemed happy to go on their way. So too was DI Barlow.

'I hope you got what you wanted,' the Inspector said as Barlow passed him on the way out.

'We did indeed. Shame though, looks like you failed to keep the buggers out.'

Chapter Twenty

Paddy

Dublin, May 17th, 1974 6.30 pm

Paddy walked on through the town, asking for The Shelbourne Hotel. With no guide, covered in dust, nothing else made sense. He crossed the Liffey and walked the length of O'Connell Street. His goal was the Shelbourne Hotel, the jingle jangle was everywhere as the emergency services tried to respond, but no boy. He asked for The Shelbourne Hotel, people with panic, anger and fear in their eyes pointed and left. The streets were emptying. No one knew if there were more bombs, or where they would be. All he could hear was the jangle. He could taste the bitterness of dust.

He walked through the entrance to the grand Georgian terrace, its cast iron and stained-glass portico held up in splendour by two African queens. The concierge was scanning the street and although he got a double take, Paddy wasn't challenged and entered the foyer. Another uniformed figure approached him. He was much younger than the concierge, he did what people do in emergencies they carry on as normal. 'Fine, Gael?'

He knew Maude was at a party.

'Follow me.' He led Paddy to a set of double doors. 'Do you have your ticket?'

Paddy shrugged. 'Errh.'

'Arrgh, you're okay. You're not the only one to forget.'

He opened the door and Paddy stepped inside.

He was in a large ballroom filled with round tables, each with eight to ten chairs. Two besuited young men sat at a table at a 90-degree angle to the door.

'What branch are you from?' the first haircut asked.

Paddy gave him a quizzical look.

Whatever order existed earlier in the day was breaking down now. Hushed conversations were happening; people were getting their coats and leaving. The noise from ambulances in the street was rising and falling but ever-present. The concierge emerged behind him making way for the manager. The manager and concierge rushed to the stage, the music was interrupted.

'Maude Carrol.' Paddy said.

The first haircut checked his papers. 'Over there, they're on the far side.' He pointed across the room.

Paddy turned and headed in the direction they pointed, weaving his way between the tables. Then he saw her rise from a table. There were few women around, but more than the previous occasion. It didn't matter how many women were there, none could compare to Maude. She was slim and graceful, gliding through the room. She went for twenties style dresses that hung off her body, not clinging to the shape but effortlessly revealing it.

'Sir, sir.' One of the haircuts was following Paddy while other people stared.

'Are you ok?' Maude asked when she reached him. 'What's going on out there?'

Paddy turned and pointed.

Maude put her hand up. 'I'm sorry, he's with me, my guest.'

'Of course.' The young man turned away, disappointed.

The Manager had reached the microphone, 'Can we have quiet, please.' The urgent sound of alarms could be heard above the hush.

'We have an emergency situation in the city, can you please take your seats. Bombs have gone off around town.' There were groans from the audience. 'Please,' he had his hands out appealing for calm and everyone to sit down. 'We don't know how many, but there are casualties and fatalities. The Guards have advised everyone to stay inside for now. Please take your seats. I will bring you more information as soon as we have it.'

Maude put her arm through Paddy's. 'Come on.'

Concern etched in her face as she led Paddy to her table, he slumped into a chair. 'Are you hurt, Paddy?'

'Were you in the blast?' A male voice asked.

'That's Thomas, my brother.' Said Maude.

Thomas reached for Paddy's hand and shook it. 'What the hell is going on out there?' He shouted at a passing waiter, 'Give this man a whiskey, he's in shock.'

The table was disordered. They had eaten, all cutlery and plates had been removed, and the empty bottles of wine and glasses remained. The event was past its peak. People circulated and chatted.

'What's all this? Paddy looked around.

'The South East party awards,' Maude explained. Then said, 'Wine?'

'If there's nothing else,' Paddy said.

Thomas poured. 'Well, how about you get this down you, and I'll see where that whiskey is.'

Maude pushed her glass forward for a refill. The hotel manager had left and the room was buzzing, voices mingled to form a haze, an aural fog. It surrounded everyone. Paddy took a decent swallow of his wine. Someone had set up a radio on a table near the stage and a growing group of people were listening to reports.

'You're just back from England?' asked Thomas.

Paddy was silent.

The waiter appeared with the whiskey, he had a bottle and a

glass. 'Leave the bottle,' said Thomas. He gave the glass to Paddy.

'Three bombs,' the waiter said, 'So far, no number yet, but lots of dead.'

Paddy threw back the whiskey and Thomas poured him another, emptied a wine glass, and poured one for himself 'Maude?'

'No, it must be loyalists again,' said Maude.'

'Where were you? Asked Thomas.

The whiskey raced through Paddy, his arms and legs were growing heavy, 'I came out of the station, was going to the pub...the boy,' he coughed and spluttered. 'The blast knocked me over, I owe him a shilling...' His head was spinning now... he didn't know if it was the whiskey or.... 'Blood...in the gutter.'

'Ok that's enough,' said Maude.

'...A leg... a woman's leg...' Paddy coughed but the cough turned into a retch and the whiskey was back out and on the table.

'Thomas help me get him out.'

'Where are you taking him?'

'To my room, he needs a doctor.'

'Dad won't like it.'

'Here, please,' Maude grabbed a waiter and with his help Paddy was half-lifted and carried through the tables, eyes following them. Paddy felt their gaze too. He glanced back at the main table in time to see Thomas lean in close to his father. Father and son turned.

Although the room was spinning, Paddy could clearly see the faces of father and son. I see you, too. They led Paddy out of the room.

Chapter Twenty-One

Anne

Wicklow, 2010

'Are you sure they live here?' Anne asked. They were slightly above the town, looking down toward the sea.

'Yeah,' said Ronan.

'How do you know?'

'It's a small town.' Ronan rang the doorbell. 'Trust me.' It was after 6 pm and the daylight was just beginning to weaken.

'They might be at work?' said Anne

Ronan rang again. Anne heard the ding-dong chime.

A dark-haired woman opened the door; she was wearing a sweat top and trousers. 'Hello?'

'Hi, is Karla there?' asked Anne.

The woman's eyes narrowed, 'I think yes, who is it?' The accent came from somewhere back in her throat, Anne thought they didn't get many visitors.

'If you could tell her my name is Anne, and I would like a few words with her. There is no problem. Everything is fine.' She tried to sound casual.

The woman didn't look convinced. 'Please, wait.' She closed the door.

A minute later, the door opened again, and Karla stood there. She was wearing a loose white tee shirt over black leggings.

Karla nodded to Anne but her surprise was clear.

'Is everything ok?' Karla asked.

'Yes, fine, sorry to disturb you at home. It's about Maude. It'll only take a minute.'

Karla checked the road behind them.

'It's just us,' said Anne. 'No one else.'

'I don't know. What do you want? Mr Simon is not happy. I get fired.'

'Oh, that's terrible you have been fired?' Anne asked.

Karla corrected herself, 'No, he says I will get fired if Miss Maude talk more to people.'

'See that's not right for a start,' said Ronan.

Anne smiled as pleasantly as she could. 'It won't take long, I promise.'

'Wait.' Karla closed the door.

'She's nervous,' said Ronan.

The door opened, and Karla stepped back. 'Come in.'

The living room was small but had a sofa and two armchairs. There was a rail in front of the gas fire, and various bits of clothing were drying. The air was warm and damp.

Karla rushed around trying to remove items of underwear. 'Sorry, you know.'

'No problem.' Anne smiled. 'I've shared before. How many of you live here?'

'My friend Jana, and two Slovak girls, four.'

'Wow,' said Niamh. 'It's a two-bedroom. Yeah?'

'We share,' said Karla.

'Of course.' Anne nodded.

'Does Jana work at Riverside, too?' asked Ronan.

'Yes, we all work there. That's how we share.'

'Oh right, I see,' said Anne.

'Why do you want to talk?'

'It's Ms Maude, Miss Carol. I don't know why Mr Simon gets so angry if she talks to us? Do you know?'

'No Mr Simon is angry man, he always complains about paying us, about the electricity, he says we use too much gas electricity, we are four girls, we shower unlike men.'

Anne laughed, 'Men just don't understand.'

'Men not so clean,' said Karla, looking at Ronan.

'Oh, don't mind me, ladies, just say what you think.' Ronan joked. 'But you mean he owns this house, and if he complains about your pay, are you saying he owns the nursing home, he's your boss?'

'Yes, Mr Simon is boss, there is Mrs Taylor in Riverside, she organises, but Mr Simon is big boss.'

'Why are you surprised?' Anne asked Ronan.

'He's bankrupt; he had two companies go bust owing people lots of money. Back in the financial crash, everyone knew about it. It's why people were surprised and angry that he's in line for a new housing development on the edge of town.'

'I don't know about that.' said Karla. 'He's boss, we sign lots of papers.'

'What kind of papers?' Anne asked.

'Contracts and agreements,'

'That all sounds reasonable, better to have contracts. You got copies of all the documents?'

'Not all.'

'Really?

'For Mr Simon, yes, me and Jana both signed, an NDA.'

'NDA.' Ronan looked at Anne,

'Ronan's face opened up. 'Aah, a Non-Disclosure Agreement, why would you need one of those?'

'Yes, we signed with Miss Maude and Mr Simon.'

'He made you both sign a non-disclosure agreement with Maude, and he signed it too?' asked Anne.

'Yes, he said we talk, we lose jobs, lose room and go home.' She shrugged. 'So, we sign.'

'Okay, yeah. I understand, but I think you have been tricked,

Karla,' said Anne. 'Whatever you signed for Mr Simon, it would not have been a non-disclosure agreement.'

'How you know that?' she asked.

'Well, if it was, he wouldn't have to sign it, or Miss Maude, just you and Jana.'

Karla's eyes narrowed. 'What we sign then?'

'I'm not sure. I have an idea, but we will need to get it to find out.'

'How do we do this? I need Jana for this.' Karla went out and reappeared a minute later with Jana.

'I hate Mr Simon, asshole,' Jana said.

Anne smiled. 'I agree.'

'I think he's tricked you and the old lady Maude. Will you help us?' Anne asked.

'If you are wrong, we lose our job,' said Karla.

'I really don't think I am,' said Anne. 'Will you help?'

The two Polish women looked at each other.

'Will it get Mr Simon in trouble?' asked Karla.

'Oh yes,' said Anne.

Jana's face lit up. 'I'm in.'

'Me too,' said Karla.

On the walk back into town, Ronan turned to Anne. 'What exactly are you doing here? I mean how can this stuff get Simon?'

'I'm not sure yet, it depends what documents they signed, but they were not NDA's so what is he hiding? Why get two of his Polish workers to sign legal documents? It doesn't make sense.'

'Unless you are doing something dodgy.'

'Exactly.'

'So how do we find out what's in them?'

'I think I know a way.'

'He won't like that.'

'Tough shit,' said Anne.

Anne's phone beeped, she read the message, 'I'm up at the

castle if you fancy a walk.'

She texted back, 'Tired going back to the room, C U there.'

'No probs.'

Anne turned to Ronan. 'Thanks for your help.'

'No bother.'

They made their way down Bridge Street. The evening closing in with a stiff breeze coming in off the sea.

'Are you working?' Anne asked.

'Yeah, 7.30 pm,'

'We might pop down when Vinny gets back.'

'Sure.'

* * *

Anne had a plan for working out what Simon was up to, she just needed a little time to bring it to fruition. If Simon and his henchmen wanted to get serious. She would need to get back down to the council office, see if Cara's guest access still worked. See what Simon's new development was all about.

She dozed as she waited for Vinny, and her thoughts turned to her new job. She was tired. The longer the trip went on the greater the distance between her and Vinny. He was moving toward his past and she was reaching out for her future. A new job and a new city. He was part of her future once, intelligent, sensitive; she could and did learn from him. She wasn't sure when things changed. Maybe it was her, she was outgrowing the space she once coveted. The older she got, the clearer saw the patterns, noticed the looks. She was no one's diversity badge. If Anthony did respect her, he would have nominated her, pushed her for promotion. Instead, he enjoyed the protégé and mentor relationship for far too long. Vinny was proud of her professionalism as long as it didn't disturb his career, meanwhile, she should 'appreciate what she had'… yeah right.

It was 11.00 pm when she woke, stretching the stiffness out

of her joints. Jesus. Falling asleep in the chair was not a good move. No Vinny yet, she assumed he would be down in the bar with Ronan refighting the civil war, at least verbally. She undressed quickly; too tired to shower, she slipped on a tee shirt and climbed into bed.

* * *

Anne realised immediately that Vinny wasn't there. She reached across to the bedside cabinet for her phone. It wasn't there. Shit. She dragged herself up and began searching. It was on the table near where she had fallen asleep in the chair. She checked the messages. Nothing from Vinny.

He wouldn't have pulled an all-nighter with Ronan in the bar? If Ronan had to do the breakfast service, he'd be dead. She dressed quickly. It was nearly 9.30 am; Jesus she had been tired.

She walked into the Breakfast room as Ronan served someone a coffee. She waited till he returned to the buffet table.

'Vinny?'

Ronan shrugged, 'Yeah? I haven't seen him, he's not down yet.'

'I mean last night,' Anne said.

Confused, he picked up a cup and poured, 'Have a coffee.'

Anne took it from him, 'I don't want coffee, where's Vinny?'

His face dropped, 'Oh right. I don't know.'

'Shit.'

'Look, sit down, here give me that.' Ronan took the coffee from her and took it to the nearest empty table; Anne followed him and sat down heavily.

'He'll be fine, don't worry.'

'So, you didn't see him in the bar last night?'

'No.'

'Then, where is he?'

'When did you last see him?'

'I got a text,' Anne swiped her phone and showed him the

exchange.

'I'm up at the castle if you fancy a walk.'

'Tired going back to the room, C U there.'

'No probs.'

'That was 6.16 pm.'

'The thing is I fell asleep. Then when I woke a few hours later, I thought he would be with you in the bar.'

'And this morning, no sign of him?'

'Exactly.' Anne took a drink of the coffee. 'Where does someone go from a quarter past six to now? In a town, he doesn't know, and the only people he does know are us two.'

'And the people who are pissed with him.'

'Really, are you trying to frighten me?'

'No, sorry.'

Ronan pointed out the window. 'Jesus Christ, is that Vinny?'

Vinny was limping toward the entrance. He looked like a zombie, half-dead, and one shoe off, his jeans dragging down, covered in dirt, wet.

Ronan shook his head. 'For fucks sake.'

'Get him inside,' said Anne.

Ronan, Anne, and Mr McDonagh, the manager, crowded around the entrance as Vinny limped in.

'Would you look at the mess of him.' Mr McDonagh was unimpressed.

'What happened?' asked Anne.

'I was ambushed,' said Vinny. 'Christ, didn't you notice I was missing?'

'Take him to your room, get him cleaned up,' said McDonagh.

'Do you need a doctor? You've got blood on your head,' said Anne.

'No, I think I'll be fine. A cup of tea and a bit of brekkie wouldn't go amiss.'

'You've got some nerve. I'm not letting you in the dining

room looking like that,' said McDonagh

'I'll bring it up,' said Ronan.

'Room service is it now?' Mr McDonagh snorted. 'Well, if you're going to do it, can you get him away from this door. God knows our reputation is suffering enough with detectives calling on you.'

'Come on.' Anne led Vinny away and up to their room. She helped him shower and change. When Ronan appeared with tea and breakfast on a tray, the table was already in use.

On a sheet of newspaper in the centre of the table was the gun. It was recognisable and partially cleaned.

'Bloody Hell. You must have one hell of a story?'

Vinny picked up a sausage 'I do.'

Chapter Twenty-Two

Maude

Wicklow, 1974

The first evening she had watched over him, he was sedated so should have slept, but he was restless. He tossed and turned for the first few hours as she listened to the awful news. She preferred the radio; the TV pictures were too disturbing. No wonder he was restless, she knew he was in Talbot St, close enough to be blown over by the blast, but not close enough to be torn apart by it. As the death count mounted, the number of women killed shocked her. A woman with a full-term pregnancy, a young girl, a grandmother, the news kept coming, three blasts in Dublin then later the same evening Monaghan, another bomb, another list of dead and injured.

Maude watched Paddy as he finally seemed to rest. She was unable to imagine what he'd seen. The first time she'd met him she thought him interesting, a confident sharp man from across the water. He had the wit and intelligence so lacking in most of the men around her, beyond the cheap aftershave, she caught a whiff of the unexpected. He was good looking, with dirty blond hair, a wispy moustache, and soft brown eyes.

She was at his side when he roused. He rubbed his face and sat up slowly.

'Hey,' she leaned across and wiped his forehead with the cold press.

'That feels good,' he said. He looked around. 'Am I really in your hotel bed?'

She smiled, 'Yeah isn't that what you wanted?'

He winced, 'You're not far wrong.'

'How are you feeling?'

'Like I've been hit by a bus.'

He raised his hands to his face. 'Jesus,'

'I know,' she said softly. 'You don't have to say anything.'

'Can you sit?' He patted the bed beside him.

He closed his eyes and leaned back against the headboard. Maude sat next to him; his hand reached out and found hers. He held her hand and with slow gentle movements, his fingers stroked hers. Eventually, he let his head drop onto her shoulder and she realised he had fallen back to sleep. She eased herself free and laid him down. He dreamed of lost boys.

The night was dark and heavy outside. She turned off the radio, she had heard enough. She crossed the room and opened the curtains, the lights of the city shone as brightly as any night. She had lived half her life in half this city. Alexandra College in Milltown, once the preserve of wealthy protestant girls, it had learned to swim with the tide and was now open to girls like her. The daughters of the new catholic elite. As a boarder, she knew the shopping on O'Connell Street, the markets in the Liberties, the beaches at Howth. She knew another Dublin existed side by side with hers, a city of tenements and alleyways, of damp and tuberculosis, crime and punishment. She didn't half know it. When she turned, Paddy was sleeping, they represented the two halves, and she knew that. She laughed at herself for thinking they might actually fit.

Chapter Twenty-Three

Paddy

Wicklow, 1974

Paddy's head was heavy. It took two attempts to lift his lids fully. The curtains were open, and the light was streaming in. It wasn't the flash of the bomb. It was a half-light, not the clear sunlight of summer, but the grey morning light of Ireland. It almost said, 'This is the best you're getting, so get on with it.'

He knew where he was because he had never been anywhere like it. The soft pile carpet and elegant Georgian furniture reminded him of Maude. He could feel her soft body pressing against him; she fitted this room, this hotel, this city. It was a weird night. Half-remembered conversations and strange sensations. There was something different about this woman, or was it him? The warmth of her body reminded him of Vinny, the way he sometimes climbed into bed during the night and would hold on to him. Maude rolled away from him. The loss of contact brought a realisation: the death and destruction, the noise and the silence of the day before. Time was closing in, he could feel it, he should have died in the street like so many others, why not him? He closed his eyes and willed his thoughts away; he wanted to sink deep into the bed, deep into the pillow.

When he woke again, Maude was in the bathroom running

water. Paddy shook his head. He remembered them holding on to each other for comfort. He didn't know how long they had lain like a jigsaw pieced together, but he remembered the soft kisses from Maude on his forehead and face and only after the longest time his lips. When their lips did meet they explored each other, slowly at first but the pressure and passions of the day meant they sought each other out urgently in the end. It was Paddy's first time making love.

Maude appeared in her gown. In the natural light of the morning her pale face and long reddish-brown hair gave her a delicate fragile appearance. Paddy already knew the steel beneath that surface.

'How do you feel?' she asked.

'Good and bad.'

She remembered her surprise at the sharp mind behind the clipped sentences when they first met. He pulled himself up to a sitting position; she sat down next to him.

'A couple of misfits,' he said.

'I had the same thought,' she smiled.

He reached for her hand; she would notice later that he always sought physical contact, as if he needed to prove the connection was real.

'Why?' he asked.

'You have a wife and child in Liverpool.'

'It's not her fault, our lives crossed, we did what couples do, I am who I am, or was. I courted her, she got pregnant, and we got married.'

'Do you love her?'

'Can you tell me what love is?'

Maude thought for a minute, 'No, I can't. The truth is we define it for ourselves, its content is infinitely variable.'

'And now? This... fear and confusion... excitement.'

'You define it for yourself,' she said.

She moved toward him and he opened his arms, there was

no hesitancy, or embarrassment, their bodies were open to each other.

'I can't though; I can't do this, not with you. Not now.'

'Why?'

She was resting her head shoulder, he gently moved her away so they could see each other's face.

'I killed a man in Liverpool.' He waited for a reaction. 'You're not shocked?'

Maude held his gaze for a second. 'Look around you, at yesterday.' She moved away from him. 'This is Ireland. Most of the old men in power were in the War of Independence or the civil war.' she paused before asking. 'Why did you kill him?'

'An accident.'

'That's a stupid reason to kill.'

'Is there a good reason?'

'There is.'

A loud knock on the door interrupted Maude. She crossed the room quickly and asked who it was before open the door.

'It's me, Maude, come on open the door.'

'I'm not dressed, dad.'

'Then get bloody dressed.'

'You'll have to wait.'

The knocking started again. 'Open the door Maude; I'm not stupid, I know he's in there with you.'

Maude opened the door a little but kept her foot firmly lodged behind it.

'I know who he is, and why he's here. Get rid of him. I've told reception I am not paying for another night so you have to leave.'

'Thanks, dad.' Maude turned back to the room and shut the door. 'I guess you heard all that?'

'He's got a point.'

'I decide who I see and when,' she collected her clothes. 'But we have to make a move, get out of here.' She didn't hide as she dressed. She put on a light grey trouser suit and pink sweater;

she had style, there was no doubt about that.

Paddy rolled over and swung his legs out of bed. He had to steady himself for a minute, to let the dizziness pass, his throat was dry and he felt nausea in the pit of his stomach.

Maude moved off into the bathroom. 'Really, we have five minutes before the cleaner comes in.'

'No problem…' he stopped himself saying 'babe.'

Paddy tried not to think too far ahead, Conor and Barlow.

'What about your da?' Paddy called out to Maude.

'What about him?'

'He was pissed off.'

'He was,' she came out of the bathroom, 'and you should be careful. I'll talk to him, but he's never listened before, so I can't see him starting now. Come on, we have to move.'

Maude picked up a potted plant and placed it next to her case.

Paddy saw his clothes clean and folded on a chair. He dressed quickly, washing and wiping away all remains of the previous day.

'What's that for?' he asked, pointing at the plant.

'It's my Arum Lily.'

The flower was weird, a single green upright stem with a white flower that enveloped a slightly yellowing stamen. 'What is it? You carry it around with you?'

'It blooms for such a short time I can't bear to be parted.' She picked it up. 'Can you get my case?'

Maude held the door open for him. 'You're going back to Wicklow?'

'Yeah, I'll go for the train.'

'Don't be silly. I'll give you a lift.'

'You've got a car?'

'Yeah, a run-around. I can take you back. I have to stop at Greystones, but that won't take five minutes.'

In the lift, Maude said, 'I need to drop my key.'

Paddy followed her to reception and waited a couple of feet to the side.

She handed in her key. 'Thank you.'

'You're welcome, Miss Carrol.'

'My father and brother?'

'Mr Carrol senior checked out a few moments ago'. He looked behind him for the key box. 'It looks like Mr Carrol junior… is here now.' He indicated across the foyer.

Maude turned to see her brother approaching, followed by two young men.

Paddy nodded to Thomas but was ignored. Thomas gave his key to the receptionist. Then turned to Maude. 'Dad was spitting last night because of you.'

Maude nodded to the receptionist. 'Okay, thank you,' and turned.

Paddy reached down for her case.

'You're making a show of yourself, acting like a tart. You give the whole family a bad name.'

He lifted the case and swung it forward. On its return swing, he let it hit Tom in the balls. Tom doubled over with pain, the two men with Tom moved forward. Paddy snarled at them. 'Come on.' He knew they wouldn't.

Paddy let Maude pull him out while still growling at the men.

As Maude pulled Paddy through the double doors, Thomas shouted, 'You haven't heard the last of this. We know who you are.'

'Was that necessary?' asked Maude.

'He just called you a tart.'

'He's my brother.'

'Even more reason to give him a slap for the disrespect.'

'Come on, let's get out of here.'

'Where's your car?'

'Just up here.'

Paddy stopped. A boy ran through the gates into the green in the centre of the square. His stomach turned, he felt a wave of fear and dread.

'What's up, come on.' Maude stopped and turned.

'Paddy, are you ok?'

'Yeah.' he lied. He turned his head and wiped the silent tear from his face. 'Go on, I'm coming.'

Maude drove well. Paddy was quiet until he wasn't, he was impressed by how confidently she manoeuvred the Triumph Herald through the busy streets. It was a beautiful car, small and elegant, with a walnut dashboard.

'You're some woman, do you know that?'

'Why?'

'There you are in your trousers, you drive, and you won't take shit from anyone. How the hell do you survive here?'

'Here?'

'Yeah, I can imagine you in London, you know, with that Kings road set, but here?'

'You've been away too long. You're forgetting your own people.'

'How do yeh mean?'

'Everyone follows what the church says, but they always have a twinkle in the eye for someone who breaks the rules. Haven't we a great history of it, my namesake Maud Gonne, and The Countess, society imposes the rules, but the people love a rebel, they just don't want one in the family.'

'What Countess?'

'You don't know your history, do you?'

'It's not my history. I know who and what I am.'

'Countess Markievicz, a rebel in the rising of 1916.'

'I'm never after celebrating losers.'

Maude gave him a sharp look. 'Jesus, don't let people hear you say that. It's a terrible thing to say.'

It wasn't her words but the sharpness of her look that cut him. For the first time his old lines, his confidence, his ability to sting, felt flat and empty.

'And can you keep your eyes on the road?' Paddy said, he pointed forward. 'Or you'll be adding a couple more martyrs to your list.'

'If I didn't know better, I'd say you cared for nothing.'

'And I'd say you care for too much, now keep your bloody eyes on the road.'

'Don't start telling me how to drive.'

Paddy threw his hands up in surrender. 'No, you're doing a grand job. Just get me to Wicklow in one piece.'

She looked again, and again he felt a distance between his words and the man he was now.

'We're gonna stop off in Greystones for a couple of minutes.'

'What's there?'

'We've a cottage, an old place, it was an uncle's or something, and Dad has had it restored. I want to set the fire and keep it warm, get the damp out of it. I have some work to do, and it's a good place to get away from everyone.'

'What work would you be doing? I thought you were fancy-free.'

'An essay, there's a new course in women's studies at Trinity in the autumn, and I've got my name down for it, but I have to show what I can do.'

'Jesus, a college girl as well.'

'Less of the girl. If I'm lucky. They'll accept the essay and me.'

They drove out of Dublin through Donnybrook. 'What's your plan, Paddy?' Maude asked.

'Get back to the digs, clean up, then I'll have to see Conor.'

'No, I meant longer-term. What do you want?'

He was genuine and knew he sounded stupid. 'I don't know. I don't have a plan.' He wasn't ready to tell her what Barlow expected and was already questioning himself.

'Will you stay?'

'I don't know,'

She turned her head to face him. He met her eyes. This time there was no sharpness, they pulled him in.

'Fuck, don't do that to me.'

'Do what?' she protested.

'You know what. Look at me like that. Jesus, it's hard enough.'

There was silence for a minute then Maude asked, 'Couldn't you get Vinny over here? If you stayed?'

His stomach flipped at the question. 'I don't know, I hadn't thought of that. His mother wouldn't come. I asked before I left, she could have come with me, but you'd think I'd asked her to go to Timbuktu the way she looked at me.'

'But if you were settled, maybe for summers, visits.' He looked at her, and without asking he knew what she was suggesting whether they could last.

'That would be good, yeah, and then I wouldn't have to go back.' And Barlow could fuck himself.

For the first time, Paddy could see a way out of the mess he had found himself in. If he didn't go back but brought Vinny over.

'That's what I was thinking,' said Maude.

'Jeez, you're a sharp one you are. I'll have to watch I don't cut me fingers on you,' Paddy smiled.

Maude laughed. 'Another ten minutes, we'll be there.'

'And what about you?' he asked.

'My plans? I'll do this course if I can get on it. Who knows, maybe, later on, teach, write, I'm not sure. Dad'll want me married off. He doesn't like the idea of women at University. What do you think?'

'If you're smart enough then do it. No skin off my nose.'

'That's what I like to see, male resistance to patriarchy.'

'You're taking the piss.'

'Yeah, I am,' she laughed.

They were passing Bray Golf Club when Maude said, 'One of dad's favourite places.'

'Yeah, I can imagine,' said Paddy.

'Bray Head is just behind us. We should walk along the cliffs.'

'I've had enough of the sea for a while.'

Maude slowed the Triumph as she managed the sharp bends

before the long straight between Bray and Greystones. Before they reached the village, she took a sharp left.

'We're here.'

The car crunched over a gravel drive, bushes brushed the sides of the vehicle. They were turning left on a gentle curve.

'Wait,' said Paddy.

Maude stopped. 'What?'

'There are people there. Are you expecting anyone?'

'No.'

'Okay, back up. Who is it?' Paddy asked.

'I don't know yet.'

'Reverse.' Paddy sounded sharper than he meant.

Maude reversed back down the track. 'Why are we doing this? It's probably my brother.'

'Let's just be careful.'

'Is someone after you?'

'No. I'm looking after you.'

Maude straightened the car back on the main road and drove a hundred yards. She pulled the car over onto a verge. 'Come on, there's a lane, runs past the back of the house.'

Maude led the way along the verge of the road, and then she turned between two hedgerows. 'Come on.'

Paddy followed till they reached the lane. 'Okay, let me go first.'

He moved forward, and within a minute, the house came into view. It was a low whitewashed cottage, recently renovated, and the garden area turned into a lawn and flowerbeds. A set of sliding glass doors led from the living area onto a patio. To the side of the house, Paddy saw two parked cars.

A silver Xj6 Jaguar and a black Rover.

Paddy was taller than Maude and could see over the hedge. 'That's Conor's car. What the fuck is he doing here?'

'Conor Walsh? Let me see.'

Paddy pulled the hedge apart and Maude looked through. 'The Jag is my dad's.'

'Jesus.'

'Okay, you wait here,' said Paddy.

'Why? Paddy, what are you doing?'

'Just wait okay, or go back to the car. I'm going to have a closer look.'

'What for? Let's just go.'

'I'm not going anywhere. Go back to the car. I'll be there in a minute. Go on,' he urged.

Maude turned. 'If they see you, God knows what they'll do.'

'Don't worry, I'll be fine.'

Maude turned. 'I'll wait five minutes. If you're not back, I'm going without you.'

'Okay, I promise, five minutes.'

Paddy walked further along the hedge till he saw a break. He squeezed himself through, ducked, and ran along the hedge till he was close to the sidewall of the property. He wanted to see Conor and Carrol, not just the cars. He had to be sure.

Paddy heard faint voices from inside the property but couldn't tell who it was or what they were saying. He moved along the wall till he was next to the glass doors. He peeked around the edge; the room was empty. He was about to move when the voices inside grew stronger. He looked again, and Carrol and Conor were entering the room. They were carrying drinks, and they sat opposite each other.

Paddy strained to hear.

'This is bollocks, I'm not interested in this petty shite. Have you seen what's going on in Dublin, have yeh?' Paddy recognised Conor's voice, he held himself out of sight.

'It might be petty to you but she's my daughter.'

'Ok ok, I'll deal with it.'

'What do you know about Dublin?' Conor asked.

'It was the Brits.'

'Of course, it was the Brits.'

'I don't just mean the loyalists, UDR, UVF, whatever badge

they're wearing. I mean, Intelligence helped in the planning and execution. Our guys tell me 100% of the explosive detonated, that's just impossible to achieve with the homemade.'

'Fuckin' bastards.'

'Come on- surprised?'

'No, not surprised, just fucking angry they had the balls. If your lot weren't so fuckin weak.

Carrol ignored the insult. 'I've got more news for you.'

'They've got someone in your crew, reporting directly to British intelligence.'

Paddy's heart almost stopped, he felt the blood draining from his head. He couldn't resist looking to see Conor's reaction. Conor stood and turned toward the window. Paddy ducked out of sight. 'That's one hell of an accusation.'

Fuck, fuck, fuck, he knows about me.

'Don't blame me. I have it from a good source, our intelligence boys. We're not talking recent, long term.'

Paddy was shocked, long-term, and not recent. He doesn't mean me, he means someone else.

'Why are they telling you now?' Conor asked.

'They are pissed at Dublin, everyone is, it makes them look incompetent.'

'They are. You shouldn't go round throwing accusations like that, you know the consequence.'

'You'd rather I kept my mouth shut? You've got a rat, sort it out.'

'Don't you worry, if I've got one, I'll smoke the fucker out.'

Paddy had heard enough. He moved back along the wall, he stopped a minute to process what he'd heard; there was someone else in the crew, another "traitor." For the first time, Paddy applied the word to himself. Traitor. He made his way out through the hedge to the road. He made his way back to the car with Maude.

Maude signalled and pulled out into the road. Paddy got into the car.

'So? Did you find anything out?' She was staring straight ahead.

'Are you pissed off?' Paddy asked.

'Of course, I am. You put yourself in danger.'

'What danger?'

'Come on, you're not stupid, you know what Conor is capable of, and my dad is just as bad. What do you think they'd do if they caught you spying on them? You could be working for the Brits or whatever.'

'Is that what you think?'

'No, of course not. I just want you to be careful.'

'I was.'

'Okay. Anyway, did you find out anything?'

'No, they were talking, having a drink, relaxed, like friends.'

'Why wouldn't they be?'

'Everyone says they are enemies, you know, hate each other.'

'Two big men in Wicklow. They've swum around each other for decades.'

'Have you ever seen them together?' Paddy asked.

'No,' Maude turned to face Paddy. 'This could mean trouble.'

Paddy stared out the window. 'I know, I know.'

Chapter Twenty-Four

DI Barlow

Liverpool, 1974

'You set him up. You did that.' Terry thrust The Chronicle article in front of Barlow.

'No. Correction, son. You did that.' Barlow threw the paper back at him.

'In front of his son as well.'

'He shouldn't have taken him then, should he?'

'Shit's hitting the fan inside the factory, splitting people right down the middle. Some of the stewards were going mad. They said it makes the union look bad.'

'And they wouldn't be far wrong, but don't go blaming me for that.' Barlow snapped back. 'What happened at the meeting?'

'There was a vote between "*No Redundancies*" and "*No Compulsory Redundancies*."'

'And?'

'Alan won, no redundancies. That's the policy. It was pretty close mind, there were speakers on both sides, but when it came to the vote, Alan swung it. It's touch-and-go for the mass meeting.'

'When is it?'

'Friday 6 am. We'll get the Assembly Paint and Trim day and night shifts, the body plant will vote separately, but the assembly usually carries the day.'

'So, it's all on for Friday then,' said DS Jones.

'Is this you as well?' Terry pulled a crumpled leaflet out of his pocket. The title was 'Whose Union?' above a picture of Alan H shaking hands with Rory Gallagher.

Terry started to read.

'*The picture above shows Alan H Transport and General Workers Union convenor of the Assembly Paint and Trim plant at Halewood. Arrested at an anti-South African demonstration recently. The picture shows him meeting Rory Gallagher well known Irish republican, and leader of the Troops Out of Ireland Movement. Gallagher from Belfast had been quoted as saying 'The Army is serving the interest of British Imperialism in Ireland and should get out before it is forced out.*

Is this what we pay our union subs for?

We demand to know what the hell is going on?

Who does our union represent?

We are moderate trade union members just trying to put food on the table for our families; we don't want our union to be dragged into politics by radicals and revolutionaries.

It is time to take our union back?'

'We've seen it,' said Jones smirking.

'Bollocks seen it, you made it.'

Barlow sneered. 'Stop whinging; we're doing you a favour, everything it says is true. These traitors need to be put in their place.'

Terry narrowed his eyes. 'And that's your job is it?'

'Yeah, if none of you have the balls to do it. Then yeah, we will.'

Terry was shaking his head. 'This is going too far; he's got a wife and kids you know.'

'So? You think that makes him special?'

'You know how crazy the Orange lot are, they could easily

have a go at him for this.'

'Not our problem. You play in the muck, expect to get dirty.'

'Dirty? That's you in one, a dirty fucking bastard.'

'Hey bollocks, remember why you're doing this? That kid brother of yours won't do so well in Walton.'

Terry screwed up the leaflet and threw it at Barlow before leaving. 'Fuck you.'

Barlow turned to DS Jones. 'He'll be alright, just needs to calm down.'

'Friday morning then, are you going?' DS Jones asked

'We all are. Wouldn't miss it for the world,' Barlow grinned.

* * *

Mass meetings were a feature of union life carried over from the docks into the car industry. When Ford opened in 1963, coinciding with changes on the docks, cargo handling had become more mechanical, the UK was in the middle of a shift as transatlantic trade from Liverpool decreased and European trade from the South and East increased. Ford chose Liverpool because of this newly available labour, but they hated the traditions of solidarity, union strength, and mass meetings the dockers brought with them. In mass meetings, workers could feel a sense of solidarity and power. Workers thought as a collective, not the individual against the company or system. There was strength in numbers and you could feel this in a mass meeting. If you had a good speaker then this doubled the effectiveness of the message.

Thirteen thousand people worked at Ford's in Halewood over the forty-four-acre site and three shifts, so getting all of them together was impossible. The change between night and day shifts offered the best chance of getting the most.

The night shift wanted to get home, but this was worth waiting for. A chance to see mates from the opposite shift and have a smoke and a laugh with the guys from the line. The mood was buoyant, the night shift had finished and the day shift was starting late, everyone was out of work. They were also in the fresh air, it might just be the car park, but it was better than the stale air and artificial light inside the factory.

A speaker system was set up, the convenor and most of the shop stewards were on the back of a lorry to give them the height to address the crowd. The full-time officer from Transport House in the City was present.

Barlow and DI Jones parked on the perimeter road outside the chain-link fence but they could see and hear everything. DC Hyde was in a surveillance van with a photographer.

The crowd streamed out of the factory, they came from four or five different exits, people were also arriving from the other car parks. There was a line of left-wing paper sellers and people giving out flyers at the gates. The mood was upbeat but there was also tension in the air. There was no predicting what would happen with so many workers together, the mood could swing quickly. The tension burst into action at one of the gates, someone giving out leaflets was being abused, a small crowd was gathering blocking the entrance. Someone grabbed a handful of leaflets and threw them on the ground. Others stepped in to separate those arguing.

'Probably our leaflet.' DS Jones lit a cigarette.

'It's too late for that, it's been doing the rounds inside for days.'

'Brothers and sisters, we have one main decision to take today, but make no mistake whatever we decide will affect everything that happens over the next few years. I'm not going to say one way or the other. What I will say is that we need everyone to get behind whatever decision is made. Through long years of experience, we all know a divided union is a defeated union. United we stand - divided we fall. We have to remember that lesson as we go forward.

'Ok, first up from the paint shop is Arthur Davis.' There was scattered applause and a few cheers.

Arthur was an experienced steward who had no fear of public speaking. He spoke directly into the mic. His voice was clear and measured. 'Let's get one thing straight from the start. As a union, we will fight against any man being forced to lose his job.' He paused and the crowd reacted with clapping and shouts of support for this statement. 'That's what we mean when we say No Compulsory Redundancies. We will not have management picking and choosing who to make redundant. There will be no favouritism in Ford Halewood.' He allowed the crowd to react. He was a good public speaker. 'The only people to lose their jobs will be volunteers. All of us know neighbours, mates or family members who after a lifetime of working will jump at the chance of early retirement with a few quid in their pocket,' he paused. 'And who can blame them?' There were some boos and cheers, there was a clear division in the crowd. 'I can hear you booing, well let me tell you this: when a few thousand pounds is dangled; we get more applications than we can handle. I'm not going to speak all day, because we all know as long as people are willing to take redundancy, we can't fight them. What we can and will do, is guarantee if you want your job, we won't let anyone take it from you.' There was loud applause and raucous cheering that drowned out a few scattered boos.

'These fellas are good, aren't they?'

'Bastards have a lifetime to practise, from father to son some of these commies.'

'Next up we have our convenor, Alan H from assembly.'

'This is our guy,' said DS Jones.

There were boos immediately and a single voice shouted, 'Fuck off to Ireland,' a few voices joined in heckling; a scuffle broke out from the area of the shouting.

Barlow smiled.

Across the Water

The chairman spoke again, 'Whooa, whoa; this is a union meeting, we'll have less of that. Can someone pull those idiots apart?' There was applause before Alan came to the microphone.

'I've known Arthur a long time and he's a good steward and a good comrade, but he is near the end of his working life. What about those young lads on the dole, in Garston, Halewood, Speke? Some of them might be your sons, brothers, neighbours and friends. It's ok for someone who's 55 or 60 thinking I could do with a few quid, a nice little nest egg for retirement. Alan controlled his cadence and intonation. 'The only problem is, it's not his job to sell.'

'That's the bottom line, this isn't about politics, no matter what some people will have you believe. This is about selling jobs that will no longer exist, jobs young people in our communities desperately need, wage packets that feed families.

'I could make the argument that as the biggest industrial workforce in Liverpool, we set the standard, British Leyland, Glaxo, Plessey, everyone watches what we do. Why? Because we have fought and won. We won equal pay for women working in the trim shop.'

There was loud applause and cheers. 'We won pay parity with Dagenham.' Cheers broke out again. 'We can win this one as well. We adopted flexible working, we adopted team working, we have increased production year on year for the last three years. Ford Europe is making more profits than ever, so we say it's time to put some of those profits back into Halewood, Speke, Garston, and Netherley. Because we are not selling jobs that don't belong to us. The shop steward's committee is asking you to vote No Redundancies!'

There was loud applause and cheering but it was scattered in groups across the crowd, and there were persistent boos. Arguments and scuffles broke out in the crowd.

The chairman took centre stage. 'Right then, quiet everybody, we will move to a vote. There will be a show of hands for and against the shop stewards recommendation of No Redundancies; if that is defeated our policy will be no compulsory redundancies. All those in favour of the policy of No Redundancies, raise your hand now.'

About a third of the crowd raised their hands.

'Thank you, and those against?'

Over half the crowd raised their hands, there was some applause but very little cheering and the crowd began to disperse immediately.

'We did it, boss.' DS Jones offered Barlow his hand.

Barlow shook it and replied. 'It doesn't matter, to be honest. Our work here is done. Look at them arguing and fighting among themselves, we've already won.'

Chapter Twenty-Five

Vinny

Wicklow, 2010

What the fuck?

Vinny's head was pounding, waves of pain were rolling in and out, his eyes were open but he couldn't see. Everything built layer upon layer, clammy cold wetness seeping through his bones. He shivered, his body reacted as he realised he was on his back and the cold was coming up from the ground. Something was sticking in him. He was lying on a rock or something. He put his hands down; the earth was hard, soaked. He tried to reach underneath but couldn't. Shit. What the fuck was going on, where was he?

He tried to lift his upper body from the ground and failed twice. The third time, he sat upright. He could taste the blood in his mouth. He lifted a hand to his head and felt the sticky flaking of dried blood. His back was wet, his jeans clung to him, sodden and heavy. He felt around, his fingers sliding over the greasy ground, there, something hard and solid, not a rock, metal.

Flashes of the previous night were coming back. He searched for his phone and felt the reassuring shape in his pocket. Thank fuck.

He pulled it out and felt a flood of relief as it lit up. Back into the real world, the reassuring icons of Google and Microsoft meant he wasn't dreaming. He hadn't been abducted by aliens and he was here in the shitty reality of 2010.

Where the fuck? He waved the phone around; there was no signal, no connection, but the blue light showed the rocky walls of a tunnel.

Vinny pointed the screen at the ground. There, in front of him, was the dark object that speared his back. He reached out and tried to lift it. It had been in place so long it was stuck to the ground. He forced his fingers under it and prised it free. When he could lift it, he felt the weight of the gun in his hand.

He stood up, his wet jeans were pulling down over his arse. He pulled them up and put the gun in his waistband. He leant down, put his hand in a puddle of water and wiped his face. The sharpness stung his skin and sent bolts through to his clammy brain. The air was still and heavy, he held the phone up in both directions, there was no end to the darkness. Opposite him was an opening, an incline, he guessed he must have slid down that. He went over, the light wasn't strong enough to show how high it was. He swiped the screen, his fingers shivering as he searched for the torch. For fucks sake, you can never find this shit when you need it. Got it.

He turned on the torch. Fuck, 21% battery life, how long would that last?

The beam was stronger and more focused. Vinny could light up patches about six feet in front of him. He shone the light up the incline. It was too slippery to climb.

Vinny pulled the gun out and focussed the light on it. It was dark, almost black mud and dirt-encrusted, so the shape was clear, but the detail was lost. He held it in one hand and the torch in the other. He remembered the fall, the shock, and the fright of sliding down into blackness, adrenalin lighting him up. Then blam, nothing. He guessed the sticky mess in his hair was where he banged his head.

He knew how he got there, the bastards. Were they waiting for him? Or was it a coincidence? Either way, I'll fuckin report them.

He waved the gun into the darkness in front of him. Try it now, fuckers.

Vinny played the scene back in his head. He wanted some fresh air and walked up the top of the town to the Black Castle. This had become his place of contemplation while in Wicklow. Something about being on a cliff among the ruins overlooking the sea, knowing almost directly opposite him was Liverpool.

He knew he was losing Anne, he could feel it, it was the absences. Absences that built into a void, around which the shell of their relationship held together, but the heart was missing. The touches as they passed, the random hugs, the smiles, the games, the laughter, ideas, and pain not shared. He knew she was right, all this time searching for his father while losing his son. Is that what it was about? He needed to find his father before he could find his son? Would Charlie become another lost boy?

He saw the red car first. The colour signalling danger as it always has. Then he saw them, the Price brothers. They were smoking outside a shop front. He thought of crossing the street, but his pride and dignity wouldn't allow him.

'Hey up, if it's not the Plastic Paddy.'

Vinny kept walking toward them 'Hi.' He acknowledged them but no more.

'Been out for a walk, have you?'

He was within feet of them now. 'I'm just on my way back to the hotel, people are waiting for me.' He hoped the last bit of information would make them think twice about doing anything.

It was early evening, the street was pretty empty, the shops were shut, there was some traffic but not a lot. They moved from the doorway to block the pavement in front of him.

'You should fuck off home, you know that?'

'I tell you what, get out of the way and I will. How's that?' Vinny had his hand up, palms forward.

He quickly looked inside the shop. The light was on, but it was empty. It looked like it was being renovated.

Across the Water

'I'll just be on my way now.'

They blocked the pavement.

'Okay, enough.' Vinny moved forward and tried to push between them.

He was pushed back, and a fist followed. It caught him in the side of the head, there was a flash, and his ear burned. Fuck. His stomach churned, he felt the adrenaline rush through his veins, he wanted to run.

Vinny stepped back, ready to run into the road to pass them, when he saw the distinctive green of a Garda patrol car. His heart leapt at the sight. 'Hey.' He waved his hand above his head.

The brothers turned and also saw the car. One of them stepped forward, grabbed Vinny, and pushed him into the shop. He closed the door behind him and then stood in front of it. They both turned to watch the Garda drive past.

Oh fuck. What do I do now? Vinny scanned the shop looking for a way out. There was a door at the back of the store. He ran to it, hoping it would open to a yard an alley, an escape.

He opened it and found himself half falling, jumping down a staircase.

Fuck, fuck.

He heard the door above open and close. He scanned the room, nothing.

'Where are yeh, yeh slippy twat, fuckin tell the Gardai on us, would yeh?'

Vinny was in a basement. Fuck. No way out.

His ear was still burning.

He tried to pull a wooden panel off the wall to defend himself. It partly came away but didn't break.

'You can't hide down there, bollocks.'

He kicked and his foot went straight through the middle of the panel. He pulled his foot back, and it brought the whole panel away.

They were coming down the stairs.

Where he expected to see a wall, there was a hole. He crouched, leaned in to see if he could hide... and boom. That was the last thing he remembered.

The next thing he knew, was waking cold and wet with a stinking headache.

Vinny had read about escapees from the Gaol and their tunnels under the town, but took them with a pinch of salt.

If the story was true, and he was in a tunnel, then one end was supposed to lead to the prison and the other toward the sea. If he went in the right direction, he would come out somewhere near the Black Castle. But which way?

He checked the time, it was morning 9.15 am, he had been there all night. No wonder he was frozen. His limbs were stiff with the cold. What happened to the Price brothers? They just fucked off and left him there, bastards.

He pointed his light at the opening above him, he couldn't see more than a couple of feet. It would be impossible to get back up that way. Anne must have the police out looking for him by now.

Which way? He didn't know the town well enough, he had no idea where he was going. He would have to take his chances. Anyway, if he reached one end and it was blocked, he would turn and come back. What if both ends were blocked? He'd be stuck down here for days if those shits up there didn't tell anyone, and why would they? Bastards.

He was going to have to make them pay for this.

He didn't want to head for the Gaol. There were stories of executions and deaths in that place, ghosts, and spirits, all kinds of nonsense. Nonsense or not, he didn't want to go that way. Fuck it.

He pointed the phone's torch and followed its beam. The floor was relatively smooth, so he just had to keep going. Maybe he would get a signal. He pushed on, the gun weighing down his arm, his jeans sliding down. One of his shoes had disappeared somewhere. He plodded on through the darkness hoping his battery would last.

Could he smell the sea? Sure, it was. He kept moving, no choice but to stumble on.

Everything hurt. He felt like an old man shuffling along, no doubt he looked like one. Eventually, he felt the breeze on his face and just as his phone gave out, the light in front of him grew. He emerged into the drizzly grey morning, to the left of the castle. The tunnel entrance was at an angle, making it difficult to see from the clifftop. Beer cans and the remains of a fire meant that local youth had found and used them.

He scrambled up and limped through town, ignoring the stares. He didn't know why he kept the gun. Probably because it was the first he'd ever actually seen. He would clean it up, find out where it came from. It could be an important part of Wicklow's darker past.

Vinny limped on towards the hotel.

Chapter Twenty-Six

Paddy

Wicklow, 1974

They loaded the guns into the boot. There was no doubt this time. Paddy knew the long metal box painted in camouflage green and brown held rifles. He had seen a similar box back in Liverpool. He went with Michael, his old mate, to Runcorn, met some guys in a pub car park and took possession of the same kind of box.

They were on the dockside at Arklow. In the grey morning light, the wind was swirling, Paddy could taste the sea spray. Declan had brought the car right up beside The Esmeralda. Ger was his same old self, smelt of rum and the sea. There were two boxes this time. It didn't take much imagination to know where they were going.

Paddy and Declan loaded them in the car.

Declan closed the boot. 'Come on, let's get moving.'

'Where to?'

'Dublin, just south of the city, we'll hand them over. Someone else will take them on,' said Declan. Paddy felt one step removed, he was listening to every word, watching every gesture for clues. Who was the rat?

It was Paddy's first time back in Arklow. They'd passed the pub a bit earlier, and he wondered how Kathleen was doing?

He felt bad about her. Things were different now. He was a different person.

It was a cold morning; the sun hadn't bothered and left the drizzle and wind to take control. Paddy drove on the way back. Declan navigated.

'So, come on, what's the story?' Declan asked.

'What story?'

'You go missing, no word or nothing. You were supposed to be doing a shift in the bar.'

'Have you not ears or eyes? I was caught up in Dublin, in the blast.'

'Well, no one knew.'

'What the fuck has it got to do with anyone else?'

'Seamus was taking the piss, back on the boat to Liverpool was his guess, couldn't take it he said.'

'Yeah, well, just goes to show how much he knows.' Paddy took the car through the largely empty streets. It was too early for most Arklow citizens, the boat came in on the early tide, and they had driven down in the darkness to meet it. Now the light was breaking on the cold, wet morning. The wipers fought against the drizzle, and the heaters struggled to push warm stale air around the vehicle.

Declan checked the mirror regularly. Paddy knew their cargo would mean twenty years if not life, and he didn't fancy any part of that. He drove carefully, observing the speed limit and indicating for every turn.

'What happened?' Declan didn't give up. 'Stephen said you had your eyes on Maude Carrol, is that why you were up in Dub? That wouldn't go down well with the boss. You know they've got history, don't you? Her old man was—'

Paddy interrupted. 'I know, I know all about it, okay.'

'So, it was her? Jesus, you don't hang about, do you? You bastard.'

'Can we leave it?'

'Ha, the hard man, getting all soft?'

Paddy threw him a look.

'Okay. Okay. None of my business.'

'First fucking sensible thing you've said this morning,' said Paddy. 'Where am I going?'

'Up to Dublin, we'll keep to the coast roads, go through Wicklow, nice and easy.'

'Have you seen Conor?'

'No, Stephen passed on the message that you would be picking me up.'

Paddy looked sideways. 'Is everything okay?'

'Yeah…'

'You don't sound so sure.'

'He's been a bit funny. I don't know. It feels like something is going on.'

Paddy knew exactly what was going on.

He followed the winding road. The light broke through, and morning arrived. They were joined by more traffic, and the world got into its stride. By the time they were in Wicklow, even the sun had decided to turn up.

'Straight through,' said Declan. 'We've got to get rid of this stuff.'

The now-familiar streets were busy with morning traffic, people going to work, kids going to school. The sight of a group of kids in uniform brought Vinny to mind. He would be going to school in a couple of years. Saint Christopher's. Paddy knew he couldn't carry on doing this. Time was running out. It usually didn't matter because he didn't think beyond the moment, but that was changing.

Michael had been right in Liverpool. He got out of the life. Paddy knew he would have to work out what he was doing. He was at a crossroads.

He watched as the cars streamed by.

'Go straight on,' Declan said.

Paddy moved forward, a car appeared from the left, and he

had to stop to let him go. He saw the passenger stare at them as he passed by.

'Do you know that guy?' asked Paddy.

'Yeah, he's a cop,' said Declan.

'Shit, what do we do?'

'Keep going. It was random, just passing in the street, nothing to it.'

Paddy looked hard at Declan.

'What?'

'Keep going, come on move or we'll attract attention.'

Paddy drove on. They watched the mirrors.

'Was he working?' asked Paddy.

'I don't know he's plain clothes anyway.'

They drove on through Conykerry and Five Mile Point and into Greystones. South of Dublin, this commuter town and resort was unaware of the deadly cargo driven through its crowded streets.

'Through the town and out toward Bray,' said Declan.

Paddy checked the mirror. 'What car was he in?'

'Who?'

'The copper.'

'It was grey, a Vauxhall Viva. Why?'

'I think he's behind us?'

Declan reached up and angled the rear-view mirror.

'Is it him?' asked Paddy.

'Fuck, yeah, I think it is.'

'Is he on us?'

'He must be, first Wicklow and now, here.'

'He got too close, though.'

'We're coming to the edge of town soon.'

'I know, I know, keep going,' said Declan. Then a few seconds later, he said, 'He's turning off.'

Paddy grabbed control of the mirror. The Vauxhall Viva was indicating left.

'Okay, put your foot down. Let's get out of here,' Declan said.

Paddy increased his speed. Within a minute, they were on the open road again, the single-lane road between Greystones and Bray. Paddy sped, overtaking slower traffic.

'He was definitely on us,' Paddy said.

Declan constantly checked behind them. 'We're clear now.'

'I don't like this,' Paddy said. 'Why would he drop us like that? He must be on the radio to others.'

'Well, he's not behind us.'

'That doesn't mean shit.' Paddy recognised where they were. 'Fuck it,' he said.

He braked hard and swerved off the road, turning into a private drive.

'What the fuck are you doing? Who lives here?'

'Never mind.' The car came to a screeching stop on the gravel.

'Get out,' Paddy ordered. He sprang from the vehicle, opening the boot before Declan was out of the car.

'Come on, bollocks, get a move on.'

'What are you doing?' asked Declan.

'What does it look like? We've got to get this stuff out.'

Paddy led the way. They put the first box to the left of the drive behind bushes and against the brick perimeter wall.

'Come on, the last one,' Paddy instructed.

Paddy broke branches off the bushes and covered the boxes as best he could. They got back in the car. He reversed, turning to face the road. They drove onto the main road and carried on in the direction of Bray.

'Whose house was that?'

'It doesn't matter; it's empty.'

'For fucks sake, we've just delivered two boxes of rifles to some stranger's garden.'

'It's not a stranger.'

'Who is it?'

'Fuck, look.' Paddy pointed ahead, two police cars were

stationed at the side of the road, and uniformed police were slowing drivers down. As they got closer, Paddy saw the Grey Vauxhall parked back from the road in the drive of Bray Golf club.

'Here we go.' Paddy slowed down and approached the officer. He wound down his window.

'Can you pull over, please?'

'What's wrong, officer?' asked Paddy.

'Pull over.' He pointed to the side of the road.

Paddy drove onto the grass verge. Three uniformed officers stood around the car. The two plainclothes officers got out of the Vauxhall and joined them.

One of the plainclothes approached Paddy's window. 'Turn off the engine and get out of the car, please.' His jacket was thrown back to show he wore a pistol in a holster at his side. His left hand was on the holster, although his weapon was not drawn.

His colleague took up position outside the passenger door. He too was ready to draw.

Paddy got out.

'Keep your hands where we can see them. Reach back in, get the keys.'

Paddy reached in, retrieved the car keys.

'Come on, move.'

Declan was spread-eagled against the side of the car. Paddy walked round to the rear.

'Open up.' The copper nodded toward the boot.

'What are you looking for?' asked Paddy.

'Just open up.'

Paddy placed the key in the lock. 'I don't know what you are expecting to find.' He lifted the lid to show an empty boot and stood back.

'Fuck,' the cop rubbed his hands over his face in frustration.

'Shit.' He waved his hand toward his colleague. 'Okay, let

them go.'

'Do you want to tell me what this was all about?' insisted Paddy.

The copper took a step forward and put his face up to Paddy. 'Get in and fuck off. Or we'll pull you in any way, just for the fun of it.'

Paddy smiled and raised his hands in submission. 'No problem, boss.' He got back in. Declan joined him, and Paddy pulled off the verge and back into the flow of traffic.

'Fuck, that was close.' Declan grinned from ear to ear. 'Jesus, you're a lucky bastard.' He slapped the dashboard.

'Luck had nothing to do with it,' said Paddy. He turned to look at Declan. 'The question is, how did they know?'

'He saw us in Wicklow, must have taken a chance. Pull over at the next phone box you see. We're gonna have to call Conor. We can't leave that shit lying around. We'll be ok as long as we get it back to Conor.'

Paddy glanced at him sideways and ignored the suggestion; he drove on to the edge of Bray. Just as they entered the town, Declan saw a phone. 'Okay. Just tell me you know where the stuff is?'

'Yeah, I know.'

'You know the address?'

'Yes, I know.'

'What is it?'

'Just tell him I know where the stuff is. It'll be safe till it's collected.'

Declan was back a minute later. 'He wants us back in Wicklow. We've to go and see him.'

Paddy turned the car around and headed back.

'Where did you leave the stuff? It was round here, wasn't it?' said Declan.

They were on the road back to Greystones

'Don't worry, I know where it is.'

'I know, you know. But I don't know. Where is it? What the fuck was that address? Who lives there?'

'Leave it,' said Paddy.

'What do you mean fucking 'leave it?"

'I'm not telling you.'

'Are you taking the piss? Who the fuck do you think you are?'

'You can whine all you like, I'm not telling you.'

Declan calmed himself down. 'Okay, look, Paddy. You pulled a blinder back there. You'll get all the credit you deserve. I can't go back to Conor and tell him I don't know where the guns are. You get that, right? He'd fucking kill me.'

'Not my problem.'

'Fuck you, not your problem.' Declan pulled out a knife and pressed it against Paddy's neck.

'Don't be stupid, Dec, put that away before you get hurt.'

'I'm not fucking kidding. I'll cut you.'

'You won't cut anyone, you cunt.'

'Don't push me, Paddy. Where are the fucking guns?'

The road ahead was clear. Paddy checked the mirror, there was a car behind, but he was way back. Paddy swung the wheel and braked, the car spun, and Declan went flying back. His head hit the side window. Paddy reacted first and grabbed the hand with the knife. He pulled back the wrist till Declan let go of the blade.

Declan tried to punch Paddy, but his head was down as he picked up the knife. With his left hand, Paddy delivered two quick punches to Declan's face. The car was diagonal across the single-lane road. The car behind had caught up and beeped; traffic was now coming from the other direction. The car stalled, and both Paddy's hands were round Declan's neck. 'I'm going to let you go, now don't fuck about.'

Paddy let go of Declan and started the car again. He lowered his window and threw out Declan's knife before directing the car back into the lane for Greystones. 'Jesus Christ, we're in enough bother without knocking the shit out of each other. Look, I'm not telling you where they are because I don't know how the cops found us.'

Declan wiped the blood from his nose on a hankie. 'You think it was me? You saw them in Wicklow the same as I did. He saw us and must have decided then to stop us.'

'Yeah, probably, but I don't know that, do I?'

'Where have you been? You're the one who went missing. What the fuck were you up to?' demanded Declan.

'But I didn't know this job was on, what route we were taking or anything.'

'Shit, Conor's going to go mad.'

'We've got the guns. They're safe. Calm down. As you said, it was pure luck. He saw us.'

'How did you know to hide them?'

'I didn't. I just don't like taking chances.'

Declan brightened up. 'Let's go and get them.'

'No. I'm not doing that. That would be asking for trouble. They're safe where they are till Conor sorts something out.'

Deflated, Declan said, 'He's going to go mad.'

'No doubt,' said Paddy. 'No doubt.'

Chapter Twenty-Seven

DI Barlow

Liverpool, 1974

Back in the squad room, DI Barlow, DS Jones and DC Hyde were in a celebratory mood.

'Did you get much?' Barlow asked about the surveillance operation.

'We got most of the shop stewards committee, the paper sellers, and some of the troublemakers in the crowd.'

'You're developing this thing into a fine art,' Barlow said approvingly.

'Someone has to. It's the interconnections that interest me, between the unions, the campaigns and the political groups. That's when things tend to happen.' DC Hyde responded.

'So today goes down as a victory? One for our side?' asked DS Jones.

Barlow beamed, 'More than a victory. I think the whole operation was exemplary.'

'At last, some good news?' Commander Marsh appeared in the doorway.

Barlow stood up. 'I think we can say that sir.'

'Good enough to share with the Chief Constable this afternoon? I am hosting him for a late lunch, it would make a nice change to have something positive to show him before we leave.'

'Of course, sir.'

'He will have DI Colman with him, you know Tom from Admiral Street, he ran the protest last week.'

'I do, sir. Why will he be with the Chief?'

'What do I know Detective Inspector? His bag carrier for the day, I expect. Come on then, give me the one-minute version.'

'Over the last month, we have managed to recruit and run an informant inside the Ford shop steward committee, and a rank and file group in Speke. He has supplied vital intelligence in connecting trade union figures with active political targets including anti-apartheid activists and Irish republicans. Just this morning we witnessed our intervention culminate in the defeat of the most left-wing leader of the union in Fords in Halewood setting their project back months, who knows, even years.'

The Commander looked sideways at Barlow. 'Can you verify all this?'

'Absolutely sir.'

The Commander looked from DS Jones to DC Hyde, who indicated their agreement.

'Ok, well we won't drag it out, ten minutes max, my office at 2.30 pm. I look forward to hearing the details.'

'We'll be ready.'

The Commander raised his eyebrows. 'I hope so, maybe you could freshen up before the meeting?'

Barlow ran his hand over the stubble on his chin, 'An early start sir, of course, sir.' He waited until the commander had left. 'I want to show them what real counterintelligence looks like. Three minutes each on the component parts. Lynda, those links you were talking about, make them clear, I want to show the connections, and how we are developing this, building a library of faces.' He turned to DS Jones. 'Use Terry as an example, how to spot, turn and manage an informant.'

'What will you do?'

'I will give the overview, the strategy, how this fits in with our role, our mission. Right, I'm off to get cleaned up. If you two want to do the same, I'll be back here at 2 pm.'

He enjoyed the drive through town, there was something special about being on the inside, with the power to make things happen. It had been a long hard road and the lessons taught by his father in the steep streets of Everton remained. The test of a true patriot an Englishman's loyalty is, was, and always will be his attitude to rebellion in Ireland.

His tyres crunched the gravel as he came to a stop in the driveway.

'Hello,' he said as he entered. He was surprised to see Julie's coat on the hook.

'Hello.' When it came back was hesitant and nervous. He kicked off his shoes and went into the living room.

His wife was sitting on the sofa with a tearful Julie. Graham, her boyfriend, was sitting in an armchair; he was perched on the edge of the seat and stood when Barlow entered. Barlow knew in the pit of his stomach what was going on, he let out a deep breath and sat in the empty armchair.

As soon as he sat down his wife spoke. 'John, we have to tell you something. I want you to stay calm.'

Julie sobbed.

'I know, I know, she's in the club, pregnant, with child.' Barlow rubbed his face.

'I'm sorry dad.' Julie held a hankie to her eyes with one hand, while her mum sat holding and stroking the other.

'It's a bit late for 'sorry' after you've been doing the dirty with goldilocks here.'

'Don't be vulgar,' his wife replied.

'I'm vulgar; I'm not the one who's been having it off.'

'Dad,' appealed Julie.

'Don't dad me,' Barlow snapped his energy coming back with rising anger.

'For Christ's sake, are you sure you're not a Catholic?'

'No, sir,' said Graham, confused.

'Never mind the "Sir" now, pretending you've got respect for me while you're giving my daughter one. If you're not a Catholic why the hell didn't you put a Johnny on?' Barlow pointed at the patio doors. 'I should take you out in that garden and give you a good hiding. You useless, good for nothing prick.'

'Yes, Sir.'

'John, we have to be practical about this.'

'Yes, be practical now she's in the club. What about being practical before? Did you not tell her about the pill? What happened to women's lib?'

'You wouldn't have wanted her on the pill.'

'I'd rather her on the pill than this.'

'I want to marry her, Mr Barlow.' Graham made his statement with all the gravitas he could muster.

'I bet you bloody do, smart, good looker like her from a good family, bet you think your luck's in. What do you even do?'

'Apprentice toolmaker in the machine shop at Ford's.'

'Brilliant, that's all I need.' Barlow began pacing the room. Decisions needed to be taken, but he wasn't in the mood to be logical. 'I told you we should have moved, Ormskirk or Crosby where she could meet a better class of lad. She can get rid of it- you can do it these days, private if you like, no one will know.'

'I will know,' said Julie.

'God will know,' said his wife.

'God knows, of course, if God knew, he could've bloody told me what was going on.'

'You're just angry, you don't mean that. We shouldn't rush into any decisions. We have to speak to your mum and dad, Graham.'

'You're gonna have to give up University. So much for being a lawyer,' said Barlow.

'I can take some gap years.'

'Gap years? You won't be travelling round Australia you'll be changing bloody nappies. And if you think Prince Charming over here is going to help you've got another thing coming. He'll be down the pub every weekend leaving you in some shitty council house. We're not having it. I'm not having it. I haven't worked my arse off to see you brought down to that.' Barlow stopped and rubbed his hands over his face. 'Anyway, I've got a meeting. I've got to get myself ready,' he announced.

'I'll organise for Graham's mum and dad to come over,' said his wife.

'Not yet you won't, there's going to be no wedding, not if I can help it.' Julie was sobbing.

Graham spoke. 'Mr Barlow...'

'You, out.' Barlow pointed to the front door.

'Sir...'

'This is your last warning lad, you either walk out that front door or I throw you out, now make your choice.'

Graham moved toward the front door. 'I'll call you.' He shouted over his shoulder.

'There was no need for that,' said his wife.

'I'm getting ready for my meeting. We'll deal with this later.'

His face lathered, Barlow looked at himself in the bathroom mirror, all the plans, the work, the saving, years of hard work, down the plughole because of some horny bastard from under the bridge.

'Shit!' The razor caught him and a line of scarlet red stood out against the white soap as it ran down his cheek.

* * *

'Very impressive, DI Barlow. There's no doubt the country is in a very dangerous position, we have the military for external threats while the lion's share of internal threats are our responsibility.' There was a common perception that Chief Constable Cambridge relished dealing with those threats. He was known for his no-nonsense approach; no-nonsense meant the physical intimidation of communities under his control. From armoured jeeps, to armour suited officers with extendable metal batons and pepper spray, he was always looking for ways of increasing the power of his officers. 'I must say I found DC Hyde's presentation particularly interesting, is this system being developed anywhere else?'

'Of course, we have the national crime database, and each force has its own records and files. But as a discipline, to identify and hone the skills of spotters, no sir, I believe my squad are first to do that.'

Cdr Marsh interjected. 'It is about being one step ahead; we are committed to advancing the practice of intelligence-led policing.'

'If I may, sir?'

'Of course, DI Colman.'

'We prepared an operational tactic at the request of DI Barlow, it was something we have only exercised intermittently before, but may well be a standard procedure in future. With a disciplined team, we were able to capture and detain a targeted individual from the crowd. We were unaware of the reason for the operation when we arrested Alan H at the request of DI Barlow.'

'Very impressive.' The Chief Constable nodded along. 'Sergeant Jones' work, should also be commended, information is the backbone of every operation, criminal or otherwise, experienced handlers are going to be like gold dust. I must say, Commander Marsh, it seems your unit really is producing the goods.'

Barlow was waiting for his pat on the back.

'The more challenging aspect of the presentation is the manipulation of the local press, while of course I completely understand and sympathise with your aims, DI Barlow, we have to be careful we do not cross the line between intelligence and intervention. We have security services who are well versed in the dark arts. Purely in terms of self-preservation, there is a mob of liberal journalists and politicians out there waiting to pounce. We must not give them an opportunity. Our remit is to protect the public within the bounds of the law, we have to be hyper-alert to our duty, protecting public order without transgressing the boundaries set by the democratic control under which we operate.'

Cdr Marsh was quick to show his agreement. 'Of course, Sir, this is a line I have drawn for DI Barlow, and one I think he understands well.'

Barlow took the floor. 'Sir, this morning the largest industrial workforce organised in one place in Liverpool, took a step back from a policy and campaign that could have seen industrial action against job losses and the elevation of a faction of union leadership that is in bed with the most radical elements of the black and Irish communities in this city. The meeting that took place this morning was a defeat for the radicals and revolutionaries and my firm belief, not only in policing but in all my previous military experience, is a defeat for the enemy is a win for us.

DC Hyde put the names and faces to the links, this is the essence of defending British values today. Unions, peace campaigns, civil rights, they can all come and go and the state will survive- why? Because any appeal to patriotism, to defend Britain, and its values will see those same people who campaigned for better pay, for civil rights, rally to the flag. In times of war and crises, British people know whose side they are on. In any crisis, all we need to do is to raise the flag and the people will rally.

These new groups, these new links, this new nexus can destroy all that- because it eats at the heart of the state - patriotism, empire, British values. They eat away at the very idea of Britain.

Above all, we should judge based on results. Not only did we set back the organised left in the factory, and the city as a whole, but one of its leading lights was sacked today, Ford management had no qualms about recognising the facts on the ground and moving to consolidate their position.'

'Is that so, Detective Inspector? Let's not get over-excited. My experience tells me that with these matters we have to be careful not to take that extra step, to in fact overreach.'

Commander Marsh was ready. 'I'm sure DI Barlow understands that, Chief Constable, we can move ahead with the gains from this operation while being cognisant of the limitations.'

There was a knock on the door, and a uniformed officer went directly to the chief constable and handed him a note.

'Do you have a radio set?'

'Of course, Sir.'

'Would you mind doing the honours, we should be able to catch the hourly news.'

Commander Marsh spun in his chair and clicked on, small radio at the side of his desk.

The newsreader injected a touch of excitement into his voice.

'Reports are coming in of wildcat strikes starting from Ford in Halewood, but spreading rapidly through south Liverpool, we are getting reports of walkouts in Standard Triumph and Dunlops, there are some delays to trains operating on lines going through Garston and Hunts Cross. The cause appears to be what militants are calling the victimisation of a union leader. The convenor of the union in Ford is claiming that he's been targeted by undercover police. For a full report on this shocking development tune into the nightly news at 6 pm.'

The Chief Constable snapped, 'Turn it off.' He waited for the radio silence then turned. 'As you were saying, DI Barlow?'

'It's a storm in a teacup, sir. Believe me; it'll be over by tea time.'

The chief constable stood. His voice rose and his face reddened. 'It better bloody had be. I don't care what strings you have to pull, you get this man his job back, and shut this story down now. Today! Do you understand me? I won't be embarrassed by a rogue, cowboy operator. Commander Marsh,

I am relying on you to get your act together and sort out your department.' The Chief Constable stood.

'Commander, I think you will have your hands full this afternoon, perhaps we can reschedule that lunch?'

'Of course, Sir.'

The Chief Constable marched out of the room quickly followed by DI Colman, who spoke to Barlow on his way out. 'Looks like this one got away, John. Better luck next time, eh.'

Commander Marsh sat in silence; it wasn't in his nature to shout and scream, however much he felt like it. 'Get on the phone, speak to whoever you have to. The only way to stop this is to reinstate this man at once, they can launch an investigation, even suspend him with pay, but this action has to be halted. Is that clear DI Barlow?'

'Yes, Sir.'

'I hope Inspector; there are no more rogue operations to surface?'

'Rogue? What I'm doing is not rogue.'

'This is it, your last warning, any more fuck ups, anything in the newspapers, if I hear a whisper that you are doing anything more than collecting information, you are finished, not transferred, not early retirement, out on your arse. Do you hear me?'

'Loud and clear.'

* * *

When Barlow walked into the squad room, DC Hyde and DS Jones were waiting. 'What the fuck is going on?'

'The rank and file committee, its members are calling people out on strike wherever they've got enough support.' DS Jones replied.

'Where's that idiot Terry Connor?'

'He's disappeared, him and his brother, his mother said they've gone to London.'

'For fuck's sake.'

'Looks like Alan H has played a blinder,' said DC Hyde.

'While our brass play like cowards, that tin hat in there is full of platitudes about democracy and rule of law. When the shit hits the fan, it's us they turn to, to get them out of trouble.'

'Us?' asked DS Jones.

Barlow banged the table. 'Counter intelligence, we are the backbone, the spine, of the British Empire here and abroad. They break me, they paralyze the whole thing. It's time to increase the pressure, not back down. It's time to take the war to the enemy. What else do they think the bombs in Dublin were about?'

Chapter Twenty-Eight

Vinny

Wicklow, 2010

'They won't know what's hit them,' said Vinny.

'Will you give over,' said Anne, reading her notes.

'I'm going to get my phone out and record it for posterity.'

'You'll do no such thing.'

'Why not, see Simon get his comeuppance.'

'I hope so, but there're no guarantees.'

'It's a public hearing, isn't it?'

'It is.'

'Well then. It'll be nice to wipe the smiles off those two goons of his,' said Vinny.

'Reporting them didn't do much good, though.'

'My word against theirs. Police will never prosecute...'

'You might be right.'

They were outside the Whitegates County Council building.

Anne's phone buzzed. 'It's Ronan, they'll be here in half an hour.'

'Come on, shall we go in?' Vinny checked his watch. They should have started by now.

The sound echoed in the open atrium when Anne asked Cara where the planning meeting was; her voice bounced off the walls. The sound threw her, and she suddenly realised what she was doing.

'Good luck.' Cara smiled.

'Do you know her?'

'Let's just say I have my sources,' said Anne.

They walked to the end of the corridor, Anne conscious of her footsteps. A uniformed porter was outside the room. 'Can you turn off your phones, please,' he asked and opened the door to allow them in. At the front of the room, there was a table with eight people seated facing the public. There were three rows of seats for the visitors. In the far right on the front row, Anne saw Simon Carrol, the Price brothers, and another man she didn't recognise.

Vinny squeezed her arm. 'Take a seat now, don't be worrying about them.'

The audience was quite lively. A reporter from the local paper wearing an identity badge was engrossed in the phone in front of her notebook. Anne was surprised to see a Garda at each end of the room.

'When are we on?' Vinny whispered.

'Not sure.'

The secretary was outlining the reference documentation for a hotel extension, and committee members were checking their paperwork. A long, complicated process was eventually accepted, and the Chairman banged his gavel to indicate the hotel extension plans were approved. Anne had been going over the points in her mind. Writing was one thing; standing up in front of people, something else entirely. She hoped her nerve would hold.

The Chairman announced a short break while the paperwork was distributed for the next proposal, Coillearnacha / Woodland Grove.

There were a few groans from the audience.

'Nice of him to name it after what he's destroying,' said Vinny.

'Hope the others get here soon.'

'Come on, let's stretch our legs.'

The meeting broke up for a short recess, Anne and Vinny left the room.

'They should be here soon. I hope they're not too late.' Anne swiped her phone, but there were no messages.

'They'll be here,' Vinny reassured.

'I didn't know you had an application in?' Simon Carrol was standing behind them. 'I hear your boyfriend likes underground spaces.'

The brothers laughed.

'We'll see who's laughing soon,' said Vinny.

'Come on,' said Anne, pulling at Vinny's arm. 'Let's go back in.'

A look of concern crossed Simon's face. 'What's he on about? I hope you're not going to do anything stupid.'

The Chairman banged his gavel to bring the meeting to order, so on to motion 533.12/C/WG Coillearnacha or Woodland Grove. 'Members of the committee, we have the full resolution before us, the secretary will read the order of documentation, and then we will proceed to the vote.'

The door opened, and there was a shuffling noise behind them. Anne turned, a smile broke across her face as Karla wheeled Maude in, followed by Jana and Ronan bringing up the rear.

The gavel banged. 'Can you find yourself a seat quickly, please? Secretary, you can commence with the order papers.'

The new group moved in next to Anne and Vinny while the secretary read the order numbers. When the secretary finished, the Chairman shuffled his papers. 'Mr Collinge, I believe this matter concerns you?'

The man beside Simon stood, 'Yes, thank you, Mr Chairman. It is simply a matter of procedure now. I can confirm that on behalf of my client, Carrol Construction, we have followed all the protocols and submitted plans. The plans have been audited for energy use and conservation, and we have fulfilled all the requirements of the conservation legislation. The finances, plans, accounts, proposals checked, verified, and approved by the planning sub-committee. All we need is your approval tonight, and the project can get its green light.'

Simon was smiling. He slapped Collinge on the back as he sat down.

The Chairman banged his gavel. 'We will proceed to the vote.'

Anne was about to raise her hand but was beaten to it by a woman with braided hair and a long dark overcoat who asked, 'Can I speak, Mr Chairman?'

The Chairman spoke 'Yes, we can allow comments on the motion, but let me warn you they must be pertinent to the application.'

'Of course. I want to ask the members of this panel who this country belongs to? Whether our fathers and grandfathers fought to win this land back from the British only to hand it over to private developers? We are rightly proud of our county, "Wicklow The Garden of Ireland," and yet we are seeing more and more of it turned over to commuter housing developments. These houses are not for local people and we will be lucky if any of the jobs go to local people. These are commuter properties built for profit, not need.'

The Chairman banged his gavel. 'Unless you have a point of procedure to make based on this planning application, I will ask you to be seated. This is not the parliament, and political speeches have no place here.'

Simon clapped. 'Well said.'

The woman didn't move. 'This is not political; it is about our future and our environment.'

The gavel struck again. 'Please sit down. We will proceed with the matter at hand.'

The woman remained standing. 'I will warn you only once, if you do not sit down, I will have you removed.' The Gardaí looked alert and ready to act.

Anne stood. 'Excuse me, Mr Chairman, can I say something?'

The Chairman looked around. 'You wish to speak to the resolution?'

'Thank you, sir.'

'I object,' Simon stood.

The gavel rang out. 'This is not a courtroom, Mr Carrol, and you are not a lawyer. If I give the member of the public the right to speak, then she will speak.'

'Get in,' said Ronan.

The gavel rang out again. 'And only the young lady who has requested the right to speak. Now young lady.'

'I haven't seen the plans for the housing, so my comment is not on the plans as they have been submitted,' the gavel was raised and was about to pound down, but held, 'and I am sure the committee has done its work efficiently and effectively.'

Members of the committee enjoyed this and nodded in approval.

'There is a problem, however, in the character of Mr Carrol as the lead contractor in this project, through Carrol Construction. I will leave aside his bankruptcy, just a couple of years ago, in which he left many local businesses and prospective homeowners out of pocket, while he suffered no ill consequence.'

Mr Collinge stood. 'Mr Chairman, none of this has relevance to the plans before the committee.'

The Chairman responded, 'Mr Collinge is right. Unless you have any information relevant to this motion, I will have to ask you to sit.'

'Mr Carrol is engaged in a fraudulent enterprise.' Anne waved a copy of the agreement. 'This document gives the power of attorney in all matters financial and legal concerning Miss Maude Carrol to Mr Simon Carrol. This document gives him the right to raid Miss Carrol's bank accounts and secure loans on her property to finance this project.'

'This is bollocks, nonsense, slander.'

The gavel struck. 'Quiet, Mr Carrol. If you don't keep quiet, I will have you removed.'

The Garda moved from along the sidewall and stood at the end of Simon's row. The reporter had put her phone away and was scribbling frantically.

'Thank you, Mr Chair. I have the evidence here. These pages show that Mr Carrol tricked his elderly aunt, Miss Maude Carrol, into signing over the power of attorney to Mr Simon Carrol; the document was witnessed by Miss Jana Matyalovsky and Miss Karla Wocjik neither of whom were aware of the real purpose of the document.'

There were gasps of surprise and muttering among the committee members.

A high strident voice rang out. 'If my Paddy were here, he would kick your greedy arse down the High Street.'

'Order, order, please. These are very serious charges you are making.'

'I know, Mr Chairman, but we have the witnesses here to prove it.'

'I never gave that man a penny of my money, the swindler,' Maude shouted.

The Chairman banged his gavel. 'I have heard enough. We will not proceed with this motion tonight.'

Simon was on his feet again. 'Liars, the old woman's senile. She doesn't know what she's saying.'

'I warned you to be quiet, Mr Carrol.'

'Look at the state of them. Are you going to believe that shower of communists and foreigners?'

'Garda, I want you to detain this man and call your Sergeant over here to examine these papers. I want this matter dealt with.'

The Garda approached Simon, the brothers stood. 'I wouldn't if I were you now, boys; you'll be getting yourselves into more than you can handle. Now, do I call on my radio, or are you going to come with me?'

The second officer had crossed the room and stood behind his colleague. 'Sit down,' Carrol shouted.

The Price brothers did as they were told, looking hurt and

confused.

'You bastards are not going to get away with this.'

'Get him out of here,' the Chairman ordered.

The Garda grabbed Simon by the arm and led him out of the room while the crackle of his radio cut through the air, clapping and whooping broke out from the audience.

The Chairman made his final gavel for the evening. 'Tonight's meeting will be adjourned, 'thank you, ladies and gentleman.'

'Now that's a sight for sore eyes,' said Vinny.

'I've got some other news you might be interested in,' said Ronan.

'Come on then, what is it?'

'I've arranged for you to meet someone who knew your dad.'

Among the hubbub of the meeting's end, the reporter spoke to Anne. 'Can I have a quote please?' She had a pen and notebook poised.

Anne smiled. 'If you don't fight, you can't win.'

Chapter Twenty-Nine

Paddy

Wicklow, 1974

It was a long and winding drive that led to his door. A bungalow outside the town in the foothills of the Wicklow Mountains. Isolated and private and yet just ten minutes from the town. Conor Walsh had fenced off his piece of Ireland.

As they pulled up outside the house, Conor appeared, followed by Seamus and two of his men.

'Good to see you, boys.'

'Conor, we had to dump the gear. We'd no choice.' Declan spoke as he got out of the car.

'Okay, enough, not out here now, wouldn't want the neighbours to hear.'

There were no neighbours.

'Come on inside.'

Paddy walked towards the open front door, Declan falling in behind him.

Conor pointed. 'No, not you, you go with Seamus.'

Declan stopped. He looked at Conor. He held his hands out palms up. 'Conor, please.'

'Son, no need to be fretting now, we just want a word privately with you, go with the boys. Seamus will look after you, won't you Seamus.'

Seamus smiled. 'Of course, no bother.' He held his arm out, shepherding Declan away to the right. The two men with Seamus moved behind Declan.

'Okay, okay, I'm coming,' said Declan.

'You come in here now, Paddy.'

Paddy stepped through the front door.

'Go on, inside.'

Paddy looked to his right and could see a large well-furnished lounge.

The front door closed, and Conor came in, moving past Paddy. He indicated an armchair; there was another opposite, and a long sofa running the length of the wall beside them. A curved bar stood in one corner, spirits in-wall dispensers, and beer pumps mounted on the counter. It was like an average family living room except more spacious. The leather sofa and chairs were bigger, the carpet softer. It had a clean, sharp smell.

'Nice place,' said Paddy.

'Thank you. The Missus does it all, but you know, it's nice to be comfortable.

'I'm sure,' said Paddy.

'Take a seat.'

Conor took the chair opposite Paddy, between them a hardwood coffee table. Conor put his hand behind his back and produced a pistol. He placed the gun at his end of the coffee table. 'Just so we understand each other,' he said.

'I understand,' said Paddy. What he understood was that this was life and death. If the shipment of weapons were discovered or went astray, someone would pay the price, and what that price would be was clear.

'Where's the consignment?'

'Inside the drive of Paedar Carrol's, Greystones cottage immediately left behind the bushes against the wall. The road might be watched, so whoever you send should be careful.'

Conor picked up the gun and left the room. Paddy wondered

what was happening with Declan. He guessed they were separated to test each other's story, but wondered what Conor already knew.

Conor returned and placed the gun back on the table. 'Why don't you tell me what happened?'

Paddy recounted events exactly as they unfolded, including his decision to hide the weapons.

Conor got up and walked over to the bar. 'Drink?'

'Yeah, a whiskey would be good.'

'A long morning?' said Conor.

'Getting longer by the minute,' Paddy said.

Conor poured the drinks out and returned with Paddy's.

'That was clever, hiding the stuff, and in Peadar Carrol's gaffe, I won't ask how you know about the place because we both know what's been going on. But it was a good call. The Gardaí are not going to rush in there. I've always said you were clever, Paddy, but Jesus, you do like trouble, or is it that trouble likes you? Whatever it is, do yourself and me a favour and give Maude Carrol a miss. A wise man chooses his enemies carefully. Peadar Carrol is a powerful man. Do you know why I'm relaxed with you now, Paddy?'

'Probably because I didn't know what the job was, where or when. So, it would've been impossible for me to tell anyone else.'

'Exactly, and why do you think I'm not relaxed with Declan at the moment?'

'Because the Gardaí who pulled us over were armed, since they have to get authorisation to carry arms, they knew something was happening and were ready for it.'

'Exactly. This was no accidental stop. Why would they show themselves in Wicklow?' He paused for a second. 'I don't know, maybe to see if you would panic, break the plan, or even bring the stuff here.'

Paddy remembered Declan suggested exactly that but didn't tell Conor.

Conor continued, 'Whatever the reason, it means we have a

problem. I have a problem, and if I have a problem, everyone under me has a problem. Do you understand that?'

'Yeah, I do.' Paddy was calm but focused. He knew he was in a dangerous situation. Conor didn't suspect Paddy, but Conor had to deal with Declan and make sure that Paddy didn't become an issue. It was looking more and more like Declan was the issue. The best thing Paddy could do was to remain calm and rational. There were times and places to lose your shit, but this was not one of them.

Conor rose from his seat and picked up the gun. 'Wait here. One of the boys will come in and keep you company.'

Conor opened the door and left. A man entered the room immediately after and without acknowledging Paddy, pulled out a chair and sat at the table at the other end of the room. Paddy didn't recognise him.

Time passed slowly, and tired, Paddy closed his eyes trying to relax. It had been an early start, being on the quayside at Arklow. The smell of the sea brought back his own journey. Liverpool seemed so far away now. Vinny and Maude were worth getting out of this mess for. It could just as easily have been him as Declan in the other room. Maybe next time it would be, if he allowed there to be a next time.

There was a gunshot nearby. The powerful explosion was impossible to miss. Paddy opened his eyes. The guy at the other end of the room was standing. He moved toward the window, then the door, spooked.

Paddy stayed where he was, anxiety increasing, heart rate rising, muscles tensed. This was real. He had no idea how Conor would handle it. Would he be next?

Was this the way he went out?

The other guy was nervous. Paddy didn't know if he was armed. He could probably get past him. Paddy stood, the guy held his hand out palm facing Paddy.

'Stay there.'

'I'm not going anywhere,' said Paddy.

He watched the guy's hands. If he had a weapon, his hand would move toward it now. Nothing. Paddy took a step forward.

'I told you, stay there.' His other hand came up in the same motion of warning.

Paddy knew he wasn't armed.

The door opened, and Conor entered.

'Sit down,' Conor ordered Paddy.

The smell of cordite followed Conor. It surrounded him and moved with him into the room. Conor placed the gun back on the coffee table. As he did so, Paddy noticed a speck of blood on Conor's cuff.

'So, Paddy, here's what's going to happen. You're going to take that gun and keep it safe. The boxes have been recovered and are now secure, so we can all relax a bit. Try to get things back to normal. How does that sound?'

'Sounds good to me.' Paddy wasn't convinced he was safe yet.

'Seamus will drive you back into town. Keep your head down for a few days. We'll let all this blow over then see where we are. Maybe even get away for a couple of days.'

'I've some family in Tipperary I've been planning to see,' said Paddy.

'There you go, great idea, catch up with the family. When you get back, come and see me.'

'Will do.'

Paddy moved toward the door.

'Paddy.' Conor nodded toward the gun.

'Yeah, of course.' Paddy went back and picked it up. The barrel was still warm as he slid it into his waistband.

Conor led the way outside. Declan's car was still in the drive with Seamus in the driver's seat as Paddy was about to open the passenger door. 'Paddy, one last thing,' said Conor from the doorway.

'A bit of advice. Don't become a problem for me.'

Paddy nodded his agreement and stepped into the car.

He waited till they were out of the drive. 'Declan?'

'Don't ask. If it was up to me, you'd both be out,' said Seamus.

'No doubt,' said Paddy. He paused, then added, 'No doubt.'

The rest of the journey was in silence.

Ten minutes later, at the edge of town, Paddy said, 'This'll do me here.'

Seamus pulled the car over to the kerb. They were near the Black Castle; Paddy wanted to clear his head with the few minutes' walk down through the town. He filled his lungs with the damp fresh air and felt the rush of, if not energy, at least wakefulness. He hadn't thought about the gun when he decided to walk, and it was now hanging heavily in his waistband. The walk didn't seem such a clever idea.

He knew Conor had given him the gun to make him complicit in what had happened. But what Conor didn't know was that this was exactly the kind of evidence Barlow wanted. If Paddy handed the gun in, Conor would be fucked. Paddy could almost see Barlow clapping his hands with glee. This was his chance, shop Conor and get back to Liverpool. It was within his grasp.

It was mid-afternoon now, and the sun had never put up much of a struggle and was giving in, giving the land back to the wind and drizzle. He was on the right-hand side of the road opposite the Gaol and the statue. He put his head down and marched on.

'Well, if it isn't Mr Connolly.'

Paddy looked sharply to his right. There, in the doorway, was Maude. 'What's this place?'

'Just an office. I'm helping out a bit. Come in, no one's here.'

'No, look, I've had a bit of a morning. I'm dying on my feet.'

'Come in, there's no one here, just me. Everyone's gone out to lunch. I'll make you a cup of tea.'

'Okay, ten minutes, then I have to get back.'

Maude linked her arm through Paddy's and took him through the shop front. There was a counter that ran half the length of the shop and a desk with a phone and chair. The place was formal, wood-panelled, clean, and stuffy.

'Come on into the back, down here.'

Maude dragged him through a doorway into the rear of the shop, and down a flight of stairs. Like upstairs, it was wood panelled halfway up the walls and a polished wooden floor. There were two desks and a settee between them, and in a corner, a sink and draining board. Next to it was a fridge and a kitchen table.

'Sit down, I'll do you a tea. What have you been up to?'

'You don't want to know, believe me.'

'Well, I've done my essay and I don't mind telling you, if those lot at Trinity don't bite my hand off, then they don't know what they're doing.'

Paddy sat and felt the shape of the gun in his back.

Maude filled the kettle and switched it on.

As she turned to Paddy, the phone rang in the main shop. 'Give me a minute, will you.'

Maude left, Paddy got up. His eyes were drawn to the side wall. The wood panelling was not a tight seal to the wall. He pulled it gently, and it came away about two inches; there was void or space behind it. Perfect, he thought. He dropped the gun behind it, surprised to hear it clatter as if falling some distance. Fuck Barlow, I'm no rat or traitor. In dropping the evidence behind the panelling, he knew he was closing off the option of returning to Liverpool with Barlow's help. One problem solved, for now.

'I'd never make a secretary. What are you supposed to say? My dad's out, probably getting drunk over lunch? Anyway, tea?'

'This is your dad's place?'

'Yeah.'

'Okay, I'd better get going. There's no point in winding him up.'

'He's okay. He just doesn't like me being with anyone.'

'Maude, we saw him with Conor. What the hell do you think he was talking about? Conor has already warned me off.'

'They don't scare me.'

'Well, they should. They scare me.'

'I thought you couldn't be scared.'

'This isn't a game. You put the idea in my head of getting Vinny over for the holidays and the rest. To do that, I need to keep Conor and your dad off my back. I think I have a way, but I need time to get out, get things straight. They scare me because they can stop that. A week, a couple of weeks, if I'm straight with him, I think it'll be fine.'

'What are you up to?' Maude asked.

'Nothing, there's something, someone I need to deal with. Then I can be clear of this shit.'

A voice behind him broke in, 'A bit late for that.'

Paddy turned to see Maude's dad in the doorway.

'Oh, Jesus, I don't need this,' Paddy said under his breath. He stood up and walked toward the door.

Mr Carrol blocked his exit.

'Look, I'm only going to ask this once. You're Maude's dad, so don't make me do anything I'll regret. Can you get out of the way, please?'

'Dad, let him go.'

Mr Carrol hesitated for just a minute, then stepped aside.

'A wise decision, Mr Carrol.'

'You haven't heard the last of this. You don't know who you're messing with.' Oh, I do, thought Paddy. Unfortunately, I do.

Chapter Thirty

Paddy

Wicklow, 1974

'No work today?' Stephen closed the front door.

'No. Conor's given me a few days.' Paddy was on the pavement with a bowl of water, some rags, and household cleaners. His motorbike was on its stand. 'I thought I'd give the bike a clean and then maybe have a run down to Tipp tomorrow.'

Stephen nodded toward the bike. 'Do you know what you're doing with that thing?'

'Just about, but a bit of spit and polish can't harm it.'

'It's alright for you fellas. When do I get my few days off?'

'Think yourself lucky you're in that bar. If you've a head on your shoulders, you'll stay there,' said Paddy.

'I guess so, can get awful boring, though.'

'A better word for it might be "safe." Know when you're well off, lad. When you see Conor, tell him I'm off to Tipp, and when I get back, I'll need to see him.'

'Shall I say what about?'

'Just say Paddy said he wouldn't turn.'

'Turn what?'

'He'll know.'

'Okay, whatever. See you later.' Stephen left for his job.

As Paddy watched him walk away, he knew that should be

his future. The daily grind, the eight hours, following someone else's rules. Truth was, he did that anyway; Power, Barlow, Conor, he was always doing someone else's bidding.

A plan, half-baked but possible, was developing. If he didn't go back to Garston, he didn't need Barlow, or to act against Conor. He knew where the gun was, it was safe. It was illegal possession at least and would be enough to see Conor gone for a few years if he ever wanted to use it.

Paddy washed the chrome exhaust down with soapy water and then took a rag to it, buffing it to get a shine.

He couldn't tell Conor about Barlow, it would be too dangerous. Conor would get rid of him, and to be fair, he couldn't blame him. He was only in Wicklow to set Conor up. But if he didn't betray him, if he could show his loyalty, he had the chance but didn't sell him out. He had saved him three times, on the border and with the rifles, and now with this gun. Three times he could have betrayed him, and three times he remained loyal. Maybe Conor would be okay with him. That was all he needed. He just needed permission to stay and keep out of the way.

It was a big risk. Fuck, anyway.

On top of all that, he now had Maude's dad gunning for him. 'A powerful enemy,' Conor said, and he should know.

He looked at the bike, the chrome was gleaming, the leather seat shining, and the tyres were jet black—just the job.

He mounted the bike. It wasn't the most powerful machine in the world, but it responded when he turned the throttle. He started the engine and moved away slowly. He turned left into Bath Street, and then up and over the Bridge. He would get out of town on the southern road through Dunbar.

Up through Bridge Street then a left, out past the Black Castle. As he left the houses behind, he opened her up a little and enjoyed the wind in his face. Fuck, this is good.

In ten minutes, he would be at Brittas Bay, a sight better than Oggie shore. He drove on, weaving the bike from side to side. He leant into the corners and pulled out of them. Fuck this is good.

The road disappeared beneath him, and moisture in the air built into droplets on his face. Paddy laughed as the water began to drip. It wasn't raining. He was harvesting his own water supply. He put his tongue out to try and catch the drops before they were blown away.

He swung the bike left, down the approach road to the sand dunes. It was quiet, a school day, so no family groups around. There was a green transit behind him, but it stopped, and he carried on to the barrier. He would park there, have a look at the sea.

The dunes were high on either side as he made his way to the beach, his steps heavy and slow in the sand. Paddy emerged on the beach, and either side of him saw the sand run for miles. No burnt-out cars, ICI, or oil refinery, just clean, clear beaches.

A hundred feet in front of him, the surf roared to the shore; the sound of the sea was immense—the wind and water combined to provide an inferno of movement and colour. The water slapped and danced, it pulled and pushed, and for the first time, Paddy didn't hate the sea. It was pure power; he could feel it. He lifted his arms and let the wind dance around him, with him. Colours and smells combined, and he knew. Knew he could start living, something had snapped, something was gone, the horror of Dublin, the bitterness, the hatred, the anger. He didn't know if it was the death in Dublin, but he knew his future was Maude and Vinny, even Ireland. Whatever it took to get there, he would do it. He would be with them.

Fuck. He was drained. The events of the day before, the tension and stress with Declan and Conor. Fuck, this shit had to end.

Paddy saluted the sea and turned. He ambled back between the dunes to his bike. He brushed the sand off the seat. He might have to give it another brush tomorrow before setting out. He kick-started the bike and moved off gently.

The green van started at the same time, the sun broke through the clouds, and Paddy slowed. Where was the van going? It moved out diagonally, and Paddy was getting closer. What are you doing?

It didn't straighten out but was now almost completely blocking the lane. He turned his throttle, and a burst of speed took him past the front bumper. He slid a bit on the sand and had to go up the base of the dune to get past. He looked back but couldn't see the driver; the sun was reflecting off the windscreen. Idiot.

* * *

It was a good outing that set him up nicely for the next day. The bike was running well. He would surprise his sisters. It would be weird, he regretted not having a photo of Vinny to show them, but all being well, they would see him soon enough.

He made his tea and climbed the stairs. He would chill today and maybe watch some TV later. The trip to Tipp would do him good. He needed to think, clear his head.

He laid back on the bed.

Paddy heard a crash; it was low and dull, the sound of wood breaking. Before he had time to get up, the boots were thumping up the stairs. His bedroom door exploded open and was followed by loud, insistent shouts of 'Police, get your hands up.'

Before he knew it, Paddy had two officers pointing guns at him.

They didn't give him a chance to say or do anything. The commands barked.

'Up.'

'Get Up.'

'Turn round, hands behind your back.'

They cuffed Paddy, the metal pressing against the bone in his wrist; the pain was constant and sharp. They pulled him out of the bedroom, knocking his tea off the bedside cabinet in the process. He watched as it ran down the side. Bastards. That would stain the carpet. Conor won't be happy with that.

Police were all over the house. They pulled him down the

stairs and out the door. Four cars took up the whole street. The neighbours were out.

The main police station was only a few hundred yards away, the other side of the bridge and just back from the river. He could walk it in two minutes. It took more time for the cars to rearrange themselves. He went with one other car as an escort while two vehicles stayed at the house.

Paddy had been in and around enough police stations and nicks not to be overawed. He took the pushing and pulling, the curses, and insults as par for the course. He was thrown into an interview room and the cuffs were finally removed, easing the pain in his wrists.

He took one of the four chairs and sat at the table in the middle of the room. The door opened, and Paddy recognised the officer who stopped them near Greystones. He didn't expect the second visitor.

'Well, if it isn't King Rat,' said Paddy.

Without expression, Barlow crossed the room and slapped Paddy across the face.

Paddy took the slap and snarled back, 'Even hit like a bitch.'

Barlow backed off and leaned against the wall. 'You're fucking stupid, do you know that? What are you here for? Do you remember? Do you? I've got you for fucking murder, life in jail without parole. All you had to do was give me Conor. And what do you do? Start playing fucking guerrilla, gun-running, and God knows what else. Gobshite, that's what you are. What was that bollocks up at the border?' Barlow paused and shook his head. 'Stupid fucking Paddy is right.' He looked toward the other officer. 'No offence.'

'None taken. This piece of shit is English. He's yours, not ours.'

'See, see that, do you? Even your own people disown you. They don't want you, we don't want you, no one fucking wants you, don't you get it? You're useless, nothing, no one would give a flying fuck if you washed up dead tomorrow.' Barlow paused. 'Do you think Conor cares? Is that it? Well, where is Declan, eh? Remember him, do you? Your mate. Where is he now? Cos his fucking mum can't find him. His sister is looking for him. We've even had his girlfriend on the phone. He'd better turn up or...' Barlow stopped himself. 'But you know what, Paddy, you piece of shit, no one is going to miss you, we won't get any phone calls for you.'

Barlow paced the room in front of Paddy, 'Look at what you can have, your son, what's his name? Vincent is it?'

Paddy hated this man. 'Keep his name out of your mouth.'

'Oh, touchy are you? Thinking of your boy being brought up by some Scouser? Your ex being fucked by a line of dockers?'

Paddy would gladly put this guy out of his misery, pull the trigger. Not out of anger, but disgust, put the dog down.

'I'm not gonna waste time with you, Paddy; here's the deal, either you give me Conor, or I give you to Conor. I tell him you've been with me all along. How long do you think you'll last if that gets out?' Barlow threatened.

Paddy snorted. 'You're just mad because you know he's smarter than you. You've got all the police, the army, all your snitches and traitors, and he's been fucking the lot of you for decades. That's why you hate him.'

'See how that helps you when he puts you in the ground.'

Jesus, shit. Paddy realised who the rat was.

'You've got 24 hours. Give me something or I'm done with you.'

* * *

Paddy got back to find Stephen examining the doorframe. 'They made a right mess of this.'

'I know, mate, I'm sorry.'

'Oh, it'll be sorted no bother. I've a guy coming round in a bit, he'll make it right.'

'I thought you were working?' said Paddy.

'I was. As soon as I heard, I came down to see the damage. Half the town was on the phone or dropping in to tell me about it. Glad they've let you go.'

'Yeah, all a bit of mess, to be honest.'

'I see what you mean. Now about the job.'

'Anything from Conor?' asked Paddy.

Stephen broke eye contact. 'He's away, not sure where. I doubt he'll be back for a couple of days.'

'You can get hold of him though?'

Stephen was stumbling, 'Erm yeah, I guess,'

'Does he know I was picked up?'

'Ahh, look now, I wouldn't know.' Paddy knew Stephen was lying. He didn't blame him.

'Look, the message I gave you earlier…'

'Yeah, I remember it,' said Stephen.

'Well, scrap that. Tell him I need to meet him, but not here. It's important, Stephen.'

'No bother, I'll make sure he knows.' Stephen looked relieved he could say something true.

'I'll ring you at the bar every night till you speak to him, then we can work out where to meet.' Paddy turned to go upstairs then stopped.

'It's important you don't tell anyone what I said about going to Tipp, none of the lads, no one.'

'Okay. I got it. My lips are sealed.'

Paddy nodded. 'You're a good lad. You keep pulling those pints, mate.'

'I will.'

'I'm off to get a kip, I'm pure done in. I'll be away in the morning before you're about,' said Paddy.

'No problem, you take care now.' Paddy knew Stephen meant it.

Across the Water

* * *

Paddy was half-asleep. The excitement of the day kept his nerves on edge. He heard the soft steps on the stairs and knew they meant no harm. He opened his eyes to soft hands stroking his head.

'Here, I made you a tea.'

'Ha, you know me, alright.'

'Looks like a lot is going on,' Maude said.

'I guess you heard about the police?'

'Yeah, and looking at the state of the door, they weren't friendly?'

'They're okay, chasing their tails. Most of the time, haven't got a clue.'

'Things are getting serious, though?' said Maude.

'They are. Can I see that paper in your bag?'

Maude pulled out her copy of The Irish Times. Paddy opened it and began a search through a list.

'What are you looking for?'

Paddy's finger went down the list, thirty-three names of those killed on May 17th 1974 by the Dublin and Monaghan bombs;

Patrick Askin (44) Co. Monaghan
Josie Bradley (21) Co. Offaly
Marie Butler (21) Co. Waterford
Anne Byrne (35) Dublin
Thomas Campbell (52) Co. Monaghan
Simone Chetrit (30) France
Thomas Croarkin (36) Co. Monaghan
John Dargle (80) Dublin
Concepta Dempsey (65) Co. Louth

Jack Byrne

Colette Doherty (20) Dublin
Baby Doherty (full-term unborn) Dublin*
Patrick Fay (47), Dublin & Co. Louth
Elizabeth Fitzgerald (59) Dublin
Breda Bernadette Grace (34) Dublin and Co. Kerry
Archie Harper (73) Co. Monaghan
Antonio Magliocco, (37) Dublin & Italy
May McKenna (55) Co. Tyrone
Anne Marren (20) Co. Sligo
Anna Massey (21) Dublin
Dorothy Morris (57) Dublin
John (24), Anna (22), Jacqueline (17 months) & Anne-Marie (5 months) O'Brien, Dublin
Christina O'Loughlin (51), Dublin
Edward John O'Neill (39), Dublin
Marie Phelan (20), Co. Waterford
Siobhán Roice (19), Wexford Town
Maureen Shields (46), Dublin
Jack Travers (28), Monaghan Town
Breda Turner (21), Co. Tipperary
John Walsh (27), Dublin
Peggy White (44), Monaghan Town
George Williamson (72), Co. Monaghan

'He's not there.'

'Who's not there?'

'The boy I owe the shilling to.'

Paddy dropped the newspaper and lay back on the bed. The Jingle Jangle, the horror of that day would always be associated with those words. The discordant notes were the accompaniment to his life.

'My dad is going nuts, too. He warned Conor about you, then there we were, in his office.'

Paddy opened his eyes, 'Red rag to a bull.'

'I'm so stupid. I put you in danger. I'm scared.'

'You will be fine.'

'Not for me, for you.'

'You know why I'm here?'

'I know you had to leave Liverpool.'

'I was given a promise.'

'You wouldn't be the first Irishman to be taken in by a British promise.'

'You're explaining it all away. You shouldn't. This is me,' said Paddy.

'None of us escapes our history, Paddy; we are all prisoners of our times.'

'Was that in your essay?'

'I'm being serious.' Maude kicked her shoes off and lay alongside him. He stroked her hair and held her.

'You shouldn't be here. It's not safe,' he said.

'I know. That's why I'm worried.'

Paddy lifted himself. 'Go home. This isn't the place for you tonight.'

Maude sat up. 'My dad, the police, who else have you upset?'

'Stop. I'll be fine. I'm off tomorrow for a few days. I know what I'm doing. I know how to get clear of all this. I just need to speak to Conor.'

'I don't want to go.'

'I know you don't, but look around you,' said Paddy. 'This is Conor's place. This is not ours. I don't want you to be a part of this. I want us to be free, clear of it all. The future will be ours, ourselves alone, we will have all the time in the world. Like you said, I'll get Vinny over for the school holidays. He can catch crabs off Parnell bridge, dodge the surf at Brittas bay.'

Tears fell, and Maude wiped them away. She smiled. 'You really think so?'

'Of course,' he lied.

Chapter Thirty-One

Vinny

Wicklow, 2010

Vinny went from a drizzly grey morning into a dark but warm bar. The windows in Maguires were permanently curtained and the only natural light came in bursts as the door was opened. Wooden floors and warm lighting gave the place a timeless feeling. Vinny scanned the room. There was someone on a side table facing the other way.

The landlord appeared from a doorway leading off behind the bar. 'Good morning. What can I get you?'

'I'll have a lager, please, a pint.'

'Is the dark stuff getting to you?'

'Not sure how much,' Vinny patted his stomach. 'But I've definitely put something on since I've been here.'

The lager was placed in front of him, and Vinny handed over a note.

The barman nodded toward the man at the side table. 'That's your man.'

'Oh right.' Vinny picked up his pint and walked over. The man was sitting looking at a folded newspaper and raised his glasses as Vinny approached. 'Good morning. It's you again, the man who was escaping the missus.'

Vinny looked closer. 'Oh yeah, on the bench.'

'That's right. Ronan tells me you've a few questions.'

'Can I have a seat?' Vinny pulled a chair out.

'As long as you leave it when I want to get back to my paper.'

Vinny sat, placing his pint on the table. 'Just say the word, and I'm gone.'

He offered his hand. 'Vinny Connolly.'

The man reached out to shake Vinny's hand without introducing himself.

'How can I help you?'

'Ronan told me you might know something about my dad.'

'Did he, now?'

'Yes, he did.'

The man half laughed and folded his paper.

'What's wrong?'

'You're going to tell me your father was Paddy Connolly?'

'I was,' said Vinny, surprised.

'I knew your dad and Conor; it was a long time ago now.'

'Yeah, I understand that.' He tried to contain his curiosity. One step at a time, he thought. 'He wasn't here long.'

'No, he wasn't.'

'What is it they say? Something about the brightest flames burn the quickest,' the man said.

'Is that what he was like?'

'Oh, he was. Your dad was, how can I put this, like a firework always ready to go off. All you'd need is someone to light the fuse, and…' he put his hands together then brought them apart dramatically. 'Boom.'

'Can I ask how you knew him?'

'You could say we worked together for a while.'

'For Conor?'

'Yeah, not long, really just a few weeks, but memorable times, you know. Sometimes life seems to go by,' he clicked his fingers. 'Like that. Decades just disappear. But other minutes last a lifetime. Guess we'd need old Einstein to work that one out.'

'You're right,' Vinny nodded.

'I'm sure you know, but for all that he was a firework, he was a smart fella. You know, had his wits about him. He saved me a couple of times, he did.' The old man nodded in memory.

'How?'

'I don't know, don't get me wrong. I don't want to go into too much detail, but his quick thinking saved me a few years inside.' He took a drink. 'I can't be sure of this, but I think he might have saved my life as well.'

'How?'

'It's complicated. Let's just say I was accused of something and the guy whose fault it was turned up dead a while later. I can't be sure of this, but I think it was your dad's doing.'

'The mid-seventies must've been dangerous times,' said Vinny.

'Very, your dad got close to it. Did you know he was caught up in the Dublin bombing?'

'No,' Vinny shook his head.

'The Dublin and Monaghan bombings, you should look into it, the Glenanne gang. It was what we always knew, everything pointed to British Intelligence. They wanted to stop power sharing.'

The man opposite had the craggy face of age, but Vinny could discern no emotion. 'And when he died?' he asked.

'Motorbike crash, wasn't it?' The old man met Vinny's eyes.

'That's the story.'

'You don't believe it?'

'Did you?' Vinny asked.

'Yeah.' He nodded slowly. 'Death was no stranger, so you didn't interrogate him. You just accepted that he was back again.'

'He?'

The old man shrugged. 'Women bring us in, men send us out.'

'Not wrong there,' said Vinny.

'The older you get; the simpler things become.'

'Less bullshit?'

'Maybe, maybe I can just see clearly now.'

Vinny leaned back in his chair. 'Now that the rain has gone.'

'What rain?'

'It's a song from when I was a kid.'

'Right.'

'Sorry, go on.'

'There's not much more I can tell you.'

Vinny doubted that but he accepted it. 'We found a bullet in the tyre of his motorbike. Sounds weird, but we also found a gun,' said Vinny.

The old man gave a nervous laugh. 'Really? Jesus, are you some kind of detective?'

'Just lucky, or unlucky, not sure which,' Vinny said.

'Here,' he showed him a picture of the gun.

'A Browning HP. What calibre bullet did you find?'

'Webley .455 according to the police.'

'Then that didn't come from this gun.'

'You sure about that?'

'Yeah, you go to an expert if you want, but they'll tell you the same.'

'How do you know?'

'Let's just say I've been close enough to the working end of these to know they use a 9mm round. In fact, a Browning just like that was shot next to me one time, by Conor as it happens.'

'Was he trying to kill you?'

'No, a warning, or a test, I took it, stopped working for him soon after that. It wasn't worth it.'

'What happened to Conor?'

'Died in his sleep, would you believe it, crafty old bastard. Had a daughter, and you know his grandson. That reminds me, wasn't your dad involved with Carrol's daughter Maude?'

'Yeah, we've met her. She's still in town.'

'Proper looker she was, crazy though. How long are you here

for?'

'Just a couple of days left now, then the ferry back to Liverpool.'

The old man drained his glass. 'Well, it was nice to meet you. Paddy would've been proud if he could see you today. Safe journey home.'

'Thanks, and thanks for the chat. I really appreciate it.'

'No, bother.'

'One last question. When I sat down on the bench did you know who I was?'

'I had an idea.' He stood and pulled his coat about him to go out into the drizzle.

'Sorry, what was your name?' Vinny asked.

'Declan, Declan Hughes. Good day now.' He tipped his cap and left.

Vinny sat back, slowly finishing his pint. It was the most satisfying pint he'd had in Wicklow.

Chapter Thirty-Two

Paddy

Wicklow, 1974

It didn't take long for Paddy to wake. Sleep was difficult with the world closing in. Things had been so hectic, Tipperary had become an escape rather than a destination. He climbed out of bed and dressed quickly. He wanted to get away. The longer he stayed, the more opportunities there were for... for who? Barlow? Maude's dad? Conor?

He threw a few things in his bag and was ready to leave. Before he left the room, he turned Connolly's picture back to face the room. Not your fault, mate; from what I hear, you didn't even get the chance to muck it up.

He poured a cup of tea and recalled the faces of his sisters and brother. They were still there. They had been filed away in those locked rooms of his mind for a long time, the pictures may have faded, but he was bringing them back out into the light, opening the doors. He had never had much connection with his sisters. There was a desperation in their affection that pushed him away when he saw them before he left for England. He didn't know how to deal with it. Marty would give him the occasional punch, or rub his head when they passed in the yard at Ferryhouse. The intensity of hugs, the warmth of their tears on his cheek was frightening. His escape from Ferryhouse and

Across the Water

Ireland was not just from the cruelty of the Fathers but from the affections of his sisters.

He took a rag and went out into the half-light of early morning, a new day was dawning, the street was quiet. This Sunday would see movement for mass soon, people in their best, going off in search of solace or hope he had found in neither God nor his buildings, but he would pay his dues to a priest today.

Paddy wiped the bike down, he wasn't afraid of much, but this trip scared him. He didn't know what he would find in Tipperary.

The country he knew before the industrial school was the one his mam and dad grew up in. He'd visited the farms and houses they came from, saw the geese and turkeys, the dogs and pigs. The lanes and hedges between fields of fertile earth, nourished with blood and bones of ancestors and struggles, the tan war when England emptied its jails and Ireland filled its ranks with young men ready and able to kill or die.

The stories lived on in country villages, so much so that they became a part of the landscape itself. A roadside cross, a shrine in a hedge, the grass was greener for the blood that fed it.

Bringing in the hay and cutting down the corn, dancing round the kitchen with a fiddle and drum, the voices like the feet, fleet and nimble. All this was before the fall; before Dad went to England and Mam had cancer, and the dancing stopped. This Ireland disappeared, replaced by the brick walls and darkened rooms, the cold, damp mornings, and the lash of the switch on bare legs and arse. There was worse, the boys knew. No one spoke of it. In the averted eyes, the frantic stabbing of the ground, there was an unspoken language of pain. Dark seeds were planted in hearts and minds; the darkness grew till it enveloped and snuffed out everything else. For most, it remained unacknowledged for decades. Many fled the scene, hoping the distance across land and sea would erase it. The building sites of Birmingham and London offered no cure; the drink only made it worse. It would remain until the love of girlfriends and wives and sons and daughters ate away at it. It could only be diminished by its opposite. Paddy had a debt to pay.

The road was flying under him, a twist of the wrist and power surged, the wheels turned, and the road disappeared. He cut through the air of autumn, the heavy damp air that resisted him. He sat tall, enjoying the fight. The road ahead was straight and empty. He was roaring through life, diminishing it, eating it. The faster he went, the closer he was to death. Death or renewal; death wasn't an end, just the start of the next phase. Who the fuck knew?

Paddy closed his eyes; one... two... three... his heart beat faster his nerves tingled, adrenalin rushed through his veins, four... five. He opened his eyes in time to see the turn. He leaned low, swinging down. Any further, and the back wheel would fly out from under him, and he would be spread all over the road. No, not now, time and time enough. I will live until I die.

Death was always a part of him, a part he knew and welcomed, like the bones in the fields, he would pay the price. We all did.

The road was straight and clear; one...two... the bike bounced but was okay ...three...he twisted his wrist, and the bike pulled him through the damp air... four... five... the sting of a bug hitting his cheek. He opened his eyes. The road ahead was good. He could have done it. He aimed to get to ten or to die trying.

The long road, the one road, the road his dad travelled before him, the road cut short for his mum, the road of the lost boy, the road ahead of his son, was this the only road? Who knows, but it is my road. Fuck them, fuck them all.

Paddy turned his wrist, he checked the clock, he was moving up through sixty, sixty-two...he closed his eyes...one ... two... three... four... five... six... he waited for impact, his heart sank, the blood rushed to his head, he could feel it, the faster he went, the slower time passed. Fuck.

The bike slipped. Eyes open, he reacted and put his legs out for balance. One foot hit the ground, he felt the leather on the road.

He wobbled and then straightened up. Fuck, that was close.

In risking death, he affirmed life. There must be a better way? To be who we are? Who we can be? He smelled the colours of the fields flashing past and saw the sounds of the silence that surrounded him.

A couple of miles further and he would be in Carrick on Suir. A town southwest of Clonmel, and the industrial school. This was the retirement home of Father Pearson. Attached to the church of St Nicholas, the priest house was large and impressive, more fortress than home, with its grey stone walls. Paddy was nervous. The Father Pearson he remembered was a bull of a man, strong and thick. He shook his head to get rid of the image of strong black hairs growing out of fingers that held him. This was the man he looked forward to taking on and beating down.

'I'm here to see Father Pearson.'

'We don't get many visitors now.'

'No, but he's kind of special to me if you know what I mean. Do you know where I can find him?'

'Sure, he's here, he doesn't go anywhere else these days. Are you an old boy?'

'From Ferryhouse, pardon me, St Joseph's.'

'He doesn't get many coming to see him.'

'Does he not now? Can I see him?'

The last time Paddy had seen this man he had broken a stick over his head and ran, he didn't stop running till he arrived in Liverpool, and now he was back.

'Well, you'd better come in.'

Paddy wasn't sure what he'd do, he'd fantasised about beating this bastard many times.

She stood back to allow Paddy in. The hallway had the ubiquitous sacred heart of Jesus. Christ with an open heart surrounded by flames and wrapped in thorns. The image was meant to portray Christ's everlasting love for humanity.

It always reminded Paddy of the pain and suffering his representatives caused on earth.

'Are you ok?'

Without realising it, Paddy had been staring at the image while the woman waited for him.

'I'm sorry.'

'If you would follow me.'

The house had the antiseptic smell of a hospital, the carpets and furniture were clean and polished but old and threadbare. It was a priest's house, larger than most homes, but without the evidence of a life lived and loved, photographs and pictures, mementoes, medals and souvenirs. Instead, every wall held a painting, crucifix or devotion.

'Father, you've a visitor,' the woman turned to Paddy. 'He doesn't speak much these days, not since his stroke, but he can hear and understand you. Would you like tea?'

'That would be lovely.'

When she left the room, Paddy stood in front of his old tormentor. What he found was a pathetic shell hanging on to existence by a thread. He looked for signs of recognition, but the eyes were glassy and unfocused.

Paddy leaned down and put his face close to the older man's. 'Look at me,' he kept his voice low and quiet. 'Do you remember? I was eight or nine, Patrick Connolly... are you there?'

There was a dark twinkle in the priest's eye.

Paddy snorted, 'You old bastard you're already in prison, aren't you? Locked up in that useless body. I came here to punish you, but it looks like someone beat me to it. '"Vengeance is mine, saith the Lord," isn't that what you say?'

The old man spluttered and a line of drool escaped from the corner of his mouth.

'Well you old bastard, you think things are bad now? You wait till you die and have to pay for your sins.'

The spluttering continued, the drooling increased, his head

shook; a sound was struggling to get out.

'You will burn, and we will be watching.'

The old lady arrived with a tray. Father Pearson was gagging, choking, as he struggled to expel the phlegm from his throat.

'Oh, dear, Father... Father?' She put the tray down and looked to Paddy. 'What happened?'

'Memories, eh? What can you do?' Paddy left the room and walked down the corridor enjoying the choking sounds behind him. He didn't know if it was sunnier outside or simply that he could see it now. A weight had been lifted.

Back on the road, he left the town and as the bike ate away at the distance between Paddy and his future, he knew there was a way he could fix things; Maude and Vinny were the keys.

A van was behind him, going fast, catching, he checked his clock, 60. He braked for a curve, moved back up 57...58... He was still coming. Okay, go on then pass.

Paddy relaxed his wrist 57...56... down to 52...45. The van pulled up alongside but didn't pass. Go on then fucker...

He looked left. The window was down- Declan. Beyond Declan, Barlow was driving. Paddy wasn't surprised; how else would Barlow have known about the border? He raised his left hand. He put two fingers up as Declan raised the gun.

There was an explosion of light and sound. Paddy shouted.

The words were still leaving his mouth as his head spread across the road.

Chapter Thirty-Three

Vinny

Wicklow, 2010

They lowered Maude into the passenger seat, and Anne sat in the back. Vinny loaded her wheelchair into the boot.

'Are you sure you're up for this?' Vinny asked.

'Wild horses couldn't keep me away,' Maude replied.

'Well, at least I know the way now. If you need to stop, just let me know.' Vinny was ready to go.

'I will love, don't you worry.'

'I have a flask here if you want some tea,' Anne said.

'Oh no, that'll have me stopping every ten minutes. Have you got my lily?'

'Your lily? No, did you ask me?'

'Of course I did. Go see Karla. She knows the one.'

Anne climbed out and went back inside the nursing home. Karla was near the entrance. 'She wants her lily.'

'Here, this is the one.'

Anne picked up the now-familiar flower. It was in full bloom, a white petal shrouded the orange stamen at the head of an upright green stem.

'I'll hold it with me,' said Anne as she climbed back in the car.

'No, best give it here. I'll look after it.'

Vinny turned. 'I wouldn't have taken my dad to be a flower man.'

'He wasn't,' said Maude.

Vinny looked at Anne in the rear-view mirror and shrugged. 'Okay, Tipperary, here we come.'

Once they reached Tipperary, Maude gave directions to the cemetery. The family were already there. There were quite a few people around, the sisters Ciara and Maeve, their husbands and children, including Sean who Vinny had already met, and of course, Marty. The scene was one of activity and organisation. The grave was cleaned and the grass had been cut.

Vinny pushed Maude along the path towards the grave. The sisters were fussing over children, getting everyone together now that Vinny had arrived.

Anne carried Maude's lily.

They formed a semi-circle around the grave and the silence grew as they realised everyone was quiet. Vinny whispered to Anne, 'I hope I don't have to make a speech.'

Maude, undaunted by the audience, clapped and was effective in commanding attention. 'Anne, can you put Paddy's flower down for me?'

'Of course.' Anne stepped forward and placed the pot on the ground.'

'No, not like that silly, cut the stem.'

Marty stepped forward and pulled a penknife out of his pocket, cut the stem, and laid it down. Anne retrieved the pot.

Maude's voice was clear. It wasn't as firm as years past, but they all paid attention. 'This is the last time I'll come. The flower is alive now. It is the unity of male and female, just like me and Paddy. It will die in the next few days, but I won't be here to see it. It is alive now, and now I am sharing it with you, Paddy's family. It and I will die, just like Paddy. Your job is to keep us alive. We don't want your prayers. We want all of you to live your best life, full and well. It's what we would have done if Paddy had lived. It's what you should do.'

There was stunned silence for a minute. Then Anne clapped,

the clapping grew, and people relaxed as the circle broke. Voices opened up and Marty invited everyone back to his place. Maude was the central attraction, thanking and lapping up the attention like an old queen.

Among the cakes and crisps, the beers and wine, Marty approached Vinny. 'I know your dad will be happy now. He has all his family with him. I think that's all he ever wanted.' He laughed. 'So, she's the one who was leaving lilies for years.'

Maude was surrounded, Paddy's sisters and Anne were chatting.

'She's pretty amazing,' said Vinny.

'So was your dad,' said Marty.

'Yeah, he was no one's idea of a hero,' said Vinny.

'Heroes are for stories. This is real. Did you find out how he died?'

'I don't think we'll ever know exactly, but to be honest, I think it's more important I found out how he lived.'

'You'll be alright.' Marty slapped him on the back.

* * *

Ciara, a round-faced woman with gentle eyes, came up to Vinny. She and her sister had hugged him, to his embarrassment when they got back to Marty's.

'Come outside.' She led the way.

Marty called everyone out. The whole group congregated in the front garden and along the path.

There was a roar as Sean drove into the road on Paddy's motorbike. He skidded around the street to whoops and claps.

Ciara slipped her hand into Vinny's. He leaned down to hear her.

'Go home and look after your son, be part of our future, not just our past.'

Vinny looked across to Anne. She was chatting away to Maude. Love and loss; how closely they followed each other.

The End

Acknowledgements

I would like to thank Maria Hunter, Paddy Osbourne, Karen O'Reilly, Carol Power, Leila Kirkconnell, and Martin Nutty for reading early drafts and pulling me up where I got things wrong. If there are still mistakes it's down to me, the guys at Northodox have worked really hard getting the various proofs checked and rechecked, and providing a fantastic cover. Clare Coombes agent and editor did a great job forcing some shape into the jelly of the first draft.

A planned third book has a working title of The Morning After, key events take place the day after the Brexit referendum of 2016. The three books together will cover 100 years of Irish and UK history. The story and it's characters, much like people in real life, flow between and over borders. As the Irish sea ebbs and flows between the land masses of Ireland and Britain so do lives and deaths. The very terms Anglo Irish, Irish, Irish in Britain, British in Ireland, Northern Irish, all speak to our common heritage of struggle and presence on these islands.

Whatever side we take in issues, the fact that we take sides puts us all in the same boat. My immediate family has lived and died in the South, the North, and England. The sooner we recognise the common interests we have the better. Peace was and is not brought by those who shout the loudest but by those who speak the quiet uncomfortable truths and accept responsibility for crimes on all sides.

Jack Byrne

Justice for the Forgotten was formed in 1996 with the aim of campaigning for truth and justice for the victims of the Dublin and Monaghan bombings of the 17th May 1974

http://www.dublinmonaghanbombings.org/home/

Keep reading for an exclusive extract of Book Three - Before the Storm.

JACK BYRNE

BEFORE THE STORM

STORM

BOOK THREE IN THE LIVERPOOL MYSTERIES SERIES

Chapter One

DI Cooper

12.10am, Friday, June 24th, 2016

Swirling, flashing, blue and red lights lit up the empty streets as the ambulance raced. No siren blared, but lights screamed through the darkness, waking neighbours in quiet dread as the engine roared through to the end of the estate, the end of the street and the end of a life.

'Junkie Sir. But you said to let you know.'

'For Christ's sake, I had to get out of bed. For him? What did the paramedics say?'

'Not much, but syringes in the living room, marks in his arm and his heart had stopped. Body cold, grey skin, blue lips, if Dulux did junkie it'd be this colour.'

DI Cooper shivered. 'Cold is right,' he walked through the disorder, chaos was normal for an overdose.

He came down the carpeted stairs and gave his instructions. 'Tape up the door to keep the rats out. There's plenty of crime here, but not the overdose. The coroner will write it up as accidental. The paramedics can take it to the Royal join the queue for the pathologist.'

'Can you sign off on it?'

He scribbled his signature on the waiting paperwork, then

walked toward the front door, but something about the quiet, empty house made him stop.

'Who called us?'

'Paramedics, dead on arrival.'

'Who called them?'

'Don't know, Sir.'

Lights enlivened the chill night air as the ambulance filled the road outside. There would be an audience for the removal, neighbours in dressing gowns and behind curtains watched the living drama. *Better than the TV*, he thought. He pulled away in his unmarked service car, heading away from the estate. A warm bed in his clean, organised flat awaited. He left death behind.

Chapter Two

Helen

9.15am, Friday, June 24th, 2016

Helen dropped Charlie at school, late again. On the drive home, her phone buzzed, she took her eyes off the road to swipe the screen.

Stay away

She dropped the phone on the passenger seat. The second message from Macca this week.

In her peripheral vision, a black car veered toward her out of a T-junction. 'What are you doing? No!'

She swung her wheel to the left, to avoid it. Her front wheel hit the kerb and bounced up. The steering wheel wrenched out of her hand as the car smashed into a lamppost with a deafening crunch. Thrown sharply sideways, her head struck the window. A flash went off behind her eyes, in front of her still silence. The shattered windscreen splintered the harsh, bright sunlight. Dust eddied and swirled. She gagged, petrol fumes stinging her throat and nostrils. The black car disappeared down the road. 'Bastard!' A thick ribbon of blood ran down the side of her face. She tried to raise her arm, but the movement sent stabs of pain across her chest. Unable to move, the last thing she heard came from within the car. The phone buzzed and the screen lit up.

Stay away

Chapter Three

Vinny

10.30am, Friday, June 24th, 2016

Vinny glanced at his watch. Time was running out. He had student papers to mark, but the all-consuming news distracted him. Britain would leave the European Union. Leave voters had won the referendum. The Guardian's front page declared, "Britain sets course for Brexit." Anger rose in his gut. He should have voted, but it was too late now. Like so many things, the realisation came too late.

The slightly open sash window brought a warm breeze into his study, disturbing the undergraduate essays on his desk.

At 9.30 am, his phone lit up. He tried to ignore the vibration, but his eyes wandered over the flashing screen. Unknown caller. Telecom, or Power companies, selling shit he didn't want. He turned his attention back to an essay on historiography. If he had to read one more cliché about history being written by the winners, he would go crazy. Two minutes in, and it was a refreshing change. He returned to the front page. Aliz Novak. Well done, Aliz. A Polish name. He wondered if she was first or second generation. He also wondered how long it would be or even if she would ever feel British. How would the vote affect her? Would the victors of this referendum write their history?

His mobile buzzed again. Merseyside Police. Vinny put the

essay down and transferred his attention to the incoming call. He swiped to answer and leaned back in his chair. He picked up another paper.

'Hello,' his eyes took in the title of a new essay *Climate Change - A crisis in Time.* He smiled at the ambition of the essay. 'Mr. Vincent Connolly?'

The authority of the voice set his nerves on edge.

'Yes, speaking...' Something was wrong.

'I'm sorry to disturb you, Mr. Connolly...' He rested the paper on the desk. 'There's been an accident.' Vinny's thoughts went to Charlie.

Shit, Shit, Shit. No, don't be sorry. Sorry is bad. No. It had to be serious. Something about the speaker's slow, careful delivery unnerved Vinny.

'This is Sergeant Collins from Merseyside Police.'

The surrounding air grew cold.

'Okay, what is it?' His words came rushing, tripping over each other to get out of his mouth. 'What? What's happened? Is it Charlie, Helen, both of them?'

'There was a traffic incident...'

The pace of the voice killed him. 'Just tell me,' he interrupted.

'Your wife is in the Liverpool Royal Infirmary, Mr. Connolly.'

He breathed out, 'And Charlie? My son, Charlie?'

His phone buzzed with an incoming call. He ignored it, waiting for his answer. 'Are you still there? What happened to my son?'

'I'm sorry, Mr Connolly...' Vinny's legs weakened. He felt sick.

'...I have no information on anyone else in the vehicle. As far as I know, your wife was alone.'

'Oh fuck. Okay, Okay...' *That's good, isn't it?* He checked the time. Charlie should be in school by now.

'You will need to arrange for the recovery of the vehicle.' *Sod the car.* Vinny rang off. He needed to get to the hospital.

The screen flashed, and the buzzing started again. Work. He swiped to reject it.

He rushed down the hallway and grabbed his jacket from the coat hanger. His phone buzzed again.

'Mr. Connolly, I think the call cut out. This is Merseyside Police.'

'Yes, I'm sorry. Okay, I got the message. The Royal.'

'I have to inform you that we will recover the vehicle as it is currently blocking a roadway.'

'Yeah, sure, okay. Do whatever you have to. Can you just let me know where you take it? Look, I'm sorry, I have to get to the hospital.'

'Central vehicle compound will contact you when they receive the car, and you can make arrangements with them for its recovery.'

'Okay. Thanks for letting me know.' He rang off.

Vinny stepped into the street, his eyes scanning the tidy row of Victorian semis in Ensworth Road, just round the corner from the busy Liverpool suburb of Allerton Road. They were ten minutes' drive from the Speke Estate, where he grew up, but a world away in atmosphere and lifestyle. The morning sun was intense, but a freshness hung in the air, under a blue sky. Not a day for accidents or anxiety. What did he mean? Brexit day was one big accident. He turned the ignition and drove out onto the main the road.

Vinny pulled into the car park of the Liverpool Royal Infirmary. Making his way through the multi-storey lot, he ended up on Prescot Street. The Royal was grey and dirty, a concrete block similar to the worst of sixties housing schemes. He walked through to the main reception desk. He passed a collection of bandaged, wheelchair-bound patients accompanied by family members — all of them a reminder of human frailty. At least Charlie remained safe.

He approached the reception. 'Helen Connolly... Dwyer, the paramedics brought her in this morning after a car accident.' He didn't know what name she would've used for the police or paramedics.

The receptionist ignored his lack of courtesy. 'How long ago?' Her fingers, practiced at protecting her painted nails, expertly floated above and tapped the keys.

'I'm not sure. An hour? Forty minutes?'

'She's probably not in the system yet. You'd best go down to A&E. I'm sure they'll be able to help you.'

'Shit. Okay, where do I go?'

'The easiest way is to go back outside, turn right, and follow the building round. You will see it.' She pointed out the main door, using her fingers and nails to full effect.

He followed her directions and left the building. He hurried round to the right, pulse racing. In front of him, the traffic edged its way into the town centre. They were close enough to the river for stray scavenging gulls to be circling overhead. He didn't know what to expect? Blood, stitches, broken bones?

Vinny turned the corner and saw the Accident and Emergency. More functional and less imposing than the main entrance, the business end of the operation. Diagonal yellow lines marked the front of the hospital for ambulance arrivals. The sliding double doors lead to a short corridor that opened into a wide waiting room. An ambulance pulled up, lights flashing, but no siren. The sight took him back. Sammo and Jaime in Garston as kids. He walked straight on and through a set of swing doors into the medical area. He knew behind those doors people were suffering, maybe even dying. A room full of the bruised and broken, of all ages and colours, representing Liverpool in all its desperation. He walked past two trolleys, one holding the figure of an elderly man, his dignity absent as he lay back half-dressed on pillows, breathing heavily through an oxygen mask, his thin, grey-haired chest rising and falling with the rasping breaths. Vinny caught his eye; he could see no emotion but blank endurance. Fuck this.

He kept his eyes on the reception window in front of him,

refusing to notice details of the person inhabiting the second trolley, except it was someone younger. An anxious mother stroked the smaller shape under the blanket.

'Helen Dwyer. Car crash, about an hour ago?' he asked.

The admin behind this desk was older and more harried. Nurses and orderlies were coming and going, leaving or collecting files and checking or writing on a large whiteboard behind her.

She swivelled effortlessly in her seat. 'Cubicle five, beyond the double doors.'

He nodded in thanks. She acknowledged him and picked up the phone.

Vinny prepared himself and went through the swinging doors. He didn't want to see blood and guts or hear cries of pain. He didn't. Instead, he saw the hustle of the reception repeated. Nurses and orderlies crisscrossed the area in a scene of controlled efficiency. The disinfectant smell of all medical facilities hit him. Voices rose and fell in urgency and volume, but never panicked.

A blue-uniformed woman stopped his progress. 'Yes?'

'Cubicle five?'

She pivoted and pointed straight ahead to the left. He walked on, each curtained area contained a casualty. He avoided the gaps between the curtains. Instead, his eyes focused on his destination, third up on the left. He looked through the curtains of number five. Helen lay immobile. Not a good sign. A shockingly white bandage threaded round her head, trapping her dark bedraggled hair and forming clumps. Her eyes were closed and puffy, her breathing regular. She looked peaceful. No blood, no scars, but a large, bluish purple patch ran down the side of her face. Vinny's pulse slowed, and he exhaled heavily. Her arm in a sling. He could see the fingers of her left hand poking out at the end.

He swished the curtain open and then closed it behind him.

He approached Helen, reaching out to touch her shoulder.

'Helen, Helen.'

Her eyes remained closed. He leaned in, his head next to hers, touching cheeks. He pulled back and stroked her shoulder.

'Excuse me.' The words and the swish of the curtain behind him were simultaneous.

He moved around and sat on the edge of the bed. 'I'm her husband.'

'Ok,' the nurse looked at the clipboard on the end of the bed. 'Mr Dwyer, your wife needs rest.'

'How is she? What's going on?'

'You'll have to speak to the doctor.'

'Ok, well, where is he?' Vinny looked around.

'She is with a patient. If you wait, I'll let her know you're here.'

'Excuse me.' The curtain was pulled open again and a police officer put her head inside. 'Mrs. Dwyer?'

'Yes.' Vinny answered.

'It's about the traffic incident. Can we have a word?'

Vinny moved to stand beside Helen. The officer opened the curtain fully, revealing her uniformed colleague. They stepped forward, and the nurse moved out of the way and let them through. Her colleague stood at the edge of the curtain with his helmet in his hands, fidgeting.

'I'm PC James, and this is PC Cartwright. We're here to get a few details regarding what happened this morning.'

'Well, as you can see, my wife is in no condition.'

'Can you take this outside, please?' asked the nurse.

'Of course.' Vinny moved out into the ward.

'Outside please.' The nurse pointed to the double doors.

'After you.' The officer waved Vinny ahead. Beyond the swing doors, PC James spoke first. 'Can I just check the basics: make of car and registration? And just to confirm the driver?'

'Do we have to do this now?' asked Vinny

'It's just to confirm the basics.'

'I haven't even seen the doctor yet.'

'I'm sorry, sir, but we need to establish what happened.'

'Ok, so what happened?' asked Vinny.

'Excuse me?'

'You're the police. You tell me, what happened?'

'Sir.'

'Sir nothing, have you been to the scene?'

The officer stepped forward. 'We're not here to answer your questions. Now—'

'Suzuki Swift, registration KLM 342,' Vinny finished.

'And the car's registered to Ms Dwyer, your wife. Can you confirm she was the driver?'

'Yes.'

'I'm sorry, but we have to ask. Had your wife been drinking?'

'Really?' Vinny asked. 'You know she's a registered social worker?'

'I'm sorry. It's a formality. We have to check with anyone involved in a road traffic incident.'

'No, she hadn't been drinking. She was on the school run, on her way back since my son wasn't in the car. Thank God. What happened to the other car? How badly is it damaged?'

'What other car?'

'It was an accident. Who was driving the other car?'

'No other car involved, Mr Dwyer.'

'The name is Connolly,' Vinny said.

'The car's registered to Ms Dwyer.'

'That's her maiden name. So what happened?'

'That's what we are trying to establish Mr.' the officer paused. 'Connolly.'

'Your wife's vehicle left the road and hit a lamppost.'

'Why did her car leave the road?'

'We aren't sure yet.'

'So, no one else was involved?'

'As far as we can tell at the moment.'

'Where did it happen?'

'Menlove Avenue, just past the junction with Springfield Road.'

'She would have been coming back from the school.' Vinny rubbed his hands over face.

'Jesus. What the hell's going on?'

'Can you think of any reason someone might want to harm your wife?'

'No, of course, not. Why would you ask that?'

The officer didn't answer. For the first time, Vinny got the feeling something was going on.

'Okay. I see. Is there anything else you want to add? Anything that could have contributed to the accident?' the officer asked.

'No, of course not.' Vinny shook his head.

'Have you spoken to anyone else? Were there any witnesses?' Vinny asked.

'If you need anything else, my name is on there.' The officer smiled for the first time since her arrival. 'I hope your wife recovers soon. Be grateful she'd already dropped your son at school. How old is he?'

'Fourteen,' Vinny said.

'Okay, well, all the best.' She turned and followed by her colleague, walked out through the main doors.

Vinny stood and watched the police leave. He waited until they were through the double doors.

The nurse in the blue uniform appeared in front of him again, carrying a large manila envelope containing Helen's personal effects from the paramedic.

'The doctor will be with your wife in about five minutes.'

She handed him the envelope.

'Thanks.'

Vinny made his way through the waiting room; the older man hadn't moved from the trolley. The harried receptionist made a flicker of eye contact, and then he was back on the street.

The noise of the street contrasted with the quiet inside the hospital. Vinny could see the growing structure of the new Liverpool Royal Hospital being built up the road. There were rumours of cracks in the infrastructure, but public money was still being poured into it. He remembered the quote from Marx: 'All that is solid melts into air.' How did it end? Something about man being compelled to face his real condition?

Cars and buses negotiated the busy road into the city centre. Liverpool bustled with activity. Instead of making his call, he opened the envelope containing Helen's handbag and contents, nothing important: phone, some makeup, lipsticks, and a compact, tissues. He looked for keys but couldn't find any. He turned on the phone after swiping in Helen's symbol, and it went straight to its last position, showing an open text.

Call me

He swiped to see who sent it. Steve McNally. What? Vinny stared at the screen. He let his hand drop, but didn't know what to do or think. Why is Helen getting texts from Steve McNally? First, the headcase Sammo shows up, then the crash and now Macca. A seagull swooped and stabbed at a piece of mouldy burger bun near his feet. What the fuck.

Chapter Four

Macca

10.30pm, Thursday, 2nd July, 1981

The time was right. Macca knew if you wanted something, you had to take it. He stepped over the low wooden gate, careful not to rattle the latch. He marched up the path and darted into the entry. Quick and quiet. The light was fading. Looking down the end of the street, he could see the sun disappearing beyond the houses into the river.

The streetlights were on, the orange glow fighting the remains of the day. Kids had been called in, football and skipping were over, the street fell quiet. TVs blared behind curtains up and down the road. Hale was better than Speke because they had more, much more, cash, even jewellery, but the walk to it from the estate was dangerous. The bizzies knew kids from Speke going to Hale at night were not out visiting friends or family. This should be easy. Macca relaxed in the entry, safe in the knowledge he remained unseen from the street. The entry ran between the two houses, giving access to the back gardens. At the end, there were two gates at forty-five degrees to each other. He moved down the entry cautiously; he knew there were no dogs next door.

Sammo was somewhere in the street and would give a whistle if anything looked out of order, so there was no rush. This was about patience and nerves.

Before the Storm

Old man Doyle turned out the light in the living room and made his way upstairs. Macca watched as the light from the living room went out. He moved down the entry to the back gates. The old man would be in the bathroom above. Macca looked up and saw the light through the window. He should wait until this light went out, too, but fuck it, he liked the danger. He grabbed the top of the gate, which wouldn't budge. Locked. He pulled himself up smoothly and eased on top of it. He was just feet away from the bathroom window. The light went out. Macca dropped silently to the ground.

The back door was half glazed, four square panes above waist height. He tried the door, but it was locked. The bottom left window in the door had a crack. Macca's lucky night. He pulled a pair of socks out of his pocket and slipped them over his hands. A precaution learned watching Kojak and Columbo, as police in Speke didn't bother fingerprinting for burglary. He pressed against the crack with his elbow pushing firmly, then relaxing, pushing, then relaxing. Each time the glass moved, it separated from the putty holding it in place. Another push, harder this time, and a new crack appeared. Now he could push and pull a triangle-shaped piece to loosen it, until he could lift it out of the frame, and discard it on the grass. Macca guessed the old man would be in bed by now. Rolling up his sleeve, he slid a hand, then an arm, through the gap in the glass. The key sat in the lock halfway down the door. Macca turned it and let himself in. His eyes had adjusted to the darkness. The kitchen was tidy; a single cup and plate were on the drainer next to the sink, a knife and fork in a glass next to them. The air was still. A dog barked in the distance, sounding an alarm for better-defended homes.

The kitchen table was against the wall. Macca reached for a shelf above it. He picked up the first of three tins, turned the lid, and his fingers went inside. Sugar. He emptied it out onto the floor. The second tin held tea bags. Maybe he would be lucky with the third. Biscuits. He took a bite of one and let the others fall. He picked up a tea towel from the drainer.

Mr. Doyle coughed and turned over. The bed creaked as he tossed and turned, seeking comfort. Macca opened the living room door. He knew these houses well. They were all the same, and he had been in this house with Helen. A cupboard occupied the space under the stairs in the hallway. Everyone had a utilities cupboard, and everyone had a lecky and gas meter. Shillings fed the meter until the money changed. Now they were ten pence pieces.

He crossed the room quickly when he heard the cough from above. He wasn't worried. If the old man came down, he could be out the door in seconds. Small padlocks fixed the coin collection tin under the meter. Macca pulled out his screwdriver and wedged it through the gap. A strong twist and the loop of metal holding the padlock bent. The padlock would hold, the collection tin was weaker. One arm of the loop snapped off with barely a sound. Macca slid the padlock off, laid the tea towel down on the ground and eased the collection tin from its place. The coins slid out with tinkles, a sound Macca loved. He repeated the exercise with the gas meter. Holding the corners of the tea towel, he enjoyed the weight of coins. He was happy. Everything was still and quiet, nothing stirred. He put the tea towel down, stood in the living room, and spun, smiling, with his arms outstretched. He bent down, picked up the tea towel, and tied the corners together, closing it tightly. The kitchen door was open, and he could see straight out to the back garden. His way out was clear, but he didn't take it.

Chapter Five

Vinny

11am, Friday, 24th June, 2016

Vinny made his way back through the hospital. Why would Helen be talking to Macca? The last time he had seen Steve McNally was years ago. Before his trip to Ireland with Anne. His recent visit from Sammo was out of the blue, and now this with Macca. He swished the curtain aside, entered the cubicle. Helen was awake, and the doctor was leaning over her, pressing her stomach. 'Hey.' Helen's smile turned into a grimace.

'How are you?' he asked.

'I've been better.'

The doctor turned toward Vinny.

'My husband,' said Helen.

'Your wife has had a serious accident. The x-ray results show fractured ribs and significant bruising.'

Vinny didn't know what to say. 'Ok.'

'We'll be keeping her in for a few days. An accident of this kind can cause trauma to the internal organs. We want to make sure there are no complications.' 'Of course,' Vinny said.

The nurse from earlier entered the cubicle. 'We'll get you onto a ward as soon as we can.' The doctor nodded to the nurse and turned. 'I'll call by and check you again when you're settled.'

'Thank you,' said Helen.

Before the Storm

Vinny handed Helen the envelope. 'Your stuff from the ambulance.' He waited for a few seconds. 'Is something going on?' He sounded harsher than he meant. Helen opened the envelope with one hand and began awkwardly searching through it. Vinny reached over and held the envelope open. He held up the phone. 'Are you looking for this?' She leant back. 'Yeah.'

'Anything you want to tell me about?'

'Yeah, just give me a chance. And can you stop being so dramatic?' Helen ran her hand through her hair as much as she could and then began pulling out strands that were trapped by the bandage.

Vinny thrust her phone forward with the message "Call me" displayed. 'From Steve McNally. Really?'

Helen tried to move forward and groaned in pain. 'What are you doing looking at my messages?'

'What's going on?' Vinny was poised between jealousy and anger. How could she do this? Secret messages with Macca?

Vinny swiped to the message again.

'Why are you getting texts from Macca?'

'Oh.' Helen closed her eyes.

'Come on. Macca, really?' There was an edge in Vinny's voice.

'It's not about him. It's not what you think.'

'Stay away, the one before says? Have you been seeing Macca?' he asked, but he didn't believe it. Not with their history.

'No. It's about Sammo.'

'What the hell has this got to do with Sammo?'

'He's been having a rough time. I bumped into his sister in town. We had a chat. She was desperate to help him. Thought you might help, too. She put me in touch with his daughter.'

'Help? How could I help? And why didn't you tell me? Keeping secrets, really?'

Vinny paced up and down in the small space beside her bed. He could've told Helen about his visit from Sammo, but he was still angry with her.

'Will you calm down? I was going to tell you, before all this.' Helen spread her hands to show everything around them.

'Jesus Christ. Sammo, Macca, what is this..? Scallies reunion class of '81?'

'That's why I didn't tell you… because of the way you are. You never talk about them, and when you do, it's nasty. You wouldn't think they were your friends. Stop pacing around. You're making me nervous.'

'Yeah. We were friends, past tense.' Angered, Vinny knew whatever it was, it wouldn't end well. His gut churned at the thought of what might come out. 'So, what's going on? You went to see Macca?' He stopped pacing and sat down. 'Okay, look, I'm calm.'

'I didn't see Macca. Like I said, I went to see Sammo. He's in Speke on Dymchurch.'

'Yeah, I know where he is. He's been in the same house since he was a kid.'

'Well, after I met his sister, I thought I would go round. He's been trying to sort himself out. Desperate.'

'I know.'

'How do you know?' she asked.

He waved his hand at her. 'It doesn't matter now. So, when did this start? And what the hell is the text about? Is that a threat? Why didn't you tell me?'

'All right, give me a chance,' Helen said. 'Look at when Macca was on the telly… how you reacted. Do you remember?'

'Yeah, I do. He's an arsehole, a bully. He's always been the same.'

'And you wonder why I said nothing?' Helen's eyes widened.

'I just can't believe you've been doing all this behind my back.' said Vinny.

Helen sighed and shifted position. 'You're a great one to talk about secrets. What was all that about your dad? Gallivanting round Ireland with Anne. So stop it, will you? Stop feeling sorry for yourself. I didn't tell you because you can be an arsehole, too.

Maybe that's the problem. You're more like Macca than you realise.'

'That's not fair.'

'What's fairness got to do with it? Let's be honest. You haven't been listening to me… us… for a while. Your meetings and your students always come first.'

'It's called work.'

'Yeah, and I wouldn't know what that is, would I?'

The nurse appeared again. 'Hi, is everything okay here?'

'Yeah,' Helen replied and with a roll of her eyes. 'Panicking husband.'

'Oh, don't tell me.' The nurse winked at Helen. 'And women are supposed to be the ones who go to pieces.' She smiled and turned to Vinny. 'Your wife is fine, but it was a car crash. She needs to rest and recover her strength.'

Vinny held his hands up in mock surrender. 'All right. All right. I get it.'

'We're sorting out a bed for you now. You should let your wife rest.'

'Yes, sure.'

Vinny waited until the nurse left. 'So… what happened?' He had a bad feeling about this.

'Nothing. I saw him last week. He got himself a little dog. Then the Social sanctioned him, which messed him right up. He kinda got paranoid. Everyone against him, that kind of thing.'

'And Macca?' Vinny asked.

'They fell out, him and Sammo.'

'Have you been seeing him?'

'No… I met him once. Macca said Sammo had lost it: his family situation, the drugs, PTSD,'

Vinny was quiet for a minute and then, in a calmer voice, asked, 'Why? Why did you put yourself back there, in the middle of all that?' Vinny had spent half his life getting away from it.

'All what?' Helen looked confused.

'That shit: Speke, Macca, Sammo.'

'Jesus, we grew up there, with them. What's wrong with you?'

Vinny couldn't hide his annoyance. 'With me? Really? You are asking what's wrong with me? I'm not having it,' he declared.

'Having what?'

'Him, them, interfering in our life.'

'They aren't,' she protested.

'Then what are we doing here? Car crash, texts, telling you to stay away. Talking about heroin and PTSD. That's their lives, not ours.' Vinny stood again. 'I'm going to see him… them… tell them to back off. Sammo. Then Macca. You're getting out of this. What the hell is wrong with you? You've got a fourteen-year-old son to look after.' He tried to sound definite, final. 'Whatever's going on has nothing to do with us. It's not our problem.'

'Let me get out of here. I'll call him, explain,' Helen said.

'No. I'll sort it out.' Vinny stood.

'Don't forget to pick Charlie up.'

Vinny instinctively checked his watch. 'Of course.'

'And you have to meet with Mrs Kane, the headteacher.'

'Oh shit, really?'

'Yes 3pm, don't be late. A chance to do some real parenting.'

'Oh, right, Thanks. 'Vinny moved toward the curtain.

'And can you bring my nightclothes, underwear, and buy a new wash bag with toothpaste, soap, and shampoo?'

'Jesus, alright. Anything else?'

'Yes. Don't do anything stupid,'

Helen's words followed him out of the cubicle and hospital.

Chapter Six

Vinny

12pm, Friday, 24th June, 2016

He drove to Speke. This needed sorting out. The first port of call would be Sammo. If necessary, he would find Macca. He wasn't looking forward to that part, but if it had to be done, he would do it. He edged his way through town, passing the neoclassical columns and portico of the once grand and now shabby Adelphi Hotel. Then the famous Lewis's department store, empty now. Stuck behind the 82c bus, he remembered the joke. 'How do you get a parrot to speak? Put it on the 82c.' There were two ways to Speke from town — through the Dingle or Toxteth. The bus took the Dingle route, and as a kid, he had done this many times. As a driver, he always chose Toxteth, then the bottom of Smithdown, down through Allerton past Penny Lane. Between the town centre and Smithdown Road, buildings were showing their age; peeling paint and untended entrances, but from Penny Lane on, it was nicer. He drove on past the parks, Calderstones, Woolton, Camp Hill, and through Hunt's Cross to the estate where he grew up.

For Vinny, it was a drive back in time. Speke was the last area of Liverpool before Cheshire; the edge of the city. He turned off the Boulevard. To his left was once the largest industrial estate in Europe. The golden years for the area were from the mid-sixties to the early seventies because there was work. Vinny's family moved from the terraces under the bridge in Garston to good family houses. He turned on the radio to drown out his thoughts and caught the end of the news. A vote in favour of leaving the EU was fifty-two to forty-eight per cent remain. A breathless reporter talked of crisis and tension. The big question was, what would Prime Minister David Cameron do?

* * *

Sammo's house was a modern redbrick at the end of the block, built in the late '70s. Flat and functional, with no architectural flourishes or individuality. A modern box that kept out wind and rain, along with any sense of style or taste. It had walls, a door, and three windows.

Dog ends and litter covered the path and a small patch of grass that was his front garden. This looks bad. A couple of youths loitered on the corner watching him, one on his mobile. A piece of wood replaced the central glass panel on the front door. Police tape hung from the bent door jamb, where the lock had shattered when forced. The guys, probably the ones that busted the door, were still watching him. He pushed it open further with growing anxiety. 'Sammo... Sam, are you here?' He pushed it open wider. A pile of brown letters lay unopened in the hallway. The door had swung to the left, and immediately on the right was the staircase.

'Sammo,' he called again up the carpeted stairs.

Nothing. A musty, damp smell came from the house.

It was quiet, strange. Vinny had been in the house as a kid. Nothing had changed. The dirty carpet was the same, the wallpaper, too. He walked along the hallway; he could see into the kitchen. 'Hello...' The smell grew stronger and stale, air gone bad.

No answer.

Everything was old and used, including the enamel on the gas cooker, stained yellow around the eye-level grill. Vinny hadn't seen one for years. Besides the back door, someone had pushed a pine table and benches up against the wall. The edging on the kitchen countertop had chipped and curled. A cupboard door hung askew with one hinge missing. He retreated from the kitchen and pushed open the living room door, revealing a sparse but liveable room. Sammo had been surviving. The three-piece suite was serviceable, and a small wooden coffee table was in front of it. It was depressing and made him appreciate the comfort of the home he had built with Helen.

'Hello?' The voice shocked him, and Vinny spun round. 'Who are you?' he asked.

'Detective Constable Peter Crowley.' The well-built man in his early thirties held out his warrant card. Then dug in his breast pocket and produced a business card. 'And you are?'

'Vincent Connolly.'

'What are you doing?' The tone was sharp.

'Looking for Sammo, Sam Maddows. The door was open. Broken.' He pointed.

'Are you a friend… family?'

'Neither, well, friend, maybe, from years ago,' Vinny said.

The officer paused before saying, 'You shouldn't be in here.'

'Why?' Vinny asked.

'I'm sorry, but we found Mr. Maddows last night. I'm afraid he's dead.'

'Dead… Jesus. How?'

'It looks like an overdose, but we will have to wait for the coroner's report, to be sure.'

Vinny leaned against the back of the sofa.

The police officer walked into the kitchen and back to the living room to rejoin Vinny. 'Looks like kids have been in. Must have seen the ambulance. Come in to see what they could find, probably after meters.'

'People don't have electricity meters anymore.'

'They do if they can't pay their bills. The lecky, sorry, the electricity company installs them, so they pay as they go, some cash, some payment cards. If they run out of money, no electricity. Anyway, there's nothing in here for them. I will get the house secured, get the council to tin it up, or they'll be setting fires, turning it into a crack house.'

'Lovely.'

The officer ignored Vinny's sarcasm. 'Are you from round here?'

'Used to be,' Vinny said. He was still processing the news of Sammo's death. 'You said overdose?'

'Yeah, that's what it looks like. He was in here, on the sofa.' The officer had led the way down the hall. He pushed open the living room door. 'No reason to think anything else.'

'Does that mean accidental?'

The officer shrugged. 'Probably. There's no note. His stuff was all over the coffee table.' He pointed.

The living room was dirty like the rest of the house, a threadbare settee and armchair filled the space, a coffee table strewn with debris, rizla papers, a broken cigarette, a scrunched up fag packet an overflowing ashtray two syringes lay at an angle pointing at each other, the dark residue of blood visible in one of them.

'Not suicide?' The syllables were difficult to produce for Vinny.

'Who knows? Sad, eh? Looks like the guy was ex-army, too. Shame.'

'Yeah, a shame.'

'Anyway, you shouldn't be in here.'

'Yeah, of course, it's just the door was open.'

The officer shook his head. 'Fucking kids.'

Vinny was heading for the front door when he stopped and turned. 'What happened to the dog?' he asked.

'What dog?'

'The last time my wife saw Sammo, she said he had a little dog.

There's a food bowl in the kitchen.' Vinny pointed down the hallway.

'Oh, right? I haven't heard about a dog, but I'll make a note of it. Thanks.'

'No problem,' Vinny replied, walking back through the open door.

He recognised the figure walking up the path. Older, greyer, but still a big man. The suit and tie didn't sit right on him. But he was a councillor now, a man who demanded respect. Not that Vinny would ever respect him. He knew far too much about Macca.

'Well, if it isn't Vinny. Vincent Connolly, long time no see.' Macca held his hand out.

Vinny ignored it. 'You sent Helen a text?'

'I was worried about her. Sammo has been so unstable recently — sadly, as we can see.'

'How did you know I would be here?'

'I didn't. Pure coincidence,' Macca said.

Vinny glanced sideways, unconvinced. The guys on the corner were still watching. He was lying.

'But I'm happy to see you, just sorry about the circumstances. What brings you here?'

If Vinny had spider senses, they would be tingling. Macca came to see what I was doing. Is he worried, hiding something?

'I came to see Sammo,' Vinny said.

'After so many years?'

Yeah, he is definitely worried.

They stopped, facing each other.

'Who's in the car?' Vinny asked.

DC Crowley had come out and interrupted the conversation. 'And you are?' he asked Macca

'McNally, Steve McNally, local Councillor.'

'What can I do for you?' the officer inquired.

'Oh,' Macca stumbled for a second. 'I'm an old friend, only found out this morning, and well, I thought maybe he had something of mine. I was just going to check.'

'No, I'm afraid I can't let you into the house now. What were you looking for? I can ask the family.'

'Nothing really, nothing important. Just something of sentimental value.'

'Well, you came here to get it, so it must have some importance?'

'Yeah, it was… a book. A book I lent him. You know we served together.'

'An old friend dies, you hear about it, and come to get a book back?' Vinny could see the answer didn't convince the officer, either.

'I don't remember seeing any books inside, to be honest,' the officer replied.

'Yeah, never mind,' Macca said with a wave of the hand. DC Crowley stood his ground. Vinny moved to go past Macca towards his car, but Macca turned to follow him.

Vinny felt a hand on his shoulder and spun round. 'Get your hands off me!'

'Woah, what's this? Eh?' Macca stepped back, hands raised, palms forward. 'This isn't the Vinny I know.' Macca smiled.

Vinny knew he was being taunted. He walked towards his car.

Macca followed. 'Maybe that university made a man of you?'

'Piss off,' Vinny opened his car door. Over Macca's shoulder, he saw DC Crowley go back into the house.

'Nice as it is to see you. Let's just say you are better off staying in Allerton.' Macca reached out and held the car door.

'I'll go where I want,' Vinny said.

'I was here to tell Sammo, and you, to stay away from Helen.'

'It's not me you should be telling. She's the one who's been sniffing round. Maybe you should have a word with your missus.'

Vinny wanted to get away now. The whole discussion was pointless. 'Stay away from us. We want nothing to do with you.' Vinny pulled the door away from Macca's grip and got in the car.

'Yeah, go on, back to Allerton. You don't belong here. This is ours.' As Macca spoke, his hand swept forward and flicked Vinny on the side of his head. Not a punch, or even a slap, but a flick. It made Vinny feel thirteen again.

Macca walked over to a waiting black BMW.

Vinny closed the door and turned on the ignition, flushed with embarrassment and shame.

Bastard, how did he do that?

Chapter Seven

Vinny

8.45am, Friday, 3rd July, 1981

Alderwood Avenue, Speke, Liverpool

Macca built the tension like a magician. He drew the chain out of his pocket, teasing his audience. Golden links appeared one by one.

'C'mon, what is it?' Vinny asked. 'A necklace?' He never really trusted Macca. He had latched onto him when he arrived at All Hallows Secondary Modern a month earlier. They lived close to each other, and Macca was hard.

'No.' Macca was grinning, his eyes bright with pride.

The chain was six… seven… eight inches long, and it kept coming.

'Fuckin'ell, we'll be rich,' Vinny said.

It was nearly twelve inches long. They were thick links, too, not the tiny ones you'd see on a girl's necklace. Finally, a golden watch, shiny and smooth.

'Wow. It must be worth hundreds, thousands,' Vinny said to please Macca. Vinny always tried to stay on the right side of him. 'Can I hold it?'

'Yeah, but I'm not letting go of the chain.' Macca carefully placed the watch on Vinny's open palm. Vinny's hand lowered to accept the weight.

Before the Storm

They were huddled in a dank stairwell, opposite All Hallows Secondary Modern in Speke, a council estate on the edge of Liverpool. The maisonettes had a common doorway and entrance. In the grey drizzle on this Friday morning, it was the first point of escape. They met just before school. Macca and Vinny came from near Western Avenue, so they usually met on the way to school. Instead of turning left through the school gates, they turned right and were waiting in the entrance of the flats.

'That's amazing.' Vinny meant it. He had never seen or touched anything gold, not real gold like this. The whole thing was glistening. He could run his hands over it, feel the weight of it all day long. He moved his hand up and down, enjoying the sensation.

'Giz it back.' Macca didn't want to let it go.

'Does it open?' asked Vinny.

'Course it does. We should wait for Sammo, though.'

Sammo was Macca's sidekick. Vinny thought Sammo was sneaky. The bell from the school rang out across the road, its dull tones reverberating through the damp air.

'Why?' asked Vinny.

'He kept dixie for us. The bell's gone. Where is he?'

Vinny cracked the door. 'Here he is.'

Macca popped his head out, too, and they could see Sammo running across the road, head down against the morning rain. His school tie flew over his shoulder. The drizzle had soaked his uncombed hair, splaying it out in all directions.

'All right?' Sammo pulled the door open.

'Yeah. What happened to you?' asked Macca, his square face set in a frown.

'Mister Thomas saw me. I had to pretend I was going in.'

'He'll notice if he doesn't see you all day,' Vinny said.

'Nah, we don't have him today. He won't know. Beep said he would cover for me, if anyone asked.'

'Let's have a look at it then,' said Sammo.

Macca kept hold of the chain but allowed Sammo to hold the watch.

'Here, let me open it.' Macca slid his thumbnail into a groove that ran around the edge of the watch. He gently pried open the cover to reveal a curved glass face that covered a white background.

'What are those numbers?' Sammo pondered.

'They're Roman numerals,' said Vinny.

Two intricate black hands pointed out the time. Inside the cover of the watch, there was an inscription. '*Faugh A Ballagh*.'

'Is that Roman as well?'

'You mean, Latin? I don't know. It doesn't sound like it.'

'C'mon smart arse? You passed the Eleven Plus, didn't you? You went to a posh grammar school. I used to see you getting off the bus with your little briefcase.'

'Piss off.' Sammo was pointing out what Vinny always knew — he was different, and the embarrassment showed.

'Shut up, knobhead,' said Macca. 'At least he knows something. What was your school called?'

'Cardinal Allen,' Vinny answered.

'And who kept dixie for you? While you screwed the house. Eh... made sure no one was coming?' Sammo answered his question. 'Yeah, that's right, me.'

'Where's the dosh?' Vinny asked.

'I hid it. We can get it later,' said Macca.

'How much did you get?'

'Not sure. We didn't count it.' Macca replied.

'Anyway, that school was shit. They didn't want me, and I didn't want them,' Vinny said. This wasn't true, but it had become Vinny's way of rationalising his failure.

'Okay. Right, are you ready?' asked Macca.

'What for?' asked Sammo.

'We have to swear.'

'Fuck off... Bastard... Twat—' Sammo had a lot more, but Macca cut him short.

'Not like that. Like a promise.'

'An oath,' said Vinny. 'Like in court.'

'I swear to tell the truth, the whole truth, and nothing but the truth.' Sammo had placed his hand over where he thought his heart was.

'But not that,' Macca said. 'Vinny, you make up the words.'

'What for?' asked Vinny.

Macca uncovered the watch again and held it in his palm in front of the other two. 'We have our gold, our—'

'Treasure,' Vinny smiled. He knew Macca would like the adventure of it. Macca was always the hero in his own story.

'Yeah, treasure.' Macca said. 'And we have to swear to stick together.'

'Okay, let me think,' said Vinny.

'You robbed it,' said Sammo. 'I kept dixie. What did he do?'

'He's my mate,' said Macca. 'And he's going to make our oath.'

'And I'm going to find a buyer,' said Vinny. He wanted to fit in, be a proper part of the gang.

'Okay, what do we say?' asked Macca.

'Put your hand on the watch,' Vinny directed. Macca held the watch while Sammo and Vinny placed their hands on top. Then Macca sealed the clasp with his other hand. 'I swear I'll protect the treasure, and my mates, against all enemies and obstacles.'

With their hands on the watch, Macca and Sammo repeated Vinny's words in unison. 'I swear I'll protect the treasure, and my mates, against all enemies and obstacles.'

'All for one and one for all!' said Sammo. 'Like the three muscleteers.'

'Musketeers,' Vinny corrected.

'Who gives a fuck?' Sammo replied.

'And we split the money three ways,' added Vinny.

'That's not in the oath,' said Sammo.

'It is now,' said Macca. 'I'll split the money three ways. Your turn.'

'I'll split the money three ways,' said Sammo reluctantly.

A regular click echoed through the stairwell. 'What are you lads doing here? Sagging school?' A woman came down the stairs; the wheels of her shopping cart clicked as they bounced down each step.

Macca quickly put the watch back in his pocket.

'Nah, we're just on a message,' Sammo said. 'I've got to get some things for me, mam. My mates are helping me.'

'Well, you'd better get on with it then, or I'll be right over to that school. You shouldn't be hanging around this doorway. You don't live here.'

'All right, missus,' said Sammo.

'Don't give me any of your cheek. Go on, out.' Her wheels clicked as she came down the last few steps.

'We're going. Don't get your knickers in a twist,' added Sammo.

Vinny opened the door, and they stepped into the street, laughing.

Heads down and blazers pulled tight, they scurried through the rain along Alderwood Avenue, towards The Parade. The Parade was the centre of Speke. Built in the mid-60s, it was the main shopping and leisure area. Austin Rawlinson's swimming baths were just along from Speke Police Station, and both opposite the shopping area.

Macca dug around under the hedges. 'It was here.'

'I don't know. It was dark. Maybe it was further up?' Sammo suggested.

'No, it was definitely here. Come on, help me look. It's in a brown cloth.'

The three boys poked about at the bottom of the hedgerow.

'Bingo. Here!' Sammo pulled out a tea towel tied at the corners. The coins inside clinked together as he swung it around.

'What are you doing, dickhead? Give it here.' Macca grabbed

it and felt the weight of money between his fingers. 'I could only get the lecky meter. Then I thought I heard something, so I got out of there quick. On my way out, there was a sideboard. I pulled open the drawers, and there it was waiting for me.'

'Good find.' Vinny nodded.

'Come on, let's spend some of this.' Macca ran off, the other two in hot pursuit.

Even with their ties off, their blazers, white shirts, and black trousers gave them away as All Hallows students. So, the shopping centre was the worst place for three truants to hang out.

Vinny didn't like The Parade. In his thirteen-year-old mind, The Parade was outside his safety zone, a place for older and harder kids. It was okay today because of the money from the meters, the sweet shop was their destination. Usually, it was just a bit too far from his home near Western Avenue. Vinny existed in a state of semi-fear wherever he went on the estate, and since it was where he lived, fear was a constant.

For Macca, Speke was his playground. Full of confidence and without Vinny's fear, at thirteen, he swaggered about like he owned the streets. Sammo would have been a happy-go-lucky boy if he had anything to be happy about. As it was, he made the best of everything.

Chapter Eight

Macca

10am, Friday, 3rd July, 1981

Loaded up with Mars bars, Kit Kats, and crisps, they walked down Central Avenue, the three-storey family houses on the right and Speke Comprehensive on the left.

'Where are we going?' Sammo spluttered through a mouthful of crisps.

'My cousin's. He'll know a buyer for us. Maybe he'll make an offer.' Vinny tried to sound like he knew what he was doing.

'He would need a few quid to get the treasure,' Macca said.

After Speke Comp, they took a right onto Lovel Road. The red brick houses had front and back gardens. An entry ran between houses, allowing access to the rear. They displayed their status and privilege through well-kept privet hedges, verdant front gardens, and gates.

'Here we are.' Vinny stopped. The misshapen privet hedge fronted a three-metre square of patchy grass. 'We'll go round the back.' Vinny led the way between the houses. The dark entry led to gates at the end. Vinny almost jumped out of his skin as the entry filled and reverberated with angry dog barks.

'For fuck's sake.'

'Woah.' Sammo was at the back. 'What the hell has he got in there?'

Before the Storm

'You first,' Macca said, pushing Vinny forward.

'Thanks a lot.'

'He's your cousin.'

Sammo backed off. 'I think I'll wait out here, keep dixie.'

Vinny lifted the latch and pushed the gate open. The back garden was in no better state than the front. There was an old sofa and a fridge in the middle. The broken fridge door hung at an odd angle, and the guts of the sofa were scattered across the garden. There was also an Alsatian dog tied to the washing line post. It was straining at its lead, snarling and barking at Vinny, it's dribbling jaw a foot away as Vinny edged towards the back door with his body pressed against the wall. Macca followed him, both boys hoping the dog wouldn't snap its restraint.

Safely in the back kitchen, they stood nervously. The sparse room was dirty and smelled of grease. Vinny looked through to the living room. The curtains were closed, and the blue light of the TV flickered with pictures of a procession. Dust motes danced in the half-light. A voice rang out. 'Who's there?'

Vinny replied, 'Me… Paul? It's me, Vinny.'

'Come in, then. What are you doing lurking out there?'

Macca pushed Vinny forward again and followed close behind. Paul splayed out on the sofa and raised himself as they entered. 'Open the curtains,' he instructed over the sound of the television.

A news reporter was speaking into the camera. 'The funeral of the latest Hunger Striker has seen huge numbers of people pay their respects for this the ultimate sacrifice.'

'And turn that shit off.' Paul pointed at the TV. Vinny crossed the room and pressed the off button, then moved to the window and pulled the heavy material aside, letting the morning light flood the room. The coffee table was full of bits, tobacco, dead matches, and cigarette butts. The room was thick with stale smoke.

'What do you want?'

'We've got something you might be interested in.'

'Let's see, then.'

Macca pulled out the watch and let Paul hold it, but he kept the chain wrapped around his fingers.

'Not very trusting, are you?' said Paul.

'Just careful,' Macca said

'Yeah, right? Well, yeah, it looks good.' He squinted at the chain. 'Looks like solid gold, not sure about the watch.'

'Of course it is.' Macca pulled it back into his hands.

'Okay, don't get shirty.'

'What do you think?' Vinny asked.

'Yeah, I could probably get rid of it for you.'

'Where'd you get it?'

Macca replied, 'A place in Harefield last night.'

'Okay, right?'

'The very end, near Damwood,' he continued.

Paul's expression changed. 'On the right or the left?'

'The left. Why?'

'The second to last house?'

'Yeah. Why?'

'Fuck, that's Joey Doyle's grandad's.'

'Who's Joey Doyle?'

'Fuck. He's a mate.' A loud rapping at the front door set the dog barking again, interrupting them.

'Who's that?' Paul got up and lifted the corner of the curtain. 'It's him, quick get out of here. Get in the kitchen.'

Vinny and Macca scrambled into the kitchen and hid behind the door. The knocking rang out again before they heard Paul say, 'Hey, mate, what can I do for you?'

Paul had brought him into the living room. 'I want you to keep your eyes open for me. Someone robbed my grandad's place last night.'

'Shit, that's bad, mate,' Paul glanced over at the kitchen door. 'What did they get?'

'Not much, the meters and a watch. Can you keep an eye out for

Before the Storm

the watch? Someone might try to pass it on. It's gold. Only thing of value he had.' Joe shook his head. 'He brought it from Ireland.'

'Yeah, sure mate. I'll let you know if I hear anything.'

'Little bastards,' said Joe. 'You know who it was?' asked Paul.

'No, of course not. If I did, I would be round there. No, but it's got to be kids, hasn't it? They got the lecky meter.'

'Yeah, probably,' Paul agreed. 'The thing is, whoever done it will regret it big time.'

'When you get hold of them?' Paul said, looking at the kitchen. 'No, not just that… grandad died last night.' He paused again, as if he was struggling to understand. 'Shit, what happened?' Paul's tone shifted to genuine concern.

'A stroke or a heart attack. They're not sure yet. But it happened sometime overnight. Probably while those bastards were robbing the house.'

Vinny and Macca stared at each other, eyes wide with shock.

Chapter Nine

Vinny

2pm, Friday, June 24th, 2016

Vinny drove from Speke along the Boulevard and turned right at the traffic lights. He was waiting at the next set of lights and banged his fist against the dashboard. Fuckin' bastard.

In one simple gesture, McNally had reminded Vinny of everything he hated about the place. Bastard.

Years of achievement and success lost. He had written books, lectured at prestigious universities across the country, and yet an ignorant arsehole like McNally had reduced him to this? There was anger, but alongside anger, there was shame. How had he let that bastard embarrass him? What was he supposed to do? Sink to his level? Start fighting in the street like dogs? He hated such a juvenile confrontation. Helen was digging up his past. A landscape of secrets and lies, better left buried. As he waited at the traffic lights, his anger and frustration grew. When they changed, he slowly pulled away. He needed to stop. Needed some air. He pulled off the road into the entrance to Allerton Cemetery, Vinny turned down the long drive. He parked on the verge and walked the twenty or so metres to a grave. It hadn't been intentional, but here he was, standing in front of his mother's plot.

The place was quiet. He put his hand on the headstone. Its coolness felt reassuring. He breathed deeply, and the air filled his lungs. He knew, as he had known for years, this was where his problems began. It took him a long time to find his father's grave in Ireland. He couldn't have done it without Anne. Now he was a parent and understood the frustration of kids. He felt guilty about not being there for Charlie when he was born, but he had never hit him and knew he never would. The outbursts of rage that resulted in physical violence had never been a part of him. He had seen it too often and suffered from it. As a boy, whenever it surfaced, he panicked, trying to shield himself from the lash of a mother's anger. The impotence, helplessness, and anxiety that coursed through his veins in the face of violence began here, and here it was back again with Sammo's death. He knew he couldn't deal with this on his own. Returning to the car, he called Anne. After two rings, she answered.

'Hey, how did you know?' She asked.

'Know what?' Inquired Vinny.

'That I was back in Liverpool.'

'I didn't.'

'Oh, right?' There was a pause. 'So, what can I do for you?'

'Well, now I know you are back. Fancy a coffee?'

'You don't drink coffee.'

'You know what I mean.' He could hear her smiling.

'How's Helen?'

'In hospital, actually. That's partly what I want to talk to you about.'

'Oh, right, anything serious?'

'It could be.'

'Okay, where and when?'

'After work today, in town. I'll message you.'

'Later then.'

Vinny climbed back into his car. The road to the past was opening up in front of him.

Jack Byrne

* * *

Vinny flashed his parking pass to raise the barrier. He was late, so he'd be lucky to find a space. He drove slowly along the lines of the car park. With a town centre campus, he didn't know why so many people drove. The world is going to shit. Selfish bastards don't care about anything.

The university was a cash machine these days, churning out degrees to middle-class kids who didn't understand or care about history. Even worse was the opportunism, cashing in on China, supplying overpriced courses to the sons and daughters of China's new elite.

Movement caught his eye, and he saw a white SUV reversing out of a space. A small sporty SUV, less than a year old. The driver was a young guy, blond crew cut with a rugby shirt and shades. He didn't recognise him. Lucky bastard.

If he was one of Vinny's students, his marks would suffer for this, Vinny would get revenge. He pulled in just along from the reversing car, his five-year-old Fiat Punto ticking over like a fucking lawnmower. He didn't make eye contact. The student waved his appreciation for Vinny's patience as he reversed. Fucker.

Vinny climbed out of the car and slung his bag over his shoulder. The day was warming up. The online timetabling system logged him as available for consultation for the next two hours. Students were supposed to book ahead, but most didn't. He would check his messages when he got into his office.

He entered the building, a low-profile concrete construction that edged the paved quad. Designers saw it as a modern equivalent of the gothic quads of Oxford. Instead, it looked like a poorly serviced shopping centre in a 70s era new town.

He said hello to Roger, the concierge. Concierge, porter, or security? Every building had to have them these days to keep the nutters and drunks out. You couldn't go anywhere without being conscious that they turned mentally ill people out of shelters and social care accommodation like overstayers at a cheap bed-and-breakfast. What was the point of teaching history in a society without a future?

Security everywhere — not that they would be much use, badly dressed and badly paid. He wondered if one required the other. He supposed the only skill they needed was to get on the radio. If a real lunatic, terrorist or madman ran amok with a kitchen knife, then Roger wouldn't be much use. Arse glued to the chair in his little room next to the entrance, he slid the window closed, glasses perched above his escaping eyebrows.

'Morning.' Roger waved as Vinny walked by. 'What about that result, eh?'

'What result?' He asked, although he already knew.

'Brexit, that's upset the apple cart, hasn't it?' he said with a smile.

'Yeah, and that's what we need, eh? Apple carts upset. That's really going to make things better, isn't it?'

'Can't get any worse, can it?' Roger shrugged.

'You know what department this is?'

Roger lifted his glasses and put his paper down. 'History,' he said confidently.

'Yeah, that's right.' Vinny nodded. 'And are you sure you want to stick to that statement about things not being able to get any worse?' He walked off, leaving Roger bemused.

Vinny fumbled the key into the lock and pushed the door with his shoulder. His office was little more than a broom cupboard. It was three metres wide by five metres deep. Longer than it was wide. His desk was at the bottom, facing the window. In consultation with students, he would swivel his chair and face the door. There were two chairs for students, although he only usually had one at a time. Bookshelves lined the left-hand wall. This is where he kept his most frequently referenced material, and, of course, titles on the student reading lists. The University supplied his desk, like the bookshelves, made of cheap pine. Functional, but without the gravitas of professorship. A small landline phone sat between the letter trays on his desk. His desk wasn't tidy, and it wasn't a mess. He knew where to find things — it was busy. But not too busy. Now he needed some space. He put piles on top of piles to clear a spot. Most of the papers needed filing away properly, and he would get to it, but not now. A large, plain clock hung on the wall, its black hands and letters standing out against a white background.

There was a knock on his door. Oh, shit. His appointment was here.

'Hey, come in. How are you, Aliz?' Vinny made a point of remembering the names of students where he could.

She took a minute to remove her jacket. Her black, shoulder-length hair bounced as she hung her coat over the back of the chair. She reminded him of a young Anne. 'How is your work going?' he asked.

'Good. I think. Your clock is wrong.' She waved towards the timepiece on the wall.

'Yeah, don't worry about it,' he replied.

He didn't keep files on his students; working on the principal that he would remember those who were worth it, and the others would have to remind him of their existence or work if they wanted his attention. He kept a sizable hard-backed notebook on his desk. In this, he entered the time and date, the name, and then any notes from the meeting. That way, he could always look back and find earlier conversations. He had a stack of them now, covering the five years he had been in the department.

'So, how can I help you today?'

'It's the essay for the end of term,' she said.

'You have the list of options?' Vinny asked.

'Yeah, I was thinking about Creativity in History. I like the idea of it, but I am not sure I understand it exactly.'

'Okay, what do you think it means?'

A look of doubt passed over Aliz's clear features, and her dark eyes narrowed. 'Well, I know it's not about making things up —

history has to have a basis in truth or fact.'

'Yeah, but whose truth? Whose facts?' he asked. It was a standard question to get students thinking.

'I know we can self-select — confirmation bias — where we choose the facts that support our version of history and ignore the rest.'

The discussion was going in the right direction, and it was a salve to the wound inflicted by McNally. 'Can there be objectivity in history?' he asked. The more he asked, the more his own situation rose to the surface.

She paused, narrowed her eyes, and her forehead wrinkled. 'In that, we can verify facts and agree on those facts, yes. But the meaning we give to those facts is different,' she said.

'Can you give me an example of that?'

'Well, we can agree about lots of things. That X happened on a certain day in a certain place. But how we explain that or its consequences depends on the view we have. For example, the invasion of Iraq; if you are an Iraqi, you could see it as an occupation. If you are a supporter of UK policy, then it is an act of liberation. So history is not independent, not in the sense that one truth serves all people.'

'Okay, all that is good, except it's not just the view someone takes of an event, but who and what they are, materially, determine the impact of events. So, where does creativity come in?' he asked.

'Well, I thought it was like finding facts and then extrapolating from those facts.'

'Yeah, good.' He paused. 'What time is it?' Vinny asked. He regularly used the clock to make a basic point.

Aliz smiled. 'Twelve.' She looked at the clock on his wall again. 'The clock is right!'

'Yeah, and…' Vinny was glad she'd noticed.

'Well, it means that even a stopped clock is right twice a day.' Aliz smiled. 'That's a pretty common observation,' she said. 'And…'

She screwed her face up as she worked through the idea. 'Okay, that if the clock is right twice a day, maybe there is a right time for things.' *There is indeed*, thought Vinny, and maybe this was the right time for him.

Aliz paused. 'Like in Ecclesiastes; there is a time for everything, a time to be born and a time to die.'

'Okay, good… but what's different in the way a historian would see that?' he prompted.

'It's not "time" in the abstract, but the conditions create the time. So, the time is right when the facts and circumstances are right. An idea can be right, say, for example, "democracy," but if people don't have the power to enforce it, then it makes no difference if the idea is right. The time also has to be right. Time is not independent of material conditions.'

'That's great. What does this mean?' His internal voice was shouting, the watch, the watch. Sammo, Macca and Jaime.

'It means that a strategy has to include time. Ideas, time, and material conditions have to be aligned for something to happen.'

'I think you're doing really well,' he encouraged, also aware that everything she was saying related to his childhood.

'You're so good at helping,' she paused. 'This is so simple. Okay, so the time has to be right.'

'And how else can we be creative with history?' he asked.

'You said in the last lecture: history is about the present, not the past. I thought about this for a long time. Studying history tells us how we get to the present. We can't understand what's happening now without understanding the things that got us here.'

'Go to the top of the class.'

Aliz smiled. 'Have you read Anton Chekov's 'The Student'?' she asked.

'No, I can't say I have. Why?'

'There's a bit in it. Can I read it to you?'

'Yeah, sure.'

'Okay, well, there's this student, as in the title.'

She was using her hands to articulate, and he liked the graceful flowing movements.

'Anyway, this student meets a couple of widows on a cold, dark night…'

'Ooh sounds scary,' he said, regretting it immediately as infantile.

'No, not like that... Anyway, I think it's near Easter or something because he talks about how St. Peter denied Christ three times, and about how frightened he must have been to do that.'

He knew he should be bored, but somehow she was speaking about his past.

'And the women start crying, feeling empathy with St Peter. Then Chekov says…' She held her notebook open and read, 'he realised the past was connected to the present in an unbroken chain of events flowing one out of another, which seemed to him had just seen both ends of that chain. When he touched one end, the other quivered.' She looked up at him, her dark eyes on his, and he could feel her enthusiasm for the idea.

'That image of an unbroken chain of time, not only that everything is connected, but that we can grasp both ends at the same time.' The image broke through to him. Is that what's happening? The broken links are being rejoined? Is that what this is? Sammo and Macca, but who is holding the end of the chain?

'Okay, I'm definitely impressed. It is an interesting quote. I will look the story up. And what do you make of it?'

'The one that I thought of is Boris Johnson blaming the EU for imaginary rules on bananas and prawn cocktail crisps at one end, and leading a campaign to leave the EU based on fears stoked at the other.'

'Sounds like you have a great basis for an essay.'

'You think so?'

'Yeah, seriously. I think you have identified something intriguing. Use "The Student" example and draw out the implications.' As he spoke, he knew the implications of his own history were about to rise to the surface.

'I look forward to seeing the essay.'

'Thank you, Professor Connolly.'

Vinny turned back to his desk and heard the door click as she left. He leaned back in his chair, his legs stretched out, and closed his eyes. Maybe the time was right for him. The stopped clock of his life was about to be the right time. He knew something had to change. The morning had left him angry and frustrated. McNally had deliberately tried to wind him up. He also tried to warn him off? He leaned back in his chair and closed his eyes. Why?

His phone vibrated. It was a call from Anne. He sat upright. 'Hey… how are you doing?'

'Fine, when are you free?'

'I can get away any time now,' he said.

'Okay, great. Cafe Tabac? Bold St.'

'Sure. I can be there in an hour. I'll just finish up here.'

He collected his things. All thoughts of Aliz had faded. Now he had Anne, Macca, and Sammo on his mind. Now, Sammo's recent surprise visit to made more sense. Vinny hadn't followed it up or paid much attention. He had just hoped he would go away, but now it was clear Sammo wanted to tell him something. The questions about what happened to Sammo were becoming larger than his anger towards Macca. He was determined to resolve both. How much should he tell Anne?

As he left the building, Vinny nodded to Roger, who held a hand up to attract his attention.

'Yeah, I get it. Things can be worse. But we're sorting it out now, eh?'

'That's the idea,' said Vinny. Time to sort things out.

Keep reading at Northodox.co.uk

NORTHODOX
PRESS

HOME OF NORTHERN VOICES

FACEBOOK.COM/NORTHODOXPRESS

TWITER.COM/NORTHODOXPRESS

INSTAGRAM.COM/NORTHODOXPRESS

NORTHODOX.CO.UK

Printed in Great Britain
by Amazon